PRAISE FOR *THE TALES OF NEDAO*
BY

To th

"Excellent … c   ntasy
season, of out   lorton

"Refreshing … a believable world!"

— Other*Realms*

"Ru Emerson has a deft and confident knowledge
of both the geography of her world, and the more
subtle inner terrain of her characters' emotions."
— Megan Lindholm, author of *The Reindeer People*

In the Caves of Exile

"Action-packed from the very first page. There is
sorcery, bravery, evil, love and hatred … a worthy
heroine … Readers will cheer!"

— *Rave Reviews*

"Emerson writes delightfully clear prose, with a
deft and loving touch for character."
— Tad Williams, author of *Tailchaser's Song*

"Ru Emerson is a storytelling wizard!"
— Katharine Eliska Kimbriel, author of
Fire Sanctuary

And now, the triumphant conclusion…
On The Seas of Destiny

"Each of her books opens new territory for me, and
takes me down unexpected trails … I specially set
aside one weekend to read *On the Seas of Destiny*
because I *knew* I wouldn't be able to set it aside,
and I was not disappointed!"

— Mercedes Lackey, author of
The Heralds of Valdemar series

"Ru Emerson has a talent for tight plotting and
strong characterization."
— Charles de Lint, author of
Greenmantle and *Svaha*

THE THIRD TALE OF NEDAO

ON THE SEAS OF DESTINY

RU EMERSON

ACE BOOKS, NEW YORK

This book is an Ace
original edition, and has never
been previously published.

THE THIRD TALE OF NEDAO:
ON THE SEAS OF DESTINY

An Ace Book / published by arrangement with
the author

PRINTING HISTORY
Ace edition / February 1989

ISBN: 0-441-80820-4

Ace Books are published by The Berkley Publishing Group,
200 Madison Avenue, New York, New York 10016.
The name "Ace" and the "A" logo are trademarks
belonging to Charter Communications Inc.
PRINTED IN THE UNITED STATES OF AMERICA

10 9 8 7 6 5 4 3 2 1

For Doug—Because. And also for the picture.
For my own Swordmaster—My Dad
And with thanks to Johannes Brahms for
Three Symphonies and Two Piano Concerti
that bound it all together

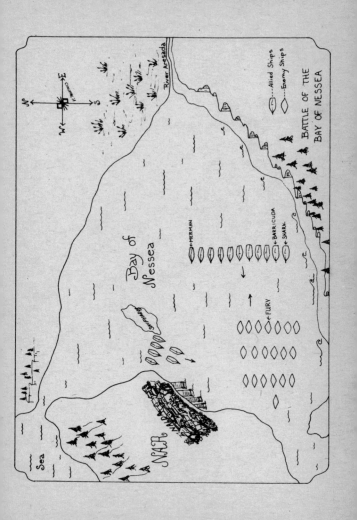

Prologue

It is curious, how time and the mind work: Now and again it seems that the attack I saw from the walls of the King's City happened in another lifetime, that the journey from Koderra to the Caves of Aresada with its dangers and evils are a tale I have read from long ago, and not a thing that happened to me. As often, it seems a five-day—no more—since I saw my beloved Scythia die, since Nedao lost a way of life five hundred years old.

But three years have passed since the Plain was taken; three years since Ylia—King Brandt's untried heir, Queen Scythia's barely skilled witch daughter—helped lead the survivors of that last battle through the mountains of Aresada: herself, King's Swordmaster, King's Bowmaster, three men at arms, an aged nurse and a nobleman's weak daughter. And I, the AEldra cat Nisana.

Ylia was a child when we fled the Plain; she did not remain one long. She learned to lead because the helpless depended on her; she became strong because she must. Cold, distance and lack of food threatened us. Evil Mathkkra, hellish Thullen, and Lyiadd, their master, opposed us. Ylia gained both sword skill and full AEldra Power in the Foessa.

We won through the mountains—with luck and growing skill and allies unexpected: the Guardians themselves; the Dreyz who are the naiads and dryads of legend. But in Aresada,

Ylia's bastard cousin Vess had proclaimed himself King; he cried her witch and would not step aside. A Champion was found among Ylia's companions; Vess was defeated and exiled.

The worst was yet before us. A remnant of Nedao hid in the Caves at Aresada with little food, less hope. Somehow, we stayed alive, but it was I who found the valley where we now live and prosper, I who found Galdan—a mountain hunter, Duke Erken's son, now Ylia's mate and Nedao's King.

Lyiadd's Mathkkra and Thullen harassed us often, attacking herds and folk alike, but many were killed that fall during the Battle of the High Ridges, and for two years after we had peace.

Ylia now bore Shelagn's Gifts: Sword, Shield and Horn bound to her by a testament a thousand years old. And in Galdan, she found support and still another weapon, for the haunted mountains that humans call the Foessa had imbued him with Power akin to hers but untamed.

And so we waited and we watched and we prepared as best we could for the day the Three —Lyiadd, his consort Marrita, his son Vess—and their allies would set upon us again.

There is a great deal of this tale I would gladly leave to another to tell. I am not often long-spoken, and much of it rekindles deep grief. But it is mind to relate; I, Nisana, the only AEldra of cat-kind to dwell among the Nedao, for I alone know the tale entire. And so, for the last time, let me begin.

1

The towers were squat, built low and thick to shelter within the surrounding crags, and ancient. Few had survived the combination of weather, continuous sea wind, salt and years: Cracked, slimed stone jutted into a stormy sky, gutted rings straggled toward the bay. Several had disintegrated under their burden of years, stone buried under vine and shore-grass and drifted sand. One was impassable: The roof timbers, rotted through, had caved in to block the passages and rooms below.

The bay was a natural harbor and so shielded from the worst of the winter storms by sandstone ledges behind the towers: Even so, the black-sailed, sleek ships anchored well apart, and they swung alarmingly as the wind rose. Two small rowboats were tied to the long stone mole on the inland side. Against the south arm of the harbor were other ships, ghosts of ships, as old as the towers themselves. Sails rotted on ancient masts. Of one or two, only the masts could be seen, the rest having long since settled to the bottom.

Mountainous slabs of rock formed a protective arc around the welter of broken towers. More water then, and beyond that a stretch of sand widening like a spear-point, wedging toward buildings, green fields, low sandstone bluffs. Fogbanks hid the land beyond.

Three of the great towers remained barely usable, and only in the most protected did light show. It stood well back from the water, so near the southern ridge one could touch tower and ledge simultaneously. Sullen candle-flame flickered in narrow, deep, glassed openings; heavy wooden storm-shutters blocked the lowest windows from without, barred many upper ones from inside. The sun, briefly escaping heavy cloud, glared mercilessly across drifting sand, greened stone, greyed wood, mildewed tapestries, then vanished again. Wind shrilled across the cliffs.

Light traveled across a low window, reappeared one level higher: A slender, golden-haired woman was climbing the winding stair that led to the topmost chamber. She held her dark fur-lined cape and mauve silk skirts close so they would touch nothing. At her insistence, the tower had been thoroughly cleaned. But they couldn't fight five hundred years of rot and neglect.

3

A breath of roses followed her; cinnamon and clove scented the hall, but under all—and far stronger—was a reek of stale salt water and mildew, dead kelp and the faint but pervasive odor of dead fish.

Marrita seldom noticed these things: Three years had inured her. Yet she was not reconciled to this place. Never that.

She kept her eyes on the uneven stairs as she climbed; to do otherwise was to court an accident. With each step, the familiar litany ran through her mind, the vow was renewed: "For his mockery of my Lyiadd, the Sirdar my father will pay. The old fools who counseled I should not be allowed to wed my Lyiadd, they will pay. The Nedaoan woman who dared set steel against him will watch all she loves die before I kill her. Beware, Father! And Ylia of Nedao, I have not forgotten you."

Lyiadd. Three years and a half since she would have sacrificed anything, everything—her very life!—to save him. Three years since she'd brought him here—weak, ill, reft of Power and memory alike—since she'd sealed the bargain with the Sea-Raiders so as to gain time and safety for him, until his recovery could be complete. It would. It must!

He was safe for now. No one would challenge the black-shipped Raiders in their own ports. And no one had believed the Nedaoan half-blood when she told her wild tale. Who would believe Lyiadd a renegade, who would believe he had found the long-deserted halls of the Lammior—the dreaded Night-Serpent of legend—or that he hoped to tap the greater Power that was the Lammior's and to turn that Power against the Peopled Lands?

Her father's Council might have searched, of course. But they would have found nothing but a deep, thickly forested bowl of a valley, inhabited by deer, bear and owls. Oh, ruins: There *were* those. Dead, empty piles of stone, with no sign of human inhabitants, no trace of Power, clean, evil or otherwise. *She'd* seen to that, for the Lammior's Power had left those walls with her, *in* her, and with her it would stay.

But Lyiadd; he was becoming restless. The planning sessions were good for him, but he was still not completely healed and that made him irritable. *He's as strong as time and care will make him*, she realized. *The transfer of the Lammior's Power from me to him will either kill or cure him. And I know he cares nothing for which way it goes, if life must otherwise drag as it does now.* It was wrong, the way things were: He'd sought that Power for so long, going without sleep, without food, searching for answers, not finding them. And then Ylia's dagger had struck deep and Marrita—who'd never used her own AEldra skills save to keep her hair soft, her skin unlined—she had offered herself and had taken it all. *Set the ceremony.*

She stopped on a wide, dry landing for breath, gazed across sand, fallen stone and the rotten hulks of five-hundred-year-old Nedaoan ships toward the gray, white-capped sea. She could sense more irritation than Lyiadd's, up there at the top of the stairs—Mal Brit Arren, Lord Captain of the Sea-Raiders; his constant companion Jon Bri Madden.

Brit Arren's anger was palpable, his thought clear: It was none of *his* bargain that brought these sorcerers to the Great Isles, and he held himself to the letter of the bargain made between Marrita and his predecessor only by what he doubtless would call the honor of his kind.

Impatience, anger—amusement. Vess' amusement. Her mouth set in a tight, disapproving line. *Three.* It had never been meant this way, it was Marrita and Lyiadd, the two of them only, his to be the Lammior's unrelenting Power, hers to support, aid and back him, to solace him when he was worn, hers to . . .

Vess. The hated Ylia's cousin, son of King Brandt's sister Nala—Lyiadd's son. He was a slap in the face, a betrayal.

She stopped, waited on the stairs until she could calm her temper: Lyiadd could still read her thought. And he knew the poor bargain he had for a son, but he would hear no word against Vess, from her or anyone else.

Had I given him a son . . . But she couldn't. That many years ago, she had feared to lose her form and beauty, to lose Lyiadd's love. But once she'd been certain enough of both her AEldra skills and his affection, she'd discovered the truth: Like many of her class, she was barren.

She climbed the last of the circling stairs, crossed a torchlit hallway that curved like a new moon around Lyiadd's planning chamber. Seven broad stairs led to a heavy iron-bound door. It had been carved by a master crafter, but time and neglect had worn the designs to vague traceries. Beyond the door was another world, a room that was warm, high-ceilinged, well lit. Delicately patterned Ragnolan carpets overlapped to cover the floor. An exquisite Osneran tapestry obscured most of one wall. The only visible window was shuttered and barred against the wind and rain. Fire burned in a central pit, drafting through a covered hole in the roof.

A chalcedonwood table was placed below the tapestry: chairs of the same rare wood, comfortably cushioned, surrounded it. It had been crafted for a Lord's halls but no Lord would have taken it now: Stained and cut, its gloss destroyed by candle wax and ill treatment, it was strewn with the remains of a meal, maps, a chart pinned down by two jeweled knives, candles, winecups and two copper jugs.

Three men huddled over one of the maps; they looked up as she let the door click shut behind her. "My apologies, if I have detained you. There were other matters to concern me."

The solidly built Mal Brit Arren cast an irritated glance at his younger companion. "Lady. Your convenience is ours."

Her eyes remained hard above a sweet smile. She seethed. *Sea-Raiders!* This Mal Brit Arren never failed to make clear to all Three of them, but particularly to *her*, that he tolerated them, but that he would never fear *or* respect them.

The boy, Jon Bri Madden, was so young his moustaches were pitiful, his thick blond braid was still covered with the red scarf of a two-year novice fighter. The arrogant look on his face meant nothing, inside he was one cringing ball of terror. Brit Arren's *gensyl*, she thought viciously. She liked thinking such things, knowing neither man could guess what she thought. Of course, she was merely tapping the anger and letting it go with that kind of thought: Raiders occasionally took boys, but Brit Arren wasn't that kind.

But he infuriated her, this boy Jon with his swagger and the sneer that curved his lips when he was away from the Three. It was the same sneer Brit Arren wore openly, even now. *Wait*, she promised herself and them. *Wait*.

Mal Brit Arren sprawled in his chair, dagger tapping at the pinned chart. Nothing about his garb proclaimed his rank: His shirt and padded jerkin were filthy from spending his morning salvaging goods from the rapidly flooding Kraken, helping the crew beach her so the hull could be repaired. His oiled short cloak had already dripped a small lake about his chair; his thick red hair had dried in sticky, salty points. He glanced up to meet Marrita's eyes, looked away again as though disinterested. He'd been drinking; there was as much red as white around the compelling blue eyes.

He resented waiting. *They could use me out there. I'd be of more real use there than here.* These Three didn't listen to him. Well, at least he had some ghost of an idea what *They* planned, if he was here. *What was she doing that was so important, rearranging her hair?*

He dragged one of the jugs across the table, shoving a sextant, a gutted candle and several loose bits of thick paper to the floor. He ignored them, poured wine, slammed the jug back to the table. Then, with a derisive smile, he stood, filled another cup and handed it to her with a flourish. She took the cup and turned her back on him.

Jon Bri Madden flushed, took an involuntary step toward her, but Brit Arren caught his arm and minutely shook his head. His eyes were hooded, blackly smoldering. *Wait*, he told himself in a corner of his mind he hoped They could not read. *Wait*.

Marrita stopped to warm her feet at the fire before she slid into her chair. "Lyiadd?"

A long-fingered hand caught hers, squeezed it, fell away. Lyiadd pushed his chair back, walked the length of the table for wine, stopped to stare into the firepit. She gazed at him from under long lashes, taking care that he neither saw nor sensed her at it. He was still too thin for her liking, though he'd regained much of his muscle. The somber red shirt was already too snug around his chest and upper arms, but the matching breeches he'd let hang over soft indoor boots were loose.

He came back to sit next to her. "Regarding our attack against Yls, and the timing of it—"

"I have said before, it is impractical, at least until spring," Mal Brit Arren said flatly. Marrita glared at him for the interruption. "Storms make the sea treacherous. The men who serve you are not seamen."

Marrita shifted. "We have waited so long, what is another winter? Lyiadd, give me your hands." She took them, closed her eyes. "We need wait no longer for the transfer, however. I will prepare for it at once."

"Good." Lyiadd spoke casually but she felt his exultation. He tamped it, hard, and turned to Vess. "You have some of the Power, as much as we can give you at present, but more will be yours. You have much to learn. There must be no weak place in our three-fold strength when we set upon the Peopled Lands, for as soon as Yls is taken we must attack Nar. Are you still willing to lead your armsmen to the Plain, and to take Koderra and its surrounding lands back from the Tehlatt?"

"I am." Vess' face was flushed.

Lyiadd smiled. "With Koderra, Yls and Nar in our hands,

there will be no escape for Nedao. I would say to take more of the Plain, but even with the blessing of Chezad, their war god, the Tehlatt are unlikely to let you far up the river."

"I know the Tehlatt," Vess said grimly. He did, enough to still give him horrid dreams. They'd nearly killed him before Teshmor's gates that first night, when he'd helped Corlin's son escape with the warning for Koderra. They'd nearly had him more than once as he fled south to the temporary safety of the King's City. But then—*Fool, to have spoken unthinking and so gained the enmity of your uncle, King Brandt!* Well, that anger had not survived long, had it? He'd seen his way clearly, then; he'd left Koderra under cover of dark and smoke, made his way north through the Tehlatt to gain Teshmor's besieged walls. There had barely been time to spread what was still the false tale of King Brandt's death, to receive the homage of Dukes Corlin and Erken before the City fell. He'd had luck, though: Wounded and weak, he'd lain among the dead until nightfall, then crawled until one of his men had found him.

Yes, he knew the Tehlatt.

The thought of facing them again chilled his blood. But to have Koderra for his own . . . ! *It should have been mine! My uncle had no right to leave Nedao to an untrained girl-child of eighteen summers, a half-blooded witch!* That thought skidded to an abrupt halt, and he cast a sidelong embarrassed glance at the tall, pale-haired AEldran at his side. *Father.* AEldran, sorcerer, Father. He and Ylia shared more than either would ever have thought.

Vess realized Mal Brit Arren was staring at him. He wanted to break Brit Arren, wipe that sneer from his face. He looked beyond the older man to smile at the younger; Bri Madden looked away quickly, his Adam's apple jerking up and down. *That is right. Fear me, never dare to not fear me. I have plans for you.* The boy would be his way to Mal Brit Arren.

He brought his attention back to the present as Lyiadd dragged the map over. "It will take time to gather the Mathkkra and Thullen again. I cannot move until there are sufficient of them here, and here," he touched rough country between New Nedao and Yls, between Nar and New Nedao, near Aresada. "Also here if possible, though I would rather not spread them thin."

Vess was still sceptical of those creatures Lyiadd and Marrita discussed so casually: A Nedaoan never really believed in what he couldn't touch, and Vess had yet to see either. At the same time, he was keenly aware of the Power Marrita had conferred upon him and Lyiadd was teaching him to use. If that was possible, anything was.

"With Nedao cut off, Yls reft of Power and therefore helpless, we can take Nar like we would pick ripe fruit. And Nedao—"

"Nedao's army was worthless three years ago, and the Tehlatt had most of it. Nedao has no chance against us," Vess said.

"Perhaps." Lyiadd closed his eyes briefly. His chest still hurt, particularly when the weather was chill and damp. Ylia's knife had severed muscle, sliced into his right lung. He still remembered none of that, but the proof was there whenever he drew a deep breath. "I do not leave anything to chance against *her*. Remember my experience, if you encounter her." Silence. "Remember your own."

Remember! Against all odds, she'd reached the Caves, challenged him for the crown, set that child Brelian against *him*, one of Nedao's greatest swordsmen! He'd lost because he'd been wounded, not due to the boy's skill, he *knew* that. And so he'd found himself afoot, deserted by his men. He'd finally been forced to accept charity—and sanctuary—from the Chosen, while she wore Brandt's crown. If not for his father, he might still be hugging the braziers in that chill hall in Osnera. He'd remember, when he took her apart a slow finger-worth at a time. "She had luck," he said.

Lyiadd shook his head. "A moment. Brit Arren, there's nothing further we have to discuss, if you wish to leave." It was a dismissal, but one as between equals.

"Wait." Marrita's voice stopped him. "There are things I need." Brit Arren leaned against the door, stared back at her impassively. "Get me silver mushrooms, a smoke pot and a small bag of Ragnolan herb. Mud and water from the footprint of a grey sea-bird, this last untouched by hands. Gather it in a dish or a spoon and transfer it to a corked or lidded jug. And," she finished cooly, "an infant."

"A what?" He started; his fingers dug into Jon's arm and kept him from retreating.

"An infant. Newborn or near it. Unmarked, for I cannot use one with gold rings already in its ears." She laughed. "A female child, of course." Jon's relief was so visible she laughed again. "Not an important child, not a boy." The laughter was gone, wiped from her face as though it had never been there. "Bring these tonight, at moonrise, to my room in the base of this tower."

"You'll have it, all of it," Brit Arren assured her grimly, and propelled Jon out the door before him.

Vess waited until the door clicked behind them. "What didn't you want him to hear, Father?"

"Things they do not need to hear. Watch against overconfidence concerning Ylia. She is more than your uncle's daughter; she is the ally of the Folk. She is the confidante of the Guardians, the heir of Shelagn. Like Shelagn, she is Catalyst."

"I—" Vess frowned. Guardians? Folk? "Who is Shelagn?"

"She was once the Catalyst by which the Lammior was defeated. Ylia could destroy us all."

Marrita nodded; she knew. But she had plans of her own for Ylia. A dead woman could not be Shelagn's heir.

"I won't underestimate her," Vess said. But as Marrita brought Lyiadd wine, Vess let his eyes close and he drifted into a familiar pattern of thought. It had come to his dreams one night, remained to tease his waking hours now and again. If someone undid her, destroyed her Power... If she became once again the fumbling, weak creature she had been in Koderra... If someone were to break her... If somehow she were his.

If only he had spent time with her before the Tehlatt had fallen upon Nedao, if only there had been time and a way! If only he had made a way under her defenses, seduced her instead of wasting his time on nobles' daughters and assassination attempts against Ylia! She had hated him, distrusted him; but she would have loved him, if he'd wanted it. She would have wed *him*, not Erken's grubby son, she would have named *him* equal and King!

Ylia. Sweet cousin. He called up a vision of her compliant, the way he could make a woman—as Lisabetha, Lord Corlin's lovely young daughter, had become, longing for his attentions. Willing to do anything to keep his love once it was hers. A way, there must be one! He passed that over for the moment, thought of her in his power. He would court her, overwhelm her, until he had what he wanted: half of Nedao, himself as her consort. If she named him King, if he had the right by naming *and* by conquest! He would be kind, he would not dispose of her even then, what man would be such a fool? Her hair was red-gold, her skin like warmed cream, her body...

He looked across the table at Marrita. How could his father love such a cold-blooded woman? Even her beauty would be no consolation! Only devotion to Lyiadd kept them from each other's throats.

Well, he would not always be under her watchful eye, serving as student to her teacher. Yls would be theirs, Nedao his. And as his strength and his Power increased—

Wait, he promised Marrita silently—her, himself and one other—from deep in the innermost recesses of his mind. *Wait*.

Strength of will: So many folk across the Peopled Lands and beyond them had so much strength of will to carry out their desires. And such varied ones: My Ysian, blistering fingertips to learn bow at her age, walking and riding in all sorts of weather, so she could return to beleaguered Nedao. Vess, casting aside prejudice and fears to embrace Power, so he could clasp Nedao's crown to his twisted bosom. The Nedaoan people, learning to fight, taking up new trades and new lives after the fall of the Plain.

Galdan, who fought the block that kept him and his wild Power apart. Together, he and I struggled against the dread fear he might never be able to use more of it than he did.

But it was pleasant for once to hear no stubborn argument when I said, "Try."

2

The wind wasn't half as loud within the thick walls of the Chosen sanctuary; it wasn't a tenth as cold, either. Ylia thanked the young novice who showed her into the small guest receiving room. It was tightly shuttered and almost unbearably hot after outside. She draped her snow-whited cloak across a chair to drip, and scowled at it. One of the seams was leaking.

She never visited Grewl so late at night, but the storm had blown up suddenly from a few fat flakes to a thick, swirling mess it was hard to see through, with a wind that went right to the bone, through lanolined wool, fur lining, thick stockings and waterproofed leather boots. And though she'd never admit it to anyone, Galdan included, it had been a long and hard six months since Berdwyn's birth. She still felt the tired of it, times like this. Odd that Selverra three years before—her firstborn—hadn't taken such a toll of her.

She stripped the thick mitts from her hands and moved to warm them at the grate. Grewl came in with a small tray holding two small cups. "Lady. You must have been caught by the storm, it's no night for a visit."

"Not an intended one." She gave one last shiver as the heat of the brandy coursed through her. "I'm sorry for the inconvenience."

"It's no inconvenience," he assured her with a smile, and stretched his feet out to the fire. She watched him. She worried about him, lately: he was old and so much responsibility had been thrust on him so late in life. Now, without him, there would be factions within the house. Grewl had kept problems at a minimum, despite edicts from their main house in Osnera, despite the one attempted take-over she knew about.

He looked healthy, though. He seemed to have adjusted to the weight of leadership and to have found peace, though he had never wanted such power, and had only taken control when it became clear he must.

"Have you any needs?" She was beginning to feel her toes again; they itched.

Grewl shook his head. "None. We won't need more paper until Nar gets through this spring. We've enough even with all the copying and the school."

"Other things for the school, then?"

"Nothing." Another comfortable silence. She could hear the whine of wind through trees, the occasional hard splatter of wind-driven snow slamming against the shutters.

"I'd better leave soon; I'll be stranded here if it gets deep, and they'll worry." She *could* leave her horse, bridge to the Tower. Grewl knew that. But Ylia never used AEldra Power on Chosen land. The fanatic Jers had been ejected from Nedao three years ago and there were no such strict adherents to Osneran policy still in Nedao. But many of them believed magic to be wrong, whatever its kind, however it was used.

Ylia paused half-way to her feet. There was another sound, rising above the wind. Grewl heard it too, and with a speed that belied his years he crossed the room to fling open the door. Ylia came hard on his heels.

Horns. She heard them clearly now, echoing through the hall, Erken's patterns spelling out the cry for help: Mathkkra. *Aid to Village Dessa, we are beset; Mathkkra!*

Dead of winter, a grandfather of a snowstorm and Mathkkra after Nedaoan sheep!

She dove back through the door to catch up mitts and cloak.

Horns bellowed out nearly overhead: Chosen sentinels were passing the cry toward the City.

"Mathkkra," Grewl whispered. Ylia passed him at a dead run. "Where?" he shouted after her. She paused at the outer doors, shouted, "Dessa!" and sped into the night.

The cold caught her as though she'd never been warm; a bundled Chosen shoved the door closed behind her, a second brought her horse from the visitor shed. Snow whirled around them, the building was no more than a black shape and the two priests indistinct forms. In the partially enclosed catwalk overhead, a priest shouted translations of the calls to his companion. Horncry was all around. She vaulted into the saddle and pressed her unwilling, skittish horse through the gates.

What light there was in the courtyard was behind her, and wind drove the snow sleet-hard into her eyes. It burned her face. 'Galdan! Nisana!' She sent an urgent, powerful mind-search for both of them as soon as she was on the road.

'Here, girl!' That was Nisana, of course; Galdan could not hear her mind-speech unless they touched. 'We can hear the horns. Galdan's gone downstairs to order horses.'

'No. Find him, tell him I said to get some men together and hurry! Tell him to let the guard ride out, but you bridge Galdan and those men out to Dessa. The snow's piling up, you know how deep it gets in those box canyons!'

No response; the cat had broken contact. Ylia urged her horse forward.

The wind was building ominously, keeping pace with the horns that still echoed across the valley. Mathkkra—a clutch of half-starved creatures—had attacked one of the other side holdings after a three-day blizzard, late at night. Village Bennan lost two sheep out of the winter pens and two herders before Erken's armsmen could get through to them; the drifts had been formidable. *If Lyiadd's behind this, he couldn't have chosen a better time to harass us with his filthy, blood-drinkers*, she thought furiously.

She clutched at mane as the horse floundered in deep snow; they nearly tumbled into a drift. No help for it; it was too bad she'd chosen to ride this young four-footed idiot instead of her best mare, who'd survived enough bridgings to take them in stride. This poor colt was shying at everything in sight, spooked by the wind, letting her know exactly how displeased he was to be out in the storm. He was pretty, but pretty wasn't going to count for much out here. Well, his first lesson was on its way.

"Brace yourself, horse." She wrapped both arms around his neck, hooked her fingers together in a hard grip and bridged.

The horse whinnied wildly and stopped cold; Ylia was disoriented from the bridging. She flew over his neck, fortunately into deep snow. By the time she fought free and staggered to her feet, he'd already bolted.

"*Damn!*" She rubbed caked snow from her eyes, dragged sword and dagger from under the cloak that was wrapping around her legs. The small shield was already in place on her left forearm. There was a fire somewhere up the road, creating ominous shadows; a woman's frightened shriek rose above the storm and horns. 'Nisana! Where is Galdan?'

'On his way. I could have told you that animal would never bridge,' the cat added sourly.

'You might have told me *before* he threw me,' Ylia retorted. She was heading for the village; the snow was blowing across the road, ankle-deep at its worst. A flare of AEldra Power between her and the first houses, and a tight knot of men were suddenly there, swords drawn, arms linked. At once they began to separate: Galdan, there, Levren on his left. Brelian's arm linked through Levren's. Golsat had braced himself against their shoulders, arms woven behind their backs. Six of the Elite Guard, old hands at bridging, were already running to aid the villagers. Ylia ran with them.

Mathkkra were pinned against the sheep pens, in the shadows between houses. Their white bodies and the pale hides they wore blended with the snow, making them hard to see. But they were not a small band of starving stragglers, and they were fighting hard. Normally, they feared fire, particularly the AEldra Baelfyr. But even when Ylia sent it among them from both hands, they held. *Gods. They haven't fought like this in three years!* There wasn't time to worry it just now, though, and no more room to chance Baelfyr; Ylia blocked a short sword with the bronze shield, brought her blade down across the creature's neck. It fell, two more replaced it. Galdan's accustomed presence against her left shoulder was not only welcome, it was absolutely necessary for several long, chill moments.

She and Galdan fell back as Levren, Golsat, their archers and the Dessan herders shot a thick volley of arrows into the enemy. Too many of the shafts missed. Levren bellowed orders, the archers took an extra moment on release and the second volley was more successful.

"Father is on his way with half a company," Galdan shouted, when he could finally spare the breath for it. "This is *not* amusing, the nasty things are too hard to see!"

"Think they planned it that way?"

"Funny woman! Watch your open side!"

"I have been. Watch your own!"

The enemy finally broke and ran. Villagers and armsmen, the village headman and his wife, Nedao's Lord and Lady all stood in the silent square and stared at each other in the aftermath. The wind had fallen, the storm was easing. Dead Mathkkra were everywhere.

Sheep milled in their locked pens; young herders ran to check on them. The headman's wife stared down at a small many-limbed body almost on her furred boots. Her lip curled. "That's no pleasant sight to haunt a body's dreams." She gazed west, up into the woods. "We'll be until full thaw, finding all the bodies."

"Set the dogs at them," Golsat suggested. He took a handful of arrows from one of the village boys, wiped them on his breeches and slid them one at a time into the individual pockets on the outside of his cloak.

The woman nodded. She turned to Galdan then and curtsied gravely. "You came with good speed, sire. We hadn't expected the horning to be so effective."

"Your own folk helped," Ylia said. "What damage to Dessa?"

The village had suffered little harm: One goat had vanished into the night, but two of the men found it in a drift near the last house. One sheep was bleeding; Ylia healed it and a villager with a bad cut. Their own small force had taken no harm.

Erken's men came in not long after; they would stay for the rest of the night, just in case. Levren, Golsat and other men borrowed horses from the night guard to ride back to the barracks; Galdan and Ylia bridged.

"Oh, that's nice." Ylia sprawled in a pile of cushions, feet extended to the grate. The room was small, easy to keep warm. It was also next to the nursery: They could faintly hear Malaeth soothing Berdwyn to sleep.

"Nice?" Galdan grumbled. "You think so?"

She eyed him benignly across her shoulder. "I'm warm, dry and drinking an excellent cup of hot wine. Two hours ago, I was wet, chilled, and I hurt from coming off a horse at high speed. Do you suppose anyone will catch him?"

Galdan shrugged. "He'll turn up in the morning, if he hasn't already. He knows where breakfast is."

"I suppose." Ylia wiggled her toes. "He needs work. I hadn't counted on snow, never mind Mathkkra, when I rode out this afternoon."

"You'll learn," Galdan replied.

"Possibly." Silence. "Did you see the difference tonight?"

"Difference?" He pulled the winejug from the ashes. "Thought you were still talking untrained horseflesh," he mumbled as he went back to his chair. Silence. "Noticed? Who didn't? That wasn't just a food raid by half a few skinny vermin. I'd say we've a nest of Mathkkra again. Close by. *I* haven't sensed one, but how would *I* know?"

"Don't start," Ylia said. "We've said all that. You're getting better. You've got Power—"

"—and I can't use it." Ylia waited, he shrugged. "All right, we've had it out, we've said all that. Go on."

"How much of that bridge was yours?" Ylia asked. Silence. She drank, inhaling the spicy, tart-apple, hot wine-flavored steam.

"Don't know."

'Half,' Nisana put in sleepily from the back of his chair.

"Same as last time," Galdan added. "So?"

"Last time you two bridged four."

"So?"

"You're doing better," she said finally. "Don't fuss so much, it's coming."

"Hah," he retorted automatically. He didn't sound quite so unhappy. "Can *you* sense them?"

"Who? Mathkkra? A nest of them? The Three? I can't sense Mathkkra unless they choose to be sensed, you know that. A nest—finding that takes luck. And the Three are still with the Sea-Raiders, that's what I think."

"Why?"

"Sense. And I know Lyiadd. He's not going to take any chances, not until they're ready to move against Yls. They'll go for Yls first because otherwise the High Council might somehow be able to stop them. Lyiadd has learned caution. So has Marrita."

"What about Vess?" Galdan asked.

Ylia scowled. "Vess wouldn't know caution if it fell on him."

'Wishful thinking, girl. His father has had three years to teach him caution.'

'He won't learn, cat.'

'Hah.'

"Nisana's right, Ylia." A corner of Galdan's mind still wondered, after a year and more, that it was Nisana he heard, her sour commentary reverberating through his thought. That he and Ylia often could share thought the same way. "Vess has always been good at taking care of himself, and you know it. He must have inherited that; your Aunt Nala certainly could not have had it. Lyiadd, of all men!" He sighed. "I rather wish word had not gotten out, however . . ."

"Why?" Ylia demanded. "Do you think we could have kept it quiet, with Lisabetha's dreams, and those of half my household women? Marckl's wife? Besides," she added with grim satisfaction, "no one speaks of him as my cousin now, or even Nala's bastard son. He is Lyiadd's." She scowled at him. "Those who never liked Vess now know why."

Galdan sighed heavily. "I suppose so. I suppose it is better for folk to know Vess is with Lyiadd because of kinship, rather than simply a twist in him."

"Why?"

"Think on it—any mother's son could grow up to become a Vess, without such a reason!"

"Hah," Ylia replied sourly. Silence. She turned her gaze to the fire once again. "He's mine," she said finally.

"If it's what you want. Just don't die with him."

"I wouldn't; that would be letting him win."

Galdan knelt beside her and kneaded her shoulders. She subsided with a happy little sigh. "Nice deep drift?"

"Not deep enough," she mumbled. "Wretched colt, I'll wring his neck when I get hold of him next."

Galdan laughed. "Not with *those* tiny paws you won't!" Her sword hand caught hold of his wrist. "Not so hard, please, I fight with that. I didn't say they weren't strong!"

"Lucky for you they are, they saved *your* hide."

"All by themselves, did they?" he retorted.

"All right, you helped a little. When you weren't tripping over your sword, that is."

Galdan laughed. "That was you, tripping over your sword. I used mine to swat my horse."

"Liar," she said sweetly. "It wasn't nice to lie to me like that." Galdan tugged her plait.

"It's not polite to call Nedao's King a liar."

"No one ever accused *me* of having manners, not even Malaeth," Ylia said with a complacent smile. "Besides, I'm Nedao's Queen. Gives me certain rights." The smile vanished. "Looks bad for us, doesn't it?"

"Lyiadd?" he asked. She nodded. "It always has looked bad. We don't know what he's up to, that's not pleasant. Not knowing when the blow is coming, just knowing it will. But I think it's him sending Mathkkra again. I think it's nice of him to warn us."

Ylia closed her eyes: she didn't need such warnings, not with Marrita sending her nightmares at least once a five-day. The dream varied, the warning was always the same: *You will lose everything, husband, children, friends. Country and people. Your own life last of all.* Death and terror held her in a cloying, sticky grasp until Galdan woke her, or Nisana did.

Nedao's allies in Nar believed in the threat of Sea-Raiders but not all of them believed the Three to be allied with their ancient enemy; Yls would not believe at all. When the blow came, how would they fare? And what of Nedao?

"I'm sorry." Marrita's whisper reached him on several levels. Lyiadd forced his head up from the small inlaid table; it took all the physical strength left in him. She held out one slender hand as though to touch his face, withdrew it as if afraid he might strike it away. He found his balance—even seated it wasn't easy—and took her hand, held it against his face, touched the chilled fingers with his lips. "I thought we could do it quickly," she went on. "Quickly and without fuss. I knew there were twins in the near village." So like Marrita, he thought; she'd never bother to remember the names of the Sea-Raiders' villages, however long they remained here.

"It's not your fault." His voice was breathy, thin with exhaustion.

"It is my fault!" she flared. "I wanted to avoid argument between myself and this bastard of a Lord Captain! Imagine if I had asked him for not merely one boy-child, but two!"

Lyiadd shook his head. He'd never seen her so angry, but he remembered a time when she would never have made the spells, gathered things for them; a time when she'd never bothered to be strong. She'd changed, since his near death; his Marrita was often a stranger these days. The compliant, golden beauty with no ambition or thought beyond pleasing him, she was gone, transformed by the Lammior's Power, filled with it—the Power he'd sought so long and *still* could not have! He could have slammed his fists into the small table until it shattered, could have slapped the concern and pity from the lovely face so near his. *She treats me like a child!* one corner of his mind railed. But even if he'd really wanted to hurt her, his Marrita—even if he'd been fool enough to dare alienate her, now his only hope for the thing that must be his—he hadn't the strength. This attempt at transfer had taken too much from him.

Marrita sank to the floor and rested her cheek against his knee. "By now, they would be too old anyway. We need two babies, though. No more than a five-day-old. Male."

"We'll send a ship to raid Ragnol, or one of the near southern ports. By the time they return, we will be ready for another attempt."

Marrita nodded. "We must. *I* must. I'm worn with carrying this Power. It should have been yours from the first. I never wanted It."

"But you have It, and you've done well with It."

"Because I had to. For your sake." She closed her eyes briefly. "That's all, all it ever was. I'd give It all to you this moment, if I could. If It would let me," she added unhappily.

"I know," he whispered. "But we will need all that strength, yours as well as mine." He patted her hair. It was flecked with blood; he was, the whole room was. The business with the child had been messy.

Marrita sighed again. "I will send word to Brit Arren to have a ship sent at once. Suddenly I fear to leave this matter. I fear she may be near finding the way to bind herself, those weapons and that man with his wild Power, sometimes I can feel it moving in her at night. If she does become Catalyst—"

"Then we have a stronger enemy," Lyiadd said as she hesitated. "Nothing more." He didn't sound as assured as he normally would; that, Marrita was certain, was exhaustion. It didn't mean anything. Couldn't. But he was staring, grey-faced and haggard into the brazier, and she knew that he did not see it.

Sometimes it takes little indeed to let one forget impending trouble: like sun and warmth, dust to stir under one's feet instead of packed snow or mud, or ice. Particularly when such things come a full two months early and out of season.

3

There was still snow, of course: in all the north-facing dells, between buildings and under trees, anywhere the sun seldom touched. Three warm days could scarcely melt it all. And likely there'd be more snow soon; after all, it was barely the end of Lambing Month—and in the three winters they'd had here, no one had yet seen flowers *in* the month of First Flowers.

So it was respite only, but more than welcome. Malaeth gathered together a merry party of Ylia's women, an ecstatic three-year-old Lady Princess Selverra and baby Berdwyn for a walk through the City and down the road. All across the City and out through the valley, shutters were flung back, doors opened to let the crisp breeze chase stale smells and smoke; several of the crafters were working from half-assembled stalls in the market-place.

From the top step of the Tower, Ylia could see one of Marckl's road crews using a six-horse drag down near the woods where runoff across the road had made it dangerous for light carts. Marckl's Road: They all called it that, even though it was originally just the Dock Road. Marckl'd all but lost his life building that road. He laughed about the name, but he took the road itself most seriously.

There were two wide, flat barges on the river, one clearing snags and deadfalls from the base of the bridge, the other checking for drowned snags and logs. No one else was out there, not just now: The river was pale green with snow runoff, bone-chillingly cold.

Everyone who wasn't cleaning seemed to be wandering the broad avenue that connected barracks to houses to market to main square to Tower. The City was crowded and there was almost a festival feeling to the air. Ylia shoved the long, red-gold plait back over her shoulder, gave her breeches a hitch and went down to the street. The pants were still loose and Malaeth was fussing at her about it: She'd lost weight after Berdwyn's birth, and it was slow coming back. *A workout, that's what I need. A workout and sun.* She tipped her face back to catch warm, glorious sun and strode across to the square.

Eveya, captain of the Queen's Elite Guard, was working with the upper novices. She nodded a greeting, set her pupils to ten sets of full pattern and walked over to meet Ylia. "Coming along nicely, aren't they?"

"You're doing a good job, Ev."

"Working on it," the young woman allowed. She ran a square hand through her hair, smoothing loose bits back from a dark, freckled face. "Be glad when 'Betha and my sister are back to help me though; with Merreh nursing the twins and 'Betha pregnant and bed-bound—there's not enough of me to go around." She cast an eye over her earnest young charges. "Nelia, get that elbow *in*, I warned you about that! Adden, you're sluffing again!"

"I'm not sluffing!"

"Got enough air left to argue with, haven't you?" Eveya bellowed, silencing her. "Come on, work it!"

"Looks like they need your attention more than I do," Ylia laughed. "Want help?"

"You? You mean it?" Eveya was more subtle about it than Malaeth, but she also fussed. Ylia nodded. "Good. I want to work the second- and third-year women today; we're getting out of shape."

"Everyone does in winter, look at the boys. Barracks practice just can't do it all. When?"

Eveya glanced up at the sun. "Second hour? After noon-meal anyway."

"I'll be here. Have you seen Erken?"

"Barracks." Eveya waved an arm in that general direction, turned back to her novices. "Adden, are you *sure* you want this? Well, then, damn ye, *work* for it!"

Ylia smothered a grin as she left the square. Eveya sounded more like old Marhan every year, and it was getting hard to remember the shy, gawky herder girl whose village headman father had wanted to forbid her sword-use. Eveya had gained more than just weapons-skill that first summer: She had developed confidence, a gift for leadership, a voice that could be heard half-way across the City and a proud father who let no one forget *his* daughter led the Queen's Guard.

Ber'Sordes was perched on a hard wooden bench next to the grounds, intent upon the exercises. It didn't surprise her to find the Narran Ambassador there: Ber'Sordes never tired of watching Nedaoan sword and dagger play, even dull practice. He smiled as he caught her eye. "Did you get the message packet from Tr'Harsen's man this morning?"

"A fat one, I suppose because it's been so long since he got through last. I wager Tr'Harsen sleeps most of today after that journey." The River Aresada was four times normal size with runoff, chill and treacherously swift; snags and whirlpools were everywhere. She could hear it at night from the Tower. She couldn't imagine floundering up that churning, raging river in one of the small Narran inland boats.

"We'll have Kre-Darst at the docks in a day or so if the weather holds."

"It's nasty out there, I wouldn't come."

Ber'Sordes laughed. "Unpleasant conditions never slow those lads, though. And I know Kre'Darst wants to finalize the contract for the dark yellow wool. He sent a message for me by Tr'Harsen; says they have a buyer Oversea that will pay just about any price for it." He snapped his fingers. "I'm reminded: Tr'Harsen has a gift for Lady Lossana—because she's done much to bring the wool trade between us to what it is. That won't offend Lord Corlin, will it?"

Ylia laughed. "You know Corlin, I don't believe Tr'Harsen could ever offend him! The wool trade hasn't hurt Lord Corry's pocket any, that I've noticed, and he'd never object to a gift to his Lady for such a fine reason."

"I thought as much." Two of the Ambassador's household came up with cushions for his bench; Ylia waved and went on down the street.

The market was crowded and there was a pleasant smell on the light breeze: Someone was selling warmed cider, hot spiced wine and venison *yushas*. She bought a tart green apple—it was still difficult for her to persuade the venders to take her coin instead of giving her things—and walked on toward the barracks.

Beyond the market were houses of noble proportion and look. Corlin, Duke of Teshmor, lived here with his Lady; Duke Erken did, and so did several of the Main Council. Past them were smaller houses such as Brelian's and Lisabetha's, those of some of the younger councilors and most of the crafters whose numbers swelled the market in warm weather. Further along the avenue was the inn that housed increasingly frequent visitors from Yls and Oversea, and more houses of the prosperous merchant class.

Behind them, separated from the houses by a wide meadow and hard against the hills, was Lossana's enormous clothbarn. Most of the City's weavers and spinners worked here, and it was seldom indeed one could not see clouds of steam rising from the open back of the building where the dye vats simmered.

"Wait up!" came a familiar voice. Ylia turned in surprise.

"Lisabetha, you're *not* supposed to be on your feet!"

"I am." Lisabetha patted her stomach fondly. "My jailers gave me leave to walk, once down the street, once back. Don't fuss."

It was hard not to fuss: Lisabetha had already miscarried twice. "Too young," Lossana had said. "I did the same, conceiving at sixteen, and I wasn't as small as 'Betha!" Unlike Lossana, Lisabetha couldn't be convinced to delay babies a few years, so when she became pregnant again, Malaeth sent for an Ylsan Healer. She and Fiyorona, the Healer, had put Lisabetha to bed and were keeping her there. So far, it was working.

Lisabetha laughed. "I'll be glad to have this baby born, just so you and Brel will quit looking at me like that! I've kept it for eight months, haven't I?"

"All right." Ylia hugged her young friend and Lady's thin shoulders. Lisabetha was much more like a sister than the formal attendant she'd once been, and a far cry from the sullen, terrified child who'd fled Koderra three years before. She'd had cause for all of it, though: The mountains had been as dangerous as Lisabetha had feared. If 'Betha ever thought about any of it anymore, no one could tell. Until this pregnancy, she'd been one of Nedao's three best swordswomen, Eveya and the Bowmaster's daughter Lennet being the other two. Ylia smiled at her; Lisabetha was strong and strong-willed both. She would be fine. "Going any further, or are you going home?"

"I had better not. I *was* going to the barracks to look for Brelian, but if I do he'll just worry." She grinned. "Don't tell him I was out, will you?"

"If you say."

"I'll go back; Fiyorona will have the bedding changed by

now." She sighed. "It's pleasant out here; I need a larger window by the bed if I'm to live in there."

Ylia watched her go. She smiled at the two young boys who came running past her, skidded to a halt to sketch a bow in her direction, and were gone in a clatter of boots. She pushed her sleeves above her elbows. It wasn't really warm, but compared to what it had been just days before, the sun felt wonderful. Her arms were pale from the long winter, making the scars even more than usually visible. She scowled as she turned them palms up: that thin line running from wrist nearly to elbow along the inside of her right arm. Three years, nearly four, and it still hadn't faded. Lyiadd's work, and not the only. She resisted the impulse to finger the one that ran down her face from temple to chin. Even Galdan bullied her when he caught her touching that, though thanks to her own healing and to Malaeth's poultices, it was even less visible than the others.

Not that it particularly bothered *her*. She had never thought of herself as beautiful, certainly not perfect of face, that a thin white line from temple to chin should ruin her life. Galdan hadn't liked that scar, though, not at first, and it still upset Erken.

She was nearing the barracks; even blind she'd have known that by the unholy din. Nedao's armed were taking advantage of the temporary break in weather. Men and boys were scattered over the sword-field, working diligently. There was Erken, and beyond him she could hear Marhan's bellow rising above the clash of steel on steel. He was working the youngest and greenest lads of all, the first-year novices. Marhan had them in a double line and he walked up and down behind them, shouting changes in a voice that had lost none of its volume since she'd cringed under it.

"Count of *four*, are ye deaf?" The boy in question jumped as the old man shouted into his ear. "Not four and something, count of four! Do it again! *You!*" The boy next to him nearly fell as the old Swordmaster turned on him. "You're supposed to be watching him! Watch!"

"Sir," the boy stammered. Marhan gave him a shove.

"Ignore me! I'm not here! You pay attention to *him*!" He turned away, shaking his head. "Well?" he demanded. Ylia grinned at him. "Distracting 'em, are ye?"

"You have them in line, old man," she retorted. Her Swordmaster snorted, stepped back a few paces.

"Huh. They come clumsier every year. How a man's to turn *that* into swordsmen is beyond me!"

"You say that every year, Marhan." He had said it every year for forty at the very least, since Brandt her father had made his awkward novice crossings under the then black-haired Sword-master's gimlet eye. "I spoiled you, learning as fast as I did."

Marhan fixed her with a glittering eye that was still formidable. "Did ye, boy?" Ylia ground her teeth, and Marhan grinned at her evilly, knowing he'd scored. He'd refused to teach her at first, he'd never tutored a girl. But she was Brandt's heir. Marhan had finally decided to take his King's order to treat her like any of the novice lads literally. "Ye weren't bad at that, I suppose." She goggled at him in mock astonishment—Marhan *never* gave compliments. "Never said ye were good, did I?"

"You did!"

"I never did. Wouldn't!"

"You did, once," she laughed. "Just once."

"Oh. That." He had, the last day of their journey from Koderra to the Caves; it had been unexpected and touching. "Huh," he chuckled wickedly. "Ye haven't a witness, tell anyone and I'd deny it."

"You'll never have to, old man; no one would believe it anyway." He merely chuckled again and clapped her soundly on the back; somehow, she managed not to stagger under the weight of the blow.

"You, there, Jassen! Count of *four*, get your mind to it!" He shook his head, watched them closely for several more passes. "All right, change!"

"You'd better get back to them," Ylia remarked as the boys shifted. Someone's sword hit the dirt; Marhan rolled his eyes imploringly upward.

"Looking for Galdan? He's down below." Marhan pointed.

"Just looking." She almost ran as Marhan began bellowing the changes with exaggerated patience: Her ears were beginning to hurt.

Erken waved as she passed him, then yelled his boys back to attention when several of them turned to stare: Unlike Marhan's, his hadn't quite learned proper concentration yet.

The straw bales had been dragged out of the barns and targets pinned to them for bowpractice. Levren was watching a number of regular armsmen and women; further down, in the smaller square, Golsat was teaching second-level bow to a mixed class.

There were several young women in the group, plus a number of herder lads beginning their second season of formal training. The lads were no problem, but Golsat was kept busy with the girls; Ylia wondered how he could manage to ignore sidelong looks, dropped items, adroitly avoiding wide-eyed or fluttering, coy stares and casual hand contact. Somehow he kept his class going, somehow maintained discipline.

Some of these same girls had been actively pursuing Golsat since the first year in this valley. That year, a self-effacing half-Tehlatt common bowman suddenly had found himself one of the Queen's closest friends and advisors, the closest friend of both the Queen's Champion and of the man who became her husband. Even then, he'd gone unnoticed by the eligible maidens until Brelian's wedding, when he'd been hauled perforce from ordinary brown breeches and armsman's tunic and bundled into the new Narran fashion of short trunks and hose. Suddenly, he'd become not only important but attractive to boot.

But for all of the taciturn and diffident Golsat, the cream of Nedao's young women might not have existed. He found such frontal attacks easy to ignore, because—though he seldom admitted as much to himself—he had other hopes. More than two years since he had last seen the Lady Ysian, but he still heard from her and of her, now and again. It was enough.

"Golsat! Tr'Harsen brought a message up-stream for you!"

"Message?" Ylia fished out the thick packet and separated the single folded page in its blue waterproofing. Golsat unfolded it and read. A rare smile lit his dark face. "She's coming back."

"I know. She's sent things, something for you besides this, I think. I got the letters but Tr'Harsen is still asleep and nothing else has been unloaded." Golsat waved that aside; he had what he wanted in the first few words of his letter. *My Ysian is coming back. And—she wrote to tell me.* He was conscious of the gulf between the two of them: Himself a Nedaoan armsman, and yes, second in command for the King's Inner Guard, second to the Queen's Champion. Close friend of Nedao's young Queen. But when he thought of himself and then of Ysian, who was sister to Ylia's mother Scythia, ten years older than he, of the Ylsan Second House, noble . . . Sorceress too, and a powerful one. She had been raised in genteel, gracious wealth. She was everything he was not, he had known that from the first moment he saw her. He had loved her from that moment.

And now, she was coming back to Nedao—coming home, she'd said—and she'd written to tell him so.

He realized Ylia was talking and he hadn't heard her. "It's still not safe here, and in a way, I wish she wouldn't come. But I'll be glad to see her."

"So will I." Golsat refolded the letter, tucked it into his belt pouch. "I hope she's better prepared this time. It sounds as though she might be."

"She had her eyes opened, before. She knows what she's facing." *I hope she knows all of it. How Golsat feels. Be kind to him, Ysian.* She turned as the Bowmaster came across to join them. "Lev, I saw your sons working under Erken just now."

"He said he'd take them. Davvel's simply terrified of Marhan, and I can't talk him out of it."

"He just doesn't want to go deaf from all that howling," Ylia said. Golsat laughed. "Now, if only Lennet would—"

Levren groaned. *"Don't* remind me," he implored. His beloved, indulged daughter had fought successfully with her mother to be allowed to learn sword and dagger, then to wear breeches. She had won honor and a place high in the Queen's Guard, she was undeniably skilled. But she still had no tact, still alienated people with her rudeness and still found herself in frequent trouble for interpreting orders to her own liking. Now she had determined she must have Marhan teach her, but he flatly refused. Ylia had stayed clear of the argument from the first, knowing Marhan would win it, but she imagined Levren's household was not the most pleasant of places just now.

"Galdan and Brelian both have offered to tutor her. I wish she'd leave the old man alone," was all she said.

"Try and tell *her* that," Golsat grumbled. He'd been one of Lennet's first instructors, and relations between them were still strained. "It's a good thing the girl looks so much like ye, Lev, no one would guess her for yours otherwise." Levren laughed.

"I haven't looked at the invoices yet, but I believe Tr'Harsen brought more Osneran steel up-river, Lev."

"Good. I'd like a pair of those rapiers, and Bos can't get the length and taper with lesser metal." Levren looked across her shoulder; the color left his face alarmingly. *Foreigners.* She knew even without turning he'd just sighted unexpected Narrans.

Golsat stepped between the Bowmaster and his phobia. "They're mooning over there instead of working," he said. Levren turned away and clapped his hands ringingly. Several of the girls jumped. "There isn't that much sun left! If you want to waste a perfectly good morning, you can do it elsewhere."

Down at the far end of the barracks, a crowd was gathered; deep in its center, she could hear the light, springy clink of rapiers, though it was almost lost in a babble of laughter and loud jeering.

Brelian and Galdan, stripped down to breeches and sleeveless linen jerkins, were dueling with pairs of the new blades. The grips were elaborate, the blades long and slender, two-edged and sharp-tipped like traditional Nedaoan swords but less than half the weight. For most trained with Nedaoan weaponry, it was like starting all over again.

Ylia clapped a hand across her mouth but those around her were laughing loudly and shouting sarcastic remarks as they watched Nedao's finest swordsmen fumbling at each other like two of Marhan's greenest.

It was partly in the stance—though men who fought Nedaoan fashion with sword and dagger knew better how to fight from a forward stance than those who used a single sword and stood sideways. The weight or lack of it was very much a problem.

Brelian's left-hand sword hit the dirt and the two broke apart; both men were laughing so much they could hardly stand. Galdan sought her eyes—it was partly the Power, partly something else, but he was always aware of her presence. "Blast the woman, Brel, she's laughing at me! Think this is easy?"

"I haven't had any problems," she retorted.

"Hah. One practice session with Marhan—who doesn't like them! Want a real challenge?"

"Not against *you*," she laughed. "I hate dueling with you tall men, it gives me neck strain. Brelian, d'you have any breath left?"

"I can try." He retrieved his fallen blade. Galdan traded her his blades for her sword belt. She tested the balance, slid her hands into the sworled basket grips and winked. "Pay attention, husband, I'll show you how it's done." Galdan hooted derisively as Brelian brought his blades up to ready.

It *was* awkward, even though the weight and balance were similar to her own sword, and her dagger was an unusually long one. Ordinarily, she would not have held out so long against Brelian, particularly so early in the year, but he was tired from fighting Galdan and the blades were giving him trouble. For one

exhilarating moment, she gained an advantage and pressed him
back into the crowd. But then Brelian dropped the left sword
again. He let the other fall, tossed his hands up and laughed
breathlessly.

Ylia mopped her forehead with a sleeve, slipped her hands
free of the baskets and bundled the swords together. Galdan
reached across her shoulder to take them, his face blandly expressionless. "Did you pay attention?" she asked.

"Hah. He was taking it easy on you."

Ber'Sordes gave a dinner that night for her and Galdan,
Tr'Harsen and his second, Lossana and Corlin. Tr'Harsen had
become prosperous indeed through trading with Nedao: A deep
blue stone the size of an egg depended from a silver chain around
his throat and he'd recently accepted a place on the Lord Mayor's
Council. He owed much of his present good fortune to his recog-
nition of a good bargain from the first: Nedaoan wool cloth was
in demand in every port where he and his ocean-going ship *Merman* traded.

He had already visited the weaving barns during the afternoon, pronounced the yellow cloth to be all his Oversea clients
desired and left Lossana a bale of silky, long-haired Osneran
wool and a contract of formidable proportions.

Lossana had been instrumental in restoring the wealth of her
house and of Nedao's herders and crafters. She still oversaw
much of the work herself, as she had when Nedao still huddled in
the Caves up-river, when looms had been rough-hewn wood
strung with Narran wire, when dyes were whatever they could
glean and wool everything from their own few shearings to gifts
and lendings from Nar and Yls, even gleanings the wild long-
haired goats left on thorn-brush high above Aresada. Lossana's
slender hands rested on the base of her wine glass; her fingers
were strong and deft, nearly as much at home on a sword hilts as
on a spindle. They were soft and unlined, fine as a girl's from the
hours she spent with them in heavily lanolined wood. This night
they were a little yellow around the nails. At the throat of her
blue gown was Tr'Harsen's gift: an Osneran brooch of silver,
shaped like a sea-bird.

Tr'Harsen had gone through his holds to bring the large pack-
age Ysian had sent: On the table stood a chalcedonwood statue of
an Yderra, tall as a man's arm. Its eyes were richly polished
malachite stones, the great jewel on its brow a faceted emerald.

Ylia's fingers strayed to it throughout the meal: The texture of the wood, the beauty of its carving—it begged to be touched, to be stroked. Ysian had tied a note to its leg: "The craftsman told me he's never made such a beauty, before or since, and he's been saving it for a special client. Clearly, this could belong to no one but you. The One willing, I shall see you before true summer."

There had also been another small packet with yet another note. "Give this to Golsat for me, if you think he will take no offense."

"At what?" Galdan wondered. "A gift from a woman? Golsat's not that sort. Particularly not where this woman is concerned."

"You noticed that, did you?"

"Difficult not to. What is it?" A piece of dark cloth unfolded from about an enameled box. Within the box was a broach, a severely plain silver arrow the length of a man's finger. Galdan touched it. "He'll like that."

"Ysian said in her letter she's taken his advice. She says she's stronger, it's given her confidence."

"Good." Galdan set the enameled box back in its soft packing, picked up the note that had accompanied the Yderra. "She'll need confidence, whether she comes here or stays in Yls."

And so it began, at last; not the first step in the chain Vess thought would lead to his victory over the Nedao—and Ylia—but we later would look back and see them as the first steps in his great push toward that goal.

4

The weather had turned nasty, and a chill wind blew sleet against the high tinted glass windows of the Heirocrat's palace. It wailed down broad chimneys, sending flurries of ash across the smooth tiled hall. Tevvro shrugged himself deeper into the fur-lined cloak· and hurried on his way, sparing no glance for the miserable huddle of supplicants around the braziers at the far end of the hall. Poor souls, they might be here a year and more, only to find their desires denied. Waste. Foolish waste. *His* wants had taken more than three years to bring to fruit: Without the inheritance his father's death had given him recently, he might still be pacing the outer halls with those fools, waiting for a response that never came.

Three years. And the Heirocrat was growing capricious. Old age, they said. But rumor said he was taking an herb in his wine, the use of which would ban a common Chosen for life. That would explain certain things Tevvro had heard recently. *When I become*—Tevvro dismissed that thought. He didn't dare think that many years ahead. For it would be years.

They actually thought he *wanted* to be Father of the Nedaoan Chosen, even those he considered allies! They were fools, who thought that. A man could die there, unnoted and scarcely mourned by the main house, as Grewl would be when he died. But for a man of ambition, a man with the backing *he* would have—the Nedao Chosen were a means to an end, nothing more. But it was as well if the fools thought they knew what he wanted, if they underestimated him in such a manner.

Tevvro tapped at the narrow door, slipped inside and doffed his cloak. The young Chosen who took it returned with wine and left him to enjoy it alone. Tevvro hitched his chair nearer the brazier, took a sip of the pale gold liquid: Ahhhh. None of the

32

poorly aged stuff he'd once shared with the outer supplicants, the wine alone could be a good omen.

He needed good omens, there were enough disquieting ones, things not quite under his control. Such as Vess. Tevvro worried about Vess' own ambitions, about Vess' sudden departure from Osnera. Oh, the man had indeed needed his own armed. "My witch cousin will not readily give up what she has taken, you know that." His words had been sensible, practical—and even so, there was something that worried Tevvro, though he still could not work it out. But Vess was back in the Peopled Lands—somewhere—raising his army.

Tevvro sat in the pleasant little room, sipped his wine and spared a brief, sympathetic thought for his fanatic friend Jers. He hadn't thought of Jers for some time, and wondered how he was faring with Vess. After all, he'd tutored Vess, and Vess needed a Chosen priest with him as much as Jers needed the responsibility, the steadying influence of armsmen to instruct.

Poor foolish, fanatic Jers. Tevvro doubted anything would steady *him* much. Jers would never learn from his mistakes; given another order from Osnera, he'd make the same frontal assault on the Nedaoan Chosen and their elected Father. Poor young fool.

Tevvro stretched his legs toward the warmth of the glowing brazier, sipped his wine. This day's meeting with the Heirocrat's personal secretaries should be among the last; before the month was out, he should be looking for a ship to take him back across the sea. Back into the eastern wilds. And then, after Nedao was secured under Vess and Osneran policy firmly instrumented, when the schism Grewl and the witch had created between them was healed—well. A step at a time. But he knew in detail how each of those steps looked. He was ready.

The red-scarved boy clattered down the last turn of stairs, almost slipping in his haste. *Ten more steps and a man can breathe clean air again!* He needed that, needed it desperately. Any time at all in the presence of Lyiadd and the concubine Marrita stopped the breath in his throat, twisted his stomach. *Magic. How does Mal bear it, that they keep him so long at their councils? And as for the third of them!* Jon Bri Madden knew *his* kind, they were common enough among junior crew: ambitious and completely lacking in scruple. Jon understood ambition, he was ambitious himself. The rest of it: a man had to have honor of some kind! Vess had none, so far as Jon could see—none of *them* did.

Magic. It washed through him like a combination of too much sweet wine and a bowl of Ragnolan steam, nearly made him ill where he stood, balanced half-way between one step and the next. He shook his head fiercely to clear it, leaped down the rest of the stairs by twos and into the real world.

It was unexpectedly warm and humid in a cloudy, windless way that felt like late summer. The smell of salt water and rotting weed was a weight against his nose and mouth.

All the same, it was better air than Mal breathed just now; Jon cast him a silent thanks. Mal was a harsh master, and Jon seldom looked to live to doff his red novice scarf, let alone to be rid of the second's blue and red one, and that as much from the course they were charted by the Three as by Mal's own personality— he'd made enemies over the years, Mal had, particularly when he challenged Nod Britt'harn so unexpectedly and snatched the ruling to himself. Mal didn't worry such things, or if he did, even Jon didn't know of it; there was no visible chink in his armor. Mal *could* be kind, though. When he chose. He knew what went on in his subordinates' minds, and he knew how the Three affected Jon. And so, an errand for the once cabin boy, now juniormost mate and fledgling sword. An errand that, in truth, wasn't so urgent as all that, but at least carried conviction: Mal's compliments to the crew, preparations to begin for the *Fury*'s departure from port on the early tide, two days hence.

And a carefully unspoken thought between them—less than a thought, for thoughts were as unsafe as words—in that brief shared look before Jon had left on his errand: At sea, a man can talk as he chooses and plan as he will.

Jon stopped short as a thin, whining voice reached him. He turned to gaze with sour impatience as a miserable creature in shabby grey detached itself from the shadow of the fallen tower and hurried toward him. Jers. Mad Chosen priest, Vess' servant —*or amusement,* Jon thought contemptuously, though given Vess' appetite for women, that last seemed most unlikely.

"Young Lord!" Jers repeated as he drew near. His voice was high, shook slightly. He brought up a fawning smile; Jon scowled at him and he took one hasty step back. "I—I have a message for your captain, for Brit Arren."

"So?" Jon folded his arms across his chest: This wreck of a human roused no pity in him, and certainly no fear. Only disgust

—he was a nasty creature, whimpering, clinging to shadows. A man was better dead than brought to that! Jon thought. Jers glanced nervously down the dock, nervously up the side of the occupied Tower. "Well? What is it, priest?"

"I—not here, young sir, not here. If I'm seen—" He dithered, caught up a length of the short over-robe and began twisting it.

In spite of himself, Jon felt a sudden curiosity; what was the man about? "If you mean to murder me," he began sternly. Jers quailed under that black regard, shook his head frantically.

"Ah, no! Young Lord, how should I, do I carry weapons, steel such as your steel, and could I hope to use it against a man of your skills? But I would not, for does not the One teach us not to kill, even a disbeliever?" Jers was babbling; spittle frothed at the corner of his mouth and ran down his chin. He drew a deep, shuddering breath, turned and fled back into the shadow of tumbled stones, rotten beams and broken glass. Jon glanced down the dock, back the way he'd come, as though Mal could know his dilemma and solve it for him. Then, with a contemptuous shrug, he stepped off the deep-worn path and followed.

Deep in the ruins, Vess smiled as he awaited them both.

It was late; a chill wind blew down across the valley from the east, bending trees and moaning around the Tower. Ylia snuggled into her cloak and followed the Ylsan Healer Fiyorona down the deserted street. Lamps burned here and there in windows, giving form and shadow to obstacles.

"How long?" she shouted. The shrill wind and the clatter of a loose barrel rolling down the cobbles nearly drowned her words.

"What? Oh. How *long*," Fiyorona shouted back. "An hour at most. She won't be long, *I* don't think."

"How is she?"

"How? She's fine." The Ylsan woman snugged the hood down around her liberally silvered hair, turned up the narrow side-street and knocked hard at the door of the last house. Brelian himself let them in. He was grey with worry.

"Lady Healer, I'm glad you're returned, she needs you."

"Her mother's in there, and so is Malaeth. They're doing all she needs just at the moment. And I needed fresh air, my young friend," she added tartly. "Had to clear my brains a bit, didn't I?" But she smiled at him in a friendly enough fashion, pushed by and dropped her cloak across his arm. "Here, make yourself use-

ful, hang that up for me, and did you get the oranges she
wanted?"

"Golsat went for them, I couldn't leave. I think he might
be—" Another knock at the door proved to be Golsat himself,
two small, soft oranges clutched in one hand.

"All I could find, Brel."

"They'll do," Fiyorona assured him. "Get Brelian some wine
and make him sit down. Lady, you come with me."

Ylia didn't want to, suddenly; memories of Berdwyn's birth
assaulted her, bringing with them such a sharp sense of recalled
pain she nearly doubled over with it. She found herself nodding,
piled her cloak on top of the Healer's and took Golsat's oranges
with her.

But it wasn't so unpleasant an experience; she was too busy
for her own thoughts to bother her. And almost before Malaeth
could finish peeling and sectioning the orange, Lossana was
holding the Good Fortune blanket she'd woven, receiving her
grandson into its soft folds.

Ylia came down to breakfast a five-day later to find fresh
messages from Nar, a letter from Ysian, a pile of contracts from
the Lord Mayor. She had expected them, but had not expected to
find Malaeth waiting for her. The old nurse seldom left the children at this hour. Ylia watched her with a curiosity that became
deepening unease while food was set out for her. Malaeth's jaw
was set, the muscle knotted under her temples. More ominous:
The small wooden box gripped so tightly that the old woman's
knuckles stood out white. Malaeth drew up a chair, sat and
waited in silence until the serving woman was gone. Before Ylia
could say anything, she drew a deep breath and plunged into
what was clearly a planned speech.

"This comes from Ysian, I asked her for it. So you can blame
us both for what it contains." She glared; Ylia closed her mouth,
successfully battled her temper—riddles before breakfast?—and
waited. "I know you'll argue with me, I expect it, but I want you
to hear what I have to say first. Every word of it." Ylia nodded.
"Good." She set the box down between them.

"This is Kabada." Ylia drew in a sharp breath. "I know ye
have heard of it, and ye know what it does."

"It's Ylsan, a combination of herb, bark and a spell beyond
most Ylsans, these days. Obviously not beyond Ysian. It prevents children. You make a tea of it, take it once a five-day, and

it prevents them until you put it aside. Or you take it once a day for a six-month, and it prevents them for good." Ylia looked up from the box with frightened eyes. "Malaeth, I can't take Kabada! Not yet!"

"Ye said ye'd hear me out!" Malaeth hissed fiercely. "Ye nearly left Galdan to raise two orphans when ye had Berd, he all but killed ye!"

"But, Malaeth!"

"Is that the manners I taught ye? Or the way to keep a promise?" Malaeth snapped. Ylia swallowed. "Ask yourself how strong ye feel yet. It took a mortal lot from ye. Another child would take more; it would kill ye for certain." Silence. Ylia picked up the small box, slipped the fastening and gazed expressionlessly at the coarse-chopped dry contents. A brief note in Ysian's fine print lay on top of the drug, explaining dosages.

"Your House has its heirs," Malaeth said. "You can die a happy old woman, many years hence, knowing your father's line goes on, as does Lord Erken's. You have Nedao, a responsibility greater than just making children. Think of the hundreds of children across the valley. In a sense they're yours."

"It's not that, Malaeth." Ylia closed the box, set it gently back on the table. Dark hazel eyes met pale old blue ones. "It's—to do something so irrevocable, to take full dose. What if—what if there was need for another child?"

"If one died?" Malaeth asked bluntly. "Or both did? Another child is the one you'd never live to see. You took the responsibility for this valley, these folk, and they need their Queen, alive and ready to lead the armies, gods help us all! If things come to the point that another child is needed, we're already lost, don't you see that, girl?"

"No," Ylia said flatly—and untruthfully. She let her head fall forward onto her hands. "Gods and Mothers, Malaeth, you *can't* just hand me this box and expect me to agree to what you're asking, just like that!"

"Lisabetha did."

"She has one, has she? You've had a busy morning, old woman. 'Betha needs Kabada, I'm not the one who couldn't carry a baby, remember?"

"No, ye just nearly died giving it birth," the old woman said grimly. "D'ye think trouble like that just goes away? Happens once and never again?"

"How should *I* know?"

"I do, and ye should listen to me. Ye listen to your Duke when it's time to fight. Such problems don't go away, they get worse. Ask Fiyorona, if ye won't trust me."

"Malaeth, I—" Ylia began desperately.

Malaeth pushed the box into her hand and closed unwilling fingers around it. "Answer me this, lass: How have you kept yourself from conceiving since Berd's birth? AEldra control or Nedaoan sops?"

"Control," Ylia replied faintly. Her hands drove into her hair; her head slumped further. "Vinegar sops aren't very effective, you know that."

"*I* do, but I didn't know if you knew."

"Well, I do. Control's simple. I don't *need* Kabada!"

"Control's easy, until you forget. Women do. Some women can afford that, you can't. Take the Kabada; start now. Don't leave your Galdan to rule Nedao by himself, to raise those two sweet babies alone, he won't thank you for it."

"I—black hells, Malaeth!" Ylia exploded. "I can't just *do* this! Give me a chance to think, will you?" She jumped to her feet, stormed out of the small breakfast room. But at the door she turned back again. "Did 'Betha cave in when you bullied her, or did she talk with Brelian first?"

"Why should she have?" Malaeth demanded. "It's her body, isn't it? And doesn't he want her alive?"

"That's all very well," Ylia said flatly. "But Galdan figures in my choice." The door banged shut behind her. Malaeth pushed her chair back, got slowly to her feet and picked up the box. Well, it hadn't been as difficult as she'd feared; at least the girl was thinking about it. She'd do more than that, though. And Malaeth would be there, every evening, with that tea in hand, watching that she took it down.

Ylia paused at the top of the stairs. *Interfering old woman!* A corner of her mouth twisted. *All right. If she's just an old busy-body, if she's merely causing trouble, why are you clinging to the railing while you try to get your breath?* Maybe Malaeth was right; she'd taken too long recovering from Berd. A month after Selverra, she'd run up those same stairs without her heart even beating faster. *Old age? Hardly.*

She pressed the heel of her palm against her lower stomach; the short, pale scar ached, now and again, as though what lay under the muscle had never healed properly. That had been

Lyiadd's worst and deepest cut; it hadn't bothered her until after Berd.

But to cut herself off from further children! She wasn't certain she wanted more, but Kabada was so *final*! And once she agreed to take it, Malaeth would insist on full dosage. As she had with Lisabetha. *Poor 'Betha. She's only the one child, only baby Brendan. It must terrify her. And poor Brelian.*

Galdan knew she used AEldra control to prevent a child immediately on Berdwyn's heels. She didn't just tell him, either, they talked about it. The children were *theirs*, not only hers. He had a right to know what she intended, and he had a right to say what he thought.

But she had no business standing and brooding at the top of the stairs with the morning slipping away from her. Two hours were promised to Eveya and the upper-rank women for practice, then a session of double rapier practice with Golsat, Brelian and a few of the advanced armed. An hour with the children, and after noon-meal the Main Council had enough small, irking matters to settle that it seemed unlikely they'd finish before dark. Evening-meal would be with Grewl and three of his clerks.

After that, she would most likely try to tutor Galdan, though she was finding it increasingly difficult to hide a growing sense of hopelessness from him. Perhaps—perhaps after that, she could talk to him.

Vess clasped a sweating, grimy-knuckled hand in his own, turned it gently palm up. He brought his amused gaze up to meet the boy's glassy-eyed stare. The smell of salt, leather, dried and fresh sweat—stale wine and onion on the boy's panting, terrified breath—assaulted him. In the triumph of the moment, he scarcely noticed it. "Take this," he murmured. A gleam of gold, a flash of red as he dropped the light chain and its token into the boy's hand, closed the fingers over it. "Take it, and keep it hidden, do you hear me?"

"I hear you," Jon whispered; he was nearly sobbing, fighting to hide his terror, knowing this horror of a man could *sense* it, however he dissembled. *Mal wouldn't be afraid*, he tried to tell himself. *Mal wouldn't, you can't!* He was. Without the wall hard against his back, without the hand that clasped his, he would have fallen.

"That is good. I am glad you hear me. You will hear me from now on in places far from this Isle, for I am part of you now. I go with you, in this gem that I give you." Jon shivered, closed his eyes. "Do not do that, look at me," Vess said in a deceptively gentle voice. His fingers curled into muscle. "Do you know what this pretty toy is? Of course you do not, so I will tell you. It is a focus stone. A magic jewel, just like in a tale. You will wear this always, from now on; you will never remove it. Swear that."

"I s—I swear," Jon whispered.

"I wear such a stone myself, do you see my ring? The ring, the pendant, they will bring us close together, nearer than lovers, Jon Bri Madden. Through this focus stone, I will hear your words and your thoughts. And you will tell me what passes when you are away from this place. Do you understand?"

"I—you want me to—to spy—" Worse than he could have imagined, worse than he had thought! "You—want me to be a traitor to Mal—!"

"How can you be a traitor, if you are loyal to *me*?" Vess murmured. "You will do this thing, just as I tell you."

"No." He shaped the word, but no sound came. The thing burned the palm of his hand, but Vess' fingers held his fist closed, he couldn't let go of it. "I can't!"

"You will. Because you are mine, now. Because I can reward you more than this Lord Captain; and because you will obey me and the stone. Because there will be great reward for you when you obey me. But because the stone will also do *this* if you do not comply with my least wish." Jon caught his breath on an agonized little cry; his hand burned, agony spread up his arm, something was pressing upon his mind, driving everything he thought of as Jon back into a dark, fetid hole. Pain gnawed at his fingers. "Do not speak, do not cry out, do not try. You cannot." The pain faded, slowly; a little of his mind was his again. "Besides," Vess purred, "someone might hear you. You don't want anyone to hear you. Do you?" Jon shook his head violently; tears flew, splattering them both. The terror crouched deep inside him, hovering just at the edge of consciousness, where he knew he'd feel it all his days—however long or short those might be. Vess stroked his cheek, gently brushing tears away. "You're mine. I own you, all of you. You will wear this Thullen, my gift, my focus stone. You will wear it as token of my ownership of you. You will tell me all your captain plans, when he plans it."

"No, not Mal, please not that!" He forced that much past chattering teeth. The blackness swarmed through him, searing pain wracked his entire body: Jon tore at his hair, writhed against the wall until the stones shredded his shirt and left his shoulders raw and bleeding. Vess maintained his grip on the hand with the focus. Silence, save for Jon's whistling pant.

"Learn from this. You do not defy me. I am not your Mal Brit Arren, I do not reward for good behavior. I only punish what is unacceptable to me. Do you understand that?" Jon choked violently, fell to his knees as Vess released him, and vomited. "Put the pendant on." Jon dragged the chain over his head and let the Thullen fall to his breast. Vess knelt and tucked it inside the boy's shirt. "You must keep it hidden, it is our secret, yours and mine." He smiled with cold satisfaction, caught the boy's head between his hands and placed a light kiss on his brow. "Bless you, my loyal servant. Go." Without a word, Jon rose and stumbled away, further into the maze of shattered buildings.

If there is anything more unpleasant than being ripped untimely from a warm sleep by cold terror, I do not wish to know of it. May the Nedaoan Mothers grant a day comes I need never hear such a summons again!

5

Marrita exhaled slowly and a red *sound* came from her lips. It tore through Ylia's inner being, ringing her like a bell. She was half aware she slept, was trying to move—an arm, even a finger—something so she would waken. Claws raked her shoulder: She screamed and found herself trembling on the edge of the bed, Galdan's fingers digging painfully into muscle. Her ears still rang and it took her two shuddering breaths to realize what it was: Horns blared across the valley and the market bell was ringing wildly in answer.

"Are you all right?" Galdan was already across the room, pulling on his breeches. Nisana came into the room as lamps were lit the length of the hall.

"No." Ylia reached for the lamp: Baelfyr crackled from her fingers, the wick spluttered. "Bad dream," she added, a little less shortly. Not *his* fault she was susceptible to such things, or that she had woven the warning horns into the nightmare. "Black hells, but I wish they'd find another hour for attack!"

"You speak for me." Galdan yanked the leather jerkin down and combed wildly tossled hair and beard with his fingers. Across the hall, through an open window, they heard a company of horse tearing by. The night guard was on its way to the fight. The message in the horn-call: "They're at Ifney's southern pastures. The company will be a while getting there." Ylia folded her breeches flat to her ankles and began pulling her boots on. "Levren is on his way up here." It was working just the way they'd planned it: A force of ten of the Elite Guard, accompanied by Levren, Golsat or Brelian, was now sleeping fully clad and armed in one of the Tower guardrooms each night. If an attack came, the regular horse company would ride out but the ten would be there and ready to bridge at once. After so many night battles with Mathkkra since the snow had gone for good, the War

42

Council and even the conservative Main Council had offered no objections to the plan.

Ylia buckled her sword belt and caught up the dagger when she heard Levren's shout. Galdan was already half-way to the stairs. Ylia caught up her dagger sheath and followed.

It was the dark of a moonless, cloudy night, the deeper dark of tree-shade. Gusts of chill wind blew young trees nearly sideways. They could *hear* fighting; could see nothing at first. With the second level of sight, Ylia saw men and women in Ifney's colors fighting a veritable horde of Mathkkra. They heard the Lord Holder bellowing somewhere deep in the woods. A spluttering and flare as Eveya got torches kindled; flame crackled wildly. She and Levren split them, shoved them into the ground in a half circle behind them. Mathkkra cried out and shrank away from the sudden and unwelcome light.

Galdan's voice rose above the noise: "The Elite Guard is here, we're coming in!" A ragged cheer answered him. "'Ware, you archers, hold fire!" Levren shouted. He fitted an arrow to his string, moved forward with four archers at his back. Moments later Ifney fought his way into the open, two lads still alive to guard his back. The Mathkkra avoided the torches; otherwise they fought with stunning ferocity.

That was no good sign, for Mathkkra ordinarily fled once the odds shifted so greatly against them. Even Ifney's company should have been large enough to discourage them, but in the short time since he'd confronted the creatures, he'd lost half his armed.

Ylia stood with her back to the torches, watching. She disliked using the sword unless she must, and the fighting was too close for her to attempt Baelfyr; she'd burn her own folk trying it. She blinked as wind-driven smoke covered her. It shifted; she rubbed her eyes, then stared. One Mathkkra stood just under the trees, well back from the fighting. Everything about the fight was odd, but this creature was the oddest thing of all. It gazed at her flatly, unafraid, almost as though it knew her. Torchlight flared in a gust of wind; it gave the Mathkkra glowing red coals for eyes, and picked out a flash of red deep in the dark red of its rough-woven short robe.

"What is that?" She was unaware she'd spoken aloud until Eveya peered over her shoulder.

"What is what?"

"That." Ylia pointed. The Mathkkra still stared straight at her, she would have almost said in challenge had it been a human foe. Something depended from a leather thong, something that glowed red in one place and seemed to swallow the light in another. "Eveya, back me, I want him." Eveya set herself against Ylia's left shoulder and the two women hurled themselves forward, leaping over small pale bodies. The red-clad shaman jerked and would have slipped back into the trees, but it was too late: Her left hand caught the thong, her right brought the sword down in a slashing sweep, nearly separating head from body. She dragged the leather thong and its jewel free; they backed away to the comparative safety of the torches.

"Galdan!"

"You're giving me grey hairs, what were you *doing*?" Galdan bellowed as he reached her side.

"Look at this!" She held the medallion before his eyes.

Galdan pulled a torch and held it up. A Thullen gazed sullenly back at him. It was plain, rough copper save for the chip stones that made its eyes. They gave back no gleam of light. "What's this? Where'd you get it?" he demanded.

"I took it from the Mathkkra I just killed, the red-robe. Shaman. This—I don't know, I took it because that thing was acting so oddly. It's Power, Lyiadd's Power."

Galdan touched it cautiously, withdrew his finger. "It's that thing you told me about, a while since, it's a focus. Lyiadd's backing these Mathkkra directly, isn't he?"

"I wish I didn't agree with you, Galdan. But—look at it, it's almost as nasty as a real Thullen. I don't like it."

"Feel watched?" he asked. She nodded.

"He is watching us. But he can't work a focus like this from the Isles! And he can't be back in the mountains!" She slammed her sword hilt into her palm. "He can't be! But that means a master focus set somewhere within a league or so, to control lesser ones like this."

The fighting flared around them briefly as Mathkkra broke and ran toward them, veering to avoid the torches; they were cut down before Ylia or Galdan or their guard had to intervene. "You can't take that back to the Tower, lady wife. I doubt it's safe for you to hold."

"I can't help that, I can't just drop it," Ylia said flatly. "I'm not giving it back to the Mathkkra, and I certainly can't leave it here. We'll have to break it. Somehow. Why isn't the night guard here yet?"

"It hasn't been as long as you think," Galdan said. "But—Inniva's warp, *what is that*?"

Someone screamed and staggered back from the front line. The torches went dim, the air was thick. The wind blew one last hard gust, fell to nothing. Swordsmen and women stood in silent, nervous groups; the few Mathkkra still alive were whimpering, fallen spills of grey and white.

Ylia fell back into Galdan. His heart was pounding a heavy, wild staccato against her shoulder-blades. The second level of sight was useless beyond the Mathkkra: A black fog seemed to be rising between her folk and the woods. She caught her breath on a frightened sob. There was something out there to fear, something whispering and giggling deep in her thought. The black of tree-shade was *moving*, humping like a thundercloud, taking shape and questingly, hellishly aware. Death was in that sooty mass, *her* death, a rending, clawed and fanged death; poison in her veins burning away what life was left to the mangle of crushed bone and torn flesh, a thing tearing at her body, leaving her thought intact to the last . . .

Galdan moaned as the full sense of the creature hit him, swayed and fell to his knees; the talisman slipped from Ylia's fingers and lay in the dirt, the red eyes glared at her. It was a focus, she knew beyond doubt now, just as she knew the thing out there sought it. *It wants the stone, more than it wants me. But it will kill us all, if it can.*

"No!" She snatched at the cord, backed past Galdan, through the torches, through Ifney's armed. The thing gave an eager, howling cry that echoed through the trees and rang her head like all the bells and horns in Nedao. It leaped.

Reflex brought the sword up to block what came at her, no thought of her own. "Shelagn!" Her voice cracked like a boy's. But for the first time, the blade did not respond to her cry. She opened her mouth to cry out again, inhaled a gust of pure, bloody horror as the thing enveloped her. She couldn't see, couldn't move. Couldn't even be certain she was still on her feet, for she could no longer sense up or down. She could *feel*, though; gods, she could! The blackness was greasy against her bare throat, slick across her hair, harsh over the backs of her fists. The thing laughed, chortled, a filthy sound that shredded her skin, smashed her bones. She could not scream at the pain; no air went in, no sound came.

And then it was gone, the sense of it already faint and distant, growing fainter by the moment. Her fingers were numb and bleeding where it had ripped the focus from her hand. She staggered, fell. Someone beyond her was screaming, someone else wailing in terror. Galdan's arms were around her shoulders, holding her while she was sick. She remembered hearing horses: The guard had arrived. Galdan's hands gathering her close, the rough cloth of his shirt hems being rubbed gently across her chin and lips, trying to blot her tears. She remembered nothing after that.

The Tower room was dark save for the sullen red of the fire, and that was down to its last coals. An unpleasant odor teased Vess' nostrils; he fought a sneeze, sniffed hard, surreptitiously rubbed his nose and eyes. He clasped his hands together under the edge of the table, then, to stop them trembling. *Tired*, he assured himself carefully. *I'm not afraid, not of that thing or of what we did. I'm just—tired.*

Neither of the room's other two occupants paid him the least attention: Until he could gain control of his—exhaustion—he was glad. Marrita's attention was fixed on Lyiadd. Lyiadd leaned forward, elbows braced on the table, his forehead in his hands.

Father. Somehow, even with all he'd seen these past three years, all he'd learned and done himself, it had never come home to him like it did tonight: Power. Black, deadly Power. Magic. He'd felt Ylia's terror and disgust when that thing went for her; he'd nearly vomited himself. Its desire had even clawed at *him*. Knowing he'd helped create it, that he was protected against it by his father's Power, that hadn't helped.

He shot another glance down the table. Lyiadd still leaned against his hands, and his shoulders trembled, but as Marrita touched him in concern, he leaned back. He was laughing. Black Fire—the Lammior's Sya'datha—hovered just above his hands in a sullen, velvety haze. He brought his amusement under control with some effort; the Sya'datha faded, taking the odd odor and the uneasy feeling with it. Marrita smiled. The old malicious gleam was back in Lyiadd's smoke-grey eyes; she had never liked it when it was directed at her, but she had missed it more than she'd known.

Marrita relaxed. It had taken a terrible effort when *she* had snatched the focus and they'd called up a Zahg to take it back. And the transfer of Power was only a five-day behind. Already Lyiadd had regained his old strength, was daily adding to it.

She felt no regret at all for that Power; she retained more than any AEldra would ever know. But she wouldn't have wanted that, except to save Lyiadd, to aid him. Lyiadd alone had the knowledge to use the Lammior's Power, it needed true malice. He must be the Primary, his the great strength.

Lyiadd patted her hand where it lay pale against the dark red of his tunic; she blinked, smiled at him. "We did it," he murmured. Satisfaction wreathed him the way the Sya'datha had wreathed his fingers. "We did it. The main focus you set in that valley works. The individual focus worked, and my Mathkkra are not unwilling to carry them. Think how frightened those peasants were tonight, that Mathkkra stood and fought! We wrought a Zahg, such as has not been seen in a thousand years, and it did *our* bidding!" He laughed again, a boy's crow of triumph. "Did you see? She feared *that*!"

"She would have to be stone, not to fear a Zahg," Marrita replied. She laid her other hand over his briefly, withdrew both and reached for the tray of wine and cups, thick slabs of bread and white crumbly cheese she had prepared before they ordered the attack. To Vess' surprise, she served him food and drink instead of letting him fend for himself as she usually did. *Father has spoken to her. Or perhaps she finally realizes my worth.*

Lyiadd lifted his cup. "You did well, my son. Your aid was invaluable." The younger man flushed with pleasure.

"Father. Thank you."

"Tonight began it. We must begin to move, now. Soon."

"But—" Marrita shifted uneasily. Lyiadd let a hand fall to cover hers and she subsided, but her expression was still worried.

"*I* am ready. Vess has his following, he has control of the boy Jon, he has the main body of the Osneran Chosen to support him—"

"If he is *careful*, he has the Osnerans," Marrita broke in.

Vess shook his head. "I know how those men think in their clawings for status and power, and I know Tevvro very well. He is not yet high-placed enough to be very useful, but he will be. He is ambitious, and he thinks I will be a rung on the ladder to his goal. He does not realize that I have ambitions also." He smiled. "I can handle Tevvro." Marrita eyed him with impatience and much of her old dislike. "He is not like my poor shadow Jers; no, not at all like Jers. I understand the difference between them. I was raised by these Chosen, remember that."

"If we begin too soon," Marrita said tentatively.

Lyiadd shook his head. "No. We have our allies, those we have bought, those we have suborned, those who will fight willingly for us. I do not intend that there will be any fighting in Yls; of course. Nar: It doesn't matter. Nedao is my son's business, or largely so." The Sya'datha was blackly iridescent around his fingers again; he smiled at them, rather fondly. "We must move soon, though, Marrita. Each day we wait means a chance of trouble. There must be no drawn-out conflict in Yslar. Also, the longer we delay, the more chance the main focus in Nedao might be found."

"She will never find it!" Marrita snapped. Lyiadd shook his head.

"We have all agreed *not* to underestimate the Nedaoan half-blood! Remember that she has a mate who controls blocked wild Power despite his own blood! Remember she was named ally by the Dreyz and by those two renegade Nasath!"

"Bendesevorian has no power among the Nasath. He is too young and they will not have looked upon him with favor, breaking their self-made exile to speak with a half-AEldra swordswoman and a cat!"

"I know, beloved. He and his sister must not have say in the councils of the Guardians, else we would not have remained free to do as we wish. They would have come upon us while we were still within the mountains. But Bendesevorian has Power of his own, and he might wear down the Council, eventually. Though I cannot believe that the Guardians, few as they are and more set in their ways than the Sirdar's Council, would interfere once the Peopled Lands are ours. Why? To begin another holy war? They have left the AEldra to go their own ways for over a thousand years. And where would they find another Shelagn?" Silence. "But that is another reason to attack soon, that last, don't you agree? Before Shelagn's heir becomes heir in more than name?" He stood, noting with pleasure how easily he moved these days. A man never paid heed to such things until every movement, every step, was an exhausting effort. "Ylia will never have the opportunity to become Catalyst, we will not leave her the time."

He started toward the door, stopped at Vess' side and dropped a hand to his shoulder. "Send a message tomorrow to the *Fury*, to

Brit Arren. He is to begin the next step in the raids on the Narran ships; all goods taken, the ships burned and sunk. No survivors." He smiled, an unpleasant expression that Vess unconsciously matched. "The Narrans will be cowed—or vanished from the face of the seas—before we ever leave Yslar's harbor to come against them."

Ylia pried one eye open to find Galdan perched on a corner of the bed, leaning over her. He smiled but his eyes remained gravely worried. She stretched out her legs under the thin cover —more than was needed, for the room was warm. Too warm for any early hour. There were a few muted sounds from the lower hall, from the street, and away up the hill behind the Tower she could hear the distant echoing *thunk* of an axeman felling a tree. She yawned. "What's the hour?"

"Fifth." Ylia levered onto her elbows in surprise. Galdan pushed her flat again. "There's food for you, I can bring it, or you can go down and eat it. Council meeting won't be for an hour yet, but you needn't go."

"Why not?" She set his arm aside, sat up and swung her feet to the floor. Her hair was damply plastered to her forehead, but one of her women had left cool washing water and fresh cloths. She scrubbed at her face, splashed water across the back of her neck. Galdan handed her one of the light grey linen tunics she favored in warm weather. She shook the last drops from her hands and slipped into the shirt. "You're awfully quiet. I don't like the look of you, just now. What chanced out there?"

"Ifney's dead," Galdan said. "Ifney and four of his sword-sworn, three of the Elite. That thing got them. We—didn't know, we couldn't tell, until we took a count of those still standing." Ylia stared at him in shocked, horrified silence. "There wasn't enough left of them to put in a small bag." Silence. "If you don't want to face the Council, you don't have to, they'll understand."

Ylia shuddered. "My fault. I had that focus in my hands, asking for trouble—"

"If you hadn't moved when that thing came out of the woods, it would have killed more of us. All the guard, me included. And you."

"If I'd left that focus alone—"

Galdan caught her shoulders and gave her a hard shake. "You

don't know that! Perhaps the creature had already been summoned! You know not to try to reguess the past!"

"Gods," Ylia glanced toward the hall. "Hssst, it's Selverra! Mind your face!"

"Mind your thought," he shot back at her swiftly. The Princess Royal was developing mind-touch at a precocious age, and would have no difficulty sensing emotion in any event.

Ylia cleared her mind carefully as she laced the lightweight tan breeches down to her ankles, slid her feet into soft shoes instead of her boots.

"Mommy?" A small golden head came around the corner. Ylia smiled—*that* took no effort at all in her daughter's presence—held out her arms and Selverra scampered into them. Malaeth peered around the door, reassured herself the child hadn't wakened her mother, and moved on with Berdwyn in her arms.

"Sel. Where have you and Malaeth been today?"

Selverra's smile marked her as Galdan's beyond question. She climbed onto her mother's lap. "Went to see Aunt 'Betha. *I* got to hold her baby," she added proudly.

"Very good. Were you careful?"

Selverra nodded gravely, paused to choose words from a child's vocabulary. "I sat on the bed first, and Aunt 'Betha let me hold him then."

"Ah. I see."

"And we got a fruit from the market, and I got to put my feet in the water, but Malaeth wouldn't let me get wet."

"Well," Ylia said, matching her daughter's grave tone, mindful of Galdan's warm gaze on them both, "the water moves pretty fast, you know."

"But I'm strong!" Selverra protested.

"I know. Maybe we can go to a place your daddy knows, where you can get wet all over." Selverra nodded emphatically, long, blonde plaits flying.

"Tomorrow," she said firmly.

"Well—perhaps. Another day might be better, though. All right?"

Selverra nodded again, jumped down and, with a quick hug for Galdan, started back out of the room. "Malaeth says I have to take a nap, so I better go now."

Both the Princess Royal's parents kept reasonably straight faces until she was out of sight and well down the hall. Ylia shook her head. "Gods and Mothers but she's funny sometimes!"

"Don't let Sel hear you say that, you know how touchy she is about being laughed at."

Ylia let Galdan help her to her feet and leaned against his shoulder. "Ifney dead. I can't believe it. Galdan, where will this end?"

He shook his head. "Don't know. They won't win, though. Don't ever let yourself think it."

"No." But she carried doubts down the main stairs to her food. There was a master focus out there, somewhere. It would have to be found and destroyed, but how? Given the size of the valley and the lands around it, how could they possibly hope to even find it? And if they did, would she dare touch it, would she dare think she could undo it, would she dare chance facing that creature again? *If I have to*—but she couldn't complete the thought.

6

It was a small bay, one mere inlet of so many along this stretch of coast: The water was treacherous with exposed and barely submerged boulders; rocks larger than a ship dotted the swells. A narrow strip of rocky beach lined the inner curve of the bay, cut off at either tip of the crescent by sheer cliffs. A steep forested slope nearly touched the water in several places. A few trees dotted the higher ledges; dark granite towered above the waves, impassable save in one or two places where water had carved falls and steps in the stone.

Little of this was visible at the moment: The bay was still, even the waves subdued under a thick fog. Men at one end of the *Fury* could barely make those at the other, and the top of the mast was lost in drifts of grey. Black sails hung limp; rowers waited tensely on the mid-boat benches. All eyes were on the powerfully built captain. Mal Brit Arren perched on the bow, bare feet gripping the rails and the jutting mast for the artemon sail. He was staring into the fog as though he could part it with the ferocity of his gaze, out toward open water.

Tension increased: Where was the Narran ship? Men looked at each other, glanced furtively at their captain, quickly away lest he catch them at it. Not all of them liked this new directive from the Three and they knew Mal Brit Arren was furious. His temper was legendary; he'd killed men when he was angered. That made them more edgy than the waiting.

Though most of them shared his anger: Their own Lord Captain, forced to accept the dictates and whims of an Ylsan! But no one had said anything when Brit Arren had called for objection. No one had dared.

They could hear it, suddenly: the mournful, deep-toned bell clanging in the distance, drawing ever nearer: Narran fog-bells. It was still muffled by the northern cliff wall of the narrow inlet, but it was drawing nearer. Brit Arren jumped down from the rails as the *Fury* slid into watery sunlight.

There was nothing to see but water and the last of the rock-teeth that guarded the inlet, making it impassable to any save a small fisher's coracle or a well-mastered fighting ship. The deep bell echoed, seemed briefly to come from all around them, and then the *Merman* was before them, its wide hull bearing down through the waves.

The *Fury* knifed straight across the swells, right for her. The bells-boy saw the ominous black shape and set up a raucous clangor; Brit Arren shouted orders, the rowers pulled, working to bring the ship in so the grapplers could do their work. The Narran cog turned away with a smooth evasion maneuver that spoke of practice and skill. Brit Arren swore, shouted another order. Half a dozen men sheathed their blades and leaped for oars; the *Fury* matched the *Merman*'s change of direction and drew close once again.

Fog stirred with a faint wind, filling *Fury*'s black sail unexpectedly. The Narran pulled away.

Not for long: The wide-hulled cargo ship was no match for the trim *Fury*. A hook clattered to the Narran deck, another and then a handful; ropes went taut and the gap of open water slowly closed. With a howl that froze Narran blood, Mal Brit Arren's crew drew long knives and swords and leaped aboard the *Merman*. The Narrans, bows and swords at the ready, grimly waited for them.

The fight was fierce and bloody, quickly over: The Narran seamen were not predominantly fighting men, were unprepared for the change in their enemy's tactics, and many of them stood in stunned horror, staring at their murdered companions before they, too, were killed. Brit Arren strode from one end of the *Merman* to the other, crying encouragement to his crew, killing any foolhardy enough to come against him. *Don't think, do!* he urged himself furiously. He'd killed before, often; his own kind, Ragnolers. Narrans such as these, now and again. Killing didn't bother him. But he'd never butchered: Fighting these underskilled and stunned Narrans was more butchery than true fighting among equals. *Damn them; damn the Three of them!*

He could defy them. He should have defied them. Perhaps it was not yet too late.

There had been heavy fighting on the low, broad step that separated main deck from the red-and-gold-canopied cabin: Best goods and coin would be there, where the captain slept. His second was directing three red-scarves to salvage there already. Brit Arren watched, then took a moment to gaze out to sea: The fog was lifting. He beckoned to his second, pointed at the roof of the cabin. "Get one of the reds up there, get him a glass, have him watch. I know a man can't see far but it's lifting, and I'm mindful there may be an escort for this one. Remember our *Spectre*? Catapults and flaming pitch, they said; lost half the crew and nearly the entire ship."

He turned back to oversee the fighting, but suddenly there wasn't any. Except in the point of the bow, just short of the small high-sided platform for the bells-boy. A Narran was trapped there, unreachable save through his blades.

Mal skirted fallen men and swore furiously as his foot slipped on bloody planks. He shouted at the men who stood three-deep around the bow and they hastily cleared a space for him.

The Narran raised a long, narrow sword and matching dagger to ready. Brit Arren glanced at the decks: Two of his men lay dead, a third had been dragged back by his mates, and lay bleeding in a companion's grip.

"You're master of these butchers?" The Narran's voice was steady.

"Mal Brit Arren, of the *Fury*."

"Tr'Harsen, the *Merman*. The *Shark* was with me until an hour ago. When it catches up, you'll be captain of the black deeps, Mal Brit Arren."

"You'll beat me there, Tr'Harsen of the *Merman*," Brit Arren replied mockingly. "Your men are waiting for you."

The Narran shook his head in disbelief. "Why?"

"Why should we share the seas with you?" Mouthing *their* words, he could even briefly believe them. Scum, these traders!

"We could say the same of you," Tr'Harsen replied grimly. "Though we've been willing to leave you alone for like treatment."

"A weak man's philosophy. But you Narrans *are* weak." Brit Arren laughed. The men behind him laughed and the rocks rang with it.

"No. Not entirely." Tr'Harsen lunged; his blade moved in a curious twisting circle, deftly avoided the parry and laid open Brit Arren's cheek from temple to beard.

He cried out, as much in surprise as pain. Trickery! Any man could take first blood with a trick unknown by his opponent! He'd make no more such scores, Brit Arren assured himself grimly.

They fought in silence, save for the occasional moan from the wounded man; that faded slowly as the blood drained from him. "Give up," Mal said finally. "I'll kill you quickly." Tr'Harsen might not have heard; an upward slash of his dagger nearly caught Brit Arren's sword hand.

But he was cornered, and that told against him; he'd already fought, more than once: Brit Arren came to the battle fresh. He waited; the moment came, he lunged, catching the Narran's sword arm in a murderous grip. Tr'Harsen brought his dagger up, too slowly: Brit Arren ran his long blade in to the hilts, pulled it back out as he twisted away.

Tr'Harsen drew his breath in an agonized shudder, staggered and fell. His long body jerked once, the sword rolled free. The men shuffled nervously, began moving quietly away from the bows. Brit Arren's voice stopped them.

"Are the holds cleared? The cabin?"

"Mostly." Jon came to his side. "They're hurrying; the wounded are off already."

"All of you, then, move it! Remember what he said? Remember *Spectre*?" The men scattered in a burst of relieved activity. "Any survivors, Jon?"

"The bells-boy dove over. He was bleeding though, Mal; I don't think he could have made shore." Jon touched his forearm. "Mal, are you all right?"

"Of course I am! Go, finish out! Hurry!"

"That's the last of it, Mal, that crate." Jon pointed as two men shoved a black-coated box out of the hold and two others staggered away with it. Brit Arren closed his eyes, momentarily sickened by all of it: Magic, blood, the sheer waste of those men, the ship—the retaliation the Narrans would surely make. The sticky red boards underfoot that had been ship's weathered grey. The unstable movement as the unmastered cog wallowed in a sudden shifting swell. *They're using me, using all of us. When they're done using us, they'll discard us like the woman throws away the ashes in her brazier.* It made him briefly so furious he didn't dare speak. Jon waited in silence, watching him.

"Don't waste any time, we can't stay here. Take two of the red-scarves and find some oil, soak down the sails and the decks."

"We're going to fire her?" For some reason this unsettled Jon.

"Fire her," Brit Arren snapped. "Fire her and send her to the bottom! Go, move!" Jon turned and sped back down the deck, tapping two of the first-voyagers and taking them with him. Brit Arren could hear them down in the holds moving through the sleeping area, heard things falling and breaking in their haste. He walked back over to the mast. Tr'Harsen lay sprawled on his back, eyes closed. "You lost, Captain," he whispered, "I'm still alive. *You're* dead." He walked back across the deck, clambered over the railing and leaped back to the *Fury*. His men lined the rails. "Fire her!" he ordered curtly.

Torches were lit, flung high. They flew across the widening gap between the two ships to land among the oil-soaked barrels. Fire ran along the decks and up the mast. The sail burst into flame. Even where he stood, he felt a wave of heat and he shouted urgent orders at the men working the lines. *Fury*'s black mainsail bellied as other men scrambled out the bow to let down the triangular artemon. The *Fury* leaped forward but a hundred lengths downwind, they brought her around again.

Silence held; save for the crackle of fire, the creak of wood, rope against tackle, the slap of a man's bare feet as he ran across the deck. A loud crack, a groan of protesting wood; the *Merman* heeled over and slid beneath the surface. The scent of charred wood and death hit them on a gust of smoke, passed over, was gone. A gull screamed; several men jumped.

"Brit Ofry, take the tiller!" Brit Arren shouted. "The rest of you, get those sails down!" Men moved. Brit Arren clambered down the stairs to his cabin. Jon Bri Madden followed.

"Mal?" It was hard to see in the lavish cabin at first. His voice wasn't working right, it wanted to go high and quavery. "I thought perhaps you'd like—"

"What I'd like," Brit Arren snapped, "is wine. Bring me the red from that last little oversea schooner." Jon found the bottle and a base-weighted cup. "One for yourself, Jon."

Jon didn't like drinking with Mal when he was in a dark mood. This time: He couldn't read the captain's mood, that could be even more dangerous. He closed his eyes briefly, found another cup. They drank in silence. Brit Arren set his wine aside barely tasted. "May all the horrors there are gnaw Bri H'Larn's bones for what he did to us." His voice was nearly expressionless, all the more frightening for it. "I would never have countenanced those Three, Jon! I should not have agreed to the killing. Lyiadd says it is to defeat Nar before war ever falls upon her, to show them how little hope they have! Only a fool would think that." He picked up his cup, looked at it, set it aside untasted again. "Such a stupid thing to die for, Jon. This plan of Lyiadd's will get us all killed!"

"By the Narrans?" Jon laughed. Brit Arren's mouth twisted in brief, sour humor.

"Remember catapults and burning pitch, even fools who cannot fight like men can sink a ship with those things, Jon." He slammed both fists on the table; it shuddered and his cup fell to the floor. "It does not matter, we are all dead men."

"Mal, I—" Jon felt the sweat running in little rivulets down his breastbone. The focus stuck to his skin.

"Well? What use will we be to Lyiadd when the Peopled Lands are his?"

"To hold the sea against—" Jon's voice trailed away. The black anger in Brit Arren's eyes slammed into him like a blow.

"Against what?" He took Jon's untouched cup, drained it and shoved it away. "Leave me, Jon. Go."

"Mal, if you—"

"Go!" Brit Arren roared. Jon fled.

As I get older, I find I take more pleasure in the small things: a narrow ledge warm with sun for most of a long day of late Floods Month. Or that Selverra's voice is so like my sweet Scythia's was at that baby age, or that I could see her semblance in Berd's large, blue eyes.

7

The sun had long since dropped behind the mountains. Ylia knew she could see the light still on the snow-capped eastern peaks if she sat up straight. At the moment, she lacked the strength for even that.

The Main Council would have been enough to wear her down; she was heartily sick of the constant bickerings, the unfortunate tendency of the old men who had been her father's councilors to live in the past. So often their recommendations were simply out of the question. Even after three years in the valley, certain of them could not be made to see the dangers surrounding Nedao, and all of the Peopled Lands. She'd hoped to avoid replacing councilors, knowing it would create hard feeling and difficulties. But the meetings themselves were difficult. Some of the eldest, like Gedersy, might even be relieved to step down.

At the outset she'd managed somehow to keep control of matters, and of her temper. But then the messages arrived from down-river: The *Merman* gone, its crew dead save for the bellsboy. Ber'Sordes' man had left the table immediately; the Council broke up moments later. Galdan was gone, too, offering the Narrans whatever aid and consolation he could—though that was unhappily very little.

Ylia sat alone at the long council table, staring its smooth length, seeing none of it. "Tr'Harsen. Gods, my friend." It hurt. She couldn't even weep for him, yet; she couldn't feel it. Nisana leaped into her lap and rubbed against her hand.

'I'm sorry for his death, I liked that man.' The cat stiffened suddenly. 'By the Nasath themselves, she's here.' And she was gone, a tortoise blur bounding across the chamber and out the open window. Ylia stared after her blankly.

"She's here?" The inner sense was sluggish, nearly as dead to feeling as the rest of her. It took a moment to understand. "Ah no! Not now!" But there was no doubting the AEldra presence. Ysian had come back to Nedao.

"Not now? What?" Galdan stood in the doorway.

"Ysian. She came on that boat, she's on her way up from the docks."

"That's good, isn't it?" Galdan crossed the room to lean against the back of her chair. His fingers rubbed the tight triangle of muscle at the base of her neck.

"Now?"

"Why should she wait? Lyiadd may attack Yls any day now. Ysian's life would be doubly forfeit as part of the Sirdar's Council and as a daughter of the Second House, don't you think?"

Ylia shook her head. "I—all right, we discussed that before. It's not safe here, either."

"Safer, though. We Nedaoans know the danger." He helped her to her feet. "Come now; bring up a smile for her and warn Malaeth she's coming."

Evening-meal was set for one more person, and Ylia managed to put herself in a better mood before Ysian arrived. Her aunt had lost weight during the past three years and gained muscle: In her breeches and plain shirt, sturdy boots and sensible cloak, her hair in a thick plait, she looked younger—more like Ylia than Scythia. Two Narrans came behind with her minimal baggage; she carried only a plain, practical bowcase.

One thing had not changed at all, however. She and Nisana arrived so intertwined it was difficult to tell where one left off and the other began. The cat was purring madly, and Ysian interspersed her conversation with whispered, cooing remarks that Ylia was grateful she could not hear.

"Ah, gods, niece, I thought I would never get here, it took forever." Ysian hefted a limp Nisana onto her shoulders and hugged Ylia hard.

"How did you do it, Ysian? They've allowed no women on Narran ships for three years now." The serving woman Therea led the Narrans up to the hastily prepared guest room; Ysian and Ylia followed.

Ysian sank gratefully onto the bed, untied her cloak and reached for the copper of warm water and washing cloths next to it. "I rode," she said. "Ah, that feels wonderful!" Damp tendrils of golden hair clung to her face. "None of the ships in Yslar Harbor would take me. But I suddenly couldn't bear to wait any longer. It took me a full five-day to reach Nalda." She smiled faintly, plunged her hands into the bowl. "I couldn't have done *that* a year ago. Even so, it was an exhausting ride. I still ache."

"Ye didn't ride *alone*!" Malaeth had come into the chamber in time to hear her last words.

Ysian shook her head, dried her hands and hugged her old nurse. "Two of Father's housemen came with me the whole way. He suggested it, amazingly enough. And for the second half of the journey, I also had three of Lord Kyeran's sons for company. Seventh House, you know, and northern border holdings; little Power among them but they're arms-trained. I was well cared for, Malaeth."

Malaeth still looked scandalized and both women knew why: one of her babies riding the breadth of Yls in breeches, in the company of five young men and no woman to chaperone! She sniffed, touched Ysian's plait and clucked disapprovingly. "It needs washing, lass."

Ysian shook her head. "Tomorrow. Tonight there's enough of me left to eat a hot meal. Maybe to climb out of these clothes before I fall asleep." Malaeth cast a scorching glance at both of them and left in tight-lipped silence. Ysian's mouth quirked. "I'd laugh if I weren't so tired. She's *dying* to tell me how awful I look. I can't think why she didn't."

"You only just arrived, and you're her Ysian. I wager she screams at you tomorrow for risking your reputation by traveling without a nurse."

Ysian rolled her sleeves down, dried her hands. "I daresay." Her face was grave, and the exhaustion was suddenly visible. "That Narran ship. You knew them, didn't you? I came barely in time; Yls can't have much longer."

"It's—Ysian, I don't want to frighten you or upset you. We may not have long here, either. Just—just so you know that."

Ysian smiled faintly. "I know. I think I can be truly useful this time, though."

"Of course you can. I want you, Galdan wants you. We all do. I just wanted you to know."

"I know the dangers. I'm ready for them."

Malaeth came back with a heavy comb and sat on the edge of the bed to loosen Ysian's snarled plait. "What's chanced here of late?" Ysian winced as Malaeth's fingers caught. "Your last letter was over a month ago."

Ylia talked and Ysian listened in silence while Malaeth mumbled to herself and loosened tangles. The nurse turned at a faint noise from the doorway and a smile lightened her face. Selverra stood there, peering shyly into the room. She came three steps when Malaeth murmured something but moved sideways to slip behind her mother.

Ysian crooked a finger at her. "Is this young Selverra? I expected a little girl. You're a young lady, Selverra."

"Sel," the child corrected in a whisper.

"Sel. That's a nice name. I'm your Aunt Ysian."

"I know." Selverra smiled enchantingly, ducked under Ylia's arm and ran.

"By all the Guardians at once, that's a love of a child," Ysian said. Malaeth nodded proudly.

"Shy. You were, at that age, remember?"

"After so many years? Where's my grandnephew?"

"Sleeping. Want to see him?"

"After food. Suddenly, I'm starving." Ysian shoved her hands through her hair and slipped it behind her ears, ignoring Malaeth's grumblings. The old nurse went back to the nursery; Ysian followed Ylia downstairs.

Ylia, Ysian and Galdan ate alone, and Ylia was relieved to see the two taking to each other readily. She hadn't expected anything else, really, but such things happened. Ysian and Ylia's father had not liked each other much, but Ysian liked Galdan, and said so emphatically when he left for the Narran Ambassador's quarters. "He suits you."

"I think so."

"I'm glad," Ysian said bluntly. "Marriage for a woman of your rank doesn't always allow that." She yawned. "Take me to see young Berd, so I can consider my duty done for the night and go sleep. Tomorrow you can tell me more about this master focus; perhaps I can find it for you."

The nursery was quiet and dark, save for the tiny blue-glass lamp Malaeth kept burning the night. Berd slept peacefully in the cradle next to Malaeth's narrow cot. Ylia reached down to stroke a tiny hand; Berd licked his lips and shifted slightly. Ysian noiselessly withdrew; Ylia leaned over the padded edge to kiss him, followed. Malaeth came out with them.

"Selverra's all right?" Malaeth nodded.

"She surprised me, Ylia. She wants that little closet for her own, and she wanted the door shut from the first tonight. All you lasses liked tiny places like that. I just checked her, she's asleep. Ysian, should I come plait your hair for the night? I can get Therea to watch them."

"I'll let Ylia, you stay with Berd. It's so good to see you again, Malaeth."

"You're a sight too thin," Malaeth said flatly. "I'll have to feed you, I can see that. Don't stay up all the night gabbing."

Ysian sat at Ylia's dressing table while the younger woman worked a plain three-section plait and bound it with one of her own leather ties. "That's better. I've become so used to a plait, it feels odd to let my hair hang loose. I've worked hard, Ylia, I won't be a liability this time."

"You said that earlier. You weren't exactly useless before, Ys."

"I was and you know it. Practically passing out before we could get everyone away from the Tehlatt, weeping myself soggy when we got back to safety." Ysian stared at the far wall. "How is he?"

"Golsat?" Ylia asked. Ysian nodded. "He's well. He'll be very glad to see you."

"He—did he like the brooch? I didn't know if I should, if he'd be offended."

"It hasn't left his cloak since it came, Ysian."

"I'm glad," Ysian said softly. She turned to look around the spacious and well-lit chamber and was suddenly all brisk business. "I like your Tower, I particularly like your rooms."

"It was Erken's doing."

"I know, you said. Let me see *them*, would you?"

"Let you see—oh." It was going to be hard to adjust to Ysian's sudden shifts in topic when she spoke, her cryptic style of conversation that was often as much mind-touch as speech. Them. Shelagn's Gifts.

The sword was in its usual place when she wasn't wearing it: slung by its belt over one of the bedposts. The shield and horn were kept in the clothing box at the foot of the bed. She laid them on the bed; Ysian came over and sat on the furs, ran her fingers lightly over the hilts, touched shield and horn. "By the One himself. The sword Shelagn used against the Lammior! I wish I had not left Aresada when I did. Another day or so—I could have been with you when you found them. But—just to touch a thing that old, and hers—! Do you feel better about it now? Not so pressured? Used?"

"Sometimes I still do. I've adjusted," Ylia shrugged. "You can adjust to anything, given enough time."

"You're proof of *that*, aren't you?" Ysian set the horn down next to the sword. Ylia laughed. "What's so amusing?"

"You're proof of that yourself, Ysian. Look at you." Ylia's gesture covered plaited hair to dark, capable boots.

"Well, but I *had* to adjust!" Ysian considered this, then smiled. "Well. I guess I am, aren't I?"

High tide had washed oddments of grass and weed onto the sand in a thick line. The tide was retreating, leaving behind mounded detritus, clouds of flies and a high, rank smell. *Fury* lay at anchor, hard against the outermost edge of the northern break-water. A candle stub guttered on the table in the captain's cabin, casting jumping shadows against the bed-curtains and the walls. The light of a moon near full touched the slow swell of receding water, the blue-white ruins of towers, the rotted pilings and ghost ships in the south crescent of the bay.

The candle flared briefly, went out. A shaft of yellow lantern-light came through the opened door then, and Jon stole in bare-foot. His shadow covered the table, moved on. Brit Arren lay face down, head pillowed in his arms, a winejug at his elbow. Jon moved forward, scarcely daring to breathe, reached for it, but as his fingers touched the unfinished clay, a square, capable hand shot out and gripped his wrist. The lad caught his breath in a startled, frightened little cry.

"Don't take it. I haven't had enough yet." Brit Arren's voice was slurred, but there was no mistaking who was captain.

"Yes—I mean, no, Mal. I just thought—"

"Don't think!" Brit Arren roared as he sat up. Jon, released, fell back a pace, dropped into the opposite chair.

Jon swallowed hard. "Mal—Mal, listen, you are doing what you told me not to do. You're thinking about the killing."

"I'm not," Brit Arren snapped. "I am thinking of a man made a fool by three foreign sorcerers. I am thinking of a man trapped by weak thinking, and I do not like what I see!" Anger thickened his speech more than the wine did. "Sorcerers. Wizards. *Bas-tards!* I have looked at it all wrong, Jon. I am not held to an old oath, not when it harms us. They need us, just now, but we don't need them, do we, Jon?"

"I—"

"We don't need them." Brit Arren's eyes were hooded; he stroked his chin. Stubbly beard prickled his fingers. He shoved the wine aside; the jug sailed across the smooth surface and crashed into the wall. What was he doing, sitting here? "Pay heed, Jon. We have always been strong, we Sea-Raiders. We have *never* depended upon any man for what we can do our-selves—and what we cannot do, we do not need! These Three will dangerously weaken us, if we sit and cringe, and fear them, or depend upon them. If we let them bluff us. For I believe there are times a strong man could overwhelm them. If he chose care-fully, if he waited and watched." He closed his mouth, com-pressed his lips. No need to say more: It wasn't safe. Jon would know what he meant anyway.

Brit Arren peered at the boy across the darkened cabin. Jon was white and sweating and his hands shook. "Well? What ails ye?" he snarled. Jon started convulsively, shook his head.

"Nu—nothing, Mal."

"Have ye been taking steam again, boy? I warned ye—!"

"No, Mal, I swear—! What's that?"

The two men stared through the open shutters. The entire Tower glowed a sullen red, as though fire burned around its base. The cliffs, clouds and even the moon went ruddy, and a thin, whistling cry rose to a shriek. Brit Arren clapped his hands over his ears, shutting out Jon's terrified cry. As suddenly as it had come, it was gone, gone on a bolt of blood-red lightning, tearing north faster than the wind.

Ylia took the horn and the shield, knelt to replace them in the chest. Ysian stood and stretched, walked toward the window. She stopped in front of the pedestal bearing the statue of the Yderra. "That's lovely."

"It is, isn't it?" Ylia closed the chest and joined her.

Ysian touched the arching neck. "Where did you get it?" She turned to find her niece gazing at her in astonishment.

"I—Ysian, *you* gave it to us—!"

"I gave you a statue of Shelagn," Ysian began. Both women stopped and gazed at each other in sudden dread. Ysian laid her fingers on its neck again. It took concentration and she was so tired: layer upon layer, deception. But that was falling away, and under all was a malice and hatred so deep and harsh she quailed before it. "Oh, gods, *no*."

"What?" Ylia staggered, caught off guard as Ysian leaped away from the pedestal and shoved her hard.

"*Don't touch it!* That's Power, can't you feel it? Not AEldra Power! Blessed Nasath, *look* at the stone!" The emerald was no longer green: It had gone deep, sullen red; the beast's eyes were a smoky, opaque grey.

"Gods and Mothers, it's *his*, it's Lyiadd's! Let me at it, Ysian, it's his master focus, it's changing, I have to get it out of here!" Ylia snatched at the statue, two-handed. Power hit her like a fist; sooty lightning arced through the chamber. The women were thrown to the floor.

Ylia staggered back to her feet, half-blinded, and flailed for the Yderra again. She froze, hands outstretched, as terrified screams came from across the hall. From the nursery.

It is the one thing of which I would not speak, ever—what happened that night. The one, worst night of my life, the one graven deepest upon my inner being.

8

The cries echoed, grew in volume as others answered them. Ylia's voice rose above them all: "No! No, not that!" She flew across the room, her shoulder slammed into the doorjamb, throwing her, but she was through it then, boots pounding down-hall toward the nursery. Blood dripped from her fingers. With a terrified look at the quiescent, brooding statue, Ysian fled after her.

The hall was a mass of frightened people, a babble of high-pitched voices. Ysian forced her way through, back up-hall. Ylia was briefly visible in the doorway to the nursery, a ruddy glow giving color to her ashen face. She shook off one of the serving women standing there and plunged into the room. Ysian swallowed, ran after her. People stepped back in sudden, frightened silence as she reached the doorway. Nisana came bounding up from the balcony, leaped to Ysian's shoulder and teetered there.

"Ylia?" Ysian hesitated, blinded by a harsh, pulsing light that filled the nursery. 'Ylia?' Nisana's inner voice echoed. But as Ysian stepped forward, the cat nudged her. 'No, Ysian. Wait. It is a trap, can you not see? Wait.' Sensible, painful advice. Ysian caught at the doorjamb with both hands, and waited.

Boots thudded up-hall, echoing in the unnatural silence—Galdan, followed closely by Erken and Brelian. Galdan pressed Ylsan noblewoman and cat aside, but he stopped just inside the room. "Malaeth?"

Ylia's weeping answered him. "I can't—I can't reach her, oh, gods, Galdan, I can't get through, help me!" Her words tumbled over each other, barely intelligible. She stood in the middle of the room.

The cradle had fallen over, spilling blankets across the floor. It was almost hidden in that pulsing red glow. The boy was a tiny huddle in the midst of the blankets, and Malaeth was sprawled between her cot and the cradle, one arm under the baby, protecting his head. As Ysian watched, Malaeth made a dreadful effort, brought her other arm up to wrap over the child. She tried to turn her head, but could not move any further. Her harsh, faint whisper barely reached them: "Go! Run!" Her eyes closed then, she let her head down next to Berd's.

"No!" Ylia's scream echoed through the hall but in the nursery the sound was curiously deadened. Galdan grabbed for her, too late. Ylia was across the small chamber, arms outstretched, oblivious to all but her son and her old nurse. She cried out in fury as her hands were stopped by the Power field. Her body shuddered convulsively. "Berd!" she screamed, and threw herself forward. She seemed momentarily to catch fire; the Power threw her across the room. She staggered, fell into the wall, and Galdan snatched her into his arms while she fought air into stunned lungs. She writhed in his grip. "Let me go, let me go, they've got Berd, let me *go*!"

"Stop it!" Galdan shouted against her ear. "You can't reach him and dying won't help Berd!" Ylia gazed at him in shocked silence and crumpled, weeping. Galdan half-carried her into the hall, handed her to Brelian. Lisabetha, her hair loose and her feet bare, a cloak thrown over her nightrobes, hovered anxiously behind him. "Hold her, don't let her back in here. I have to get Selverra!"

Ysian backed out of the chamber, eyes still fixed in blank horror on Malaeth and the baby. Nisana pressed against her ear, hard; one hand came up automatically to steady the cat. The Power in the little nursery was pulsing, spreading ever so slightly. "No," she whispered. There was another cry deep within the room; she started.

'It's Selverra, Ysian.' Nisana's thought was meant to soothe but it was as ragged and frightened as her own. The cat glanced at Ylia. Brelian had her by the shoulders, holding her against the wall, and for the moment she wasn't fighting him. Her eyes were closed; her hands were twitching where Lyiadd's Power had burned them; her sword hand still bled sluggishly from the initial contact with the Yderra statue. She appeared to notice none of it. 'Galdan has gone to get Selverra, he'll bring her out.'

Galdan emerged a moment later, his badly shaken daughter clinging to his neck. He whispered against her ear. Her tiny hands gripped even more tightly. "Brel, bring Ylia. Everyone else, stay back from that room, what is there is black Power and nothing to trifle with!" He needn't have worried; most of the people in the hall had already backed away. Ysian stood alone, Nisana on her shoulder, staring into the chamber. Galdan carried Selverra down the hall, down the main stair. Brelian caught Ylia by the elbows, pulled her toward him; she reached for the wall, missed it completely and fell. Lisabetha knelt beside her. "She's fainted, nothing more." People moved aside as Brelian picked her up and followed Galdan.

'Ysian, you may not be safe here.'

'I can't leave, cat. It's—still moving.'

'You can't stop it. I can't.'

'I don't know that. I might be able to slow it.'

'I think it *is* slowing, else it would be in the hall already. But Ysian, don't trust that. You're in danger, standing here. Come.'

'I can't leave Malaeth, I can't leave Ylia's baby!'

'You can't help them here.' There was subtle inflection in the cat's thought. Ysian turned her head to meet the green eyes so near her own, and Nisana returned that gaze levelly, her inner voice oddly silent and a warning in her look: *Speak and think nothing. The Three watch and they listen.* Of course they did; but she must do something! Destroy the Yderra? But she knew she could not, not with it fully activated. To try would be death. But to stand and wait—?

No! She kept her own thought carefully blank, but she knew what Nisana wanted. What they must do. They exchanged that look again, and this time it said, *Watch me. Be ready.*

Malaeth drew a slow, shallow breath. The pain had subsided to something she could bear. Old bones felt so much in a long life. She knew how to fend pain off, how to deal with it. Pain didn't matter. The babe had no such defenses. Had nothing but her. 'Shhh. Hush, small love, I'll take what I can of the hurt from ye. Hush, small precious love, I'll keep ye safe.' Berd's infant mind-touch clung to her desperately. Terror, pain. Poor child, too young to understand. *That* was the worst of it, worse than the fact that he hurt. But she could not cure it, she could only help. She fought her own panic, her own pain and fear, and soothed, calmed, lulled. *My little one, my Berd. I won't let them hurt you, won't let them have you. My Ylia will save you, your mother will find a way to save you.*

It hurt to think, hurt to try, and her formidable will was briefly shaken. What could Ylia do? What could any of them do? Berd whimpered as fear pressed him again. Malaeth cleared her thought of anything that was not this baby. Ylia would find a way. Meantime, she could keep Berdwyn calm, could keep the pain from him. Ease his terror, protect him. She could do that. And she could wait.

Galdan left Lisabetha with Ylia and Selverra and came back up the stairs, Brelian, Erken and a dozen of the Elite Guard at his back. The hall was immediately cleared, the upper chambers evacuated, the household shifted into the great reception hall. Silence reigned once again.

Ysian and Nisana still stood in the nursery door. In that spill of light, the cat's eyes were coals, Ysian's hair a banked fire. Galdan touched the Ylsan woman's shoulder and Ysian cried out, started away from him. Her eyes were wide and blank. *She was less prepared for this than we*, Galdan thought, and strove to make his thought and the hand that reached for her a reassurance. "Ysian. It's all right," he soothed. "Ylia needs you. Come away from here."

"Don't touch me," Ysian whispered. She slid down the hall, hands braced against the wall.

It worried him, this on top of the rest. Had they attempted to enter the nursery while he was gone? Galdan turned his attention to Nisana, and found still greater cause for worry: He could not read her thought at all, the cat might not have been AEldra. Nisana clung to Ysian's shoulder, claws drawing blood, but neither she nor Ysian noticed. The cat's dark fur stood up along her spine and made a ruff around her neck. Her ears were flat, her eyes all pupil. They were terrified, both of them; he could feel it and it nearly drowned him. He blocked what he could of it. "Ysian, come away from there, you'll be safe with Ylia. Nisana, we have to get her away from here." Nisana growled; Ysian stared at him in black-eyed horror. She edged another step away, another. Erken came up the hall.

"What's wrong with her?"

Galdan waved him back, extended his hand another few fingers' worth. Ysian cast one frightened look through the nursery door, another at Galdan and beyond him to Erken, stumbled back along the wall. "Don't touch me, don't!" And as Galdan lunged for her, she and the cat vanished.

Someone down by the staircase cried out as the two AEldra disappeared. Galdan staggered back, stunned. Erken turned and bellowed at the guard: "That was nothing to frighten any of ye, she bridged, nothing else! Hold steady there!" He caught his son's arms in a rough grip. "You've had enough. Take the advice you gave Ylia and go. You can't think, standing here."

"I know." But Galdan stood where he was, staring blankly into the nursery. Malaeth—his son—there, within reach, if a man could reach them. But Ylia had proven he couldn't reach them and he wouldn't try. There might be another way, he would wait—he realized he'd taken a step forward and his father was trying to drag him back. "Gods. What's in there—it's pulling at me." He let Erken lead him back toward the stair.

They stopped on the top step. Erken still held his arm tightly. "What must I do?"

Galdan tried to think. "Watch. Stay clear of the nursery and our chambers, both. The statue, the Yderra. Somehow it's *theirs*. The focus we have been looking for, it's in that statue. It's—that's where the Power is coming from. Stay away from it."

"We will. What else?"

"If it moves, if it spreads, get away."

"I doubt I'll have to order *that*," Erken said; he gazed uneasily up the silent hall. "And?"

"Let no one into the nursery. Not even me," Galdan said bleakly. He turned away and went down the stairs.

Erken watched him go, then turned back to the silent huddle of guard. "You heard. We'll spot ourselves two lengths apart all the way from here to the royal bedchambers. We can see the nursery from the west wall and from the bench there." He pointed. "Stay clear of the entrances to both chambers, the source of the Power is in there, you don't want to stand between it and the nursery."

The air was still throbbing, pulsing with Malaeth's laboring heartbeat, and there was a faint, unpleasant giggle just at the edge of hearing. Berd stirred, whimpered. It was harder for Malaeth to move than it had been, just flexing her fingers took all the strength in her. Hard to remember she must be strong. She touched the baby's cheek. 'Shhh. Rest, Berd. Rest, my heart, my little love, my sweet. I won't let them harm you, no one will hurt you while Malaeth is here.' A velvety soft little arm rubbed against her hand, tiny fingers clutched her thumb and held. The baby subsided again. Malaeth swallowed, closed her eyes. She could retain the least contact with Berd, still. There wasn't much else she could do, save wait. Red stained the insides of her eyelids, pain flared across her skin like fire and she bit back an outcry. Old bodies could still feel pain. *Be strong, old woman, the babe needs ye strong. Wait.*

Lisabetha had built a fire down in the small dining room and was cuddling Selverra. Ylia lay flat, a fur pulled up to her chin. When Galdan came, he took his daughter and sat against the wall on the nest of sleeping furs and cushions where Lisabetha had been sitting. "She hasn't spoken. I don't know if she's still unconscious, Selverra needed all my attention."

"It's all right. You'd better go back home, Lisabetha, you'll catch your death like that."

"I'm all right. There's wine by the fire. I'll return." She had to pause just outside the door until she could stop trembling. She'd *felt* that horror when it struck, had left her startled mother with the baby and run as she was, knowing only that something was desperately wrong, that Ylia needed her. Ylia's baby—*it could have been my baby!* She flew across the hall, pushed through the still crowd gathered in the square and ran down the avenue for home.

Galdan's foot was going to sleep. He shifted carefully, leaned back against the wall. Selverra, wrapped in her father's cloak, slept in the crook of his left arm, fingers still twined in his. Ylia slumped against his left shoulder, eyes closed.

"Why did Ysian run like that? Why did Nisana?" Ylia's voice, a cracked whisper, broke a long silence.

"Shhh, don't waken Sel. I told you, I don't know." Another long silence. "Father will come to tell us at once if there's change. If it retreats."

"If it—" Ylia swallowed, buried her face in her hands. Galdan's arm tightened around her shoulders. "She told me. Marrita did. I should have known, should have—"

"Should have what?" Galdan demanded as her voice broke. "Known that gift wasn't the one Ysian sent? How? You've touched it daily, and so have I! We've slept in the same chamber with it for months and until tonight it never gave any sign it was evil, that it was their focus." Silence. "They can't maintain that spell for much longer, Ylia. Not at such a distance."

"They can hold it long enough to—"

"Don't endow them with strength they don't have, lady wife," he interrupted her gently. "Despair can defeat us also, you know. They tried to reach Selverra; they couldn't. They tried to trap me, tried to kill you, and they couldn't."

"She won't kill *me*," Ylia said bitterly. Her voice was muffled by her hands. "She said that, too: You'll all die first. All of you. *Then* she'll kill me. I should have tried again."

"You still could have died in there. I remember what it did to you. You're not thinking clearly, beloved." He leaned down to kiss the top of her head. "You can't trust what Marrita says, and you don't when you're able to think." Silence again, a long one. The fire burned down until it was a bed of coals; the room was overly warm. Neither of them noticed the heat. "They can't hold it forever, when Father tells us it's fading, we'll break it."

"They'll be dead by then," Ylia whispered.

"No. Don't think that, you're giving in to fear and misery, they want that. Maybe it even feeds that field, up there. Rest. Be ready when our chance comes." Ylia's head came slowly up. Galdan kissed her brow. "Will you?"

She closed her eyes. Nodded. "I'll try." A tear ran down her cheek; Galdan caught it with a gentle finger and blotted it on her shirt.

"Then so will I." He settled against the wall, shifted Selverra's slight weight to a more comfortable position. Ylia's breathing slowed and became more regular, and he thought perhaps she slept. He made himself relax. But his thought ran wild. Ylia. The nursery. The missing AEldra. Poor Ysian! But Nisana. What had it done to them? Or—or had it? Something deep down stirred, a fragment of a thought. He wouldn't pursue it, it might not be safe. But suddenly he was not quite as worried about them as he had been. Because just perhaps he knew where they had gone—and why.

Nisana cast about for direction. It was like walking through fog, like trying mind-search with blocked Power. But it seemed —she could only act on what she *felt*. 'North again, Ysian.'

"I can't." Ysian knelt, head even with her knees, breathing deeply. Everything had gone black after this last bridging. But even after her vision cleared, there was nothing to see but trees, everywhere trees. Moonlight slid between them in narrow shafts, but gave no clue to their whereabouts. Nisana willed her a tiny burst of strength, all she had to spare.

'Again. We can rest then, I'm certain of it. Now.'

'We'll have to rest, there's nothing left in me to bridge again, after this.'

'We'll rest,' the cat assured her. Ysian brought her head up carefully, flailed for a handhold and scraped her palm against harsh bark and the thorns of a low-growing berry bush. 'I'm sorry for this, Ysian, but there isn't time to waste. It has to be now.'

'I know. Go, I'll back you.'

Every candle, every lantern in the lower hall had been lit, throwing the upper end into even darker gloom. A faint ruddy glow still pulsed in the nursery. The guard was nervous, silent. Erken strode from watcher to watcher, moved back now and again to gaze down the empty stairway.

"M'Lord! Erken!" He turned back from one such tour to see Eveya, who had the far post, wave at him urgently. "Look, it's fading!" It was, beyond all doubt. Erken ran up to her and gave her a shove toward the stair. "I'll take your place, go, get Galdan!" Eveya was already on her way.

Malaeth choked. It was harder to fight air into her old lungs, to force it out again. Berd's mind-touch was nearly gone and her own was fading. Tiny fingers tightened on her thumb. 'I know, shhh.' She could have wept, but there were no tears left, no breath for it. He was frightened, a void lay before him and he feared it. She couldn't let him die like that, trembling with terror. 'It's not so bad, dying. It's a pity you should have had so little life first.' She wrapped him in love, all the love in her, felt it shield him from the fear. 'I'll be with you, sweetest, only precious, I'll stay with you, don't be afraid. I won't leave you, not ever.' The room was fading, the pain fading with it. For one glorious moment, it was gone: pain, warped Power, exhaustion, fear. Malaeth inched forward with the last of her strength, gathered the baby close and fell back, her arms and body curled protectively around him. Berd let out one final, long breath and his tiny body went limp, but his fingers remained clasped around her thumb.

'Ysian?' Nisana's fur was warm against her cheek. Ysian could feel that warmth and the cat's fear; there wasn't enough strength in her to so much as move a hand. Even the mind-touch was mostly gone.

"I'm sorry, cat," she whispered. "It was a fool's notion. We've lost."

Nisana rubbed against her again. 'It was a good idea. We can't stop, Ysian. They're near, I *know* they are, they must be!'

Golden light flared over them, over the tiny meadow. Ysian blinked, rolled over and pushed herself partially upright on shaking arms. Someone there . . . "By the Nasath," she whispered in sudden awe. Bendesevorian knelt beside her, one hand on her shoulder, willing her strength.

"I felt your fear and the urgency in you, even across the barrier. I am here. What is your need?"

Ah, gods of my ancestors, that I lived to see such a night! Would that I could believe in Fate and not torment myself even now with the certainty that some act of mine might have prevented what passed. Malaeth, friend of my childhood, companion of so many long years, the One bless you for such unswerving devotion, and tiny Berdwyn, may your mother and father hold you again, a long day hence.

9

Galdan came up the stairs two at a time, Ylia close on his heels, but half-way up the hall, Erken blocked the way; he and Galdan held Ylia back when she would have forced her way past them both. "Father? Eveya said—"

"It's still there, son. But much less strong than it was, I think."

"We'll wait. Ylia," he spoke gently against her ear, accompanied it with a little shake. She came back from a long inner distance, blinked at him. "We can't go in there yet. It's fading."

"I know," she whispered, and pulled against his grasp again. Galdan's fingers tightened, she subsided unwillingly against them.

"We'll wait here." One of the armsmen brought a wooden bench over for them. There was uneasy silence in the hall. Outside, in the street, they could hear worried voices muffled by distance and closed shutters. One of Ylia's women crossed the hall below with a click of heels, vanished into the small dining room where two of the others sat with the sleeping Selverra.

"How long?" Ylia's whisper broke the silence; a near guardswoman started, drew a disapproving glare from Erken. Galdan shrugged, she slumped against him, closed her eyes. *Berd, ah, my baby, I can't sense you, can't touch you at all!* It tore at her: he'd be terrified, and she could do nothing, *nothing*, to ease that fear. And Malaeth—she was so old, so frail after the past two winters. Her Power had never been strong, never much but mind-speech. How long could she hold out against that? Galdan's

75

arm was warm around her shoulder, she could feel his worry, his fear and a rising grief, the attempt he was making to hide it from her, to reassure her. His child, too. His son. She couldn't even console him. She turned, buried her face in his shoulder.

She sat up suddenly, the hairs on her forearms tickling with the least of presentiments: "Galdan, something's happening."

"Something—?"

"There—*look*!" She pointed toward the south balcony now shrouded in gloom. The air was eddying there.

"I don't—" Whatever he intended to say was cut off by a blinding, golden light and the powerful surge of an inbridging. The Elite Guard stumbled away from this sudden new threat. Erken shouted a warning. "Wait, all of you!" Galdan topped the older man's wordless cry. "It's all right, they're ours!" In the fading glow were three: Nisana, Ysian and a man taller and more fair than she. The light seemed to cling to him even as the balcony went dark again. Ysian swayed; Nisana toppled from her shoulder into her arms and lay there unmoving. Bendesevorian touched Ysian's hand, passed them swiftly. He slowed at the nursery, stopped before the royal bedchamber. Ylia had already slipped from Galdan's loosened fingers. She caught at his sleeve, opened her mouth but no words came. Bendesevorian gripped her arm in turn, pulled her into the chamber with him and gestured Galdan to follow.

"Come with me, both of you. The Lady Ysian told me what is there. I may not be able to destroy the thing myself." They vanished into the gloomy chamber. Erken started after them, stopped in the doorway. Ysian laid a hand on his forearm, shook her head as he would have followed. Her face was drawn and white, and there were faint lines around her eyes he hadn't seen before; what she'd done had taken a toll from her. Nisana was a curl of still dark fur in the crook of her left arm. Ysian shook her head again. "Stay here, Lord Erken. It's not safe in there."

Erken shook his own head impatiently. "I know that. But they can't—"

"They have protection you do not." Ysian leaned against the doorframe for support. "It's faded, hasn't it? It was much stronger when we left."

"You went to find him?"

"Say that we hoped we could."

"But who is he?" Erken was peering into the darkened chamber; the air about the Yderra pulsed, a dull ruddy fog spiraling slowly out from its brow. To one side, hands extended, fingers tinted the color of an old wound, stood the one Ysian had brought. He was like no man Erken had ever seen, and even Erken, pragmatic Nedaoan that he was, could tell the difference went beyond height and coloring; he had felt *something* as that other passed him.

Ysian shuddered, closed her eyes. At the moment, the chamber beyond was fairly crackling with opposing Powers. "Who? He is Bendesevorian, of the Nasath."

"The Ylsan Guardians—?" Erken's voice trailed away, and he stared in astonishment. "To *our* aid?"

"He assisted Ylia once before, did she never tell you?" Erken shook his head. "I knew. Nisana told me, else I had never thought to try and find the Guardians. Who would?"

"Who would?" Erken echoed blankly. "But—you *did* find them!"

"Bendesevorian found us, and left his own kind to do it. I fear I've done him irreparable harm, seeking him out, bringing him to the Peopled Lands. Well, it can't be turned back. And I would have done more or worse, if he can save them." Erken glanced at her, went back to watching his son, his joined daughter, their companion. Ysian wasn't making much sense, but he didn't have time or energy to try and sort it out.

She turned away, her eyes worried indeed as they sought the nursery. The least ruddy glow still spilled out into the hall and darkened the doorsills. *If he can save them.* Faced with the focus and the malice in its spell, she felt her hope falter. *Against Three who could contrive such a spell, who could reach from the Great Isles to Nedao with it; who knew my gift to Ylia and found a way to substitute that horror for it—what chance has even one of the Guardians?*

"You speak in riddles, Lady Ysian." Erken's voice roused her.

She came back to the moment with a jolt, smiled a wan apology up at him. "I am sorry. I am too worn even to think, just now. Pray your gods and ours we were in good time."

Erken merely nodded, but his face was bleak and Ysian remembered with a sudden pang that this was Galdan's father and the babe in that small room his only grandson. She would have spoken again but his attention was all for the three in the chamber beyond.

•   •   •

Bendesevorian studied the Yderra in silence for a long moment. He detached Ylia's fingers from his arm, gently pushed her back. "Let me try to break it alone, first."

"All right." Galdan drew Ylia toward the bed with him; they watched, scarcely breathing. For an even longer time, there was nothing to see. Bendesevorian's hands were outstretched, fingers spread wide, the muscles of his bare forearms corded, but whether he was attempting to destroy the Yderra by main strength or by some knowledge of his own, he made no headway. He let his hands fall to his side, finally, and walked slowly around the thing again. Baleful, smoky eyes watched him.

"You can't, can you?" Ylia said. In the still room, her low voice echoed. "Not alone."

"No. It's too well formed, too carefully set. But there is another way." He gazed at her thoughtfully. "Perhaps, with your help—"

"Tell me what to do and I'll do it," Ylia said flatly as he hesitated.

"The sword. It may have the necessary Power." Ylia silently drew the blade, set Galdan's hands aside and walked across the room. Galdan came up behind her. "I will do what I can first; wait. I will tell you when, and you must behead it."

Ylia stared at the statue. She could feel the pain where her bloodied fingers gripped the hilts. If even *he* was unable to breach that shield, how could Shelagn's sword better him? She could still feel the pain in her fingers from when the statue had exploded with Lyiadd's Power; still felt the shock of its touch in the nursery. *It might kill me, this time.* "Behead it. I shall." To her surprise, she sounded calm, almost as though she believed what she said, and somehow, that helped her actually believe it possible. Perhaps, a little. *I can do that. For Berd, for Malaeth. I must.*

Bendesevorian touched her arm gently; warmth coursed through her, almost reaching that core of ice that held grief and fear at bay. She fought that; she dared not let herself feel, not yet. The Nasath seemed to understand, for he withdrew his hand at once. "There may be backlash. I will try to protect you, but I am not certain I can. Know that."

"I know it," Ylia said. "It doesn't matter, the choice is mine." Galdan made a faint, protesting sound deep in his throat.

Bendesevorian closed the distance between them. "My Lord, I am sorry. There is risk here, you can see that. If the focus breaks the way I intend, its Power will turn back on those who sent it. But we all know such things do not always go according to plan. If this does not—" He spread his hands wide. "One of you must survive, if only for Nedao's sake. The sword is our greatest hope, and only Ylia can wield the blade." His hand touched Galdan's. Galdan gazed back at him in sudden astonishment as Bendesevorian's strength touched something deep in the center of his own untappable strength. "Yours is the hardest part, to wait and not know. I am sorry."

Galdan closed his eyes briefly. Nodded. "I—I understand. I will wait." He brushed a kiss against Ylia's cheek, clasped her close as she turned to cling to him momentarily. It took all the strength in him to back toward the door as Bendesevorian turned his attention to the Yderra and brought his hands up once again.

Erken was waiting for him. "What chances in there?"

"They're going to destroy it." He looked around; the guard was clustered behind them. "There may be backlash, and this doorway will not be safe, if so. Father, move the guard back."

"And you? If you were sent back to safety—"

"I'll follow. In a moment." But as Erken drew the Elite Guard down to the main stairs, Galdan moved toward the nursery. He stopped half-way between the two chambers. Ysian, her face a pale blur in the dark, pushed away from the wall to join him. Nisana stretched as tall as she could up his breeches leg, delicately extended claws until he became aware of her and bent to pick her up. "I won't go any nearer the nursery. If they break the Yderra, I want to be close." His face was grey in the half-light.

"I know," Ysian whispered. "I'll stay with you, we both will. It may help." She looked over her shoulder. An ominous, barely audible hum came from the bedchamber, and a greenish light flickered, vying with that pulsing red. The Elite Guard retreated. The hum increased, vibrated Ysian's sinuses. Nisana's ears went down, and she flattened herself into Galdan's shoulders, pressing her head into his neck. Galdan turned away, but the sound pressed against the back of his head, hackling his hair.

Someone in the guard screamed; Ysian clamped her hands hard over her ears. The hum was rising to a shriek and a nasty scree now wove in and out of it; under all there was a furtive little whisper, a horrid susurration of almost-words that crawled across AEldra senses. Galdan staggered back into the wall. Faintly, he could hear Ysian chanting in High AEldran, trying to weave a protection around the three of them. So far as he could tell, it wasn't working.

"Are you ready?" The pale hair was plastered to the Guardian's brow; a drop of sweat clung to his chin, fell to join the others darkening his shirt.

Ylia, so much nearer the source of the sound and Power tearing at those in the hall, was beyond speech. She nodded, shifted her grasp on the sword, took the hilts two-handed and fought to raise it over her head. The air was like clotted cream or syrup, movement nearly as impossible as speech. *Berd.* "Berd," she whispered. The sound was muted at her lips. Bendesevorian met her eyes across the wooden statue. He was blinking against the acrid smoke that spread from the pedestal. Ylia kept her eyes on Bendesevorian's, avoiding the baleful thing between them, for she knew it would trap her if it could. *They're watching, gloating. They know my grief and they rejoice in it.* Fury filled her, releasing strength.

Bendesevorian watched the purpose rise in her, turned back to the statue. A last, least thing to neutralize. Malice, evil and more malice; he had been right not to attempt to merely break the spell with a straight blast of Power. *You thought, Night's Heir, that I would not see that final trap and avoid it?* he whispered. *As though I had not seen such traps before, as though in a thousand years I could forget?* There: It took an effort that left him half-dazed, for he had attempted no such feats in long years, but it was done. "Now," he whispered, and there was a half-breath of relief in the pressure from the wooden horror under his hands. "Now!" he cried.

"Berdwyn!" Ylia's answering cry tore the air; strong hands and wrists swung the sword and brought it down hard. Blue flame enveloped the pedestal as the blade sheared through the wooden neck. The head fell to the floor with nightmare slowness. Her point, wedged in the pedestal, came free as she braced her foot against the base and pulled. She went over backward and landed hard as the statue and the fallen head burst into flame. A towering shriek burst the glass window behind it. Ylia rolled away from the sudden heat, watched in stunned silence as Bendesevorian stood before the pedestal and brought his hands together in a clap that thundered. A ball of flame rose above the pillar. "To those who sent you, go!" It shot from the room as if catapulted, shattering what was left of the windows.

It was suddenly, blessedly, quiet in the upper hall. Ylia caught hold of the bedpost and pulled herself shakily upright. She stared at the shattered windows. There was nothing where the Yderra had stood but a pile of ash.

It was quiet in the harbor, save for the distant whisper of water against sand, the lap of waves against hulls and the stone quays. The stars were fading, a faint, greyish line to the east showed the hour. Now and again a figure moved across a deck, change of guard or someone unable to sleep. In the one occupied Tower, a sole red light shone around an imperfectly fitted shutter, and smoke trailed in a thin line from the chimney.

One of the watch shouted the warning as his attention was caught by movement from the north and out to sea: Men clambered from below deck to stare at the swiftly approaching fireball, crouched down in fear, stoppering their ears against the wail that froze the blood of the strongest of them. Several flung themselves overboard but the approaching horror had no business with them; it passed over the crescent shoreline with a howl that seemed to shake the very rocks and turn the water to blood before it enveloped the Tower. Mal Brit Arren stood on the foredeck of the *Fury*, blinking wine and sleep from his eyes, as the uppermost chamber of the Tower shook with the desperate force of opposing Power. Then, with a roar like an explosion, the shutters blew out, and the seaward portion of the roof collapsed inward.

The unnatural light slowly faded, darkness and silence returned. From the Tower came no sound or movement.

Galdan straightened; the burden was gone as if it had never been. Anxious mind-touch assured him Ylia was unhurt. He set Ysian's restraining hands gently aside, pushed past her and walked into the nursery.

Dark. There had always been a lantern burning; Malaeth kept one for the children. It had gone out, long since. Someone came up behind him with light.

But he didn't need it. *This Power in me is no use at all*, he thought bitterly, *I cannot even protect what is mine, but it works to tell me where my son lies*. He knelt. Malaeth's arms were still protectively around the baby. *My son*. He loosened the fingers gently, picked up the small body and sat back on his heels.

"Galdan?" Ylia's voice roused him—a moment later? a lifetime? He shifted, came partway around, shook his head. He couldn't speak. Ylia knelt beside him. Galdan released Berdwyn into her arms, held them both. His head came down to touch her bowed head, his tears dampened her hair. Ysian gathered Malaeth's frail body into her own arms and wept into her old nurse's nightrobe.

Erken set the lantern carefully on the small table just inside the room, and walked slowly down the hall to dismiss the guard. He stopped short of the bedchamber; Bendesevorian leaned against the doorjamb, his face pale and still with exhaustion. The Duke had to try twice before words would come past the tightness in his throat. "The thing that did this—is it gone?"

Bendesevorian nodded. "It is safe to send the guard away. But you are needed down there." He gestured toward the nursery.

"I know." *My grandson*. He couldn't think about Berd just now, he didn't dare. This Nasath was right. His son had loved Berd beyond sense or proportion. And Ylia: She'd bury her grief, hide it from everyone including Galdan, tear herself apart with it. He'd have to be strong. *Mothers aid me, this once I've no heart for it*.

10

The sky was a glorious pale blue bowl, the sea a deep green mirror; the pre-dawn alarums might never have chanced—or so Brit Arren thought as he stepped onto the *Fury*'s deck, shielding his eyes against the level rays of early sun. He stretched, inhaled fresh salt air and let it out with a sigh. All that wine the night before, next to no sleep, and not even a headache to show for it. *The old man's not so old at that, is he?* he thought in some satisfaction. And today—but *that* a man of sense would keep to himself. His temper was back under control, caution again well to the fore.

He stole a covert glance at the Tower. At this hour, with the sun beating mercilessly on those piles and heaps of greened stone, the damage might have been ancient. No smoke issued from the roof this morning, no candles flickered against grimed windows. No sign of life anywhere, save his own men lining the rails to stare at it. His and those on every other ship in harbor.

Well, let them stare! There was nothing uncommon in curiosity, was there? *Draw no attention by the unusual, Mal Brit Arren, and you'll live to see another dawn and others after that.*

He stretched again, ambled across the deck to the main mast, back to his cabin. On impulse, he climbed the narrow ladder to the rudder-post, gazed out over the heads of his men. *Aye, this is the time, we might never get such another. Something came back at them, last night. What's left up there, if anything is, could be a clever man's, if he were quick about it.* He brought his gaze, now thoughtful indeed, down from the Tower to the *Fury*'s deck, picking through the men there, choosing, discarding, selecting—setting aside, until he had a tally of eight. Counting himself and Jon, ten, a good round number in case of trouble. Solid men, who'd no more fear of magic than he had . . .

He paused in his consideration, struck by another thought as Jon emerged from the crew's hatch, the blue and red scarf dangling from his fingers, his shirt all untucked, feet bare. Gods of the green deeps, what had done that to the boy? *How long has he looked like that and I haven't seen it?* Jon Bri Madden was the color of the Tower stones, and even at a ten-length distance, he looked unwell, his eyes red-rimmed, his

lower lip trembling until he caught it between his teeth. He
glanced around, almost furtively, saw Brit Arren and started
sharply. The scarf fell from nerveless fingers, dropped back
through the hatch to the planking two lengths below. He swore,
ducked back down after it.

Brit Arren stared at the place Jon had been. *He's terrified,* the
older man realized. A sudden pang stabbed at him. Jon had done
what he could to disguise his fear of *them,* but Mal had known
from the first how strong it was. He'd pushed the lad into a
corner, bullied him into actively going up against the Three . . .
well, but that was how such things were done, wasn't it? It was
how he, Mal, had learned. No different rules for the frightened or
the weak. But Jon—*he'll crack.* The thought gave him pause;
suddenly. He didn't want that.

The discovery shook him. "Unlike you, Brit Arren. Why?" he
whispered to himself, and turned into the full glare of early sun to
puzzle the thing. He was fond of the lad, certainly. But that was
all the more reason to push him past fear, into action against the
Three, to help him prove to himself that fear—even that much
terror—was surmountable.

It surely wasn't that Jon might be his son. A few men had
always claimed sons, and more were lately. That often made
men protective, possessive toward the lads in question. Fussy,
like mother hens. Well, he'd had Jon's mother, but then, he'd
had plenty of women and fathered plenty of sons. He had
never felt the need to claim any of them. Stupid notion. No, it
wasn't that.

He turned back to stare out across the water. *Venom*'s captain had let one of his boats down and part of its crew was
rowing in; up on shore, several men were working at an
upended rowboat. The smell of smoke and patching tar came
across the water to him. Three men sat on the docks mending a
sail, and along the northern crescent, women combed the
shoreline for shellfish and hauled in pots. All very normal. *Go.
Go now, before it's too late.*

Too late. Perhaps it was, already; some of the anger and the
depression that had washed in on the anger's heels was clawing
at him again. He swore and jumped down to the main deck.

Jon stepped out of shadow and touched his shoulder. "Mal,"
he whispered urgently. "You won't go on with this—this—"

"Shhh. Thought carries, remember?" But Brit Arren grinned
at him like a man with no such worries on his mind, clapped the

lad a sound blow across the back. Jon brought up a wan smile, but his eyes were black, all pupil, and they strayed toward the freshly toppled roof across the bay.

"Mal, it's not safe!"

"No. Nothing is, since Nod sealed his bargain. You and I talked about the lesser of dangers, Jon. Remember?" He clapped the boy on the back again, but gently this time. "Ye look dreadful. What, did ye take both watches after ye left me last night?"

"I—I slept some."

"Ah. If you say." The lad hadn't closed his eyes all night, Brit Arren would suddenly have banked half his take from the *Merman* on that. A momentary pity for such terror filled him. He shook it off. Pity was for fools. *He's a good lad. But I won't take him, we can't afford a weak splice in this, the entire plan will unravel.* Jon would feel shamed, when he found out. He'd learn from that, if he was as good as Mal thought.

"Mal?" Jon was gazing at him nervously.

"Well." He drew a deep breath, let it out as a sigh. "It was what I asked of you, wasn't it, Jon? When I first took you as my back man?"

"I—Mal?"

"Don't you remember?" Brit Arren grinned at him cheerfully. "To serve as my common sense when I wanted to go headlong into some wild scheme. Never mind, Jon. We'll try another time. I'll go ashore in a while, speak with old Brit Unliss."

"If you—" Jon began anxiously, stopped short as Brit Arren shook his head.

"To cancel our plans, that's all, lad." Jon's relief was almost comic, it was so sudden and complete. "In the meantime, I need you alert; *Fury* goes out again tomorrow. Don't want the men to think the old man can't take it, do we?"

"They'd never think that, Mal."

"Some might, if we gave 'em the chance," Brit Arren said flatly. "And you know it. We won't give 'em that chance, though, will we, Jon?"

Jon grinned widely. "No, sir—Mal."

"Good. Alert, I said. Means you take two full watches in my cabin, where it's cool and dark, and you get some sleep." And as Jon Bri Madden hesitated, "That's an order. I can deal with Ban Brit Unliss without back, I hope! This old man's not so feeble as all that!" That brought a laugh from his companion—not much of a laugh, but the lad was coming out of his funk. "That's better.

Get yourself a few hours' sleep. I may go on into the village for a meal, but I'll be back by nightfall." He strode off across the deck.

Jon moved back into the recessed doorway and stood in shadow, idly watching as the captain's own boat was lowered. Mal and four of his men set out for shore. Another boat followed moments later. Ten men altogether—

Ten. Heat flooded his face as realization struck hard. He ducked into the captain's cabin, slammed the door and leaned against it, his face red; he was weeping in shame. *Mal's gone to do it without me. Couldn't even tell me the truth.* Aghast, he bit his lip. *He's right not to trust me, even though he doesn't know why.* Despair washed through him, leaving him drained.

Someone was shouting up on deck, and a voice from the *Venom* shouted in reply. Another voice, much further away, yelling something at the female gleaners that brought a roar of laughter and snickers from those still aboard the *Fury.* Jon pushed away from the door, strode across thick rugs, skirted the table and dropped down onto the bed. He caught up one of the silken cushions piled on the floor, pulled it against his chest and fell belly down onto the soft fur cover. The fragile fabric caught on his chin stubble, scraped against the metallic thread that edged the collar of his unfastened shirt. He wrapped his arms more securely around the cushion, buried his face resolutely in it and closed his eyes.

Silence. The ship, suddenly, might have been deserted but for him. It rocked gently on its two anchor-ropes; overhead and beyond the closed shutters, the tiller creaked softly as it moved back and forth in its oiled locks. There was a mingled smell of salt air, stale wine, oil smoke from the lanterns: all reassuring, normal, familiar. He drifted, the room fading as sleep slipped around him.

A vague discomfort touched his thought, sudden fear: *Mal, don't!* It drifted away; he snuggled down into the soft fur and fine pillow and let the ship lull him to sleep.

Deep in the folds of embroidered silk, buffered from young skin by a twist of the heavy shirt, the medallion pulsed, matching the boy's heartbeat. The red stones that were its eyes glowered in their fabric cocoon, but they were already fading, the warmth of the metal faded, until even Jon—sensitized to its presence as he was—would not have noticed it had been active at all.

• • •

The air was already warm when Mal Brit Arren stepped out onto the docks; men sat along its planked length mending, splicing, gossiping. Two other boats were departing after dropping off crewmen; three others were behind his.

By mid-day, there wouldn't be anyone sitting here, the heat would be overwhelming. By mid-day, two boatloads of men coming ashore from the *Fury* might attract attention—if there were any with attention left to be attracted. At the moment, it was unlikely any eye would mark him and his men amid the friendly turmoil of Sea-Raiders coming and going. He waited until the second boat unloaded, started casually along the dock toward the path that skirted the towers, worked between the slabbed peaks and led back inland. A lot of men were doing *that*, too.

Once beyond the last heap of rubble, where the path veered south around dressed stone and fallen rock and into deep shadow, he stepped back into the shelter of the remnants of a stone lintel. Nine men moved with him, sliding through that opening, down an ever narrowing alleyway between man-shaped and natural rock, into a shallow cave formed by long years of wind and fierce rain. Two men were waiting there: Ban Brit Unliss and his grandson, Den.

Brit Unliss had aged in the three years since Mal Brit Arren had killed Nod Bri H'Larn and become Lord Captain. The lad Den hovered near him protectively, forming a new and stronger hand to replace the fire- and curse-withered right. Brit Arren gazed at the lad thoughtfully: *grandson*. Brit Unliss had claimed the woman Ettra's second boy as his; claimed, too, this youngster as his son's son. Part of Brit Arren sneered at them. To claim so much of a woman as to be certain of her womb! But . . .

But to have the unswerving devotion Den gave old Ban. Hah. Jon was also useful without such pointless ties, this of fathers and sons was counter to sense: where there were fathers and sons, inevitably would come daughters and mothers—wives, such as other men took. Already that woman of Ban's dared raise her voice against him.

"There's been no sign of *them*," Brit Unliss whispered against his ear.

"Good." Brit Arren settled his back against rock and stretched out his legs. "How long since any man saw them?"

"I did." Den's voice was still a boy's treble. "Two bells after sundown, yesterday, at full dark. *She* went up, said they were not to be disturbed." Like his grandsire, like most Sea-Raiders, Den Brit Unliss would not call Marrita by name, would speak of her only as "she," or "the woman." "I offered to bring them food."

"She was rude," Ban said angrily. "There was no cause for it." Brit Arren waved that aside impatiently. The lad whispered something to the old man that soothed him for the moment, then turned back to the Lord Captain.

"A short time later, the other went up also—Noble Lord Vess. Most Noble Lord Lyiadd had not left that chamber."

Lyiadd never did, save only the once, when Vess first came. *On my ship*. He pushed that thought aside; too late to do anything about *that*. He fought off anger at the boy's granting the two men the titles, that was foolish. Den had to serve them, there was no point to his being beaten for forgetting the proper form of address.

"They were up to something. A major spell, I thought. You could smell the witchcraft even at the base of the Tower, and the light through the shutters was very strong. Smoke poured from the chimneys. The moon was well up when something went hurtling across the sky—*their* doing, it must have been, though I saw nothing of it, only felt and heard it—and there was silence for a bit. And then, near dawn—" Den stopped.

"I know. I saw it."

"I heard it," Den whispered. "I moved just in time. Stone hit the ground where I'd been standing." Ban Brit Unliss stirred, opened his mouth to speak, but subsided as Den said something to him again. "Since then, I've seen and heard no movement. I didn't try to climb the stairs, but I looked up them."

"They're still clear?" Brit Arren asked.

"What I could see from the main doorway."

"Good." One of his own men stirred; he waved a hand for silence. "Let me think how to proceed from here." He glanced at the men with him, the old man and the lad huddled against his other side. "I'd lose none of you, if the choice is mine." His crewmen settled into what comfort they could find as Brit Arren drew his feet in and wrapped both arms around his shins, let his chin drop to his knees.

But if there were any way besides frontal assault, he could not see it, not for men who could not fly, coming against those who stayed in the uppermost chambers of that Tower and never came out. He peered out of the rubble toward the silent Tower. From this side, the damage was scarcely visible. A qualm touched him;

anger pushed it away. *Now. Delay only serves them, and lets them regain strength.* He jumped to his feet. "Let's go." As one, the men rose, silently drew swords and knives and followed him through a maze of fallen stone, crushed rubble and rotted timbers.

There was an unpleasant odor inside the Tower: Burnt hair and flesh, some kind of thick incense, an underlying faint reek of decay that teased at the edge of the senses. Eleven men and a green boy slowly, silently moved up the circling flight of stairs. Brit Arren found himself grateful to Marrita for her fussing about the steps: They need fear no slimed rock underfoot.

He'd cautioned against the least noise, though each man of them knew the Three used more than ears to sense approach. He'd tried to assure them on that point, too: The Power *they* drew on was strong, but it wasn't infinite. Overuse of it, or a spell that had come back on them, might temporarily drain them. Perhaps that was a flimsy hope to build an assassination upon, but it was the best they had. He'd been willing to chance it, and so had his men.

That smell—death and must combined—was increasing as they mounted. An opening, any opening in the walls would have been welcome indeed, but the damage did not seem to have come down so far. The men were at his back now, for he'd put himself two paces in front of them and they came on resolutely. He was glad all the same there wasn't much further to go. No Sea-Raider liked fronting sorcery, it wouldn't do to give them long to think about that, and the smell of the place wasn't helping.

He came up the last step, started across the open tiled floor toward the short staircase that led to the topmost chamber. There was visible damage here; stones had fallen from the walls and he could see the brilliant blue of distant ocean, a little of the bay. Oddly, the odor was stronger than ever; the breeze hadn't slackened but it seemed unable to make its way through the cracks. He shrugged that thought off, it wasn't a good thing to think, just now.

The men spread out as they reached level floor, and Ban and the boy came to his side. Den's face was greenish. Brit Arren held up his sword hand, the curved blade briefly reflecting light as it crossed a stray sunbeam. At the signal, four men dropped back to form a rearguard at the top of the stairwell.

He and the rest started up the shallow steps that would take them—

Odd. The air was becoming thick, hard to breathe, like Ragnolan steam. He caught at the wall, skinned his knuckles and swore under his breath. The silence was uncanny.

Behind him, someone cried out in surprise. *Silence! They will hear us!* He wanted to shout that; the thought echoed through his mind, but his tongue refused to work, the air wouldn't move into suddenly agonized lungs, and the floor was sticky under his feet. He tried to focus on them. The stone floor was bleeding; dark red liquid was puddling around his boots. It dripped from his fingers; his forehead—he shifted the grip on his sword to wipe his brow; his hand came away stickily red. The cries behind him faded as horror gripped him. His gaze went up to the door—so few steps away, so distant!—and then, unwilling, past it to the ceiling. A crimson wave poised there, and as he looked up, it fell on him.

Dark pain surrounded him like a stifling blanket. "Bah!" he told himself angrily. "Dark doesn't hurt!" The words rolled through his thought, thundering from ear to ear and back again, and he wished he could recall them. A wave of nausea gripped him, receded a little as he bit at his lower lip. His fingers throbbed; the stone floor was cold beneath his cheek. "I must have been drunk indeed to pass out like this," he thought, and braced himself for more pain. But it was less this time, almost bearable. He ventured to open one eye.

His right hand lay against his nose. No wonder it hurt; the tips of his fingers were scraped, swollen, bleeding in places. He'd gripped the wall with them, he knew that suddenly; gripped it for his very life, to stay upright when the ceiling turned to blood and came down on him. When he—a foot moved into his line of vision, a dark, well-cared-for, soft boot. Lord Captain Mal Brit Arren, with a jolt he could almost hear, was suddenly very much aware of his surroundings.

"Treachery." That cultured, slightly nasal voice with its half-heard undercurrent of whine or sneer. Vess. *He knows I am conscious,* Brit Arren realized. *Of course. He. They. They know it all, just as Jon feared, just as Jon tried to warn me. And I was fool enough to think it was his fear.*

"I have never met a genuine traitor before," Vess continued conversationally. The Sea-Raider couldn't decide if the man was speaking *at* him or *to* those others, Lyiadd and the witch. It didn't matter. *They get no satisfaction from me, I will not crawl.* He considered that thought, amended it carefully, *If I can help it.* He let his eyes close again.

"Of course," Vess went on, "there are such as my cousin, who could be construed as a traitor."

"We will *not* speak of her," Lyiadd broke in harshly. His voice changed, concern etched it. "Marrita, please speak to me!"

"I'm all right, my Lord." She sounded short of wind. *Someone nearly had them*, Mal Brit Arren thought in brief satisfaction. "No, we will not speak of Nedao or Nedao's Queen, not tonight." A chill silence. "If it does not discomfort *you*, of course, Lord Vess."

"Your servant in this, dear Lady, as in all things." The sugary venom practically dripped from Vess' lips. "But to return to this creature—what, I wonder, should we do with it?"

"It broke its vows, kill it," Marrita replied shortly. Vess laughed.

"Yes, how simple! And how foolish of me not to see that!"

"Stop, both of you!" Lyiadd overrode Marrita's sharp retort. Vess took a step back. "I would like to sleep a while, at least rest, so that I can put my mind to what passed here, and prepare to deal with it. Marrita is right, slit his throat and have done. Not here, you'll soil the carpets." Brit Arren forced himself to lie still. To die with no chance to defend himself—

"Ah, but," Vess said. He sounded a little subdued but no less malicious. "This is the Lord Captain of these uncouth louts, if we kill him, it might precipitate—difficulties, shall we say—among his following."

"I doubt that," Lyiadd returned evenly. "Remember how he became Lord Captain. By slaying the previous one! How much loyalty would you have for any man, knowing he'd killed for his place and might hold it four years? With luck?"

"Well, but," Vess protested mildly. "He might have his uses, you know. It seems a waste to simply kill him. Besides, consider his intentions. Read him. He's conscious."

"I know that," Lyiadd returned in some irritation.

"Read him," Vess urged. "He's hoping to die quickly, can't you tell? I personally feel very strongly, Father, about giving this creature the very thing he wants."

"Well—" Lyiadd's voice trailed away. Silence for some moments, save the high, thin scree of wind between shifted stones, well up in the wall. Vess' toe dug viciously against Brit Arren's ribs.

"Rise, you! I want to see your eyes!"

Somewhere deep in his mind, Brit Arren shrugged; it began, now, and it wouldn't be easy for him. He could only hope those who'd come up the Tower steps with him were dead; that the Three would believe him when he said no one else knew his plot. Likely that was the only thing he could still do, protect—he closed the thought away from him. Poor brave men from the *Fury*; poor old Brit Unliss. He could sleep away his curse forever now. His woman would mourn him and Den. No one would mourn Mal Brit Arren.

He rolled over as the foot came for his ribs again, managed to get his feet under him. Vess was waiting, fixing him with a chill look indeed.

The chamber was a mess: The table had been thrown against the far wall, the large tapestry was half-torn from the wall and wind hissed between the mangled shutters; the brass fastenings had burst, and someone had nailed extra bars across to hold them shut. Thick shards of glass lay everywhere; ash was smeared on the carpets and the chairs he could see were gritty with grey and brown soot. Lyiadd was hunched down in a chair well away from the door; Marrita hovered near him. Her gown was filthy, one sleeve torn nearly off; her hair had fallen in grubby spills and tangles across her shoulders.

Vess had fared no better: A smudge of black ran down his face, one eye was swollen and purple. The hand holding the dagger between them was nearly as scraped and battered as Brit Arren's own. The two armsmen who barred the door with long pikes were hurt, too; one wore a bloody bandage over his brow and one ear.

"A poor way to dissolve our bargain," Vess said coolly.

"It was no bargain of mine, and so I told you more than once." Anger gave Brit Arren back his tongue. "It was Nod Bri H'Larn's."

Vess laughed. "And you think that will make a difference to us? Well, however you savages look upon such contracts, we intend to hold it, and you know that. Don't you?" His gaze caught the other man's and held it. "Don't you?"

Brit Arren's skin crawled and he clamped his tongue firmly between his teeth. It moved of its own, his lips did. "Yes." Pure fury glared out of his blue eyes, and for a moment, Vess wavered, almost retreated a pace. "You'd make me speak, would you? Aye, I knew you'd no intention to break Nod's bargain. Just as I know you've no intention of leaving us alive when you quit the Isles."

"Ah?" Marrita had come silently across the room and now stood next to Vess. "And how do you reason this, seaman?" He closed his mouth, thinned his lips to a disapproving line and resolutely kept his gaze from her, lest she trap him as Vess had.

"My reasoning's my own, I *know*. And now you can do as you like with me, let one of the younger lads take command. Let them do your bidding, commit murder and rape for you!"

"Brave words," Marrita said finally, her voice ominously gentle. "You might have provoked another of your kind to kill you with such words, was that your intent? We are not ruled by such emotional trickery, Mal Brit Arren. I fear no such simple death will be yours."

"I had not thought it," he replied shortly, and fixed on another spot well above her head.

Silence stretched. Brit Arren concentrated on the stone wall, and when Marrita spoke again, he started. "Vess. When do you leave for Koderra?"

"Two days. Those I hired to clean and rebuild the Tower should be near done."

"You will take the women, children and the boys from the inland villages for our surety? Your Ragnolan mercenaries, your personal armsmen?"

"Seven ships go with me. That is not counting those already in Koderra and those I expect from Osnera in a five-day or so."

"Surely, you will have room for one more man? A prisoner?" Out of the corner of his eye, Brit Arren could see Vess nod in response to each of Marrita's questions. "One who should be saved for a very special execution, who could serve as an example when Yslar is conquered?"

"What an excellent notion! My Lady, I quite like the way your mind works." Even Brit Arren could sense the antagonism underlying the sweetly spoken words, but Marrita pretended to take them at face value, smiled and inclined her head. "It behooves us not to move rashly; treason requires particular care in its treatment. But just now, there is one small matter. Something the Lord Captain—but you are not Lord Captain now, are you, Brit Arren?—something requiring your talents."

"No! I refuse—"

"Silence," Vess whispered. Brit Arren trembled, but even anger was of no use; words would not come.

Vess reached into the throat of his tunic and drew out a long, fine chain. Something depended from it, but Brit Arren could not tell what without looking at it directly: bird, perhaps. Red stone eyes glittered even here in shadow. He shuddered; Vess laughed. There was eagerness in his laugh, anticipation. Brit Arren swallowed hard and closed his eyes.

Silence, a long, tense silence. Then sounds in the corridor: reluctant footsteps mounting the last short flight of stairs. Vess laughed triumphantly; Brit Arren's eyes flew open as a terrified sob filled the room. *Jon?* Vess waited; the boy stopped before him. A pendant like Vess' swung from his neck, clearly visible against the pale shirt.

"Mal?" Jon's whisper was scarcely audible, and it trembled so with tears no man would have known it for Jon Bri Madden's. "Mal, I am sorry, it wasn't my choice! They trapped me, *he* did! But I was afraid, so afraid, and I didn't want you to know—!" His voice broke. Tears ran down his face, following tracks left by earlier ones. Brit Arren stepped around Vess; he touched Jon's face, wiped the tears away with gentle fingers no man would have known for Mal Brit Arren's.

"I know, lad, I know," he whispered. It was all he had voice for at the moment. "I know you were frightened, there's no shame to that. It's all right." He turned his head. "Bravely done, Noble Lord Vess! So that's how your sorcery works! Not great spells, but the terror of a poor young lad! You vermin, you filth —you coward!" Vess moved back out of reach. Brit Arren would have lunged for him but his legs would not obey.

"Be still, you give me a headache," Vess said evenly. Brit Arren opened his mouth to bellow a retort, but no sound came, no words. "I wager you would ask me not to harm this poor sniveling rag—if you could talk. I have no intention of hurting the lad. In fact, I shall reward Jon Bri Madden. Perhaps I shall let him serve *me* personally, as he served you." Jon caught back a sob; he closed his eyes and went even paler than he'd been.

"Ah, but he betrayed his captain," Vess went on softly. He laughed. Brit Arren closed his eyes and desperately wished he could close his ears as readily. "Treachery, service, punishment, reward—how to deal with this?" He contemplated the two for a long moment. Brit Arren opened his eyes as Vess bent down to release a thin-bladed dagger from his boot. The gems in the handle glittered, almost like the little red eyes of Vess' medallion and Jon's matching one. *Ah, Jon, no!* It was suddenly more than he could bear, that Jon had been the means of his undoing."

"Take the knife." A gentle voice broke in on his agonized thoughts. Brit Arren blinked. There was a narcotic flavor to that voice, it soothed, lulled—he found his hand reaching for the blade almost before he was aware it had moved. He caught his breath in a gasp that sounded overloud in the still chamber, tried to pull his hand away. He couldn't. The air was sluggish, hard to breathe—like Ragnolan steam. "Take it." Square, capable, red-freckled fingers wrapped around the hilts. "Take it, and kill the traitor."

"Traitor," he whispered. *No!* He was himself for one brief, terrified moment. *That is Jon! He'd have you kill Jon!* 'Kill the traitor.' The words swirled through him, drowning his thought. The Sea-Raider swayed on his feet as the conflict pushed him back and forth, but the hand was going back, fingers tightened on the jeweled haft. Jon whimpered, his eyes wild, and he fought with all the strength in him to move. Vess' Power held him still; he could not so much as turn his head to avoid seeing Mal Brit Arren's blank face, the intention in his eyes.

"Mal," he breathed as the blade came up in a shining arc and plunged into his chest. He choked, caught at the older man's hand as Vess' holding spell dropped away from him. His hands went limp and he fell. Brit Arren stood over him, dagger still clasped in his hand. Vess took it from him, wiped it across Brit Arren's palm and restored it to his boot.

"That was well done, my friend. We'll speak of it another time. Perhaps I shall even reward you for the deed. Perhaps *you* will serve me, as he served you. Or perhaps I shall grant you death not long removed from his—so you need not re-member for so long a time that it was your hand that killed him." He turned and left the chamber. Marrita followed, her arm around Lyiadd, his around her. They skirted the fallen boy, the standing, stunned Sea-Raider, took the guards out with them. The door slammed shut and the bolt fell into place with a final, heavy clang.

Mal Brit Arren shuddered as the sorcery fell away from him.

Jon. He dropped heavily to one knee, touched the fallen lad. Jon's eyes were wide and fixed; terror still gripped his face. The neat little wound just under his ribs had bled very little and now had stopped. Brit Arren clasped Jon's body to him, closed his eyes and wept.

The funeral was a large one, attended by almost every single person in Nedao—or so they tell me. I could not have borne it, however much comfort that ceremony gave others. I pitied Ylia and Galdan, for they had no choice but to face that ordeal squarely, and to accept the overwhelming burden of their people's sympathy and their sorrow.

11

"Finished," Ylia whispered as she dropped to the edge of the bed. There was silence in the Tower and down in the street, people were still subdued after the funeral for Berdwyn and his nurse. She worked her low boots off with her toes, started as a shadow filled the door; it was Galdan. He sat next to her, put an arm around her shoulder and drew her close. They sat like that for some time. Galdan finally stood and went into the dressing room. Ylia picked up her soft boots and followed.

"Ysian has Sel?" It was the first thing Galdan had said all day; his voice was rough. He cleared his throat.

"She and Bendesevorian. I—I couldn't—"

"Shhh. Don't." He drew a shuddering breath, wrapped his arms around her and pulled her close. Ylia closed her eyes and leaned against him.

"I'm all right."

He shook his head. "You're not all right. You don't have to be. I'm not." She pushed away from him, nodded. Galdan finished unlacing his dark tunic, pulled it over his head. Ylia let him undo the back of her own close gown rather than send for one of her women: She knew she couldn't face one more tear-stained face just now. She reached automatically for the lightweight breeches, the loose shirt, the thin overshirt and dressed in silence, then caught up her boots and carried them back to the bed to finish. Galdan came back in, his everyday jerkin half-laced, took the comb from her and worked her hair into a plait.

Ylia sat staring at the wall after he finished; suddenly movement was more effort than it was worth. Tired—she hadn't slept

97

in two nights, no, three now. And—why? Why bother, what use
to anything? Galdan gripped her shoulders and he drew her to her
feet. She turned, held out her hands. "He'll pay, they will. I
swear it by all that's sacred, Galdan, I swear it."

He swallowed hard, nodded. She gripped his fingers, released
his hands and turned away. Deep down, mostly buried under grief
and pain but not buried quite deeply enough, was her own separate anguish: Kabada. Malaeth had grimly spooned it into her,
carefully measuring dosage, watching to see she took it. There
could be no other son, no other child. Galdan would never hate
her for that; just now, she hated herself for it.

Galdan waited for her at the door. "There should be food
down in the small dining hall."

"I'm not—," she began automatically.

"You know you must eat. Strength. You'll need it." She
couldn't argue with that. In truth, she felt hungry and hated herself for it. *When did I eat last?* Galdan was right, though; however much she resented any inner signal that her own life was
going on while her son lay dead, she needed to eat.

Galdan was waiting for her. She caught up the sword belt,
buckled the weapon low on her hip, and went to join him.

It was a cold morning, overcast and drizzly. A wind blew
steadily from northeast, straight across the harbor and the docks.

There were few men about and they were subdued. A boatload
of women and young children was shoved away. Herd Brit Ofrey,
acting Captain of the *Fury*, leaned against the tiller, watching
shore for the rest of his passengers and trying hard to stifle his
nervousness. The crew were silent, stunned as they set about
preparing for the voyage to the mouth of the Torth.

The boatload of women and children drew alongside; Brit
Ofrey barked orders, got them loaded below. Out of sight.
Women aboard the Fury, *gods aid us, we needed only this!* At his
gesture, the boat went back to the docks to await the last of the
passengers.

Lord Vess was traveling with them. Brit Ofrey found himself
praying for good wind and a fast journey. Whatever followed—
well, whatever did. No one had said what the *Fury*'s fate might
be, once they reached Koderra and unloaded their passengers;
Vess might well have it holed and sunk, crew and acting captain
all killed.

Herd Brit Ofrey had made it very clear from the moment he

assumed temporary leadership of *Fury* that he would not try to hold her, *or* to take Brit Arren's rank. *Ah, Mal*—! He didn't dare think of Mal, and that hurt. *They'd* warned him, though.

Movement on shore drew his attention; a clutch of men coming from the towers. There, the dark red that was Most Noble Lord Lyiadd, and there his consort, Her Excellent and Gracious Lady Marrita. Before them, in somber silver-edged black, Noble Lord Vess and a dozen armsmen. Brit Ofrey threw himself down the ladder and began working his way along the deck, stopping now and then to warn the crew: "It's Mal, they're bringing him *here*! Remember, no speech with him, that's death for certain! Gods, don't even look at him!"

Vess stood on the dock and gazed complacently after the rowboat carrying half his personal guard across the cove. Four other ships out there carried his armsmen and took women and children from the inner villages as surety for the continued support of these barbarous pirates. Not that Sea-Raiders would be subdued by threat to their women, of course. But their male children—they'd think carefully before chancing the loss of most of their sons.

In two days' time, he'd be in Koderra. *Koderra! Ah, Brandt, if you knew! And cousin Ylia—but you will know, won't you?*

"It's what you want?" Lyiadd's voice interrupted pleasant thoughts. Vess nodded.

"What I always wanted. If it's not quite the way I wanted it—well, things seldom come the way one wants them. The end result is the same. And my Ragnolers are not comfortable here, they do not mix well with these pirates, it's as well that I go, and take them with me."

Lyiadd gripped his hands. "Hold yourself ready."

"I shall." The boat was back. Four of Vess' personal guard moved forward, Mal Brit Arren in their midst. He was securely shackled, his gait made awkward by the overly short hobble on his ankles. Most of the men on the docks turned away, as much in shame for their fallen leader as for fear of the Three and their directives. Brit Arren's shoulders sagged, his head was down, his eyes dull. He plodded where pushed; stumbled once and nearly fell. It took them a long time to get him down the ladder and into the boat—grief and hopelessness had overborne him completely and he moved like an old man.

"He *is* broken—for now." Lyiadd followed Vess' thought eas-

ily, responded to it. "I doubt he will remain broken. Have an eye
to him."

"I will." Vess didn't seem particularly concerned.

"He thinks himself defeated; he is not, entirely. Read him, my
son." Vess considered this, nodded finally. He turned to bow over
Marrita's extended hand; his lips did not, quite, touch it. He
clasped hands with Lyiadd, then.

"I—when I was a lad, in Teshmor, I wondered what sort of a
man my father was." The words came stiffly and rapidly as
though Vess wanted to speak but found it hard to bare so much of
himself. "My mother could not have given me a better." Lyiadd
gripped his hand, wrapped the other arm around his son and held
him briefly. Vess smiled, turned and motioned his remaining
armsmen to join him in the waiting boat.

Night. There were ten sitting close together on and around the
raised dais in the Reception: a small group indeed for the size of
the room. A fire burned in the grate, more for the cheer of it than
the warmth.

Ylia and Galdan were side by side on the top step of the dais;
Bendesevorian sat between them, a step lower. At Galdan's left,
much as they'd stood for him at his wedding, were Golsat, Brelian, Erken; on Ylia's right, Nisana, Ysian, Lisabetha.

Grewl sat a little apart, by himself, for he alone was to take no
active part in the night's labors. Bendesevorian had asked his
presence, and Grewl, ever willing to hear a new tale or to watch
one made, had eagerly agreed. Now, under the strain of waiting,
he was growing uneasy; knowing the cause was no help. The
Nasath had warned him: What they sought to do was dangerous,
someone might die.

Such a foolish thing to fear, that this matter of magic might
kill him! It was only death, after all. *But I'm not yet ready to die,
there's too much at stake for Nedao if I do. And I haven't seen
and done so many things.* He leaned forward as Bendesevorian
broke the long silence.

"Queen Ylia—"

"Please," Ylia interrupted him. "We're friends here, and here
as friends. Just Ylia and Galdan."

"Ylia, then. I asked you to bring these others. Tonight we will
do what we can to break the block on Galdan's Power. There will
be need for each of you. Ylia, Lady Ysian—Ysian," he amended
as she stirred, "and Nisana will back me with Power. Lord Erken,

you may be needed to aid your son." Erken nodded. Galdan smiled at his father; Erken smiled back. Neither was convincing.

Bendesevorian went on. "You all know what chanced here, a bare five-day ago, how the Three breached this house's defenses by the substitution of a gift, and wrought grievously. The Power we threw back at them may slow them a while, and it may teach them caution. It will not stop them, and it will doubtless not delay their plans long." He half-turned to gaze up at Galdan, who stared back at him somberly. "In a war such as this, we must put aside personal wants, needs, even fears, to consider the greater need. Galdan has done this."

Erken shifted uncomfortably, subsided as the Nasath turned back to look at him inquiringly. Erken shook his head.

"And so we are here," Bendesevorian continued. "An exiled Nasath; three wielders of AEldra Power; Galdan's father and sworn brothers; one who dreams true and so holds what Nedao holds of Power. And a chronicler." Grewl nodded faintly.

"Exiled." Erken caught at that. "You are exiled, sir?" Bendesevorian nodded. "Why?"

"The whole is a longer tale than I could tell tonight. My part of it—yes, you have a right to know my part. And there is time before we can begin.

"We are not native to the Foessa or to the Peopled Lands at all. I myself scarcely remember the other place that *was* ours, save for a child's memory of burning and death. I recall the night the Elders made the bridge and brought us safely over it, casting it down in the very face of pursuit. I remember those first years in the mountains, in what is now Yls—lean years, indeed, until we learned how to live in the wilderness. The Dreyz—the Folk—found us, and gave us what aid they could; we in turn gave them much of the Power they now possess. Though they were not without Power when we first met, for the Foessa have always been wild with Power.

"Enough years passed that we came to consider the lands ours; we multiplied and prospered, and we perhaps began to think of ourselves as invincible. Of course, we were not. We learned this when the Lammior made himself a place in the Foessa and warred against us.

"After that war, we were again few and nearly all of us were so weary of fighting that the mountains seemed an ill place. The Elders decided then to give what land was ours to the AEldra, along with the Gifts of Power, and to step away from folk and lands alike. Not so far a step as we had taken in coming to them, this time. Fortunately, for one as young and relatively unskilled as I can cross the gap without effort.

"The Elders had decreed the Peopled Lands were barred to us forever. The humans had everything we could give them, we had balanced the scales of debt and would not tip them again.

"So for long years, we were content. I had fought and killed for so many years I was sickened by thought of the Foessa. But eventually, I grew curious: What chanced here among our once allies? Had any human gone in search of that valley to become another Night-Serpent? My sister and I felt there could be no harm in a single visit. We could assure ourselves that nothing ill prevailed—and we agreed we would not interfere."

He sighed. "That we ourselves felt such a concern at the same time, that we chose the time and place we chose to return to these lands—I can only believe we were guided. We first set foot in the garden you call Hunter's Meadow. The Folk had once dwelt there, but it now reeked of evil, the whole of the mountains did. Beyond the mountains, eastward, north of the Plain, we sensed an old Tehlatt shaman gifted with his war god's dread Power urging his chief to destroy the Plainfolk. Against such Power and such a force of armed as the Tehlatt had, we two were helpless.

"But then, out of that wrack and destruction, came a little clutch of folk, moving northward, set on a course that would take them into the Lammior's valley." He stared down at his hands. "Even then, we dared not interfere; dared not and did not until it was nearly too late. Then—well, we had violated our law by leaving sanctuary, what did a second transgression matter? I set Ylia's AEldra Power free.

"Later—" He shrugged. "A second time the law was broken, what did a third or a fourth matter—given the need? We revealed ourselves to Ylia, spoke to her and gave her what aid and warning we could. We told the Folk of her coming, that she and they might perhaps make alliance against this new threat.

"When we returned home—" He went back to a contemplation of his hands. "The Elders were most displeased. Fortunately our kind does not punish as humans do, or I would likely not be alive to aid you now. They confined us for a long time. But even that is strong punishment among us. At length they chose a way to ensure neither of us would leave again: Nesrevera would be free to go where she chose so long as I remained sequestered. I was free to move about if she was confined."

Ysian had gone pale. "She's not—they won't hurt her!"

Bendesevorian smiled at her wanly. "They will not harm her, no. That is not our way. They will hold her until I return. And if I do return, they will doubtless not allow me freedom again. But that is why I am here and why Nesrevera stayed. We planned it when they began to use us each as surety for the other. We knew one of us must return to the Peopled Lands, and of us two, I am more suited to aid you. I speak Nedaoan, Ylsan and High AEl-dran. I have killed before, and though it has been long years, I would kill again, in need." He smiled briefly. "But more importantly, I am more blunt-spoken than my sister. If one of us is to persuade the Elders to reconsider our exile, or perhaps to convince the younger of us to come here, that is no task for me. It is one I know Nesrevera can accomplish."

Silence. He stood, cocked his head to one side as if listening. "The hour has come. Galdan—rise and come with me to the center of the room. Ylia, accompany him, Duke Erken and you other men, at Galdan's right arm. Ysian, Lisabetha, at his left. Nisana—to me, please." Ylia moved around the silent little group, sword, shield and horn bunched in one hand. Her face, like Galdan's, was set and pale. Grewl shifted his chair so he could see and wiped damp hands down his grey-robed lap.

It was very quiet in the Tower, so silent in the Reception that the snap and flare of torches sounded overloud. Bendesevorian closed his eyes briefly, opened them again and extended his hands. Galdan swallowed hard, reached and caught them with his own. They knelt.

'Close your eyes, man of Nedao, and seek the innermost core of your strength.' Galdan started as Bendesevorian's mind-speech rang through him. He licked his lips and shut his eyes tight. Erken exchanged a brief, worried glance with Golsat, brought his gaze back to the top of his son's head. 'Not deep enough, Galdan, search!'

'I—can't!'

'You can, you must!'

'I am!' Galdan felt sweat trickle down his ribs; his lip was salty with it. Somewhere, somewhere deep down, so deep he'd never yet found it, a core of Power—*But I don't want it!* an inner voice wailed.

Ylia's mind-touch reached him. She was worried. *What I might become—if she fears that—*'Never!' she reassured him passionately, and he knew that was true. But—*Marhan lives be-*

cause of what I did. With that block in place, I made a dead man live. If Bendesevorian removes that block, what might I become?

'Do you fear that? Enough to block your own efforts to find the innermost core of Power in you?' Bendesevorian's thought demanded.

'I could work evil against my own people!'

'Anyone can do that, if that is what they choose to do with the Power that is theirs. Power is. Nothing more, nothing less.'

'But I know I would work evil, if it took evil to reach those who murdered my son!'

'If. That against a certainty! Without use of all our resources, Nedao is lost and Lyiadd has won. And your son's death, Malaeth's death—those who died at the hands of the Tehlatt—those will be all to no purpose.' Galdan's fingers tightened convulsively on Bendesevorian's, and the Nasath winced.

'Beloved—' That was Ylia; her thought was ragged with renewed grief.

"Don't," he whispered. "It's all right. I'm—I'm afraid."

"I know," she whispered in reply. "You needn't go on. Don't."

"I must, Ylia. He's right, we need all our weapons. I'm—I'm one of them." He became aware of the physical pain he was causing Bendesevorian, loosed his deathgrip on the other's hands. "I can sort the fear later. We can, together. It isn't important." And as Erken took a step forward, "It's all right, Father. Just a last thought in the face of the inevitable." Erken looked from one to the other of them, baffled, but returned to his place. Golsat gripped his arm, nodded faintly as Erken looked at him. *It'll be all right.* The dark man might have mind-spoken him, so clearly did the thought reach him.

Galdan was still afraid of the Power itself, of what he might do with it—that it could change him so he was no longer what he knew as Galdan. What he'd said to Ylia was suddenly true, though: It didn't matter. All sense of the chamber faded as he withdrew into himself, searching with all the single-minded strength of purpose in him.

Bendesevorian blinked. "Ylia. Grip the hilts. Give Brelian the shield, Golsat the horn. Brelian, when I let go his hands, you kneel beside him and hold the shield over his heart. Maintain it there, no matter what."

"I will." Brelian cast Lisabetha a reassuring smile, took the proffered lozenge and ran his fingers across the carven edges. A shiver ran through him. *Magic. My poor friend, would I be as brave in your stead?* Out of the corner of his eye, he could see Golsat carefully unwinding the frayed silk banner and let it hang loose at the Nasath's direction. *This Nasath—when did Ylia meet with him? Once I would have sworn nothing happened to one of us on that journey that all did not know.*

His attention shifted. Galdan still knelt, eyes tightly shut, but he was swaying, as though to some music only he could hear. "Galdan." Bendesevorian gripped his hands hard. He spoke aloud for the benefit of the watchers. "You've nearly found it. A last try."

Last try. He was exhausted already and that worried him. If he needed strength to survive what followed, he might not have it. He was uncomfortable, uncertain how much those with Power could sense of what he picked through, searching for what he needed. Even Ylia. For there was much of Galdan he found wanting, there were things he'd greatly prefer no other living creature knew.

Something walked along his nerves with catlike feet, then, and he *knew.* 'I have it!' The Nasath was waiting for him.

'I know. Hold ready!' *Brace yourself,* he might as well have commanded. 'Look at me.'

Unwillingly, afraid he might lose his grip on what he'd quested for, Galdan did. The room swam in an odd light: It was as though the air itself had turned, faintly, yellow-green—or as though the light of a spring sun through aspen leaves had come into the chamber. He looked at everything with new eyes, or with a newly heightened sensitivity, he wasn't certain which. It was decidedly unnerving and rather dizzying, and he was glad he had Bendesevorian's hands to steady him. The Nasath gave him no time to analyze it, or to let the sensation build from unnerving to fear.

"Ylia. To my right side. Galdan, when I release your hands, grasp the shield along with your friend. Do not let go."

"I won't."

"Golsat?"

"Here." The dark man came forward.

"Set the horn to your lips. When Ylia touches Galdan's shoulder with the sword, blow through the mouthpiece and think only of that sword upon your friend's shoulder. The horn will know what notes to make from the air you give it." Golsat eyed it warily, but nodded. "Ysian, you and Lisabetha come to my left side and join hands. Ysian, take hold of my arm. Back me." He smiled at Lisabetha. "You may feel weakened, but I will draw as little upon you as I can."

"Don't worry for me," Lisabetha replied as she took Ysian's hand.

'Nisana.'

The cat pressed against his ear. 'If this goes awry, I will shield as many of the untalented as I can.'

'Good.'

"What must I do?" Erken asked. He was tense and pale.

"Be ready to catch him, if he falls," Bendesevorian said.

Galdan managed to laugh. "That is a task for you, Father. You've done that since I first learned to walk!" Erken snorted, but he looked suddenly less nervous. Galdan turned back to Bendesevorian. He nodded once. Bendesevorian let go his hands. Brelian knelt and held the shield out. His knuckles were white from the intensity of his grip on the edges. Galdan caught hold of it, top and bottom.

Ylia gripped Shelagn's sword and at Bendesevorian's gesture let it down to rest against Galdan's shoulder. Golsat raised the horn to his lips and blew.

The yellow-green of the air intensified, until it was more like staring up into leafy sunlight from underwater; there was *sound*, but afterward none of them could have said whether it resembled horncry, music, or if it was merely vibration. It shivered through them like a wind, intensified, was suddenly gone as Bendesevorian threw back his head and cried out.

Words, or song, or merely sound? There were words in the cry, Grewl thought, though no language he'd ever heard before.

Nedao's King shuddered under the multi-fold assault. Brelian's grip on the shield tightened; he somehow kept it over Galdan's heart. The sword bounced on Galdan's shoulder. Ylia pressed it firmly against his jerkin. Bendesevorian's voice rose, filling the chamber, setting the light to swirling in a dizzying fashion. Grewl moaned, closed his eyes. Lisabetha sagged and but for Ysian would have fallen.

Galdan's cry suddenly topped Bendesevorian's: "No!" The torches were extinguished by a sudden blast of wind, the lanterns went out as though snuffed. There was only the swirling, greenish light.

The horn blazed with light of its own; Golsat shouted as it fell from his fingers and clattered on the tiled floor. The sword flared and brought forth an answering blaze of light from the great topaz at the shield's center.

"Take that which is yours!" Bendesevorian cried out. The words echoed through the chamber. Galdan's lips moved soundlessly; topaz and sword were pulsing wildly with his heartbeat. "Reach for it; *take* it!"

"I can't! Ah, Mothers, it hurts!" It was tearing him apart, burning through his inner being like fire, it was agony! "I *can't*!"

"You must! Do it *now*!" Galdan's hands moved, slowly at first, fingers crawling across the shield's face until they met over the center stone. He jerked once, color flooded his face, and with a last cry, he fell as though struck, taking the shield, Brelian, Erken—and the light—with him.

*Poor man: so soon after the death of his be-
loved son and his heir, to have to fight so hard
for what was his, but beyond his reach. And
then to endure weary days and more days with
Bendesevorian, with Ysian or with me, learning
to wield his Power. But he did all that without
complaint. I think only Bendesevorian and I
knew how near he came to death when he tried
that one last time to refuse his gift and to take
shelter behind the barrier of his Nedaoan blood.
If Galdan knew, he never said.*

12

It was a subdued Council that met to discuss final plans for
Midsummer Fest—as subdued as the folk without who were dec-
orating stalls, finishing crafts for sale or dressing out fresh beef
and venison, washing fruit and setting it in baskets in the River to
chill for the next morning's festivities.

In her seat at the head of the table, Ylia pushed hair back from
her brow and again wished Galdan at her side. He was better at
settling arguments or leading the discussion in the right direction.
She could have particularly used him just now: There were entirely too many niggling matters, and she was nearly asleep
where she sat.

It had been her night to lead the Elite Guard against any raids,
the last night, and so she had been dozing only when the alarm
sounded at second bell past middle night. She and ten of the
guard bridged out to the trouble—one of the western pastures
adjoining Bnolon's lands. She'd returned to the Tower when
Bnolon's guard reached them, but was on her feet less than an
hour later responding to a second alarm.

It was tiring, this splitting of the duty. But Galdan had been
secluded with Nisana most of the night, and the War Council had
been firm in its decision, after Ifney's death; no longer would
both King and Queen battle Mathkkra together.

And so it had been near dawn when she'd tumbled back into

bed. The meeting was thankfully brief: The only urgent matter was the unexpected arrival of twenty young Ylsan nobles for Fest. Ysian had warned them the Sirdar's grandson and several companions intended to come. But Ylia assumed the Sirdar would prevent the visit, and no one else took the notion seriously, that Ylsan nobility would chance the dangerous journey to Nedao all for a chance at the Fest and its tourneys.

"Unexpected," Vedrey said. Ylia repressed irritation; this *was* only his third full council meeting. She hoped for better of him, if he ever got past his nervousness. "My son has been guiding them about this morning; he tells me they've come mostly for the contesting."

"We know that," one of her father's men said testily. She looked at him; the older man, sensitive to the Crown's subtle signals, leaned back in his chair and got a grip on his own irritation. His next words were more mildly stated. "They should have a formal reception, Lady."

Already decided, Ylia thought, but she merely nodded. "They will. Tonight, after evening-meal; that is for the Narrans, of course. Vedrey, is your son still showing them around?" He nodded. "Have him extend the invitation; go ahead and send someone now." Vedrey hurried from the chamber. "We will need to fit them into the contesting. It will be well worth the trouble to place them with care, so they aren't over- or underchallenged."

"Well, of course," one of the other older men began. He stopped as Ylia held up a hand.

"It's a matter of different styles of fighting; archery, sword, wrestling," she said. "It won't be as simple as devising levels for our own. I'll speak to Marhan and Lev this afternoon and see how best we can gauge and sort the Ylsans without offending anyone."

That should have satisfied the Council; of course, it didn't. Several of the men wanted to argue for more prizes, more divisions, even more placings for prizes. Ylia turned all that down flatly. "The Ylsans would not appreciate our making it simple for them to win, as though they were spoiled children. If the events were to be changed or more prizes given, do you think they would not learn it was done simply to give them a chance to win? They'd find that more of an offense than not winning at all. I would."

That did not set well with most of the older council-members. Ylia knew they likely did not understand what she'd tried to tell them. Too few of the men who had been her father's were or had ever been fighting men.

Ylia watched them file out finally, stood and stretched hard. A late noon-meal was waiting for her. Galdan and Nisana were not long ahead of her, Galdan eating bread and fruit like a starving man. Nisana was sitting near the end of the table, her back to them, batting a seed back and forth. As Ylia came in she gave it a final shove off the edge, and stared down at it with intense concentration.

"Ah. Lady wife. What were the alarms last night?"

Ylia sliced off a thick piece of the dark bread, smeared it with runny butter from the pot and sank her teeth in it. She chewed, swallowed and tucked another bite into her cheek. "What, you haven't been down to the barracks yet to find out?"

Galdan scowled at Nisana. "*She* won't let me."

'No such thing,' the cat retorted stiffly. Nisana was never in the best of moods when she taught, particularly when things weren't going the way she wanted them to. Her present preoccupation with the appleseed, Ylia realized suddenly, was an attempt on the cat's part to separate herself from a formidable attack of temper. 'I told him to bridge there; *he* won't.'

Ylia leaned back in her chair, let her head fall back and laughed. "It's not funny," Galdan said stiffly; he was as near anger as Nisana. "I keep *trying*, and all it does is make me sick!" Ylia sat up to gape at him; she smothered a giggle with one hand, clapped the second over it, finally gave it up and roared with laughter. "It's not funny, I lost my breakfast, trying to get from the Reception to the barracks!" Nisana transferred her scowl from Galdan to Ylia.

'Stop that. I don't find it amusing, either!'

"*You* wouldn't, cat," Ylia replied. She drew a deep breath, let it out as a sigh, fought another fit of giggles—this time almost with success. "You never listen to *me*, do you, cat?"

'You bridge,' Nisana said flatly. Galdan was looking from one to the other of them, following the conversation with considerable confusion, but without effort. *At least*, he thought sourly, *I can do that now!*

"I do bridge. I—" She realized Galdan was watching her. "Sorry, we're talking riddles. I had the same problem, bridging. It was too much like high places, they still make me sick." She frowned, transferred the frown to the cat. "Odd, though. Galdan was bridging before."

"I was going along for the ride," Galdan said dryly. He broke off another piece of bread. "It's different since the other night; everything is. The few things I used to be able to do, I can't work the way I did. Others like the bridging, things I didn't have, I can't seem to work at all, and some things—hells. Doesn't matter, I'll manage, eventually." He popped the bread in his mouth, mumbled something around it.

"What? Galdan, you can't eat and talk at the same time, *think* it, why don't you?" Ylia demanded.

'I *said*, how did you finally master it? The bridging? Maybe I can do it that way.'

"I hope not. It just happened, all at once, because I found something that was more important than being afraid. I—here, I'm forgetting now, *look*." And she brought up a four-year-old memory: the Tehlatt camp on the night they rescued the Nedaoan captives from certain death by fire. Golsat had been stranded among his half-kin, and Ylia had had no way to reach him save to find the bridging and simply do it. "I had to, there wasn't anything else. It hurt almost worse than anything I've done, before or since.

"But I couldn't have done it just for the practice, or for anything less than Golsat's life. I still think Nisana hesitated, though, in hopes I would find a way to bridge without her."

'I swear, girl, I would *never* have risked the man's life so! Poor Ysian was hysterical, who else was there to keep her from screaming so the Tehlatt could come for us? And I was already worn—' The cat eyed her tiredly. 'Think what you want, you do anyway.'

Ylia merely shook her head. Silence. Galdan was peeling an early apple, letting the skin fall in a bright green coil to his plate. "Nisana was right to force me to learn," Ylia said finally. "Making me try when I *knew* I couldn't, that I'd never be able to do it. Because once I *had* to bridge, *how* was reflex."

"Oh, I'm not giving up," Galdan said grimly. He sectioned the apple, cored it and held out a wedge; she leaned forward to take it with her teeth. "Anyway, enough of that. Tell me about the raids last night. And this other thing: What do we do with these wretched young Ylsans?"

• • •

Galdan left with Nisana not long after, but promised he'd be back early for the formal reception. "I'll meet you down at the barracks, in a couple of hours," Ylia called after them. Galdan turned in the door, made a face that left her laughing again. He vanished down-hall, Nisana curled around the back of his neck like a collar.

She consulted the list Lisabetha had left in its usual place, under her winecup. War Council next. She'd better finish eating quickly, she was running late. Then a walk through the market, a meeting with Lossana at the clothbarn. Lossana was working on a new felt and the Narrans were pressing for samples.

Barracks, then: She needed to work with the women in her Elite Guard. One or two of them had seemed weak lately. That wouldn't do. And Ylia needed the workout herself. *Neglect no skill, when any of them might prove the one needed*. She should know that better than anyone else in Nedao: She whose Power had been strong, if only roughly managed, when she'd been captured by Lyiadd. Power hadn't been *his* downfall.

She finished her bread, set the list aside. Nothing else on it; but her evening would be quite busy: The reception for the Ylsans, then the Narrans: Ber'Sordes always brought his new household for introduction, and they changed annually on Fest Eve. Galdan—if she could help him at all, if he'd have her aid—*He'll be worn from Nisana, but if there's anything left of him, perhaps we can find something together.*

'I am not pushing him that hard.'

'That was a private thought, cat. Save your attention for Galdan, why don't you?'

'If it's a private thought, keep it to yourself,' Nisana responded huffily, and before Ylia could reply, the mind-touch was gone. Ylia rolled her eyes, caught up the last two sections of apple and walked back to the council chamber.

The War Council discussed the two raids of the previous night, the step-up in patrols and the change in times and patterns to these. A plan had already been worked out by Lord Corry, and Erken presented another plan to allow the parameter guards as much time at Fest as possible, while still maintaining tight watches. Unlike the Main Council, the War Council seldom wasted much time, and when it broke up moments later, Ylia slipped away to the weaving barns.

Lossana was busy enough for three women, even with Ysian

and Lisabetha to help her, and with the support and assistance of the other women who worked the looms and spindles. There was a consignment of wool to go out after Fest, another of linen and another bale of the unique yellow. And she was participating once again in the Women's Sword Crossings and Women's Bow. Somehow, she never looked harried and somehow, everything would be accomplished.

Ylia took the piece of felt Lossana gave her and let sunlight fall across it. It was soft and much thinner than ordinary felt. It was a smooth thickness, without lumps. Lossana had dyed the sample a rich, deep blue. "The Narrans will like this, Lossana."

Lossana pushed hair back from her brow and tucked it into the loose plait. Over the past winter she'd lost weight and there was as much grey in her hair as dark brown, but her eyes were as lively and young as her daughter's. "I hope they do; it's a good use for the second-grade fleeces and this piece has goat hair worked into it for strength. I lined my old woven red cloak with some and it's nearly windproof."

"The Narrans *will* like that." Ylia handed back the sample. Lossana took it. Her eyes were grave.

"How are you, lass?"

Ylia shrugged. "I'm all right."

Lossana shook her head. "You don't have to be, not with me," she said. "I know what it is to lose a son."

"I know you do," Ylia whispered. She couldn't manage anything else. Lossana wrapped an arm around her, held her briefly.

"I couldn't talk about it for a long time, not even to Corlin. It was different, for both of us; I think that was the first time neither of us could fully understand the other. The first time I realized that we both loved Gors in different ways. Maybe because I carried him in my body. Corlin didn't have that." Silence. "So I understand in a way perhaps even Galdan can't. If you need that. Remember, will you?"

"Thank you, Lossana. I will."

Lossana glanced out the open doors. "Mothers, it's past third hour already, my red dye will be burned to the pot! Are you fencing Marhan again tomorrow?"

Ylia laughed faintly through a tight throat, but it was loosening already; trust Lossana to bring her back firmly to safe ground before sending her on her way. "I have to; the old man's made a thing out of it, and Ber'Sordes' new household has already been primed for it!"

"Good. I won't dare leave here tomorrow except for my first-round bow and to watch *that*. Usual hour?"

"Yes." Ylia walked toward the doors, turned back just inside them. "Lossana—thank you."

"Certainly." And Lossana was gone, practically running into the open-backed dye shed to check her kettles. Ylia shook her head in mild amazement and headed toward the barracks.

She and Eveya worked the new women exhaustively, then Ylia watched while the third-year Elite Women went through daily crossings. It was hot out in full sun, would probably be hotter the next afternoon for the competitions. It was too bad they'd never found time to cover the main square save for a covered seating area and the royal platform where she, Galdan and their personal guests sat. *This year, we'll get it covered*, she resolved. *This year if there's time, and Nedaoans left to do it.* She sat back to watch Lennet and Eveya; the two were working out the practice maneuvers for paired rapiers.

"Huh. Look at her, numbing her backside on the bench. Is that how I taught ye?" Ylia started as Marhan dropped heavily onto the bench beside her, then drew herself up indignantly.

"I was out there—!" she began defensively. Marhan laughed.

"Huh! Of course ye were, until just this moment, no doubt! I'll have ye easy tomorrow, boy."

"Don't count that victory yet, old man," she warned him. Marhan chuckled evilly. "They're good, aren't they?"

"Hah." Marhan would never admit to such a thing, however good any of them were. *Women.* She could almost hear the single word rising like a curse, just the way he thought *magic*. Women wielding swords and daggers, wearing breeches, standing shoulder to shoulder and fighting with men. "Lev's girl, isn't that?" He knew full well it was.

"And Eveya," Ylia said. Marhan scowled at her.

"I *know* it's Eveya. Old man hasn't lost his memory yet. Lev's girl's got guts, I like that." He silenced the remark Ylia would have made with another hard look. "Won't teach her, don't ask. *Ye* were enough." He watched in silence another moment or so. "She doesn't need my teaching, and I'm too old for those silly blades."

Ylia laughed. "That's a challenge if I ever heard one!" Marhan turned to face her with slow deliberation. One eyebrow went up. And don't tell me you haven't tried them, I know you better."

"Hah. *Hah!*" The Swordmaster leaned back against the wall. "Don't have to prove anything to *you*, boy."

She could have bullied him into it, she was certain of that. But a sudden flare of Power caught her completely off guard. Marhan scowled and Ylia turned to look. Galdan leaned against the barracks, to all the world relaxed and unconcerned, Nisana on his shoulders and a complacent smirk on his face.

"Well. Look who's come," Marhan snorted. "Your lady wife is trying to tease me into fighting her."

"Foolish woman," Galdan said. He sounded rather winded. "He's at least as stubborn as you. Moreso, actually. Comes of being older, I suspect." Marhan laughed.

"Hah. Listen to *you*. He's breathing heavier than the old man ever did!" Marhan turned to scowl at the silent, staring armed: Some of the lads looked as though they thought Galdan might jump all over the cheeky old Swordmaster. "Well?" Marhan bellowed. Novices scattered back to their practice ground. Marhan followed them, shouting changes as he went.

"*You!*" Ylia turned on Galdan. He smirked at her. "Of all the rotten timing! He started it! I wanted a go at him with those rapiers, and I swear I could have had him!"

"Never mind the rapiers, you know how he is. And get him tomorrow, isn't that the one that counts?" Galdan demanded reasonably. Nisana poked his shoulder with one delicate claw and got his immediate attention.

'You used entirely too much Power. I *warned* you about that,' she began. Ylia shook her head.

'Nisana, by all the gods at once, let him use more at first, if that's what it takes!'

'Who,' the cat demanded frostily, 'is teaching him? You or me?' Silence. 'If you want the task, say so and it's yours.'

'Mothers no, she'd kill me, first night,' Galdan said anxiously, but he was grinning widely.

Nisana turned on him in exasperation. 'Come back to the Tower when you're done being pleased with yourself, there's more you need to know.' And she dropped to the ground and vanished.

"Galdan, she's grouchy when she teaches, haven't you learned that yet? I can't think why you want to push your luck like that, she'll skin you alive yet." Ylia laughed then. "How'd you do that? And how'd you get the *nerve* to bridge into this crowd?"

Galdan shrugged. "To be honest, I didn't think about *that*.

Nisana said I had to bridge to the barracks if I wanted to come
here. I got that stuck in my mind. Eveya saw me, and I think Brel
did, and of course Marhan. If anyone else did, I couldn't tell; no
one takes it seriously."

"They shouldn't."

"Well, then, that's all right. I suspect I ought to get back to the
Reception the same way, maybe Nisana won't clip my ears for
me. Want to come? For the ride?"

Into the Reception? She opened her mouth to say no. She
hated bridging into buildings; despite Nisana's assurances, it
never felt like a safe thing to do. But Galdan—he was so very,
very pleased with himself. And he had every right to be proud.
"Sounds much better than walking in this heat," she said.

Galdan clapped her on the back. "You said that so well, a man
could almost believe it if he didn't know you. Not inside. Into the
meadow behind the outdoor kitchens, all right?"

"All right. But not from here, in the open. No point to showing off, is there?" She led him back into the shadows. Only
Lennet, who had stepped back to let Eveya get a rock out of her
boot, saw them vanish.

It had been many long years since I had seen so many young Ylsans. My usual caution assured me they could not all be like these brave and sensible lads, but I was glad to see that they at least were not so passively certain as most of their elders that they were the sole worthy strength in the Peopled Lands.

These lads, the Sirdar's grandson Alxy among them, were the core of a recently formed Yslaran league. Little was required of any who wished to join them, neither high House affiliation or wealth. What each must have was belief and desire to work in the knowledge of that belief. And each swore an oath on joining, to work to improve his Power—or hers—and to bring it to its greatest strength. To learn weapons-skill and to hone it; to be ready to kill in need. And with those skills and those weapons, to protect their land from decay within and invasion without. For unlike the Sirdar and his Council, they believed Ylia's tale that the Lammior had heirs. And that those heirs would not rest until the Peopled Lands were theirs.

13

"Perhaps I should go to Yslar." Bendesevorian was pacing the floor of the Reception; Ysian sat on the topmost step, watching him prowl back and forth across the chamber.

"If you think it might do good," she said doubtfully.

"You would know better than I. What do you think, Ysian? You were on the Sirdar's Council. You know the Ylsans, you are AEldran. I knew your folk when they were AEldra, much too long ago."

Ysian considered this in silence for some time. "It's difficult for me to say. Yes, I am Ylsan, but I do not think much like the Council. That was one reason I left Yls four years ago and came here. They wouldn't believe Ylia's letters, and they wouldn't listen to me. I went back, of course. Things didn't change. They weren't any different when I resigned my post for good and came here to stay." She shrugged. "Then again—even the most hidebound of the old fools had to admit the truth of the Lammior and his valley when confronted with proof. Perhaps if they were also confronted by one of the Guardians, they would believe in you. The One knows they invoke your name often enough!" she added bitterly.

"Ah?"

"By the Nasath," Ylia said. Bendesevorian laughed.

"I see. Well. The question is, what can they do to thwart Lyiadd and his allies, if the Three are intent upon taking Yls?"

"But if you were to back the Council with your own Power?"

He was already shaking his head, and she stopped. "What I have, what any of my kind have—I can wield Power, of course. But our strength is not individual strength, Ysian; it works best with many of us, and against a force such as the Three could bring—one of my kind, even two or three, would be utterly helpless."

"I—see." She smiled faintly. "That wouldn't be a sensible idea, then."

"No. Should I go?"

"I don't know," she replied honestly. "But remember the young Ylsan company that is here. Alxy—Alxeidis—is the Sirdar's grandson, after all, and he knows the household situation better than I would. I think you should speak with Alxy and his friends before they go home." She sighed. "*I* doubt there is sufficient Power in the entire Council to battle what Lyiadd was before he left the Lammior's hold for the Isles." She spread her hands, turned them over and gazed thoughtfully at the palms. They were hard, now; hard like they'd never been in her pampered life, and there were calluses at the bases of her fingers, calluses where she'd gripped a bowstring, practicing until her arms ached and her neck was stiff. "I knew about Alxy's group. They began it soon after Ylia's message about Lyiadd leaked out. I thought they were just—oh, talking. Playing. One never takes the young seriously, you know."

"I know," Bendesevorian said. He did.

"I don't think that of them anymore; anyone can see they're

ready to salvage what they can, if—when—Yslar goes under. It's not a child's game, when they see the need for *that*."

Bendesevorian resumed his pacing. Ysian watched him. He was not handsome by the standards she applied to men: His nose was too long; his mouth overly wide. His cheekbones slanted at a sharp angle, casting strange shadows over his face. His eyes were the nicest thing about him: Wide-set, warm, an almost luminous green. *Overwhelming*. He was that, however unconsciously. After all, he was not only a Nasath, giver of the Gifts—he had spoken with Shelagn, he had touched the sword that Ylia now wore when it was still Shelagn's.

He was also worried, and that worried her; the Nasath should be invincible, should be gods, should not show such a weakness. That was unfair, and she knew it, but it was hard to ignore the teachings of her childhood. No, he wasn't a god. He was a tired and worn being, young among his kind and now exiled from them.

"I'm sorry," she said, suddenly, impulsively. Bendesevorian stopped his pacing, turned back to look at her.

"You mustn't be. Our decision was already made, mine and Nesrevera's, that I must come back and aid you. We knew the risks and the effects of our actions. I would have come anyway, even without your call. Though if I had come sooner—but my fate is not your fault." He came to help her up. "I think I shall go explore the hillsides. I walked these mountains once, but this valley retains nothing familiar. Perhaps if I can no longer see people and change, I will know it better." And he was gone. There was no feel of a bridging, no sense of Power. Nothing.

"Just like that," Ysian said to herself. The words echoed through the empty Reception. She shook herself. She'd had noon-meal, but was hungry again, maybe there was still bread or fruit in the family dining room. It was quiet in the Tower: Galdan and Nisana were gone, Ylia was down at the docks. The women were either in the outdoor kitchens preparing for the reception dinner that night or down in the market helping with preparations there.

Selverra was with Lisabetha for the afternoon. Ysian shook her head. After she ate something, she ought to go get the child.

Poor Sel. Poor Ylia. Ysian had never had a child to lose and while she ached for her niece, she could not really understand Ylia's way of dealing with her pain. *If I lost one child, I would cling to the other. I know I would. I wouldn't desert her*. But that

wasn't fair. Unless it happened to her, she couldn't know. *And I
am not likely to have a child, at my age*. Galdan spent time with
Selverra, the women did and so did Lisabetha; Ysian did. But
Ylia could not look at her daughter without weeping, and so
hardly looked at her at all.

Selverra was subdued these days; she seldom asked for her
mother and never for Malaeth or Berd. She accepted the attentions of her father, her great-aunt and her honorary aunts Lisabetha and Lossana. She let the household women fuss over her. *I
hope the child doesn't hold it against Ylia, later*.

Perhaps before she got Sel, she ought to track down Alxeidis
and his young cohorts. Perhaps they could turn the favor back:
Alxy had sought her out three years ago in hopes of getting information he could not milk from his father. She'd been weeks away
from the Council; Alxy could tell her what had happened of late.

And while she was looking for the Ylsans and their guide, she
could walk down toward the barracks. Golsat might be there.

There was an unpleasant smell in the air: Tevvro had forgotten
how very much he disliked the odor of sea-wind blowing across
those southern marshes. Well, with the One's aid, he'd be here no
longer than a few hours. And it was his own caution that set this
meeting aboard his Osneran ship, rather than in Vess' newly
taken Koderra.

I don't trust him, quite. No, he didn't quite trust Vess, not
anymore. The man's outside allies were disquieting: Sea-Raiders,
by all that was holy, and this unseen Ylsan and his lady! The
whole reeked of blood and sorcery; there had been rumors as far
as Osnera before he left; the docks were rife with them. The
seamen on this ship and its captain had told him worse, and little
of *that* was rumor.

Of course, the Ylsan *was* Vess' father, or so Vess' messages
said. And a man was to hold faith with his father. But—if the
father were a black sorcerer? Tevvro prided himself on being a
little more worldly than most Chosen. There was magic and
magic—there were allies and allies. A man thought carefully and
long, whether it benefitted him to follow the teachings literally or
to turn his face from things it was better he not see. But, if half
the tales were true, he was not certain he could countenance this
Lyiadd as even the most distant of allies. It might be necessary to

tread very cautiously; he must keep all his wits about him. There were more ambitions involved here than his, and more at stake than he had ever thought possible when he had first allied himself with Vess.

Movement up the Torth caught his eye: A small black-hulled galley was coming down-river. Tevvro glanced at the sky; with luck, his ship could be back out to sea, back in one of those sheltered coves west of the Torth before night fell.

The sun was down, the streets torchlit as merchants and City-folk worked to put the last touches to their stalls. A steady hammering echoed up from the east end of the square; half a dozen men were at work on the Royal Pavilion. It was three times the size it had been its first year. The Queen's arms and the King's were both painted on the front; a canvas shadecloth in the blue, white and gold of the House of Ettel lay in a roll on the floor, awaiting the posts and overhead latticework it would cover.

The Great Reception was ablaze with light: A carpet of deep blue, bordered in figured gold and white—a gift from the King of Gehera for the latest wool contracts—led from the Reception doors to the thrones on the shallow dais.

Galdan forced himself to sit upright, brought up a smile as the Narrans were announced, though at the moment all he wanted was sleep. Ylia had warned him about Nisana's single-mindedness. If anything, she'd understated. Between the cat's intervention and his own strong intent, he was sleeping like a log when he finally tumbled into bed, but never for long enough to erase the exhaustion that overlaid numbing grief.

He settled the sleeves of the voluminous rose-colored shirt—they were a little snug at the wrist—and resisted the urge to tug at the waist of the new doublet. The Narran fashion had gone shorter, and he wasn't used to it. His hose were figured down the outsides, burgundy on rose. Soft, half-height boots of black and burgundy suede completed his share of the Narran gift.

He preferred blue for himself. But he matched Ylia, and he liked the rose and burgundy on her better than blue or green she usually wore.

Ylia looked radiant in the new Osneran women's fashion: A low, squared throat edged in deep burgundy with a velvet bodice that ended just beneath her bosom and voluminous skirts that swirled to the floor. The wrist-length sleeves were slashed and tied all the way down, to let the rose brocade lining show through. A cloak in the same satin as the sleeve lining lay across her chair and she wore slippers of softest Ylsan leather stamped in gold. And there were stockings of a wonderfully fine thread and weave. Lossana was going to be entranced by those stockings.

Ylia claimed she felt half-clad with her bosom swelling above the throat of her gown, and Galdan was glad young Ang'Har had never seen her dressed so. Of course, he hadn't been jealous of the Narran for years; Ang'Har wasn't here, anyway. He had gone down-river the day before to be with his father, who had suddenly taken ill.

There'd also been a hat of some sort, a silly affair that was half stiff framing, half a swath of veils. Ylia had stoutly refused to have anything to do with the hat, and Galdan was glad. It would have hidden her hair and he loved it unbound as it was tonight, falling across her shoulders in a glorious red and gold wave. In place of a crown, she wore a strand of grey pearls that had been Shelagn's across her brow.

Her face was tired, seen close. But the smile for Ber'Sordes was warm, and the Narrans with him would not have guessed, just looking at her, what she'd endured the past days.

Ber'Sordes bowed low and formally before them. "Your Majesties." *Odd*, Ylia thought. *I once flinched from that title. It's hard to remember that.* "With Your Majesties' permission, I present my new household."

"It is our pleasure to receive them," Galdan said. He still wasn't quite comfortable with such formal speech. Ber'Sordes brought them forward one at a time, pronounced names and household or ship affiliations of each. There were many of them, and Galdan was certain he'd be weeks sorting them out. Of course, he had thought the same thing the year before, and the year before that.

Ylia came down the steps to clasp Ber'Sordes' hand. "You must give me the names of the women who crafted this," with a sweep of her hand, she indicated the velvet, "so that I may properly thank them."

"I shall," Ber'Sordes replied gravely. He smiled then. "One hopes you will not need to fight in it, however. It seems even less suited than your green was." The other Narrans looked at each other, uncertain whether to smile at the Ambassador's joke; uncertain what the joke itself might be. Ylia laughed.

"It's safe, so is Galdan's. The Lady Ysian and Nisana will bridge the Elite Guard out if there is need."

Dinner was a pleasant meal, if not so merry as in former years. Ber'Sordes followed the lead set by Ylia and Galdan and made no mention of the recent tragedies, concentrating instead on the expected trade at Fest, the sword crossings which he dearly loved to watch, matters Oversea and in Nar. Even then he spoke of lighter matters, and avoided the Lord Mayor's failing health, the latest attacks on Narran ships by Sea-Raiders and the loss of the Narran *Hippocamp*. Though unlike the *Merman*, most of that ship's crew had been pulled to safety by the warship *Gar*, and the Sea-Raiders' *Viper* had cautiously withdrawn.

The food had improved since his first Fest, the Ambassador thought, though the Nedaoans had done well with what they'd had that year. The meal went quickly; his new household was eager to explore the market again, marking which stalls they would visit as soon as Fest opened the next morning, talking to any merchants they might find out at this hour, finishing up work on their craft or the housing for it.

They passed Alxeidis and his companions on the outer steps.

"Curious, m'Lord," Tre'Dorret ventured as they stopped in the main square to watch workmen unroll the canvas shade over the pavilion.

"What's that, man?" The Ambassador's attention was fixed on two men teetering on rough ladders, tacking cloth in place.

"Those Ylsans. Had anyone asked me whether Yls grew men like that, I'd have said no."

"It doesn't have many." Ber'Sordes turned to walk back to the Embassy house. "Unfortunately for Yls. May come a day not too far hence, they'll need them."

There was no answer to that; each of the men with him had sailed the increasingly perilous route between Nalda and Yslar, and Tre'Dorret had been second mate on the *Shark* until this last month. They knew.

"By the Blessed One himself," Tevvro hissed, "what have you *done* with him?" His voice was pitched so only Vess and the two guards at his back, the two Chosen at Tevvro's, could hear him.

His eyes lit with fresh shock on the half-mad rag of the man behind Vess.

Jers ignored them all. He sat on the block near the left tiller, picking at loose threads on his sleeve and whispering to himself. Vess smiled reassuringly. "It's nothing, really."

"Nothing, really? *Nothing?*" Tevvro's voice echoed across the water, and several of the rowers started; Jers might have been deaf for all the attention he paid.

"It's a passing thing; I had not realized his state until we left the Isles. I knew he was unwell, but he is truly better than he was. A passing thing. I doubt he was deliberately poisoned, I think it more likely to have been fish. Or eels; he's fond of them, you know, and they can be a danger this time of year. He was quite ill, and raving until a few days ago. Bringing him away from that island hold has already worked wonders with him; now that I have time and energy to spare, I shall see to it that his recovery is complete." Tevvro gazed at him, transferred the look to Jers. "It is too bad he would not accept healing. I—ah—I could do that now. My father's gift, you know. He has taught me that much of it. But of course I must respect Jers' beliefs."

Lie. Tevvro knew it was a lie. Vess was making no attempt whatever to even make it appear truth. And the Power—by the One, the rumors were a joke!

"You dare not let him die, Lord Vess. We need him. I have Osnera's papers and guard with me so I may take control of the Nedaoan house. I am ordered to send Grewl back to the Heirocrat for correction."

"And my cousin. Of course, she will sit calmly by and allow that?"

"I said I had orders. I did not say how I intended to carry them out."

Vess laughed. "You have papers that are utterly worthless until Nedao is mine. But that will be before snow comes," he added, forestalling the Chosen's next question. "We have already discussed this, there is no need to do so again. I know you do not wish to remain in Nedao. Jers will be ready to take command of that House and I will gladly have him. The people have strayed from the truth since my cousin took the ruling and forced this Grewl upon the Chosen."

Another lie, at least in part. Vess cared little or nothing about the Chosen way. He would use it as he used everything else, as means to his desired end. Jers—well, perhaps Jers could be useful to Vess. The proof of that was that Jers still lived.

"Your ambition goes beyond that valley, Lord Vess," he said finally. "I know it. My own does, also. But—we have discussed this before." Tevvro smiled coolly. "Certain men in Osnera think me buried in the Foessa, and that pleases them, because I am thereby out of contention for higher position."

"I know your ambition. You will be Heirocrat one day," Vess said. "Jers will manage the Nedaoan House. He is only temporarily unbalanced, though I think he was never truly a balanced man. But that is not important. He is strong in his belief and a fanatic will be useful to us once the House is mine." Silence, save for the lapping of the river against the side of the ship and the ever present wind whispering through tall shore-grass. "There is more you do not know yet: More than Nedao will be mine. Yls will be my father's. Nar, mine. But a thing occurs to me. Once Yls is reft of Power, might the people not be turned to a new religion—to the true Way?" He paused. Tevvro caught at his beard, tugged a hair or two loose unnoticing as he concentrated on this new idea.

Yls! The priest who brought that proud nation of sorcerers to the Chosen fold would be strong indeed! It would take time—it might take years. But Tevvro was still young and the new Heirocrat a vigorous man of fifty-five years. Yls. The timing could be right; his successor could well be Tevvro.

Vess watched him closely. *I knew that would be the play to capture this ambitious noble's son. It will not hurt me if he fails —as I know he will.*

Tevvro gave his beard one last tug, cast Jers a businesslike glance. "You'll care for him?"

"I will. You want him in Nedao; he'll be there for you."

"He had better be."

"Trust me." Tevvro looked at Vess sharply; Vess made him a deep bow and Tevvro laughed.

"Certainly! As well as you trust me." He glanced at the sky. "I must leave; I want my ship anchored before dark. I'll sail to Nar and see what can be learned there. I'll send messages to Osnera that all is proceeding according to order. Thereafter, my ship will be anchored in that cove south of Nalda. You know the one."

Vess walked him back toward the railing. "Keep that red flag on your foremast at all times, it's your safety against attack. We attack Yls very soon. You and I will talk again after that." He watched the Osneran boat cast off, watched until it was well on its way, then climbed the ladder to the rudder benches. "My poor, abandoned friend Jers." Jers started, looked up in mild confusion. "Tevvro didn't even bother to speak to you, did he?"

"Tevvro? My friend Tevvro—here? Where?"

Vess caught at his arm, pulled him to his feet, pointed downriver. Jers stared slack-jawed after the tubby Osneran ship. "I asked him but he refused, Jers. He said he could not think of a reason why he should speak to you. Poor friend." Silence. Jers continued to stare down-stream. A tear ran down his cheek. "I warned you, do you remember? He has ambitions and has cast us both aside to pursue them since we cannot elect him Heirocrat. But I am your friend, Jers, your good friend." Jers turned to stare at him; Vess smiled and the Chosen shuddered. Vess caught him by the arm as he flailed for balance, but Jers tore free and staggered into the bench. He sat, hard. "I *am* your friend, Jers. Remember that." Vess turned and clattered back down the ladder. Jers stuffed grubby fingers in his mouth, stared after him. Another tear made a black streak down the side of his nose.

Another Fest and another five days of con-
testing, trade, show and pomp dedicated to the
high days of summer. This year, no one but the
Ylsans had much heart for it, though we all tried
to put as good a face on the Fest as we could.

14

Ylia spent most of first Fest day in the pavilion, watching the
crossings with only Ber'Sordes for company: Galdan was off
most of the morning judging bow with Golsat, and the Ambassador's household were out bargaining. Ber'Sordes left such trading
to them: He enjoyed everything from the novice crossings to the
exhibition fighting, and the first day was a full one. Galdan and
Brelian had followed Ylia and the Swordmaster for the past two
years and this year Lennet and Eveya were showing rapier.

The Narran sword competitors had come a distance since their
first Fest. One of the household had made third in his sword class
the previous year, while two others had come second in novice,
and that against determined and strong Nedaoan competition.
This year—well. Ber'Sordes had actually wagered a full purse
this morning on Dri'Hamad's son. The lad was good enough to
draw praise from the Queen's Swordmaster.

One of the novice crossings was over, and the competitors for
the next not yet ready. Ber'Sordes glanced across the square to
see five of the Ylsans near the southern corner of the square,
watching in astonishment as two of the Queen's Elite Women
walked by. The Ambassador smiled. It had been long since *he*
had found the sight of a woman's breeches unnerving, so long
he'd forgotten how it might affect others. And these were Ylsan
and young: The young were often the most hidebound in their
clinging to convention.

Ber'Sordes wondered how much truth there was to what he
had heard: That these young men would welcome women to their
company. Of course, he had never seen an Ylsan woman save
Lady Ysian in breeches and with bared forearms. He doubted
very much that Alxy had intended his ranks to include swordswomen. *I do wonder,* the old ambassador thought, *what they'll
make of the Bowmaster's lass.* He'd seen Lennet earlier, coaching

two novice girls, and even he had been surprised: *That's Tr'Kedias' old doublet and hose the lass is wearing!* There she was, bold as a jay, the only female in Narran masculine garb in sight. Lads were staring openly, many older women glaring at her, some of the girls giggling nervously. Lennet pretended not to notice any of them but Ber'Sordes knew full well she was aware of the fuss; she was a little too outwardly unnoticing. *Ah, yes,* the old Narran thought as he leaned back against his cushions, *this will be a most interesting Fest, and not merely for the competitions.*

One of the watching Ylsans gazed absently across the still empty square, then froze. "Ssst! Alxy!"

"Not so close to my ear, Geit, what?" Alxy sighted along his friend's hand. "Narran hose, too dark and years out of fashion; a dated doublet. So?"

"Look again," Geit urged, and smothered a grin as his friend did and this time saw the long plait, the slender hand, and then Lennet's fine-boned dark face as she turned to speak to someone behind her. Alxy actually blushed as he turned away. "It's a *girl,*" Geit said, rather unnecessarily.

"I can *see* that!" Alxy retorted in an annoyed whisper. "By the Guardians and the One, what kind of folk are these Nedaoans, to let their daughters expose themselves so?" Vysat leaned casually around Alxy's other shoulder to see and rocked back on his heels.

"She's pretty," he said finally. Geit cast him a repressive look, the Vysat blushed. As the only one of the twenty with no Great House blood, Vysat never knew when he might say something wrong, though Alxy tried to teach him the niceties. They all did. Alxy shrugged.

"I suppose she is rather pretty," he said finally. "Not a *lady,* though. She'd be the mark for rude comment at the very least, back in Yls. And just look how her own people are staring at her!"

"Well, I'd wager," Geit said thoughtfully, "the way she wears those blades, she doesn't get much insult to her face. Did you see the Lady Ysian this morning? She's in *breeches*!" He laughed with good-natured malice. "Her father would die of shame. And her poor stupid brother! I know, let's persuade her to come visit, clad like that. It would be the end of Ardyel, the Council could only benefit."

"Well, but breeches are practical, and even the Queen wears

them here," Alxy said dubiously. He stepped back into the street, drawing his friends with him. "But hose on a girl!"

"I can think of several girls who should wear—" Geit began in his high, carrying voice. His friends shushed him vigorously.

"Jadyan has bow within the hour," Vardyel said. "We had better be there to cheer him on, or we'll never hear the end of it if he loses."

"When he loses, you mean," Alxy laughed. He glanced over his shoulder as the foot traffic caught them; Lennet was standing on the opposite side of the field, staring after them. Her gaze met his; her chin went up defiantly.

That first night, most folk ate at the banquet held in the main square and the surrounding streets. Ylia and Galdan hosted a dinner in the large dining chamber for the Ylsans, Ysian and Bendesevorian.

"I agree with Bendesevorian," Ylia said. Therea was lacing her into pale green brocade in the new fashion and she was fussing with the bodice. Galdan nodded.

"There's no reason he should follow stupid protocol that insists he receive the Sirdar's permission before he talks to any other AEldra. This is the real world and we haven't time for such foolishness."

Ylia tugged at the bodice. "Therea, I feel half-dressed, I don't think I can walk around like this tonight."

"The gown reveals less of you than the breeches show leg, and a more proper portion of you," her chief serving woman retorted. "The color's a good one, and as for the style—well, my Lord, you tell her."

"It's wonderful," Galdan said. One of his two lads was pulling yellow brocade undersleeve through slashes in the green velvet sleeves of his short doublet. "I like it."

"You would," Ylia said darkly. "It's too snug, I can't breathe properly and my breasts are squashed."

"If it were looser you'd fall out of it and into your soup." Ylia turned to glare at him and Galdan leered. She shook her head and laughed. Therea adjusted the flowers plaited through Shelagh's pearls, turned the whole so the teardrop emerald was between her brows and stood back to admire the effect. "You can wear the short cloak, if you feel unclad."

Ylia was still giggling. "There's a kerchief I can tuck into the throat; I'm just fussing. I'm just not used to the fit, but I'll adjust. Therea's right. And it's no worse than *your* legs, Galdan, when you began wearing hose instead of loose breeches." She shook out the skirt. There were lengths of it and it trailed behind her. "It's time they met, Bendesevorian and Alxy," she went back to the original subject of discussion. "And if it's not the War Council we need, it's something. A start. *I'll* feel better for it."

"You're not alone," Galdan said. He donned the informal gold circlet, smoothed the hair under it and dismissed his dressers.

Ylia eyed herself critically in the mirror Therea held up, adjusted the pearls. "I think indecision is going to tear poor Bendesevorian apart. I hope he has a better idea of what to do after tonight."

"Maybe we all will." Galdan held out an arm; she took it. Merreven, now Master of the Household, waited at the foot of the stairs to escort them into the main dining hall.

The Ylsans were waiting at the chalcedonwood table. Ysian came behind Ylia and Galdan, glorious in deep red silk. But for once she went unnoticed: Alxy and his friends saw no one but the tall figure at her side. Bendesevorian wore plain dark blue hose and an unpatterned doublet—Erken's, all that would fit and all he would take—but there was no doubting who he was.

Alxy could never remember how he got from his chair to kneel before the Nasath. "By the One," he whispered, and his voice shook, "by the sacred memory of my ancestors, by holy Shelagn herself, you've come back."

This meal had been the hardest part of it all, Bendesevorian thought. It was difficult, being deep in the dealings of humans after so many years. Though he had dealt with many of them before, save Shelagn. He was still not certain he'd convinced the Ylsans he was mortal. *To be thought a god*—had the Elders realized that would follow when the Nasath gave such a gift and then went away? That was not a pleasant thing to think upon.

Fortunately, several of those present were intelligent and resourceful enough to accept his presence after the initial surprise, and to treat him as an ally. Between them, he learned very dismaying things about current affairs in Yslar. As the meal was cleared away and more wine poured, he decided: He would go with them when they returned home.

"I am glad, for my sake and for our league. But my grandfer Asselman won't listen to you, sir," Alxy said. "After all, you know, that's his daughter that's one of the Three."

"I understand. But I feel I must try."

"I appreciate that, sir. As for us, we intend to work harder than ever to increase our ranks when we return. Of course, there are those like my brother who have held out to see what we might learn. There isn't much outside news in Yls, only rumor, and to get that a man often has to talk to the Narrans, down at the docks. That is how we know the Sea-Raiders have increased their attacks, and that it may be the work of the Three."

"It is," Galdan said. "That much we know."

Alxy shook his head. "That's not a pretty thought, Sea-Raiders allied with *them*. But I would rather know than try to sift rumor back home. So we have justified coming for your Fest. Beyond—" He met Bendesevorian's eyes and managed a true smile. He turned back to Galdan. "The Fest itself would have been sufficient reason, of course, if times were not so difficult. I trust it will not be our last, and that the next we attend will be held in more pleasant and peaceful circumstances."

"We can only hope," Ylia said with a smile, but she felt no hope: How many years would pass before such a Fest?

The final evening of Fest, Ber'Sordes, his household and the Ylsans all made a snug fit in the Royal Pavilion, but a merry one. The last prizes were given out: Sword firsts mostly to Erken's lads; Marhan's lads would have a hard practice the next day. Women's sword firsts had gone to Eveya—her last contest, she announced as she took the coin and ribbon. No one looked more pleased at that than Lennet, who had once again come second behind her. The Ylsans had placed often enough to make them happy. Lossana had taken the coin and ribbon for older women —a field much larger than it had been the first year in the valley, thanks largely to her skill and effort. Ber'Sordes' man had justified the Narrans' faith in him, and the Ambassador was in an expansive mood as the prize-giving ended and the musicians came forward to begin the dance.

Bendesevorian sat well back in the Royal Pavilion. He liked the music and enjoyed watching the dancing, but he would not try himself. Ylia danced often: with Alxy and Geit, with Ber'Sordes, with Galdan. She danced once early with Golsat, who danced thereafter only with Ysian, to the visible dismay of the girls who still had hopes of him—and the young men who had looked forward to escorting the beautiful Ysian across the square.

Galdan danced with Ylia and with Therea, once with Lossana and once with Lisabetha. He spent most of his evening sitting, talking with the Ambassador or with Bendesevorian. The Ylsans were never in the pavilion while there was music.

"They're doing a wonderful job of improving relations, those Ylsan lads, aren't they?" Ber'Sordes touched cups with Galdan. Ylia was dancing with Vysat at the moment and save for the Narran, the Nedaoan and the Nasath, the pavilion was empty.

"Too bad it's so little, but I'm proud of Alxy. If the Sirdar had sense, he would be, too." Galdan peered across the crowded square as the music ended. "Who's that dancing with Levren? I've never seen—Lel'San's spindle, it's Lennet!" It *was* the Bowmaster's hoyden daughter, unrecognizable in ivory silk, her black hair a raven wave that touched her knees. Pink rosebuds, white wildflower and pale ribbons were plaited down one side of her face—but even the face was not immediately recognizable as Lennet's. Galdan could not recall having ever seen the girl look like that: Shy and frightened, as though she wanted to bolt. Levren handed her through the formal set with a glow of pride almost visible around him. He was clearly aware of the attention they were drawing but Lennet kept her gaze fixed on her father.

"Now, I will wager," Ber'Sordes remarked, "that the lass did all that less to please her mother than to startle the southern lads out of their sneers at her hose. And I'll further wager you she wishes right now she could turn and run."

Galdan laughed. "No take. I've never seen Lennet so miserable because she's being watched. That's her favorite pastime, next to causing trouble, of course. You've a keen eye, haven't you?"

The Narran shrugged. "I watch a lot; it's one of the things I was trained to do. I thought at the first, this might be a most interesting Fest, and I think now this dance might prove the most fun of it all. Look there, watch." The formal set had come to an end, the Narran minstrels were discussing the next piece. Ylia and Vysat were on their way back. It looked to Galdan as though Levren wanted to dance again, but Lennet seemed to want to leave. She glanced around nervously, and even across the crowded square Galdan could see her fingers tighten and Levren wince as Geit began making his way toward her. But as he opened his mouth to speak, Alxy brushed past him, inclined his head in the Bowmaster's direction and bowed over Lennet's fingers. Lennet gazed over his blond head in shock. Levren pinched her arm, smiled encouragingly and vanished into the crowd. Ber'Sordes leaned back against his cushions and drank wine. "Indeed. A most interesting night."

Often I am frustrated because I do not have certain AEldra talents I need: I cannot heal, though I can aid others. When Ylia was injured after her battle with Lyiadd, it would have been so much easier if I could simply have healed her!

But the One balances all things, and properly so: I do not dream as humans dream and I do not foresee. I do not have the Sight that brings visions one cannot turn aside.

15

Alxy intended to strike a wandering path back to Yslar through the northern villages, for the northern towns and farmlands were seldom in touch with events in the south. And few northern Ylsans, particularly villagers, had Power. Alxy worried for them indeed, for it was likely they knew nothing of the Three. He explained as well as he could to the War Council just before they departed. "Word always gets around Yslar, however secret my grandfer Asselman seeks to keep things. The Great Houses know eventually because they are represented in the Sirdar's Council. But the villagers—they'll have less warning than we, that is not right. So we will return home slowly and tell folk as we go."

"No." Erken shook his head. "Your place, Honored Sir, is in Yslar. You must expand your group. Before trouble comes."

"Before the Three come, you mean," Alxy said. He was as direct as Nisana, a curiosity indeed in a young man being raised to Ylsan politics.

Erken smiled faintly. "Just so. There will not be time for both things, unless we are gravely mistaken in our reading of events. We have men here who can visit your villages. They will pass on your messages and if they must, they are skilled in the art of fighting and moving in secret. If there is trouble, I would prefer Golsat and his trained men there, not you. They have experience, and you, Honored Sir, have not."

The Ylsans finally acceded to the wisdom of this course. Alxy wrote out numerous short messages and marked them with his seal.

Bendesevorian agreed to accompany Alxy back to Yslar. Ylia worried, and woke from unpleasant dreams she could not, quite, recall. *If they come to Yslar while he is there.* Bendesevorian tried to set her fears to rest. "They cannot see or sense me, if I do not wish it. The Lammior could never sense the least of my kind, and their Power is his. If there is trouble, I will return at once." *Trouble.* The word was beginning to haunt her.

The Ylsans decided to take horse and ride most of the way down the Aresada before branching off toward Yslar. A tragic-faced Lennet accompanied them as far as the docks and stood watching and waving until long after they were out of sight. Alxy's red and gold scarf was in her hand, his ring on her thumb —the only finger where it would stay. Alxy had been nearly as miserable at the parting, and he rode twisted around in his saddle so far down the trail, watching his lady and then watching for the least glimpse of scarf, that he ached the whole next day. *They will make quite a pair,* Ylia thought with amusement, *provided the Sirdar doesn't have Alxy's head for trothing himself to a Nedaoan knight's daughter.*

It had been difficult to convince Lennet to remain behind, even more difficult when Golsat and twenty of his hunters took Geit's maps and set out to visit Ylsan villages.

Three days past Fest end, Ylia found herself in the nursery for the first time since Berd's death, staring down into the street. Folk were still cleaning up, they would be for the rest of the five-day. The pavilion, minus its canvas top and the piled cushions, still stood against the east end of the square. The rope lines marking the fighting square had long since been removed: the judges' bench was back down in front of the first barracks. Banners hung dusty and limp from the bridge, and the market was frankly a mess.

Berd. She swallowed hard. Berd and Malaeth were safe— safe and loved and cared for, pain and grief behind them forever. She knew; she had *dreamed* several times and Galdan had, once. She suspected the dream to be Bendesevorian's doing, since it was he who had once shown her King Brandt, Queen Scythia and Brendan, her first love, in the White Halls. And now her son and her old nurse were there, with her mother and father. *You have no right to weep for Berd, knowing where he is, knowing he is safer than you could ever keep him,* she whispered. Tears spilled down her face; she shook with them. It had been a mistake, coming in here.

Wait. She could not go among her women like this; they watched her too closely, fussed over her too much. She waited, wiped tears away and walked into the hall; she nodded to the two women who sat by the open window, but they watched her worriedly.

With Fest over, Galdan returned to his lessoning with Nisana and with Ysian. Ysian was already busy, honing her bow skills, aiding Lossana with her own considerable knowledge of dyes, sitting in on the Main Council meetings. She rode occasionally with the daytime parameter guard to keep her strength and to learn tracking. Aiding Galdan helped keep her from worrying about Golsat—at least while she was tutoring.

Galdan was finally making progress; bridging had either been the worst of it or the most difficult task because it was first. Other talents began to manifest themselves with increasing ease. He could heal, which surprised none of them. He had something similar to Ylia's Baelfyr, but it came from a different place and at a different command. It had to be worked much differently—all of which had led to furious argument between himself and Nisana and resulted in the cat leaving him on his own for a full two days. Ylia prudently limited her assistance to a word of help only when Galdan specifically asked it.

But beyond the AEldran basics, there was not much the AEldra-trained could do to help him expand his skills. Nisana bullied him into learning to conserve his strength, as she had once done with Ylia. Galdan found it much easier to work with Ysian. She gave him support, information, and put no pressure on him; she knew he was already putting desperate pressure on himself, and grief haunted him constantly, though he concealed it well from most people. He still feared he would be unable to learn enough to use against Lyiadd—occasionally feared he would turn evil—or that Lyiadd would be able to manipulate him should they come close enough to each other.

And so, rather than drilling him in dull basics as Nisana did, Ysian taught him Scythia's trick of juggling the fragile bubbles and how to build fantastic *seemings* of light and color to delight the eye. They were only tricks, of course: But they were amusing and the very things he'd wanted to learn when he was a boy. He found they took his mind from that which plagued his thought, and Selverra was entranced.

It was late: Ylia knew that, and knew that she slept. She moaned faintly, turned over and sank into a black dream, a well filled with night into which she slowly fell.

At her side, Galdan stirred; he, too, dreamed, but the dream was so vivid—so unlike his usual dreams—he felt as though he lived it.

It was warm where he stood, warm and damp. He felt uneven boards under his feet; a low fog coming off the sea rose from the harbor. Cloud and fog covered the moon, lending an eerie light to the mist. Here and there a torch or a lantern made a ring of ruddy orange light against some building. He couldn't make out features, he had never stood in this place before, but suddenly, he knew where he was: Yslar.

He peered into the gloom: Even the waves were subdued. The ancient mole and the broad stone dock that led out toward open water, the curving arm of stone that enclosed the harbor were almost dry. He walked slowly, feeling his way with his feet. He could see, somehow, though he should not have been able to see in such a soup of fog. Odd, for this time of year, so much mist.

A few ships were tied near the dock's end, where there was still water; the rest were anchored in the bay. Two Narran traders were in the deep harbor.

A night watch slowly paced the long mole. He gazed at them, felt himself briefly watching the harbor through their eyes. They were both bored, the night long and muggy. One of them thought longingly of his bed, the other of a flask left with his cloak back at the head of their route.

Why am I here? Galdan wondered. There was no answer. No sense of anything beyond his sight or ears. He stood on the docks, listening to the ship nearest him creak faintly as the tide began to turn. The Ylsan guard passed him unaware: They were discussing the Sirdar's grandson Alxy and his journey to primitive Nedao for a weapons-match. Neither seemed to think it had been a good idea. They vanished in the fog, heading toward land.

Galdan knew he was dreaming. *Something I ate,* an inner voice said dryly. But something out to sea caught his attention and turned his blood to ice. A sound? Barely that and not yet

identifiable, but it was steady and coming nearer by the moment.
A gull, startled from its perch on the mole, flapped upward with a
raucous cry. Even through that, though, he could hear the furtive
thing that had wakened the gull. Boats. Rowboats filled with
Lyiadd's sworn armed. *Yslar! 'Ware, Yslar, your doom comes!*
The cry stuck in his throat; he could not shout, could not move.
Could only listen as the steady, whispery sound of muffled oars
came nearer; could only watch in horror as men rose out of the
mist and moved in silent ranks on the sleeping city.

Ylia moaned again and tossed, trying to waken, but somehow
Marrita was always there, blocking her. Smoke, fog and blood
filled her dream, battle that was hardly a contest. So complete
and overwhelming was Lyiadd's attack that Yslar changed allegiance before the sun rose. People died; those few who tried to
fight, those already marked for death by the Three.

Everywhere as the sun rose, Lyiadd's men, moving with the
satisfaction of possession through streets never before conquered,
and stunned AEldran watched with a growing sense of hopelessness. The mercenary invaders wore Thullen brooches that bound
AEldra Power, carried swords with the ease of men who knew
how to kill with them. Ylia ground her teeth in frustration. Yslar
was broken, and where was Bendesevorian? Where was Alxy?

Wake! Do it! She tried; nothing worked, and Marrita's laughter sent shudders through her. The street she watched faded and
the laughter grew: When she could see again, she stood in a room
that must be part of the Sirdar's apartments. For surely that bent
and shaken old man was Holy Lord Asselman himself. Two
guards held his arms or doubtless he would have fallen. He
would not look up, even when Marrita stepped before him. *Father. What, no kiss of welcome, no kind words?* Silence. *Not even
a plea for mercy? Ah, but that I can arrange.* She smiled and
raised one hand; Black Fire wreathed it.

"No." Ylia writhed, but she still could not waken and could
not turn away as the Sirdar died a slow, painful and utterly silent
death.

Lisabetha lay still, aware she dreamed true, fearing to move
and waken Brelian who would in turn waken her—for he sensed
her least sleeping distress. She must not waken yet, she knew
that; Ylia must know what chanced.

She became aware of dream first as sound: Battle and frightened cries and she thought it yet another Koderran nightmare; Koderra and its fall had haunted her of late. But when sight came, she saw Ylsan faces and heard Ylsan speech. Everywhere, strange and harsh men, terrifying in their certainty of victory. Red-gemmed brooches were everywhere, the Thullen clasping cloaks or banding wrists, and she sensed their purpose. *Ah, Mothers, the poor folk! At least we had no such terror of loss to face when the Tehlatt came against us!*

Without warning, she was in a deep cellar, one tiny opening giving onto the street and a faint musty smell in the air. There were folk there—Alxy, Geit and several of their friends. Bendesevorian squatted on his heels, his back against the wall, his eyes closed. Alxy paced nervously. They were safe because the Nasath was hiding them. For how long—Bendesevorian was confident, however frightened the others were. Geit was trying to persuade Alxy to leave with the Nasath as soon as it could be managed. Alxy didn't want to go. A terrified cry from the street startled them all and Lisabetha moaned in her sleep. She woke a moment later, Brelian's hand on her shoulder.

Ysian's fingers tightened on her blankets and her thought cried out: *No more, I can't bear it!* But the vision moved inexorably from street to street until it reached the Sirdar's tower. No flame had touched its walls, no rams had torn the carven gates and no hand had damaged hangings or furnishings. There was no mud on the familiar carpets. But before the doors to the Great Council Hall, there were bodies—the Sirdar's own guard had fought to the death, trying vainly to protect the terrified old man beyond the gilt doors. She passed beyond them to gaze with stunned pity upon the huddle of terrified councilors. Not all of the Council was there; Ysian knew that moment when the final member was brought would be their last.

The Sirdar was gone, dead. Old Odic and her sister were talking in frightened whispers; Marrita herself had come for him. Two of her guard had dragged him from the chamber: The Sirdar's legs would no longer support him.

Ysian moved among them, searching. There, in a corner by himself, was her brother Ardyel. He stared at the far wall, blankly; he was hugging himself, hands clamped under his arms to keep them from shaking. There was resentment in the set of his

mouth, and she could almost sense his thought. *She was right.
Ysian—damn you, you had no business being right!* She couldn't
touch him, couldn't even give him the final pleasure of lashing
out at her. *Poor Ard. I'm sorry Ard.* She woke with a cry as
Nisana came awake with an ear-splitting yowl.

From one side of Nedao to the other, there was pandemonium
as women long gifted with the Sight and many others who discovered it for the first time woke in terror from the same dream:
A silent wharf, a still City, its folk sleeping peacefully; and then
doors kicked in, people torn awake and dragged from their beds.
Now and again a man or his son was dragged away while helpless, frightened women watched. Other men—a very few—tried
to fight and died at the feet of their women.

The Tower woke to the same wracking cries; half of Ylia's
women were Sighted. Galdan—still caught in his own vision—
shook Ylia. It seemed to take him forever to waken her. Ysian
came stumbling and weeping from her chamber, her plait half-
undone, a light cloak inadequately wrapped around bare
shoulders. Nisana was right behind her, trying to find a way onto
her shoulder or into her thought. But Ysian was half in and half
out of the vision that had dragged her from sleep, unaware of the
cat, and Nisana was fighting a stunning blow of her own. She had
not dreamed, but the multi-fold terror that was Ylia's, Ysian's,
Galdan's had nearly overborne her before she had been able to
shield from it and wake.

Selverra and her nurse came through the crowded hall; the
child was more excited than frightened by all the fuss. Therea
caught Ysian as she passed, dragged the cloak around her and
clipped it in place. Nisana took advantage of the moment to leap
to Ysian's shoulder. Ysian instinctively held her there, but it was
doubtful she noticed the cat's presence yet, more than she did
Therea's.

One of the house guard was turning up the lanterns; Ysian
sagged back against the wall, let her eyes close. The guard got
her by the arm and Galdan took her other arm. They brought her
back into the royal bedchamber, got her to sit on the bed next to
Ylia, who was shivering despite the fur-lined cloak draped
around her shoulders. Galdan sent the guard back out for wine
and started lighting lamps from what was left of the fire.

"Ah, gods." Ysian's teeth were chattering, her lashes damp.

"Shhh." Ylia patted her hands, though she herself looked in no better shape. Nisana walked from one lap to the other and back again. She was trying to soothe them both, without much success. The cat was shaken herself: For a moment, it had almost been as though Ysian's *dream* was hers, something the cat had never experienced before. Galdan went into the hall to make certain someone was bringing wine. He came back with a bottle in one hand, Selverra on his other arm. Ylia bundled the child under the furs with her and gave her a cup of well-watered wine.

It took Ysian some time to swallow. She was still shaking and her teeth chattered on the cup. "Shhh," Ylia soothed. "I know. Yslar."

Ysian nodded; Galdan pressed the cup against her lips, held it there while she drank. She slumped against him, suddenly limp. "I saw it; I dreamed. The Sirdar—"

"I know. I saw, too." It would make her ill, if she let it, and she desperately hoped Ysian had not seen what she had. The Sirdar had been dreadful enough; Ylia dared not remember how Alxy's father had died. She hugged Selverra close. "Did you have bad dreams?"

"No. I had a funny dream. I saw a lot of water and it was a little scary. But that was all I dreamed, Mother," Selverra finished gravely.

"Good," Ylia whispered. However it happened, Selverra had been spared. She took the child's cup and let her nestle down in the warm covers. Selverra clung to her fingers, sighed and slept.

"Ard," Ysian whispered. "Poor, poor stupid Ard. I saw him—there. In the Council. He's dead by now."

Nisana rubbed against her arm. 'He is. But it was quick. He didn't have long to fear.'

"Bendesevorian," Galdan said. "Did you see him?"

Ysian shook her head. "I never saw or sensed him."

"I did." Lisabetha came through the doorway, a cloak wrapped over her nightdress, her baby Brendan in her arms and Brelian behind her. He stayed only long enough to make certain she was all right, then went back out to help restore calm out in the street. She took the chair Galdan brought her but refused wine. Her voice was steady as she told them what she had dreamed.

"He's well protected; he and Alxy will be safe," Ylia said.

Galdan shook his head unhappily. How could they be, after all he'd seen? And, gods, how did Lyiadd's men *stand* the touch of those focus brooches? His skin crawled.

Ylia slipped her fingers free of Selverra's, stood, swayed and caught at the bedpost. "He said the Three couldn't sense his kind. We *have* to believe that, don't we?"

If the alternative is that the Three found him, bound his Power and slew him? "Where are you going?"

"Down to my women," Ylia replied from the doorway. "Many of them won't know what they saw tonight: The Sight is not always specific." Lisabetha and Nisana went with her.

Galdan closed his eyes. His own mother had been spared *that* vision, at least. He refilled Ysian's cup and held it out to her, but she pushed it away.

"Drink some yourself, Galdan. I'm—all right."

"You're not."

Ysian considered this for some moments. "No, I'm not. My homeland is fallen, my brother dead—my House won't survive him long, you know. Second House, Scythia's House. There won't be two bricks together to go back to, when this is over. My poor brother; he was a fool, and I could never persuade him to see what was coming. Nor Father." She picked up her cup, swirled the wine and stared down at it. "I feel—I shouldn't have left them. I deserted them."

"I know. I understand what you feel."

"Do you?"

Galdan nodded. "I was in the Foessa, living as a mountain hunter when the Plain fell. I had left everything behind: Father, Teshmor, what Father called my responsibilities. If I'd been there instead of deep in the Foessa I'd very likely have died. That doesn't make me feel any better, Ysian, when I think of my friends who did die in Teshmor. I feel I deserted them, I feel guilty for that still, and knowing that isn't sense doesn't make the feeling any less strong."

Ysian sat a while, head bowed over her empty cup, finally put it aside and stood. "Since I did decide to live, perhaps I'd better make myself useful. I'll dress and go down to the street. Maybe I can do some good out there."

"Good. Do that." Galdan watched her go. He stripped out of the long shirt he'd thrown on when he ran into the hall, rummaged through the chest at the foot of the bed for breeches and shirt. He'd better go down to the barracks. The warning system of horns and bells would be inadequate for the messages he'd need to send; they'd need riders. He spared one worried thought for his friend Golsat, bent down to kiss his daughter's damp forehead. At least one of them was sleeping comfortably. He was afraid it would be a long, weary time before he got back under those furs.

No, I cannot be sorry that I do not dream. Though being torn from sleep by the concentrated terror of the woman who shared her pillow with me, the echoing terror that was Ylia's and Galdan's, the horror of women from one end of the valley to the other, that was no pleasant thing.

Nor the certainty—as strong as Ysian's—that the Second House would soon be no more.

16

It was nearly a five-day before the valley returned to something near normal: women with the Sight woke, trembling, after Yslar's fall for many nights.

Golsat and his company came back across the Aresada to report sudden fog in the valley they were to visit the next morning —fog that later rang with frightened cries. They had remained where they were, and the next morning had looked down upon a stilled village, bodies stacked near the well, stunned silent women. It was late that night before Golsat dared order cautious withdrawal from the overhang where they hid. They had counted only eight armsmen in the village, and Golsat had clearly seen the red-eyed Thullen around one man's wrist.

"We had already visited sixteen villages before we came to that one." Golsat sat at the head of the table, the silent War Council grouped around him; he was rumpled and grubby, his eyes red-rimmed. Ysian sat at his side, slicing and buttering bread for him. She still wore a haunted look. Golsat emptied his cup, poured wine and more water into it. He took the bread, ate it in four swift bites, washed it down with wine; took the second slice Ysian had ready for him and smiled his thanks. She began cutting an apple into sections. "For all the good it might have done," Golsat added.

"Why?" Erken asked. "Didn't they believe you?"

Golsat shrugged. "Most did. We had Alxy's written warning, of course, but many of them had to take it on my word what the words said. Only a few of the northern Ylsans can read. No, it wasn't that—thank you, Lady." He squeezed Ysian's fingers, chewed apple and swallowed. "That attack—I've never seen anything like it. Even if those villagers had wanted to resist, I don't see what they could have done. And if Lyiadd need only send a few men to take villages, it's not like sending out a full company, is it? He'll never be at risk of spreading himself too thin." Silence. "I'm sorry. That sounds defeated, but it was bad and I'm tired."

Corlin was turning his dagger over in his hands, staring at it as though that act needed all his concentration. "You have a point. He could hold villages with a man or two each, leaving himself a formidable main force. It may not be possible for us to aid the Ylsans after all."

Erken leaned forward. "But only four armed men against as many of our armed? We would not be affected by Lyiadd's magic-killing gems, nor would we be frightened into capitulating by loss of our own magic."

Ylia stirred uneasily. "Lyiadd must have contact with his armed. If they vanish or die, he might take reprisals against the villages."

"Then we will avoid the villages, lure his men away. Lyiadd intends to come against Nedao anyway," Erken said. "We know it is only a matter of time until he does. So we should harry the Ylsan border, keep Lyiadd off balance if we can. Let us make the choice of time ours, not his."

"I think—" Marckl began loudly, but stopped short. His shoulders sagged. "I think Erken's right. Don't like it."

"None of us *like* it, man," Erken replied mildly.

"I know," Marckl grumbled. "Doesn't make it any better, does it?"

Marhan stirred but whatever he intended to say went unsaid as the doors opened; Bendesevorian and Alxeidis staggered into the room, the former paler than normal, the latter nearly out on his feet. Galdan rose swiftly and pulled out chairs for them. "We had just about given up on you both. Here, Marckl, get that wine down here!"

"We had to stay hidden for so long," Alxy whispered. "And then—they took Geit's father and mother. We spent an entire day in the old root cave, under the cellars, hiding." He buried his face in his hands.

Galdan took Alxy's hands and wrapped them around a cup, pushed it toward his lips and saw that he drank. Alxy's blue eyes were very young indeed. "They're dead. My grandfer. Father. All my family except *her*." He obediently drank as Galdan pressed the cup against his lip again. "Marrita." He looked as though he would have wept, if there had been enough of him left to weep. "It's over."

"It's not over." Marhan slammed his fist against the table, shaking cups and rattling the knife against Golsat's empty plate. A silent War Council and two exhausted outsiders stared at him in blank surprise. "Nar's still free and Nedao. And Oversea is. Remember that, lad—and all the rest of ye, too! They've taken one land, one unprepared land, less willing to see danger and avert it than Nedao was, four years ago. *We* fell, we lost. Look at us now.

"Look at Nedao's Lady, young master. Came a time, four years ago, when there were only eight of us got free of the King's City, after the Tehlatt took it, and this same Lyiadd thought he'd have our king's girl for his own, the rest of us dead. Didn't she strike him down? Gave ye—gave us all!—four years to prepare! Gave ye warning, so that now there are men in Yslar preparing against the time when Lyiadd can be overthrown. He's a man, for all his evil! Puts on his breeches a leg at a time, like any man! Think of that, when ye would give him all the strengths of the Dark One himself!

"And this, too: Ye in Yls, ye never lost, never a thousand years ago, never until now. We have, and we can tell ye, we Nedaoans. We know. There's tomorrow, or next year. Nothing is permanent, is it?"

"You've allies and friends." Levren came down-table to stand next to Alxy, and if it cost him, none of that showed on his lean dark face. "They've won a battle, not all. Remember that."

Alxy brought up a faint smile. "I'll try, sir." He held out a hand; Levren took it.

"You need sleep, both of you," Galdan nodded toward Bendesevorian, who had remained silent throughout. "Unless you have urgent news." Alxy shook his head. "Go, then. We'll talk later. Golsat, go with them, you sent your men for sleep, but I wager you need it more."

"I didn't keep all the watches myself," Golsat laughed, and smothered a yawn.

Ysian held out a hand and he helped her up. "I will walk with you. I promised Lossana I'd help her this afternoon." They left together. Alxy went out moments later, with Erken to see he got up the stairs, into the right room and into a bed before he fell asleep. Bendesevorian followed. There was a long silence in the council chamber.

"We'll take Erken's suggestion as given," Ylia said finally. "Golsat and Brel are two of the best trackers we have, and they know who to send out, how many armed per company. Alxy can make maps for them, once he's slept. But he must not know where and when the attacks will be. I do not want Galdan involved in that. I do not want to know. The Three are no longer so distant as they were. I fear Marrita's ability to send me dreams may allow her to read my thought—or that of any of us with Power. We won't chance it."

"That's only sense," Levren said. "Parameter guard?"

"It's adequate," Marckl said. "But we'll run an additional spot guard, and I'll change the pattern of patrol on my lands. Ivanha?"

Ifney's daughter nodded. "We'll do the same. Odd hours, different route each time, no set pattern."

"Good lass. Other matters?" Marckl added sharply to the rest of the table. "I've a long ride and my Lady's been nervous the past five-day."

"Nothing else, just now," Ylia said. "We'll meet again tomorrow after evening-meal; they should be slept out by then."

"Maybe," Marckl said doubtfully on his way to the door: The boy looked half-dead, and the other one—whatever it took to make an Ylsan Guardian look like *that*, Marckl wanted no part of it. He quickened his pace: It was a long ride back out to his halls; he had to make it before dark, for Lyva's peace of mind.

Golsat was gone again three days later, twenty armsmen with him. Alxy had fretted at being refused a place in their ranks but he'd already known they wouldn't take him: The last heir of the First House had to be kept alive. Since he was to remain, Lennet made only a token attempt to be included and took the denial with something like relief. Ylia took her aside later. "I'm sorry you can't go, but we'll need you later, Lennet. You're not as good at tracking and hiding as the ones we chose. Save yourself for what you're best at."

"If you promise me—" Lennet began, but subsided as Ylia shook her head.

"Only a fool would promise anything, just now. I can't, and I won't. Everything's uncertain. I might not even be here to keep that promise."

Lennet looked at her in sudden alarm. "You won't—!"

"I didn't say won't. But no one can say something might not happen to any of us." Ylia's mouth twisted with grief; she turned away. When she turned back a moment later, her face was carefully blank, and Lennet, tears of sympathy in her own eyes, impulsively gripped her hands. *My stupid mouth again, she's only just lost the baby and I remind her of it!*

"Mothers, I'm *sorry.*"

"Shhh, don't say it. Please don't. I know. Anything might happen, though; we've all been through it. Go keep Alxy from fretting himself to a shadow; he's raw with loss, don't add yours to his load."

"Mine?"

Ylia managed a faint smile. "There isn't anyone in the valley can't see it. We'll make him your responsibility, just now. It's a big one, mind that."

"All right." Levren was already out the door; Lennet bobbed a brief courtesy and ran after him. Certain of Ylia's words would come back to haunt her later, but at the moment, she was blissfully unaware of that.

There were refugees—one or two at first, shocked and worn folk Golsat had found and sent on to the Aresada. Others followed, until the temporary camp they'd set up beyond the barracks was overflowing, and it became necessary to find additional shelter. Individual families took in what folk they could, Marckl moved his household armed into his own hall and made his barracks available. Erken did the same. Before the five-day passed, however, the number of refugees halved, halved again, slowed to a trickle.

These were all from the border villages, only two women from further south. Nothing beyond that. Since Bendesevorian's return, there was no word from Yslar or the lands around it.

"Lady?" Ylia was in the small dining room, alone, toying with the last of her evening-meal, when her door-warder tapped on the sill and leaned into the chamber. "There's a man here, a hunter. He says his name is Verdren, and that you know him?"

"I know him." Ylia pushed back from the table and shoved the unappetizing food aside as a skinny old man came cautiously into the chamber, stopped just inside the door and knelt. A fox-head, its forepaws tucked firmly under his chin, bobbed as he inclined his head. "Rise, Verdren." It was four years since she'd seen him, when he'd helped her small company out of a tight place in the southern mountains—no trail to follow, no food, no fire. The old hunter had brought them down out of the treeless heights, and thereafter vanished. Since then she'd heard from him, but always indirectly: Three years ago, a villager near Mt. Yenassa had come to the Caves, with word Verdren had found them, that he was searching for others. A few more folk had come straggling in after that, bringing Verdren's name like a talisman, and the old man was a legend among the valley folk: An ancient hunter who appeared out of nowhere, set their feet on the right path and then went his way.

"Lady." Bright eyes darted around the chamber. "Odd, being in walls. Haven't, not in years. Caves, now: Visited the Caves a while since."

"Any folk hiding there?" She knew already; she or Nisana would have sensed them, or Ysian would have. Verdren was reassured by the simple conversation, though, and noticeably relaxed.

"No. Save myself."

"Good. Would you like wine?"

He considered this, shook his head. "Nay. Haven't had wine in so many a year, likely I'd make a fool of myself. No, came because of these new folk, these Ylsans. All about the place, these days. Found a few wandering where sensible folk wouldn't and set them on to come here. Trouble in their own lands, seemingly."

"Bad trouble. We appreciate your aid." He waved that aside. Nisana padded into the room, leaped to the table and lapped at Ylia's water. Verdren stared at her, brow puckered, then laughed.

"Remember her now. Rode in a bag at your back, didn't she? Queen's cat, magic." Nisana regarded him gravely over the cup. "I need your aid. Can't manage it myself."

"Trouble?"

The old hunter nodded. "Just south of the Caves, there's marshes, a stretch of woods, heights?" Ylia nodded. "There's some shallow caves up there; I use 'em now and again, store grain and dried meat. Went up there, two—no, three days back now. Children there."

"Children," Ylia echoed blankly. She shook herself. "Children? *Nedaoan* children?" It almost stopped her breath. Children living in those mountains for four years?

"Said so, didn't I?" the old man demanded peevishly. "Ate all my grain, everything I left there. Two dead little ones. One of 'em—older one, boy—said they'd been in a barbarian camp, one of the women was raising 'em, working the older ones hard. They got away, spring sometime. Afraid to move from the caves, and two—well, the boy said they'd had to carry 'em. Woman beat 'em so they couldn't walk. One still can't."

Gods, gods! "Older—how old?" Ylia was pulling her boots back on.

"Couldn't say," Verdren shrugged. "Matter of—ah, eight or nine summers." His hand measured half-way up his own chest. Ylia's eyes went wide.

'Ah, mothers—Nisana!' Her mind-speech was wildly out of control.

'It isn't safe out there, just the two of us,' the cat replied. 'Wait for Galdan or Ysian at least.' But Ylia waved her silent. *Her mind's set; look at her,* Nisana thought unhappily. If that old man had tried to find words that would upset her most, he couldn't have done better. *She'll go, and that means I will, too.* Because Ysian was sound asleep upstairs; there'd been a bad fire on Erken's northern pastures and she'd been out the entire night, helping to dampen it with Power, then healing burns and other injuries for hours after. Galdan was off with Erken, following a trail that might have Mathkkra at its end; if she bridged for him, Ylia would already be gone.

They could call to him, of course. But even sensing Ylia's current state, Galdan might try to convince her that children who had been living in the open for so long would be safe there another few hours. The cat tried anyway, but though she could sense him, she couldn't reach him. *Wild Power!* she thought furiously, and, tiredly, *If I say her no, she'll go without me.*

Something did not feel right, she couldn't think why; the backlash of Ylia's wildly frayed emotional state, no doubt. She put aside her usual fastidious dislike of the act and invaded the old man's thought. He was telling the truth, no doubt whatever about that. She could see the ledge, see the children—*Ah, gods, it's going to tear her to bits, to see them.* Worse by far than the old man had conveyed. *If I went alone, brought them back—*but Ylia would not permit that, either. She'd follow if the cat tried to leave her behind.

A brief, fatalistic gloom filled her. 'Let us go, since you're set on it. Now, quickly.'

"My cloak—blast, it's upstairs with the sword!"

'You won't *need* any of that, let's go!'

Ylia turned to the old man. "Verdren—"

"I don't ride so quickly, Lady," he began.

"We won't ride. Let me touch your thought so I can see where to go. You stay here; the door guard will bring you food." The old hunter eyed her doubtfully. *Magic*; distrust and fear stood out all over him, and he was shaking as she released him. 'Oh, gods. Cat, you saw?'

'I saw. Let me go alone, Ylia, look at you! You cannot deal with this.'

'No!'

'Hells. All of them,' the cat responded flatly as Ylia bridged. Verdren cried out as they vanished, sank down into the nearest chair. His face went blank, he seemed scarcely to breathe. Galdan found him there hours later, staring without seeing across the polished table.

It was chill at the northern edge of the marshes. Ylia had forgotten how cold the wind was, coming across so much damp green, and there was a fog drifting up from the wet places and numerous little streams. They rested briefly, despite the smell of damp and decay; a single bridge from the valley had brought them this far, Ylia's doing, and she was paying for it. Nisana curled up in her lap, sheltering as much as possible from the wind, and kept prudently quiet.

"I'm sorry, cat; too much at once."

'Two bridges might have been easier on you. Take the rest of the distance in two steps, it won't take that much more time, and you need strength to bring the children back to the valley.'

"I know." Ylia pushed loose hair back from her forehead. "I just—" she swallowed, "children. And all I could think was, Berd—"

'Don't,' the cat urged gently. 'I know what you thought, I felt it. But I still wish we had waited for Galdan or Ysian.'

"No. If a child died because we waited or hurt longer than it had to—Nisana, I couldn't face that. You saw them."

'I saw them.'

Ylia let the cat clamber onto her shoulder and stood. Nisana's thought touched hers, fed her power to shape, and they were again gone.

The woods were eerily silent. If any of the Folk were about, *she* could not sense them. Ylia was too single-mindedly concentrating on that ledge, now just moments away. Nisana put aside all thought of again asking Ylia to wait so she could try to reach the Dryad Eya. She doubted if Ylia would have heard her just now, let alone agreed to such a delay. They joined for the final bridge.

"Cat?" Rock crunched underfoot, and wind howled around them, moaning through the tops of trees far below them. The dark was absolute. "Cat, I can't see, what's wrong?" *There was a moon below, a thread of moon, there's nothing now, I can't see!* "Nisana?"

'Trap!' The cat's thought vibrated between her ears. Ylia's fingers moved along her left sleeve, freed the dagger. 'Bridge, girl! Join now and bridge! Ylia!'

But she was *trying*! "I can't!" Terror was crawling up her back, the certainty that someone stood there—she whirled, but there was nothing, nothing to see, nothing to sense—nothing to *see* with the inner sense, as though absolute darkness shrouded it, too. She could no longer even hear the scrunch of shattered rock under her boots. She felt pressure against her leg, stooped to gather Nisana close; the cat's fur was standing straight out, and she was growling low in her throat. Ylia was whispering in a thin little voice unrecognizable as her own: 'Nisana, help me, Mother, help me, oh, gods and Mothers, someone, someone, help, please help me—!'

Power caught her by the throat, held her upright, kept her knees from buckling. The air was no longer opaque, she could see the rock ledge behind her, a spot there the size of her spread hand reddening as though it smoldered. It was pulsing, keeping track with her heartbeat. For one long, horrifying moment, she could not move at all.

'Focus. It'll bridge us to *them*—!' Nisana's thought reached her faintly: The link between them was being severed.

Trap. "My fault," Ylia whispered. "No, they can't, not both of us, not you, Nisana." She bent her head to brush a kiss between dark ears, pivoted, scooped the cat's small body into one hand and threw as hard as she could. Nisana's startled shriek faded as she fell out and down the sheer ledge.

Ylia drew her breath on a sob, tightened her grip on the dagger hilts as the ruddy glow spread and enfolded her; a breath later, she was gone.

*Pain; so much pain. I fell what seemed for-
ever, my inner strengths fragmented by the pull
of that focus, and then Ylia's ripping me from it
perforce. I do not remember the moment when
my body struck the ground.*

*For long I lay there, unable to feel or see,
scarcely able to breathe. Sensation came back
first; pain like fire, so much of it that I knew my
hurts to be grave indeed. I dared not move; I
was unable to sense beyond myself, unable
even to see.*

*So much time passed before I was able to
dampen the pain enough to call upon the
Power, and to move myself by miserably short
bridgings, back to the Tower. And I cursed myself the while for not sensing that trap beforehand, for not obeying my impulse when
Verdren spoke; that I had not somehow kept my
Ylia from harm.*

*The outside world faded around me as I
bridged, until there was nothing but myself,
pain, the drain on my strength I could ill afford
and a growing sense of urgency and fear. Then
only the pain, and the thought that I must find
Galdan and lay fresh grief upon him.*

17

Ylia woke to such complete darkness and silence that she was
certain at first she'd gone deaf and blind. The faint rustle of straw
beneath the rough blanket on which she lay assured her she could
hear beyond the scree in her ears. Vision, though: She felt for the
second level of sight, but there was nothing there.

She sat up abruptly, one arm clawing for support as dizziness
swept over her. Stone: *Indoors. Cellar, dungeon—Lyiadd's*

halls? But there was a scent teasing the back of her mind, a tart, fruity scent—*wine. Father's wine!* The odor was unmistakable: not just any wine, but the special vintage Brandt's father had laid down, the dark red they used only for midwinter banquet. It was the first wine she'd ever been permitted, a smell she'd have known anywhere. And the inference was as unmistakable as the red: *Father's winecellar.* But there'd never been any kind of cot in the cellars at Koderra. Exploring, trembling fingers assured her she sat on a narrow pallet, affixed to the wall, a layer of dry straw laid over bare board and a rough woolen blanket over that.

She felt further: The dagger was gone, blade and sheath alike; the small blade gone from the holder inside her left boot. But in the place of the forearm sheath, secure around her wrist, was a bracelet: Thullen, her fingers told her. A goodly length of fine, strong chain led from the bracelet to a ring in the wall.

Trapped. It was worse than it had been in the Foessa; she huddled into herself for a long time, shivering with terror. Scythia's calming charm did not respond; like the rest of her AEldra Power, it was gone. The thing about her wrist had the Power buried so deeply she could not feel it at all.

She hugged herself, closed her eyes, spoke to herself aloud. The words were muted in the small stone chamber—an inner chamber, lowest level of Koderra's cellars; she remembered its exact location. It didn't matter: Koderra was so far from her own kind, from any aid—"Shhh. There is a way; there is always a way. Shhh. Relax. Whichever of them it is, don't show fear." It seemed to take hours; her throat was dry, the words were a mere whisper. Slowly her hands relaxed, a little, but the fear was still a vast knot in her stomach. She gazed into the blackness vainly seeking anything to see. Nothing. The dark was oppressive, frightening. Anything could be there, she couldn't tell. Anything —*Hands, feel where you are, see with them.*

Time passed; she had no way to guess how much. The Thullen bracelet was snug against her skin, but no more than snug. No catch her exploring fingers could find. The chain, though long and light enough not to hamper movement, had no weak point, and the staple that attached it to the wall was thick as her wrist.

She could move as far as one corner of the room but not as far as the opposite wall. Back past the cot—she stumbled into it, bruising her knees. She could feel the other corner with her outstretched foot.

It was smotheringly dark, oppressively silent in the boxlike chamber, and the pervasive odor of wine was making her ill; her head still ached from the forced bridge. *Nisana. Oh, gods, how could I forget you?* They couldn't have taken Nisana. *Somehow she got away, she'll warn Galdan. He'll find me, he'll get me out of here.* But there was no conviction in that thought, none at all.

Her mouth was dry. She wasn't hungry; that might have been as much fear as time. "Hours," she whispered to herself. "If it were days thirst would be painful. They won't leave you here forever; someone will come to gloat." She clenched her jaw to keep her teeth from chattering.

More hours or minutes. She blinked, rubbed at her eyes and sat upright on the uncomfortable bed. She hadn't imagined it: There was light almost directly across from her; the faintest hint of it, a thin band limning the door. Someone was coming. Someone—her throat dried further. There were voices now; murmurs and one rather reedy voice ordering something—*Ah, Mothers, no!* But there was no mistaking that voice: It belonged to Vess.

At first she could see nothing but a painful glare of light as the door opened; then a body blocked most of it. The outline was Vess', that unpleasant laugh unmistakable. Anger shot through her, shoving fear aside. She stood, blinking as her eyes fought to see. *Wait.* He would come nearer.

Vess took one of the lanterns from his guard and pulled the door to, behind him. Brandt's seal was impressed on the cellarer's table next to the door. It was one of the few things the Tehlatt had not found to burn. Vess eyed the little table complacently as he set the lantern on it and turned the same possessive eye on the room's other occupant.

"Well met, sweet cousin." He smiled, reached for her hand as he came across the small chamber. Ylia stiffened; his fingers wrapped around hers, he took another step forward. She brought her knee up, hard. His elbow came down in a blurring arc to intercept it and she doubled over, hissing with pain. Vess gripped her manacled arm tightly, backed her against the wall and held her there, body pressed hard into hers.

"I can play rough if that's what you want, sweet cousin. But it's not my style." He gripped her chin and forced it up. "Look at me, please." Silence. "Look at me!"

She tried. Could not, quite, meet his eyes: Hers were watering from the pain in her thigh and the sudden light; she nearly trembled with the need to fight free of him, even knowing he was stronger, his balance point better—and that she was at a double disadvantage. "That's better. Only a fool fights a lost battle, and you, my fair cousin, are scarcely a fool."

"Not often." Her voice broke and she hated herself for it. Vess laughed in quiet satisfaction.

"No, not a fool. Perhaps too trusting."

"Perhaps." Steadier this time. He was still pressed against her. His skin smelled of soap and smoke; there was wine on his breath, some strange and unpleasant spice, but he'd chewed mint since he ate and drank; that lay incongruously over all.

"Now that you've come to me—however unwilling for the moment—"

"I will always be unwilling!"

Vess' fingers tightened on her chin. "Do not interrupt me, I do not tolerate that in my women. For now, unwilling. Such things change. Women are changeable, and you, for all your mannish attire, are very much woman." Silence. "Mine," he added with an unpleasant smile, "just as Nedao will be mine. Doubly mine —by conquest *and* by marriage. That marriage will already be consummated, of course. And what better protection for Nedao's widowed Queen than that her cousin should wed her and take the overwhelming responsibility of ruling from her?"

"No!" Fury overcame sense; she fought his grip. Vess merely laughed, pressed her against the wall until she was forced to subside.

"I told you, do you remember what I said? You are just like any other woman. You all struggle—knowing you have no strength to match a man's. You cry out 'no' in such loud voices, but you never mean it. Hold still." He leaned toward her; she twisted her face away from his. With an exasperated oath, he yanked on her plait. Her head went back into the wall with a crack that left her stunned. Vess' mouth was on her throat, her eyelids, her mouth.

She tried again to turn away, gasped as he tightened his grip in her hair. "Be still! If you insist upon this pretense of protecting your virtue, I will have you held. I would prefer to be kind, but it is your choice. It would be embarrassing for you, but that also is your choice. Your only choice."

She sagged against the wall, horrified and furious to find herself weeping. Vess gently wiped a tear from her cheek. The scent of him was overpowering on her empty stomach; it heaved.

His grip was hard on her shoulders, his voice all around her, thick with Power. "I *forbid* you to be ill, do you hear me? I forbid it!" The nausea was gone, as suddenly as it had come, and he was whispering against her ear. "You must not fight me, you must not be ill. You must trust me, my Lady. I want only to make you happy, Ylia. Sweet cousin." Silence, save for her ragged breathing. "You will forget everything, everyone that is not me."

She would have denied that; would have tried again to push him away, but her body wouldn't obey her. He picked her up and carried her back to the cot. She watched, numbly, as he moved to latch the door, to turn the lantern down. He was a shadow coming for her, a shadow that grew until it filled all her vision. A shadow and a presence that pressed down on her, driving bits of straw into the skin of her shoulders and back, cutting off breath and light and hope.

It was near midnight, but every window in the Tower showed light. People stood in the square and the street; a murmur of hushed, worried speech drifted through the open doors. Something wrong—what, no one had yet said, though many of the Sighted had *seen* a terrified Queen and her cat vanish from a high place, the reek of black sorcery all about them. Coming and going all day, the Elite Guard here and everywhere—the King shouting and cursing. Folk drew together for what comfort they could find in each other, and waited.

"I can't just stay here!" Galdan wasn't shouting now, but there was hysteria in his eyes, and his voice shook. Ysian gripped his shoulder, handed him wine; he shoved it aside.

"You must stay," Bendesevorian said flatly. "Lyiadd tampered with the old man. But Verdren must have sent them *to* someplace. We may discover where they went once I find a way to read him. The Foessa are vast, can you search them all by yourself? And where will you start?"

Galdan slumped in his chair, buried his head in his hands. "I can't wait. If I do, if she dies because I—" He couldn't go on.

"You cannot run wildly, that will not help her or Nisana. Nedao cannot afford to lose you also. You know that." Silence. Galdan started as the Power backwash of an inbridging touched him.

"Oh, gods." Ysian dropped the winecup and flew across the chamber. "Nisana." The cat stood just within the room, swaying; as Ysian dropped to her knees, Nisana made one faint mewing sound and fell over. "She's—help me, one of you, she's hurt, she's terribly hurt!" Galdan caught her shoulders, pulled her around and turned her head away; Ysian clung to him briefly, but then pushed away. Bendesevorian touched dark, sticky fur. One of the cat's hind legs was bent at an unnatural angle and skinned well up the hip. Dried blood darkened her nose; her eyes were half-closed, unseeing.

"She will live," he said finally. "But she's taken a dreadful fall, I wonder she was able to bridge at all."

"Ylia—" Galdan turned away and slammed his fists against the wall.

Bendesevorian closed his eyes, remained hunched over the cat for some moments. He shook his head reluctantly. "I am sorry. There is only fear, blackness that hid everything. She suffered her injuries when she fell—or someone threw her? Surprise and terror, then dreadful, overwhelming pain. Your face, Galdan. She was determined to find you. I see nothing else."

Bendesevorian's voice was as gentle as the fingers that straightened Nisana's back leg, pressed torn skin back onto her thigh. "There is one other thing. She feared a trap before the trap caught them. Lyiadd's Power has touched Nisana. I can feel it in her and on her." Silence. "I do not think Ylia fell with Nisana. I cannot yet tell."

Galdan stared at his knuckles: He'd hurt them on the wall; blood ran down his wrists. He walked back to the council table and dropped into his chair and buried his face in his hands.

Vess sat up. "Now. Was that so terrible after all?" She closed her eyes. He sighed, stood and rearranged his tunic, brushed straw from his sleeves. "I could have been harsh with you; I know men who would have been harsh. I was not. I will never willingly hurt you, my Lady. Because I want more from you than harsh men might want. Think of that, before I come again to see you, sweet cousin."

Silence. He ran his finger along the line of her jaw. A muscle jumped under her left eyelid. "You are a stubborn and foolish woman, my pet. Think on this, then: If you repay my kindness freely, I shall see you housed in proper chambers—in say, a day or so. It will cost you nothing but cooperation, cousin; cooperation and—a little gratitude. Is that so difficult for you, considering what I give in return?"

He kissed the pulse in her throat. Ylia swallowed. Other than that involuntary movement, she gave no sign she felt or heard him. "I ask so little of you. Kindness and a lady's favors. I will go now, but you may have water and freedom of this chamber." He unlocked the chain, crossed the small room and tapped on the door. The guard opened it, set a small jug on the table and took the lantern. Vess pulled the door behind him. A bolt clattered into place. The line of light around the doorway faded, faded again, was gone.

Ylia stared dry-eyed into the darkness. *Water.* She sat up slowly. *Water.* She kept her thought carefully blank beyond that. She brushed straw from her hair, pulled her breeches and shirt straight with slow and deliberate care. Felt for her discarded tunic—it was gone, somewhere on the floor along with her belt. *Find them later. Water.*

She groped her way to the door on legs that threatened to fold at every step. Her hand brushed the table, touched the clay jug. The water was warm, the jug had held cooking oil and been imperfectly washed. She held the liquid in her mouth, swallowed reluctantly. Not much there; she had better save some. There might not be more for a while. She took it back to the bed, set it where she was not likely to kick it.

She lay back down on the cot, stared at the ceiling she could not see. Tears slipped silently down her face.

Vess fought to keep his face expressionless all the way up from his uncle's cellars. After so many years, she was his! She would be! The scheme was going as he'd planned and its conclusion—he could almost grasp it. Though it was odd, the way she'd reacted to his skilled touch: One or two maids in Teshmor had gone limp on him in just that way. After all, Ylia was scarcely fifteen and protecting her maidenry! Married women had no such virtue and no right to pretend to it, in his opinion. They seldom pretended to it when *he* seduced them; what was the matter with her?

Perhaps she was still shaken from the bridging she had not initiated, or possibly frightened for the cat. It was too bad he could not have reset the bridging focus to go after the hellish beast and make certain it was dead, but his father had been adamant: The trap could be used once. The reason hadn't made sense: something about leaving trails for skilled eyes to follow.

Nisana didn't matter; Vess had the one thing he wanted. The horrid cat had to be dead, nothing could survive such a fall, and whatever else it could do, it couldn't fly. That must be Ylia's problem, though: She was grieving for the cat. Women were sentimental over pets, and this one had been with Ylia all her years.

Vess fought a shudder, dismissed his armsmen at the foot of the main stairway. Magic: Yes, all right, *he* had it now, and it became easier by the day to think of it as his own, as though it always had been his. After all, *he* was half AEldra, just as Ylia was. That cat, though: No loss to *him* if it was dead, and as for Ylia, he could comfort her. He was good at that. She would forget it, before long, she'd forget all of it: Cat. Galdan. And he could give her another son, that would please her, wouldn't it? That would bind her to him as nothing else would, though by the time she bore his child, she would be long since his. If not wooed and won, then turned with drug and Power; he'd prefer the former but the end was more important than the means it took. He wouldn't let false pride keep him from altering her thought, if it took that.

It likely would not; he knew how to bind women to him, and Ylia, most definitely, was woman. A little after-shock of pleasure washed through him.

"Patience," he whispered. "She'll be mine." And through her, once Galdan and the girl-child were removed, Nedao would be *honorably* his. Just as he'd always planned.

*I remember Galdan's face, and Ysian's. Ben-
desevorian's touch. Nothing then, save dreams
of falling—falling—*

*I could never understand Ylia's fear of
heights. But now it is I who find it difficult to
stand upon an edge, who cannot sleep upon a
balcony in the warm sun. I who fight irrational
terror each time I bridge.*

18

Galdan sat in his chambers, as he had for so many long hours,
his attention fixed upon the pile of cushions on Ylia's side of the
bed and its small, sleeping occupant. Ysian had healed Nisana's
ribs, the torn and smashed hind leg, the internal injuries. The cat
slept, completing the healing. They could only wait.

Galdan was numbly aware of Ysian's coming and going. She
resolutely held him to eating and drinking, and somehow, he
could never put her off as he would have anyone else.

Bendesevorian slept on a pallet near the bed. His face was
pale and drawn: He had taken Galdan's place among the Elite
Guard when Mathkkra attacked and had been awake most of the
night.

Galdan stared down at Nisana. Berd's death hurt; he still
couldn't think about Berd. But Ylia was all he had. If she was
gone, there wasn't anything. *If she is gone, I am Nedao. Inniva
help me, I cannot bear it!*

Selverra came in before her nap, again before bed, worried
about her mother, in need of her father's reassurance, frightened
for Nisana. He soothed her somehow, though later he could never
remember what he had said. But he sent her to her room with a
smile on her young face, in company with her new nurse Chedra.
There's Sel; she needs you as much as Nedao does. Words; they
came out in certain shapes and made sounds. They made no
sense.

He sensed Erken hovering uncertainly in the hall. Galdan got
half-way to his feet once, thinking to go to his father but he sat
back down on the bed. It took too much effort to move; besides,

Nisana might waken. "Poor Father," he whispered. "I know he wants to comfort me. He and I still aren't good enough at showing love." *Learn, before it's too late and he's gone, too.* But even that thought was dulled and couldn't move him.

Hours passed. Bendesevorian was gone again, so was Erken. It was quiet in the hall, quiet out in the streets. Nisana's side rose and fell smoothly; perhaps she was breathing more deeply. Perhaps she'd fallen into true sleep; it might be hours, yet, before she woke. *Gods and Mothers, Ylia might be dead by then!*

He shook himself, walked across the chamber and back again; his legs were stiff, his hair matted and snarled, his eyes overdry from too many hours awake. His mouth too was dry. He found the water jug, poured, drank, and let his head rest against the stone of the windowsill. *Two days. Nearly three.* How many more would he have to count, before he gave up? *How many are there left in my life?*

'Galdan—' The faintest of mental whispers brought him around and sent the cup flying across the room; it shattered against the wall, but Galdan was already kneeling beside the bed. Nisana opened one green eye, reached with one tiny paw to touch his trembling fingers. The paw fell against them, her eye closed again. 'Tired.'

"Shh. Rest." And, in a mental shout that reverberated through him, 'Ysian!'

Nisana moaned, shifted uncomfortably. 'Don't—it hurts. My head aches.'

"I'm sorry, cat."

'Galdan?'

"I'm here." Gods and Mothers, she was so weak! He was suddenly terrified for her. Ysian came flying barefoot into the room. "Ysian's here, Nisana. Wait, rest."

'No, I can't. Ylia—'

"Precious, don't." Ysian, a thin cloak wrapped around her for modesty and warmth both, laid a light hand between the dark ears. "You're hurting, let me fix it."

'That's better.' Nisana opened one eye again. 'Head still aches.' Ysian merely nodded, concentrated. The fingers moved across the fur on the cat's spine. 'Much better. Thank you, Ysian.' Her mental voice was hard to hear, each word spaced from the next, as though she must think them individually or not at all. 'Bendesevorian.'

'Out. He will have heard me, Nisana. He'll come.'

'Good. I—' Her breath went out on a sigh. 'Won't wait for him. Can't. Galdan.'

'I'm still here.'

Nisana cast him a sour look. 'I know you are, don't coddle me! I'm—worn. Not lackwitted. The old man, Verdren. I *read* him, things didn't feel quite right. But—he was all right. I know. Children, Nedaoan children, Tehlatt prisoners, south of the Marshes. I *saw* them, in his thought.' She let her eyes close. 'But—children—not there. Trap. Caught Ylia. She—' A longer silence.

Ysian laid a light hand on the cat's flank. "The old man was tampered with," she said.

'Tampered?'

"One of them interfered with his thought in such a way you could not tell. We could not read the truth in him, and we can't find anything of his inner being now the lie is gone."

Galdan shuddered. He couldn't look at the old man without hating him, however unfairly; but he pitied him too. It horrified him to touch the shell that had been a man, to sense the hollow where there should have been Verdren's thought.

'Gods. I *knew*, somehow, it was all wrong. But children—she saw them and that was—I could not stop her from going. I tried to.' Galdan closed his eyes. '*Show* you where we went.'

"Later," Ysian said. "First finish telling us."

'A set, focused bridge. Lyiadd's only, I think. Sensed no one else. It caught us both. I would have been drawn through also, but she—threw me. I fell—gods, I fell. Was black dark when I woke. Waited until I could see a little, until I could move. Had to bridge so many times, such tiny distances—' Her thought trailed weakly. 'I failed her.'

"No." Galdan touched her forepaw. "Don't think that. Wherever she is, she must be glad to know at least she got you free. You know she'll think that. It's not your fault, any of it, cat. But this thing—do you know where it went? Where she was taken?"

'No. It was un—undeniably theirs, the Three. Set just to take Ylia. Reeked—of Lyiadd.' Without warning, she closed her eyes and went limp.

Ysian touched her ribs; shook her head as Galdan leaned forward. "Sleeping," she whispered. "Oh, gods, Galdan! If Lyiadd has taken her to Yslar!" Galdan merely nodded; words wouldn't come. He closed his eyes and waited.

She was losing track of time, here in total darkness. Vess had come six—no, seven times. *Do not forget*, she admonished herself, *not even the least of things*. Not even the worst of things, Vess. She felt unspeakably soiled, all of her. Just to touch her own face took courage; she hadn't much courage left.

They'd brought her food—dry bread and a few strips of jerky that was too spiced for her taste—and two other times, someone had come with water. She ate and drank, not really caring what it was.

The dark was wearing. Even after days, her eyes could not adjust. She hungered for the moments when food and water was brought, fought with herself not to weep and beg them to leave the light behind. There was light, too, when Vess brought his lantern and—and stayed. Though once he had come without it. She had wakened with a sudden, horrid certainty of *someone* standing there in the total dark. When he'd touched her, she'd fought, but Vess had merely laughed, overborne her with nightmarish ease. She'd felt him, never seen him; had not even seen the door open and close as he left her.

After that, she slept poorly and woke often: Panting, terrified she would find him there again, standing in the dark, waiting.

Her hair was pulling from its plait, she was desperate for light and clean air, a comb, a change of shirt and breeches. But mostly, passionately, for light and air.

There was light around the door again, coming near. She threw one arm across her eyes as the door was flung open. Torchlight blinded her.

"You are sent for." She blinked, rubbed her eyes, blinked again. Two of Vess' Ylsan bodyguard stood there, but Vess was not with them.

She bridled at the man's flat voice. "Who sends? And why?" she demanded.

"We were told not to answer questions. We obey our orders and you are to obey ours. Here are clothes, water and towels. Wash and dress, now, or we are to do it for you."

"No."

"If you make a fuss, we will take the things and leave you here."

Dark—deathly silence—*Gods and Mothers, no.* "Give me

the clothing," she said. There was a gown of brocaded rose silk
—the thin, rare stuff that came across the deserts east of Holth—
a sleeved underdress and soft leather slippers. She held the gown
like a shield, painfully aware of her disheveled shirt and
breeches. "I cannot undress with you here. And I need the light to
wash."

"No. No light in here without a guard."

She could have laughed. "Why? I can't burn this room! Or do
you think I'll set fire to myself?"

"No. Orders." He stared at her; she gazed back. And, just as
she thought she must give in, lest they leave her in the dark
again, he sighed loudly and said, "Foolish. But I will mount the
torch in the hallway and leave the door open. We will stand
where we cannot see you."

"That will do." She wouldn't thank him, not for such an ordinary courtesy; and he obviously still thought she was making
unnecessary fuss. He watched from the door as his companion set
a bowl of water and cloths on the floor by the bed, then turned
and left.

"We have been overlong already, woman. Do not dawdle, or
we will take the light and leave."

She waited until he was out of sight, then knelt to dip one of
the cloths in the water. The water was scented with rose and
clove, but it was some time before she could smell it above the
reek of herself. Foolish: The Ylsan was probably right. Why
should she care if he watched while she shed her filthy shirt and
breeches? *Because some things still matter. They must. If I lose
the sense of what matters, I lose Ylia.*

It took her a while to work the shirt sleeve over the Thullen
bracelet, and she could feel the impatience out in the hall. The
underdress had sleeves that were too long but fortunately not
snug fitting or she'd never have gotten it on. It laced up the front.
The rose silk was cut lower than she liked and it trailed on the
floor; the lower edge of the sleeves belled nearly to her ankles.

Her feet were swollen or the slippers would have been too
wide. It was not new, any of it; Vess had borrowed or taken from
some woman near her size. There was a plain kerchief of the
same brocade as the gown stuffed in one of the slippers; she
tucked it across as much of her bosom as it would cover. She
drew a deep breath, settled the skirts and stepped into the hall.

Surely the hallway to the cellars was never that narrow and
long when she had lived here! Two men couldn't go abreast,

even one—she froze, breath stopped in a tightened throat. *I've been buried, buried in a hole at the end of that*—!

One of the Ylsans grabbed her shoulder. "Hair. Unplait it."

She couldn't hear him, couldn't see anything but a narrowing tunnel; a high scree filled her head and set her swaying. The men exchanged irritated looks; the nearest pulled her face-first into his jerkin and the other undid the plait. *I can't breathe!* she thought, and fought to free herself, but the Ylsan merely tightened his grip until she went limp. As soon as her hair was loose and the larger bits of straw picked out of it, he released her.

Ylia caught hold of the wall for balance. "How dare you?" An ungentle hand stopped her mouth.

"Be silent." They put her between them and started toward the stairs. Ylia opened her mouth as they started up the stairs and the men moved to flank her. She closed it again as the man on her right gripped her arms and shook his head. "This is as much for your protection as to guard you. Keep still." She did. They both had her arms now, but left her hands free so she could lift the skirts of the gown as she climbed. They were long enough to trip her anyway; stairs would have been dangerous.

What, Ylia; afraid you'll break your neck? Somehow that wry thought gave her a little courage; that and the knowledge that she was climbing toward honest daylight.

They emerged in the back hall short of the winter kitchens. The stone walls had been recently whitewashed, and the heavy doubled kitchen door was new. Gone the wonderful carving that had covered the doors to even this mundane chamber. She doubted they would remain plain for long: Vess would never be satisfied unless his Koderra outshone the Koderra that had been Brandt's.

Her eyes prickled and she swallowed tears as they came through the side door into the Great Reception. She had stood here that last day when Brandt had again named her heir, had sworn the nobles to her. Here, Lisabetha's brother Gors had died, bringing news of Teshmor's fall. Here—it didn't bear thinking.

The chamber was too white, the wash on the walls thick. Vess had replicated most of the flags that had hung from the rafters and had added his new arms: Those of the House of Ettel left, divided, palewise, and on the right, gules, a Thullen, displayed, noir, above three chevrons, gules, braced. Over the throne hung the arms of the Three: The Thullen as on Vess' arms. The whole was on an enormous red banner with Mathkkra supporters on the left, a black-hulled ship of the Sea-Raiders on the right.

Her guard had slowed—deliberately she thought—to allow her to take that in; then with a jerk that nearly took her off her feet, they propelled her out of the Reception by its main doors, into the narrow hallway that divided Reception from Formal Dining. Left would have brought them eventually to the main doors, and outside; they turned right.

But except for that one moment in her father's reception, she felt like a stranger in unknown halls. She had been born here, grown to girlhood here, overnight to womanhood and Queen's rank—and that only four years ago. It might have been a lifetime and another person entirely. Another city.

The narrow hall gave way to a wider one, became narrow again as they walked through a maze of chambers and toward the staircase that had once led to the family apartments. She was no longer certain where she was: Doors and chambers were not where they had been; unfamiliar furniture, carpets, tapestries and paintings, mosaics—the ones she had known had been ash for four years. *Don't think, Ylia. Don't.*

Two chambers had been opened out around the base of the broad stairway and there were some tables and a few backless benches near one of the many fireplaces. Ylia smelled stale ale and wine. *A tavern? Here?*

A number of wild-looking young Sea-Raiders lounged on the benches and had taken over the bottom steps. They were drinking and laughing. Ylia's guard pulled her through them and up the stairs. Whistles, howls and remarks she fortunately could not translate followed them.

They slowed at the turn in the stair. A small set of steps branched to the left, leading to the room that had once been Brandt's private library and accounting room. The entry gaped at her, dark and doorless. She turned on the senior guard; he tightened his grip on her arm and held up a hand.

"That was the only way to reach this part of the Tower. If you once lived here, you know that. And Lord Vess suggested it might be better that you know what dangers there are. Should you contemplate escape."

"All right, I know now."

"Do not speak. Listen. The crews of three black ships are within Koderra's gates at all times. There are always twenty men at the foot of this stairs. They would not use you kindly. Remember that."

"Remember that! Remember that!" a mocking voice replied. It echoed over the landing. Her guard pivoted toward the side steps and his companion drew a dagger.

"Who is there?" the second man shouted. A giggle answered him. He rolled his eyes and sheathed the blade. "Only the madman," he mumbled under his breath.

Madman? she wondered.

"Let's go, then." They started up the steps; a patter of slippered feet came down the small staircase and up behind them.

Ylia stared, aghast. Jers stared back at her, unblinking. His pupils were pinpoint, even on that dim landing. He was hunched in on himself, and he seemed to have somehow shrunk. He bared his teeth and giggled as she recoiled. "Hee. He said he would and he has! He's tamed the witch!"

"Step aside, you." The second armsman shoved; Jers staggered back into the wall, recovered his balance and came hurtling up the stairs to stand in front of her again.

"No, he did! He swore it, a—a time since," he finished doubtfully, and a frown creased his brow. It was gone in a moment; he bared his teeth and giggled shrilly. "Our most noble Lord Vess embarks on the holiest of wars! He and his allies will strike down the evil dabblers in magic so the true faith may prosper."

Ylia laughed; she simply couldn't help herself. Of all the things to happen, of all the *people* who might have confronted her here! The feared, hated, fanatic Jers, made as a frothing rabbit, spouting Vess' rubbish—for even Jers could not have thought up such a mouthful of stupid lies himself! "He's using magic himself!" she shouted over her shoulder as the guard dragged her away. "Black magic that will foul you forever, Chosen!"

"Liar!" he bellowed from far down the steps; he bounded up two stairs at a time to pass them and stand waiting in the hallway. Light from an open window showed him in all his unlovely state: His hair was wild, matted into his beard. Spittle ran from his mouth, unnoted, to dampen the front of a greasy robe that might once have been the pale grey Chosen roughspun. His hands shook and he plaited his fingers incessantly. "He has been blessed with Power beyond that of yours, but only so he may overcome you. Who should grant him such Power but the One? Repent of your ways, woman!" he thundered as they neared him. "Recant the witching, give over the heresy of witching and save your life!"

Her guard shoved Jers out of the way and started walking faster. Ylia laughed again. "You're mad, priest!" she shouted. "Why don't you go find some children to warp, it's what you do best!" Jers was screaming at her; she couldn't pick out words.

The guard stopped at a white, plain door, its only ornament a cast brass handle. Ylia gazed at it with a sinking heart. Her own apartments. *I should have known where Vess would put me.*

The door opened and Vess was there. "My sweet Lady. I have been waiting for you. And I see you have company." Jers was abruptly silent. Vess smiled at him; he returned the smile nervously and began pleating his robes again. "You've been lecturing my Lady on her duties, haven't you, my friend?" Jers nodded warily. Vess laughed, clapped him on the back and sent him staggering against the wall. "That was kind of you; I appreciate your care for things that are mine. I will let you instruct her in the proper faith, my friend Jers."

"You will?"

"Soon. Perhaps you will be able to persuade her from her blasphemous ways, if I cannot." Vess leaned down to whisper against his ear. Jers clapped his hands together in a dreadful and unwitting parody of a small child promised a treat, turned without further word and scampered away. Vess watched until he was gone, a complacent smile on his face. "Thank you for bringing my Lady here. You need not wait." He held out a hand as the guard turned away. "Sweet Lady?" Ylia drew a deep breath as Vess took her arm and led her through the door.

I knew from the first that it would be bad,
whichever of them had her, but I feared Marrita
the most, Vess the least—

I was not with her and so I could not know all
the reason why Ylia hated him; and it was not
for a very long time that I learned for only then
could Ylia bear to tell me all of it.

19

The shape of the rooms—that much was familiar. The furnishings, the carpets, the hangings, like those in the rest of the
King's palace, were new, dissimilar enough to those she'd known
since childhood to render the entirety strange. Here, in the
chambers she'd known all her growing years, the strangeness was
disorienting; she clutched at the nearest wall. Vess' hand on her
arm stayed constant; she tried, briefly, to dislodge it, but he
merely tightened his grip. She *must* remember not to fight him,
but it was humiliating to be helpless against a greater physical
strength. *If I had my sword, or use of the Power*—but her sword
was in her true bedchamber, and the bracelet was securely in
place. She'd spent enough time trying to remove it, gaining only
a skinned and sore wrist for her pains.

"A gift for you, my Lady. Favor for favor, as they say." He
smiled widely. "Favor for favors, might come nearer the mark."
She closed her eyes, turned away from him; Vess caught her chin
between his fingers, brought her face around. "Do not look away
from me." The fingers tightened, almost enough to be painful,
loosened, though he did not let her go. "I thought you had perhaps learned manners, and behavior fitted to a Lady. If you feel
the need of more time to learn these things, I can have you returned to your former chamber."

Gods, no! Horrified denial echoed through her mind, and she
was almost certain at first she'd cried that aloud. Not the dark,
the long hours, the uncertainty—the dark was the worst of it,
suddenly; she couldn't bear it again. Her face must have reflected
the thought, though: Vess laughed, shook his head.

"You have learned—haven't you? Favor for favor. Behave

and you shall remain here. Guarded or with me. Or locked securely within these apartments, of course."

"Of course," she echoed faintly.

"As much for your safety as for fear that you might try to leave me—which, dear Lady, I would not recommend. Not all my allies are—tame."

"Point taken," she said dryly. Vess laughed.

"You retain your sense of humor, I like that, sweet cousin. Humor in a woman is a rare thing, all the more to be appreciated when found. No, the guard is—let us say *mostly* for your safety. Food will be brought to you shortly, and wine. I may not be able to join you for that, but I shall later." He bowed low, his lips lingering on her fingers and was gone. A key turned ponderously in the enormous lock—that *was* new. Ylia stared at the closed door until she could no longer hear his footsteps down the hall toward the stairs; she turned away, then, scrubbed the back of her hand viciously across one of the tapestries and crossed the room to the nearest window.

It was much narrower than it had been; once she could have climbed onto the ledge, if she'd been fool enough then to tempt such a long drop—ten or more lengths to hard paving stones. They'd narrowed it to half its original size. She could see mountains, a corner of the stables, part of the city—it was still largely rubble, and the folk walking through the streets were too few, subdued. Not Nedaoan, any of them. A gleam of light beyond all that that might be sun on the Torth.

Trapped. She was, still. The Thullen bracelet was a heavy weight on her left wrist, she was aware of the edge of a nasty headache she could not heal. But the mere fact of light, and fresh air, a clean body and clothing that was not stiff with dirt and sweat—such small things, such simple things, to give her so much hope.

'Galdan?'

Galdan started, shifted his weight and leaned across the bed. "I'm here, cat. What do you need?"

'Information, mostly.' Nisana had napped the morning, wakened to eat the bits of cooked and boned fish Ysian had brought her, lapped at a little milk and gone back to sleep. So, amazingly, had Galdan slept, though on waking he wondered if Ysian might have had something to do with that. Ylia could not send him sleep; something in his form of Power blocked her from doing that; it should also block Ysian. But the wine he'd drunk with that plate of soup had been fairly tart.

"Information." He laughed mirthlessly. "I could do with some of that, myself. What I know, though." He sat up, stretched. Perhaps Ysian had been right, if that wine was her doing: He'd needed the sleep. It felt disloyal, but the pure sense of the thing was he couldn't help Ylia if he was worn to a thread on lack of sleep and fear. Eliminate one, if possible. He'd done that, or she had for him. "Bendesevorian is going to bridge to where the fixed focus was set."

Nisana looked alarmed. 'He can't—!'

"He says he can. He's Nasath, remember, cat? Different protection. He's out readying now: something to do with gathering strength from the sun, the earth, the wind—I was too tired to understand. He says it works better when there's more than one or two of them, but that he is safe even without this extra protection. With it, he told me he could walk through the Sirdar's palace undetected by all Three." Silence. Galdan shifted uncomfortably. "I hope he doesn't test that, myself. I don't like it."

'If he says he can, it's so.' The cat's thought was stronger than it had been, and she cautiously levered herself up, licked one shoulder and stretched. "I know only the form of Power is different. Where is Ysian?'

"She has gone to be with Golsat; he's just come back from the Ylsan border again."

'Again?'

"Bringing in refugees. Not as many, the last two days. But he's still finding some."

'Good.'

"If you need—I can cure headache," Galdan offered tentatively. Nisana unwell, so shaky—he hated it. It was like being a child again, the first time he'd seen his father afraid. Nisana fixed him with grave eyes.

'I know, I taught you how, remember? Thank you, I haven't one.' She let her eyes close. 'I would like sun, can you open the shutters?' Galdan walked over to the windows and let afternoon light fall on the bed. 'I know how hard it is to wait, Galdan. I'm sorry.'

"It wasn't your fault, cat." He watched as Nisana stretched, stepped into a pool of sun and collapsed gracefully into his side of the bed.

'Not my meaning. Sorry that you must wait. Because Bendesevorian will not let you go with him. You know that.'

His shoulders slumped. "I know. I guess I know."

'You must stay, and always for the same hard reasons. Selverra must have one parent to raise her in the ways of both her mother's and her father's kind. Sel is only three and Nedao must have one grown ruler alive and on the throne. You know that. Particularly in the face of things as they now are. It is harder to wait than to wield. I know that, too. But,' she added in the most gentle mind-touch he'd ever felt from her, 'it must be painful indeed, to wish to rescue your beloved, to deliver her by your own hands, and not be able to. I love her, too, of course. But I know it is not the same thing.'

Galdan dropped back to the bed, buried his head in his hands. "I—to just *wait*! Berd, Ylia—I've had to sit and wait and there is *nothing* I can take sword to, nothing I can battle! Nothing I can do!"

'I know,' Nisana replied, still gently. She eased forward to rub her chin on his hand. 'We will get her back.'

"Mothers, cat," Galdan whispered. "I don't dare think—that far ahead."

Ysian came an hour later with a tray for them both: Milk and a cooked piece of hen breast for the cat, bread and wine and the rest of the hen for Galdan. She refused his offer of part of the food, saying she had eaten with Golsat, but took a cup of the wine. Only then would he drink from his own cup; Ysian laughed briefly, but her eyes stayed sober. "Bendesevorian reached me, about an hour ago."

"He's—where is he?" Galdan stuffed bread into his cheek so he could talk.

"Don't stop, keep eating. He's nearly ready; he needs your aid, before he goes. Said you'd need your strength for that. Eat." Galdan pulled a leg joint loose and neatly stripped it down to the bone in a few bites. "He won't go until middle night. Nisana, he'll need you to show him where."

'I'll be awake.' The cat was working through her food with a near-normal appetite.

"Good. I'll be back later, I promised Selverra a walk down to Lisabetha's, to hold the baby. Chedra's busy drying fruit."

"Go." Galdan spoke around a mouthful of chicken. "We'll—black hells." He shrugged. "We'll be here, won't we?" He peeled off more meat. "Cat?"

'I had enough. Thank you.' Galdan picked up the tray and set it on the chest at the foot of the bed, finished his wine and set the cup back on the tray with the bottle. He lay back on the bed and his eyes closed; he shifted once or twice, relaxed into the blankets. Ysian came into the chamber, tiptoed across to adjust the shutters so he was in shade. Nisana curled up in the pocket of his knees where sun still hit.

'Very clever, Ysian. But he won't thank you for putting sleeping draft in his butter.'

Ysian ran a hand over warm fur and she laughed quietly. 'He'll thank me tonight, when Bendesevorian wrings him dry. Besides, Galdan admires initiative; I wager you he'll be more proud of me than not.'

'No take.' The cat rubbed against her hand, hard. 'I gave up years ago trying to keep such foolish human notions straight. Go back to your Golsat, I want more sleep.'

'Cat, he's not *my* Golsat.'

'Not much. He knows, I know, all Nedao knows. Like that hoyden Lennet and the Sirdar's heir.'

'Go to sleep; you're babbling,' Ysian replied firmly, and strode from the chamber. Nisana opened one eye to watch her go, mentally shrugged and closed it again. Human notions of love and courting and all the rest of it had once irritated her very much; they seemed to get in the way of everything sensible. Anymore, they just amused her. *Getting old, cat,* she admonished herself, but the notion didn't upset her much.

She was drifting toward sleep, drifting—falling—momentary terror filled her. She jerked awake, felt Galdan's knee warm and solid against her neck, the other one as warm and solid where she braced her hind feet. *Safe—one of us is. Two of us are. She will be.* She let her eyes close, pressed her neck and cheek hard into Galdan's knee and this time slept.

The sun was nearly behind the mountains, level in her eyes, when the tap at the door drew her attention. "Enter," she called, momentarily transported back beyond the past four years by the view she'd stared at the past hour or so, the familiar mountain shapes, the shining band of Torth that was now lost in mountain-shade and tree-shade. Reality jarred her hard; she turned and leaned back against the window ledge as Vess came in followed by an old woman bent near double under the weight of her tray.

She set out wine and cups, a bowl of fruit, two deep bowls of a cool green soup, a basket of bread, another bowl of soft white cheese. Vess locked the door behind her, leaned against it and looked across the room.

"Sweet Lady, I put them to considerable trouble to prepare you a meal, things I know you like. Come and eat with me." She crossed the room without comment and sat, waiting quietly while Vess poured wine. She waited until he, with a deprecating smile, took an ostentatious drink of his own before she drank hers. Vess sampled everything else with that same broadly sardonic air. "You *might* thank me," he said finally as she began to eat.

"It is good. Thank you." She took the bread he smeared liberally with cheese, bit into it, washed it down with a little more wine. Vess watched her, biting back irritation.

What was the matter with the woman? As much attention as he'd rained upon her, as much care as he'd taken not to force her, not to hurt her, only to give her pleasure—and then finally, to bring her *here*, to clothe and feed her! Well, she no longer treated him with open contempt, but it was just below that carefully cool surface. Any other woman would have been hanging on him by now, pouting if he left her alone for hours at a time, blushing and giggling if he brought a meal such as this and hand-fed her as he was hand-feeding Ylia.

Where was he failing? He'd been so gentle, so kind, and she still loathed him; he didn't need to read her thought to tell *that*. But why? He'd forgiven her everything: Nedao; the petty remarks—even that slap in the Caves. Another man would have set her ear ringing for a week. *He* had been kindness itself, and she still—*Ah, well*, he thought comfortably as he refilled his cup, added wine to hers and handed it to her, *in an hour or so, these things will change. I've done everything that Father said.*

Why would Lyiadd not increase his Power? *That* irked him badly. It hadn't failed him so far. But it had been Lyiadd's Power that had set the focus; it was Lyiadd's Power that wrapped Ylia's wrist and kept *her* AEldra Power at bay. *It's that bitch Marrita. Her doing.*

He ate soup. It was poultry, fresh chilled cream, herbs, greens—nothing *he* liked. But she did and he'd have to eat it to assure her it wasn't poisoned; that was how her nasty, suspicious mind worked. Vess kept the grin from his face, but it warmed his belly: *I shall have to do something about that nasty, suspicious mind, as soon as I have opportunity. And that will not be very long at all.*

Down on a landing which was even gloomier than it had been mid-morning, Mal Brit Arren hovered undecided near the staircase leading to the old library. He had had the freedom of the Tower for a five-day now, ever since they'd taken his cell for that woman. *I'm not mad,* he assured himself. *Jers is mad, I'm not.* He wasn't completely sure of that. It was hard to focus his thought, his wits were too often scattered. *Ah, by the black depths, why bother?*

Because of Jon. Because you own Jon a life. Why did Vess let him run free, knowing Brit Arren still wanted to kill him? *Am I as helpless, as ruined, as that, that he no longer fears me?* Vess *had* feared him once. His hands wanted to fold into heavy fists; he restrained them. Given opportunity, there was a face he'd smash—that before he gutted the man! But to do that, a man would have to hold his brains together and think.

The Nedaoan woman was Brandt's daughter Ylia, Queen of the Nedaoans. Nedao's Queen? Vess' bedsheet, now. He grinned at that, briefly. But he'd heard more of this Ylia than just the name. She was witch, of course; an Ylsan mother guaranteed that. But she carried a sword, they said, and knew how to use it. She'd fought beside men like an equal, led Nedao's armies; she'd earned her blades. *I'd like to see that, a swordswoman. But what is Vess doing with a woman like that?*

Because she hated him, if gossip below was true at all. Some —those who bothered to speak to him, now Vess' rule permitted —said she had tried to kill him once. Or perhaps he had tried to kill her because she stood between him and the throne. That could possibly explain why he wanted her. Rumor also had it she would still kill him, even though he had bedded her, even though he claimed her as his Lady. She'd worn fair garb and no fetters when she came up from the cellars, but Vess' Ylsan guard had held her and there was a lock on her door. No one really believed the lock was there to keep men out; who would dare take a woman Vess named his?

But Vess! He'd gone down those cellar stairs like a puppy after a bone! Fortunately the men in the upper halls had held back laughter until he was gone from sight and hearing, and fortunately his attention had been so single-directed.

Brit Arren grinned suddenly. "If Vess wants her," he whispered with rising glee, "he can't have her!" But *he* must not kill her, no. Someone else, someone Brit Arren could denounce, and then, if a man could seem to come to his senses and take Vess' part? It might work. He had freedom of the Tower and its courtyard and while Vess didn't trust him yet, unlike Lyiadd, Vess could possibly be manipulated through his pride. If he thought he had broken Mal Brit Arren, he might well accept that—long enough to die. Now—a dupe to kill the woman. He took the narrow steps two at a time.

"Who is it?" Jers rose from his improvised prayer bench. His voice quavered nervously.

"Is it the religious?" Brit Arren demanded.

"It's F-Father Jers," the grubby little cleric replied with what dignity he could muster. "I cannot see you."

"Well, make a light! 'Tis I, Mal Brit Arren."

"I—what is it you—you want?" The stutter was suddenly pronounced. Jers backed away, stumbled over his bench, and both fell to the floor with a clatter. Brit Arren strode across the chamber to right them, turned aside to light the room's single candle.

"Sleeping here, these days, are you?"

"I—um—yes. No!"

Brit Arren turned back to lean against the room's only furniture, a long, narrow table holding the fat red candle. Strange shadows crawled up the walls; the light bleached the Chosen's face. "Think I'll come back tonight to slit your throat, do you?"

Jers shook his head wildly; stringy hair flew. "L-L-Lord Vess —I'm under—his protection."

"Worth a man's life to go against that, is it? But perhaps I don't want to. If it's Lord Vess' order, perhaps that's good enough for me, eh? My Lord, too, perhaps. Spared my life, after all."

But Jers knew little or nothing of the events that had passed that night in the tower, save that men were dead in a fool's attempt at coup—supposedly this fool. Brit Arren had lost his ship and command but he was alive. Not even a prisoner anymore. Did that mean Lord Vess—?

Brit Arren laughed, shattering what little concentration Jers had managed to pull together. "I'm not going to kill you, little man, stop shivering! I only want to talk to you, nothing more."

"Wuh—what?"

"I heard you today, exhorting the witch." Jers drew himself up a little straighter. "Good work, too; though I hear witches don't repent. Safer dead, aren't they? She might kill us all, mightn't she?"

"I—the One teaches that. But—but only as—last resort. After—only after they refuse—refuse to recant. And he—Lord Vess holds her powerless. Did you not see the bird about her arm? She will not harm you, if you feared that."

Bird. Like Jon's, Brit Arren thought savagely. His hands gripped the table behind his back until the wood creaked. "So he has." His voice remained level, vaguely amused. Jers seemed reassured by the distance between them, the Sea-Raider's relaxed stance and voice. "But I still worry. She is a powerful witch, you know that. And you *do* know what they are doing—she and Lord Vess?"

"He—he is teaching her, he is correcting her—" Jers faltered to silence as Brit Arren roared with laughter.

"Correcting her! Teaching her! Well, yes, so he is, isn't he? He is rumored to have certain talents where women are concerned! And what he is teaching her, my fine religious, has nothing to do with renouncing witchcraft!"

"He is—he is not—"

"No? Ah, my stomach hurts from so much laughter, little man!"

"He is not—he cannot!"

"He can and is! Do you know what they are doing in that room? Did you not see that fine bed, perfumed sheets, soft pillows? Did you not see her, clad in pale silk herself, with her hair all unbound and her breasts half-uncovered?"

Jers clapped his hands over his ears. "I will not listen to this! It is evil, it is blasphemy!"

Brit Arren launched himself off the table and closed the distance between them in one long stride. Jers yelped as heavy hands descended on him, and he tightened the grip on his ears and hunched his head down between his shoulders, trying to protect it from an anticipated blow. Brit Arren took hold of his wrists and pulled them away with no effort at all. "It is not blasphemy. It is not evil. It is a thing as old as men and women, and I am certain it is much more amusing to Lord Vess and the Nedaoan woman than you picture it."

"Do not tell me, I will not listen!"

"Stop blubbering! You will listen! Are you not curious? Perhaps it is not witchery on her part, it may be merely lust on his. Could you look upon such a woman and not think of perfumed sheets?"

"I *will not* listen!" Jers closed his eyes tightly.

"You will. Can you not imagine, Vess and that woman?" Brit Arren let his voice fall to a whisper. Jers flailed at the wall for balance, turned and leaned against it. He caught his breath on a sob; tears ran down his face and he stared at Brit Arren miserably. "Now, I do not care. But you! A man who follows the ways of the One, will He not hold it to your account that you condoned this lechery? And do not your laws say that witches must die?"

"Witches?" Jers giggled faintly, clapped a hand over his mouth. "Aye, kill the witches, kill them all. Shhh!" He held up an admonishing hand. "The bell for evening service, do you not hear it?" *Mad,* Brit Arren thought in disgust. *Mad and worthless.* He pinched out the candle, turned and strode from the chamber. A mumble of prayer followed him, and something that brought him up short: "Kill the witch." Perhaps he hadn't failed, after all.

"More wine, my Lady?"

"No." She pushed the cup away. "Thank you." *Chance no offense, he'll bury you alive in that cellar.* The last rays of evening sun touched Vess' face. His smile sent a chill through her gut; she gripped the edge of the table, shifted her gaze in sudden horror as her fingers seemed to meet right through the wood. Her eyes reassured her this was not so, even while her sense of touch tried to convince her otherwise. It was getting dark—or, rather, it should have been: There was a golden light touching everything. The cup at her right hand was glowing a sultry red, like coals in a fire long burned down. Beyond it, on the wall, the hawker and his bird, the dogs on the tapestry came to life, moving gracefully across the fabric with underwater slowness. And between the tapestry and the cup, Vess, his pale brown hair shining like gold, his hands setting off sparks as he moved them, his eyes pale brown fires.

One hand went to her throat, the other sent the cup sprawling across the table; somehow, she forced the chair back, pushed to her feet. Vess smiled; the sun no longer touched him, but his eyes still glowed with it. "You look unwell, my Ylia."

"You've—" She dragged her voice down from that high pitch of hysteria. Something was coursing through her veins at double speed, giggling through her body, trying to smother sensible thought. "What have you given me?"

"Something rather amusing—you'll like it. Ragnolan herb, distilled to a paste and smeared across the bottom of your cup. I've only inhaled the steams, those are quite pleasant. This is of course more potent. I will try it another time." He came around the table and held out his hand. Ylia backed away from him. The smile stayed on his face; he walked toward her, waited until the wall stopped her, then caught her wrists in his hands and pressed them against stone. Her eyes were all pupil and blackly furious.

"I will kill you for this!" she whispered. She twisted and one wrist came briefly free; he recaptured it, slammed it back against the wall. "Are you afraid of me, Vess? I wager I could take you, my AEldra Power against your warped Power, just as readily as I could gut you with a sword." The words brought a brief, intense sensation of color, sound and *feel* and threatened to make her sick, but fury temporarily slowed the drug.

"You are forgetting, sweet cousin. Manners. A proper respect."

She laughed, silencing him. "We had this conversation once before, do you remember? In the Caves, before young Brelian brushed the sword out of your hand and cut holes in you, because you were *afraid* to face me! I would have killed you then, Vess; I'll kill you now!"

"You couldn't have touched me," he snarled. His grip tightened savagely, pressing the Thullen bracelet into her wrist.

Ylia laughed wildly. The drug was making her light-headed, burying fear and sense both. Vess was a blur, near as he stood, but she was grateful for that. "I never hated anyone as I hate you. I will always hate you, whatever you think," she whispered. "Give me a blade, one chance, do it!" Silence. "You always *were* a coward, Vess. Sweet cousin," she mocked viciously. "But you're one of the Three! What, haven't you sufficient Power to stand on your own against another half-AEldra? Against me? But my AEldra blood is Second House, not Fifth. And my parents were honorably wed when my mother bore me!" She cried out as Vess slammed her back into the wall.

"You will not, *ever*, say that again!" he hissed. With visible effort, he brought his temper under control. She sagged as his grip relaxed. The Ragnolan drug was swallowing her whole, she heard Vess from a distance and he echoed. "My father warned me how you goaded him into battle, how you tricked him. You will not trick me that way. And you are my Lady, now. A Lady does not duel. The bracelet stays where it belongs, you stay where you belong—in my bed. Count yourself fortunate that I permit that, instead of sending you back to the cellars. My uncle was a fool, your husband a greater one, that you are so willful. That is behind you now. You will obey me."

"Don't wager on it," she whispered. "I'll kill you, I swear it. You must sleep sometimes, and most men sleep with their eyes closed."

"No. After tonight, you'll never want that chance. You will only want me." He was not certain she heard him; she sagged against his hand. When he released her, she slid rather gracefully to the floor, skirts billowing out around her, and rolled over onto her face. He watched as she tried to push herself up with her arms, but could not. He began to count, then. Slowly, as he had been told. *Awareness of the drug first, then it quickly distorts vision, balance and strength. Then thought. A count of 500 past loss of balance, and it will have taken its strongest hold.*

He hoped it hadn't been too strong a dose: Ragnolers only inhaled the stuff, and those who ate it or drank it were men twice her size. He'd not quite halved the dose. It might still be too much. But it would serve her right. She'd always known how to go for the throat; he smarted, remembering the things she'd said, and his hands twitched.

Her body would be undamaged, whatever the drug did to her mind, and he had plans for her thought, anyway. The Ragnolan paste would lower her inner shields, and she'd never taunt him again. He continued counting, ticking off the numbers on his fingers, right hand, left, right again.

Ylia gazed at the floor. It shimmered, and just at the edge of sight it was blossoming. There were *things* beyond the flowers, but they stayed almost out of sight. Wood hard against her cheek —as though they were melting together. The sensation wasn't pleasant, but she could not bring herself to move.

That curiously shaped thing, what was it? She closed one eye to try and sort it out: Her eyes weren't focusing together just now and she saw five of everything that way. Five? Some number. The thing—what? Sense of the floor, flowers, all of it faded. *Boot—no, two. A pair of them.*

Lyiadd? For one shuddering, dreadful moment she was

sprawled across Lyiadd's floor, Marrita's boots under her nose, Brendan dying and herself not knowing, not able to change any of it. The sensation passed. The boots belonged to Vess, the floor had once been her floor. She sighed faintly, let the eye close. *Not Lyiadd's halls; not the Lammior's.* She was no longer afraid. But deep down, she knew she should be.

I would have done anything to aid Bendesevorian, but neither I nor Ysian was able. I was too weak, but even so AEldra Power could not have helped him. Galdan alone had the Power to reinforce and strengthen the Nasath. But we waited with them, Ysian and I, and we watched. An eerie, bluish light touched both of them for what seemed hours. Then Galdan cried out in pain, and fell to his hands and knees. But Bendesevorian—he was gone.

20

He found the ledge without difficulty, found a place to sit and waited. He needed sun and wind for his Power, but the Folk were a night people: He needed their aid, if he was to find Ylia. Eya came and listened in chilled silence as he told his story and asked for help. She left at once, returned with many of her people. Between them, they would scour fallen Yls for Nedao's Queen, as well as the lands south—avoiding only the Lammior's valley —and west.

It was near dawn before Eya returned. "She is not in any of those places. We even searched as much of Yslar as we dared, all but its Tower. She is not in Yslar. I am sorry."

He shook his head. "Do not be. We have eliminated a vast area of land. Yslar and its Tower would be the greatest threat to Ylia, and to our hope of freeing her. I can now search other places and in my own way." He sighed. "I had hoped to avoid what I do now; I have not expended so much Power in a thousand years, and no Nasath wields well alone."

Eya touched him. "We will aid you in any way we can. But the sun is hard on us."

He nodded. He was glad for her touch: Like Ylia, he loved the outward forms the Folk took. And so strong was their Power of shape even he could feel the touch of dry, slender fingers on his arm. "Go and rest. When I come back to this place, with Ylia, then we may need your help."

"Send," Eya replied simply, and was gone.

His shoulders sagged. At the moment, he keenly felt the mortality Ylsans denied he had and missed the company of his kind. "An itch in an unscratchable place for each of the Elders, to be so stubborn and unyielding when the need is so great!" He laughed at the image and felt better for having laughed. The sun topped the eastern ridges as he stood with a refreshed sense of purpose and sought the place upon the rock ledge where Lyiadd's fixed focus had been.

It was not as difficult as he had feared; it might be use was honing his own skills. *Waste no time on Yls: Try north first, then east and south.* He clasped his hands together, extended his arms and slowly pivoted on one heel.

The sun was an hour higher when he stopped: The faint line that had never been an actual one, that was only the ghost of an image of the faintest of connections of Power, point to point, led him past the Lammior's valley; past the Lake of the Falls. Past the Hunter's Meadow and the Yls Road. To Koderra.

Lyiadd had set a fixed focus in Yslar that had caught Ylia *here* and dragged her perforce to Koderra? *Lyiadd is more powerful than even I feared. Once he has the Peopled Lands—and perhaps the lands across the sea as well—might he not take the step to bring him against our kind? And what is to stop him taking the Elders as simply as he took the Ylsan Council?* It wasn't a pleasant thought.

Sudden realization set that aside: "Vess has Koderra." *Vess* had Ylia. He sought the ruined city with far vision.

First sight showed him ruins: deserted, burned, torn ruins. But that was *seeming*. Lyiadd's spell, and a strong one, too, reinforced by focus stones embedded in the outer walls. It wasn't an easy spell to break through, even for him, but by dint of strong concentration he could see black-hulled ships tied to the quays, men and wagons going back and forth between the harbor and the main gates; Ragnolan fishermen casting nets up-stream from the City; smoke from many hearthfires; Sea-Raider women and children working small garden plots, or herding goats and sheep on the hillside.

The Tower was harder to breach, but he had it in the end. Two full companies of Ylsan guard lived there: Men sworn to Lyiadd and his House. Vess' Ragnolers and Holthans, quarreling, gambling and drinking in their barracks or guarding the south walls. Sea-Raiders—younger men who followed Vess in open admiration or fear. Mercenaries from Osnera.

The One guard me, that I can remain hidden and protect Ylia.
In Yslar he had had the strength of Alxy and his companions to
create the insubstantiality that had screened them all from the
Three and their servants. Here: He was alone, for Ylia might not
be able to help him and he dared not count upon her.

He must find where she was so he could reach her without
delay. She *was* there; he sensed her with a relief that momentarily
left him weak. There was a block on her Power, but she was
alive. He sat back and closed his eyes; Koderra was gone. The
sun was warm, the wind pleasant. He had better take what energy
he could. Using insubstantiality to walk through Koderra's gates
would be foolish. Shape-changing was safer, for he would be lost
in his flighted form, even from Vess. Surely he could reach the
ravine in safety and from there find the hidden entrance to the
Tower.

He was glad now he had taken so much time to read Galdan's
thought. Neither of them had thought of Koderra, but Bendesevorian had gathered Galdan's slight knowledge of Koderra's secret ways along with so much else the man knew. *Poor Galdan, I
warrant he's sleeping well at the moment.* Vess would of course
know the escape tunnels but he was a cautious man; it was very
unlikely he would have allowed the main tunnel to be blocked.
Bendesevorian closed his eyes and began to concentrate on the
change. He would know what Vess had done to Koderra before
many more hours passed.

Ylia became aware by slow, fuzzed stages: She couldn't feel,
though blurred sight confirmed she had fingers, and feet. *Drug.*
A fragment of thought surfaced from the rubble of her mind,
connected to nothing else, was gone again. The chamber was
dark—*Ah, Mothers, he hasn't put me back!* Panic threatened to
engulf her until she realized she *could* see shapes. In the cellar
there was no light, ever. She could feel fresh air, too; there was a
window somewhere.

She blinked rapidly and that brought a least moment of clear
sight. This was a nice chamber. It had windows. The furnishings
were good ones, well crafted. Why, then, was she seated on the
floor, back against the wall, a soft hanging rubbing one bare
forearm? She tilted her head back; she could not see the top of the
tapestry, though her eyes weren't trustworthy. *Drug.* It was a

narrow tapestry. White wall on both sides, where she could almost touch.

Get up. She couldn't; her legs would not support her and her mind wouldn't hold the thought long enough for her to act upon it. She leaned back against the tapestry. Let her eyes close.

Silence. Silence that stretched a lifetime, two. Until a voice broke it. "Ylia," it whispered. It made her ears buzz. She shook her head in irritation but the buzzing persisted, and so did the voice. "Ylia. Ylia. Listen to me."

"Go away," she whispered finally.

"No. Ylia. Listen to me." It wouldn't leave her alone. She scowled. "I am here, Ylia. Listen to me. Can you hear me, Ylia?"

"Leave me alone!"

"Ah, no, I will never do that." Silence. "Ylia." The voice did leave her alone, long moments at a time, but it always returned to whisper her name. She clapped numbed hands over her ears, her head rocked back and forth against the tapestry; nothing blocked it. "Ylia. Listen to me."

"Where *are* you?" There was no one near and everything else was a blur, laughter her only answer. *Fight it, fight!* She dragged herself upright, clung to the wall until her fingers ached. She could feel them, suddenly; it was fading, it *was* fading: The wall was *there*, she felt rough-hewn wood under the soft wool of the tapestry. *Drug*, she told herself, and this time it made sense. Vess had put a drug in her food. But no drug lasted forever.

Vess—*his* voice! He was here somewhere, here in this half-darkened room, tormenting her! "Bastard cousin," she whispered "where are you?"

"Why, here of course. Where else should I be but with you?" Vess lay on her bed, among her pillows. He smiled and his mind-speech rang through her. 'Ylia, I can touch your thought. Is this not wonderful?'

The blood drained from her face. "Get out!" she screamed. The sound split her in half.

"Out? Of this chamber?" He laughed as he sat up. "As you please, sweet cousin, but I would rather not. I am enjoying myself."

"Get out of my mind!" Her legs were shaking, threatening to go from under her; she clutched at the wall, closed her eyes and fought the drug as she had fought for balance. Vess was laughing, trying to tell her something, laughing at her, but she heard none of it. And then nothing of his mind-speech as her inner shields slammed back into place. The effort left her half ill. Sweat beaded her lashes and burned her eyes. She scrubbed her face on her sleeve.

Vess sat up slowly, shook his head to clear it. He could not stand at first, and when he tried he fell back among the cushions. He lay there panting for several moments, then came across the room and caught her by the elbow. "How dare you?"

"I dare?" She forced a breathy laugh. "You've fouled my body, Vess, that had better be enough for you. My thought is my own!"

"Don't wager all your tossing sticks on that, cousin." There was sweat on his face too; his black tunic reeked of it. He hadn't found it easy, breaking an AEldra's natural inner guard, even with Lyiadd's Power and the drug. And she'd hurt him, throwing him out. His face showed it; hers showed she knew. He turned and left the room, slamming the door behind him. The sound of the key turning in the lock rattled through her.

Ylia staggered across to the bed and fell onto it. *I cannot bear much more of this. How long before he decides to abandon his present, stupid quest, and calls upon Lyiadd for aid?* Down in the courtyard, she could hear chickens and geese. It sounded like home. The drug was nearly gone, and she was suddenly terribly tired, horribly depressed. *Home. I have no home. Only this. This and death.* She was too tired to care, too tired and miserable even to weep. She closed her eyes and hoped for sleep, but it was long in coming.

She woke late to find a bowl of water and cloths; she stripped out of the silk gown and washed. The water was cool, faintly scented, pleasant against overly warm skin. She found a piece of bread in the basket on the table, used her fingers to smear it with cheese and ate it. Food seemed to lessen the residual effect of the drug; and she was hungry. The soup was curdled in the bowl but there was an apple. Vess had not forgotten to take the knife with him, of course. She bit off several large chunks, discarded the core and dipped apple bites in the last of the cheese. It didn't feel like enough food but it was better than none. She draped the silk gown across the foot of her bed, loosened the lacings on the undergown and fell back among the cushions. Sleep claimed her almost at once.

She woke to the grey light before dawn. Her heart lightened with it, and it took her a moment to realize why. Dawn in Koderra: Her favorite time. So many mornings she had watched from her windows as the sun touched the always-snow-covered Foessa, moved down their unclimbable faces to sparkle on the Torth and turned the hillsides to golden. Koderra's walls always looked new, seen at first light. She had seldom missed a sunrise, though often she went back to sleep for another hour before Malaeth came to rouse her.

Malaeth—no. She couldn't. *Take the moment, Ylia; pretend, if you can. A sunrise in Koderra; once you thought you'd never see another. Here is one for your taking, however you came by it.*

And so she stood at the window, shivering in the undershift as first light slid down the towers, the walls, the long grass on the nearest hillside. That hill had been thick with Tehlatt, four years ago. For a moment, she saw them again; she closed her eyes, shook her head. The drug was still coming at odd moments to catch her off balance. "If it doesn't all go, if it damages me forever," she whispered. But Vess would feed it to her again, and next time, he'd increase the dose. Or he'd feed it to her before the previous dose wore off, until she went mad or gave in to him. Or he'd fetch her to Lyiadd, or Lyiadd to her, and that would be the end of it.

A weapon, any weapon—*Kill yourself, and have done. If he somehow uses you to conquer Nedao!* But a survey of the chamber showed no possibilities: no knife, no sharp utensils of any kind. There was nothing she could use to open a vein. The water bowl where she washed—not possibly deep enough to drown in. A very young child might force his way through the windows to fall to the ground smashed; she could not. She crossed the chamber, peered into her old dressing room, into the tiny latrine beyond it. Nothing.

Her shoulders slumped. "Go and dress," she ordered herself, but for the moment it was nearly too much effort to move at all. Only thought of Vess coming upon her as she stood, laces undone, hair wild and loose, and half her body exposed, sent her back into the main chamber, snugging the underdress back into place as she went. The rose silk was no longer fresh, and one sleeve was stiff with dried blood; there was a tear in the right shoulder. The slippers—she finally found them under the table. No, nothing was fresh, but it was covering.

Be ready, she ordered herself. *Any chance that offers, any at all, be ready to snatch it.* For freedom? No, there would never be freedom for her, not now. It was better that Galdan never know what Vess had done to her, anyway. She bit her lip, fought tears.

A tap on the door roused her from a long, black silence. "Enter," she called impatiently when no one came. Who would wait for her permission *here*? But the woman who brought her morning-meal looked half-witted. Lady's chamber: One must seek permission to enter. Whatever her orders, she wouldn't know to behave any other way. She set the tray down, made a low curtsy and bowed her way out the door.

Food. Strength. Eat. Strength to find her way out of this chamber, into the lower halls. There would be a sword there, either for her hand or one she would throw herself upon. Soon, while she could still think to do it. While she had the will. *Now, before I lose the nerve to do it*. It should have frightened her, knowing she planned her own death and would carry it through. She was too tired to care.

There was a bowl of warm corn porridge, a ripe apple, two thick pieces of bread and a crock of near-white butter to spread on it—with her fingers, for they had not even given her a spoon for the porridge. There was a mug of cool goat's milk, a jug of water. The milk had an odd taste, but it took her a moment to place it: Someone was letting the goats graze on the pastures north of the city, there was an unmistakable tang of sage. She laughed faintly, a laugh that had an edge of tears to it. "The things you remember!" The taste stayed in her mouth until she washed it down with a bite of dry bread. The water was cool, tasted of the great wooden cisterns, but nothing else.

She stood, went to wash her face. And stopped, water dripping from her chin, eyes on the door. The old woman had come in with the tray, had set it on the table, had gone out again—"I did not hear the key. Gods and Mothers," she breathed, "it's not locked!"

She stood frozen one long breathless moment. To touch the ring and find the door wouldn't move—*Coward. Stupid coward!* She strode across the floor with a step that twisted underskirt and silk around her calves; she caught up the hems and knotted them on one side. She gripped the heavy bronze ring. The door swung in silently. A step, a cautious glance to assure her there was no one in the hall; the key hung on its chain next to the door.

Go, now. A desperate urgency filled her; she fled. She hesitated at the head of the stairs: There was laughter down there. She threw herself downstairs at breakneck speed; caught her balance at the landing just before she crashed into the wall, and teetered at the head of the next flight.

But someone came from behind, someone who had been waiting in the shadow of the landing, and hands caught at her shoulders, spinning her around and pulling her off balance. When she would have cried out, they tightened hard around her upper body, driving her face into a rough cloth shirt, driving the air out of her. "Be silent!" a voice hissed; the accent was thick, the words, for a wonder, Nedaoan. *Not Vess.* It was all she could coherently think. She went limp. "Swear you'll be silent!" *Silent? Why?* She tried to twist free, but her captor picked her off her feet and carried her into the small library.

Brit Arren flung bits of cloth from Jers' stool and dropped her onto it. "Your word, silence," he said as she tried to catch her breath. She stared at him, pulled her mouth closed with an effort. "It's my death, if I'm found with you. I thought I wanted that at first. I do not now, there are more important things than dying." He smiled faintly. "I wondered how I would reach you, but someone's gods are smiling on you, woman."

Ylia shook her head. He was talking in curious circles, and his eyes weren't quite sane. Sea-Raider. Perhaps that explained the eyes. Hers didn't feel quite sane just now, either. But something filled him, something she might have been able to name if the Power were not dead. "Reach me? Why?"

"I am not certain." Brit Arren shrugged. Behind the carefully expressionless face, he was thinking furiously. *If I simply let her run down those stairs, and Vess learned I was on the landing . . . if I killed her myself . . . no. The plan I had was a good one. She cannot read me, that much is obvious. Tell her anything, let her think what she likes. Get her back where Vess wants her.* "There are those here who would aid you, but you may ruin all by being here, now."

"Riddles."

"No. If I had not stopped you just now—"

"I might already be dead," Ylia said flatly. "Do you think I was unaware of that?"

"Not a pretty way to die."

"Vess is killing me a breath at a time; is that prettier?"

Brit Arren shook his head. "We are wasting time, any moment your absence may be noted." He tightened his grip on her arm. She twisted against his grip as she read the purpose in his eyes.

"No. No! You cannot take me back there! I won't go! I can't!"

Ylia caught at his hand with her free hand, sought his eyes with hers. "Can't you see what he is doing? He intends to turn my thought, to warp me, to make me betray my own people! Can you not understand that?"

Brit Arren shuddered. His pain was so intense even she felt it, Power-reft as she was. He pried her hand loose with unexpected gentleness, and she saw to her horror his eyes were bright with unshed tears. "I know, woman, better than ye can imagine!" Ah, gods! In a breath, his whole world had shifted and only one course was left clear to him. "He will not do this to you; I will find a way to prevent it. I swear." Ylia ran a sleeve over her own eyes, swallowed tears. Brit Arren pulled her to her feet, gripped her shoulders lightly between his hands. "You do not believe me. I do not blame you, and I admit I was not candid with you just now. My own reasons. If what you just said is true—" Silence. "Then I will do what I can for you. But there is no way out of this Tower, not with Vess here. Save death. And if I can wait for death until there is no alternative, you can wait, woman."

"I cannot."

"No? I am no man who understands women, I do not know gentle words. But you are different, swordswoman. You have fought, and killed, or so they say, and you see the world as it is. You have sworn oaths as men do. So. I swear I will free you, or I will bring you a blade to die upon myself."

Ylia considered this. "I do not know your name."

"Mal Brit Arren. Captain of—once *Fury's* captain." His lips twisted as her eyes went wide. "You have heard of me, haven't you? No matter. Here, I am nothing. Less than you are. Vess' prisoner, a discarded toy. My vow holds, Ylia of Nedao."

"I believe you." She extended her hand. Brit Arren was startled but took it and gripped it as he would an equal's. Ylia sighed faintly. "Take me back, before I lose my courage."

He gripped her arm. "In case there is guard in the hall." She let him lead her down the little stair, up the main stair and down the hall. Neither saw the shadowy figure hugging the wall, creeping toward the stair a step at a time. *After me!* Terror froze Jers' heart as he heard them. Horror had imagined Vess following him stealthily through that open door, into the bedchamber and across to the bed where he had left his gift half-buried in cushions, or perhaps waiting to pounce on him as he emerged. He backed away soundlessly, then stopped and stared the way he'd come. *Mal Brit Arren, and he has the witch!* Jers clutched two-handed at his mouth to keep the laughter in.

At first he'd thought it Vess' doing, the door open and her gone. It occurred to him only after he'd hidden the weapon and its note, after he'd reached the hall, that perhaps she'd somehow escaped. By the One, if she had, and Vess had found that paper! There was no signature, no proof Jers had written it—Jers would surely never call himself *her* friend! But Vess had ways of learning things. Unpleasant ones.

But now! She'd tried to escape and that beast of a Sea-Raider had caught her! Jers turned and fled, still trying to stifle a giggle behind trembling hands.

Brit Arren handed her through the door in silence and locked it securely behind her. She leaned against it, listening to the sound of his boots retreating down the hall. "Ah, gods and Mothers, what have I done? My one chance to die with a little honor intact, and I lost it on a half-mad vow! But I was fully mad to take it."

She sagged, all at once exhausted. It took effort to walk across to the bed; she dropped down onto cool sheets and shook air into a cushion, plumped another. A third fell unnoted from her fingers.

Her dagger lay there—Brendan's dagger. *Illusion. The drug again.* But the hilts, with its copper ship, felt very much real; the leather smelled of the oil she'd rubbed into it just before Fest. She gripped the hilts, drew the blade partway out; stopped. Something had come loose; something mostly white, crumpled —she let the knife fall, picked up the note Jers had written. Smothered a giggle that was half-hysteria. *"You will know what to do with this, to deliver yourself. A friend.* Gods, I find myself surrounded with friends!"

Who had done this? When was easy, the dagger had not been there an hour before. But who? She reread the note, smiled grimly. It was in Nedaoan, the writing that of a man comfortable with Nedaoan script. And the intention was ludicrously clear. Only Jers would have such ease with her language *and* wish her dead by her own hand. *But before I kill myself, this blade will kill another first.* How had he got hold of it—sly, sneaking creature that he was? It scarcely mattered. It was hers again.

She glanced over her shoulder. Vess might not come to her so early in the day; he never had liked mornings. Nothing to trust.

She cut a hole in the mattress, resheathed the blade and buried it deep in the straw filling, piled sheets, blankets, pillows back over the top. Unless he *searched*, he'd never know it was there. And there was no reason for him to *search*.

The note—in tales, folk usually ate them, but she knew a more sensible way to dispose of it. She tore it into lengthwise strips, crossed the chamber as she tore the strips into bits and then smaller bits still and threw all of them down the latrine.

She lay back down, shoving most of the cushions aside, pulling two under her head, feeling cautiously under them. She could, with a little cautious maneuvering of her hand, get a grip on the hilts. She shifted her position, shifted the blade so she could get at it with the least amount of movement. Finally satisfied, she pulled the linen sheet up over the hole in the mattress, curled up and slept.

It was early afternoon when she woke. Someone had brought her wine, a wooden jug of fresh water. She drank some of the water, left the wine. Harder to tell if wine had been tampered with. Vess hadn't come yet; it wouldn't be long now.

There was heavy activity down by the river: New ships in, most of them Sea-Raider hunter ships; one or two of the heavier oared, open-decked Holthan warboats. She could see Vess on the docks, arguing with a pack of Ylsans. Something was afoot. At the moment, she didn't much care what, so long as it kept him out of Koderra, out of the Tower and out of her bed.

She gazed out the window. The wind was strongly west to east, fortunately, because they were killing pigs somewhere beyond the north wall; the horrid squealing was unmistakable. Carrion birds were already gathering, waiting. Someone shouted at them, a voice briefly rising above the shrieks of terrified beasts, and they rose in a clatter of wings to circle the corner of the Tower where she watched. One of them caught her eye: It was brown, white-bellied and half again the size of the normal Plains-vulture. She glanced back at the docks. Vess was still there, now standing on the deck of one of the Holthan vessels, talking with some brightly clad sailors.

She went back to the table for more water and a piece of bread to dip in the now runny butter, and so did not see the great brown and white bird launch itself from the wall to circle high and sail down across the south walls. Two Ragnolan commons at guard

on the south tower stared after it. "A sea-scavenger, isn't it?" one
of them asked. His companion shrugged.

"Perhaps. If it builds a nest here, though, that ought to be
luck, oughtn't it?"

"Ah—might be. Back home, it would." They turned to watch
it out of sight.

There was little sun left in the narrow ravine. The bird landed
in one of the remaining patches, folded his wings and stared up at
the sky. Slowly, his legs lengthened and straightened, and became thicker; the claws on his feet retracted, became flat, part of
stubby, pale toes, part of long, high-arched feet. The wings
shimmered, spread again, the feathers shrank, faded, were gone
—replaced by arms covered in sturdy blue Nedaoan cloth. The
neck moved back on broadening shoulders, thickened, the head
blurred, shifted. Changed. Bendesevorian drew a deep, shaky
breath, and dropped down to sit in the warm sunlight.

But only for a moment; he was not as worn by half as he
thought he'd be. And there wasn't much time. *Vess*—at this
range, Vess was simple to find; out there, on the river. Further
cautious touch showed a disquieting matter: Vess was sending
advance ships to Yslar for Lyiadd to send against Nar. And there
was urgency involved: A five-day, two at most.

Bendesevorian set aside what little he learned in that brief
touch for later, after he came back to Nedao. Ylia. She must be
his first, his only concern.

Find the entrance to the tunnel to begin with. It took time,
more than he could have wished. But he finally located it among
rock and brush, unexpectedly on the left flank of the ravine and a
full four lengths from its upper end. It had been blocked by falling dirt, stone and the brick that had once made the lintel; he
managed to squeeze through and walked the dark tunnel beyond
it.

The blank wall was where Galdan's thought had placed it, and
the least bit of mind-touch showed him the trigger. The wall
eased back silently, with a strong odor of fresh oil. He found
himself behind an enormous, heavy woven woolen hanging.
There was no one in the chamber when he came from behind the
tapestry. *Now.* He stood still, reinforced the place that created the
insubstantiality. It should hold even against Vess, but with luck,
he would not need to chance that. *Get her and go.*

The guard at the door was talking to the woman scrubbing the hallway. Neither noticed as the Nasath walked lightly past them.

With the sense of Ylia strong here, he had no difficulty find-ing the stairway to the family apartments but at the base of the stair, he had to wait until chance moved some of the young men lounging there. He took the stairs two at a time, paused on the landing to test the air.

Something unpleasant, there, to his left. But it did not seem enough of a threat to chance a search. He moved up the narrow stairs and stood just inside the chamber. Ylia had been in this room, recently. And the passage he had seen in Galdan's mind— he crossed the room and laid a hand on the wall. It was still there, and recently repaired.

He turned aside then to move silently into the main hallway. That door almost to the bend. A key hung from the lock. Per-haps, with Vess temporarily out, with that escapeway so near—

He pressed himself into the wall and reinforced the insubstan-tiality as two men came up the stairs behind him. They moved down to the window, opened the shutters and stood in the warm afternoon sun, talking and watching the locked room.

Well, luck had held well enough. And he hadn't been caught. But he couldn't go in after her, not now. He couldn't cover her, he couldn't maintain a cloak of insubstantiality to shield himself and her. He would need to find someone whose mind he could bend to aiding him. One of these men? It would have to be both, but could he manage both?

He stood irresolute only a moment. For just then, coming from the other direction, was a tall, red-haired Sea-Raider. Mal Brit Arren ignored the guard, slowed as he passed Ylia's door. He shrugged faintly and moved on, so near Bendesevorian the Nasath might have touched him. His thought was a roil, difficult to sort through. At the very heart of it all, though... Bendesevorian turned to follow. He had found his ally.

21

Bendesevorian caught up with the Sea-Raider just past the turn in the stair. Brit Arren leaped as an unseen hand touched his arm; he staggered back into the railing, tearing himself free. "What is that?" he whispered; his voice wouldn't hold any more volume. Was it Vess, testing him again as he had over and over in that wine-scented, black cellar?

"Come with me," Bendesevorian whispered in reply. "The small chamber behind you."

"I—" Mal Brit Arren pulled his mouth shut with an effort. There was nothing there! Nothing to *see*, he amended hastily, and fought a shudder. But not Vess; unskilled in sorcery as he was, Brit Arren *knew* he could tell if it was Vess. He fumbled at his belt, found the warding charm his first captain had given him and clutched it before him like a shield as he started up the narrow stairs.

The Sea-Raiders on guard waved at him, but he didn't see them; they looked at each other as he vanished into the library and one shook his head. "He still hasn't all his oars down, does he?"

"No." *He has cause*, was on the other's face, but he prudently did not say it.

"Where are you? Who are you?" Brit Arren whispered. He stared wildly around the small chamber, the charm held at arm's length before him.

"You may put that aside, it cannot affect me, but I do not intend you harm." Bendesevorian emerged from the corner where Jers' prayer bench and his blanket were. Brit Arren kept the charm where it was. "I am real enough. Feel, if you wish." The Nasath extended a hand; the Sea-Raider touched it gingerly. "I came to find Queen Ylia of Nedao. Invisibility is useful to me, as you might think." Silence. Brit Arren gazed at the Nasath as though he might vanish at any moment. "I have found her. I must free her."

"Free her." Brit Arren pulled himself together. "You'll die for even thinking it. Vess will read your intention, even if he cannot see you."

"No. You did not see me when you passed me in the hallway,

near her door. Vess will neither see nor sense me. What you think
is dangerous to you, Mal Brit Arren."

"How—how did—?"

"I read your name when I read your thought. I am sorry but
my need is great and so is the need for haste."

"Greater than *you* know," Brit Arren replied grimly. "He has
given her Ragnolan drugs. Already she thinks of death."

"Your risk is no less. If Vess read your thought now, he would
kill you."

Brit Arren shrugged. "If he dies also, I do not care." He
turned away, drove his hands through his hair. "I owe Jon that."

"I know." He pitied Brit Arren; he kept that from his voice,
knowing the Sea-Raider would not thank him for it. "I must free
Ylia."

Mal Brit Arren turned back. "The halls are thick with men,
and I no longer control any of them, even those who once obeyed
my orders. You can get to the woman, if you wish suicide as your
cup; you will not get half-way down those stairs with her."

Bendesevorian shook his head, crossed the room and felt
along the wall. Little of the ornamentation remained. But the
triggering device was still there, near the ceiling. He pressed his
ear against the wall until he heard the latch open. "Listen carefully. The spell I used to be unseen in that hall covers only me. I
cannot shield another with it."

"Sorcery." Brit Arren spat.

"If you like. I will not be able to fetch her; Vess cannot sense
me now, but he might if I attempted to shield myself and her. I do
not wish to chance Ylia, having come so far to save her, and I do
not want Vess to know of my presence, not until he comes
against Nar or Nedao and finds me there." Brit Arren folded his
arms and leaned back against the wall, a thoughtful look on his
face. "So I need you."

"Me. Why?"

"A man with nothing to lose, a man who is not loyal to Vess.
A man who stands and listens while I speak of these things." He
paused. "Find a moment when she is alone and unguarded. Bring
her here and use the passage behind this panel. I will await you
both below. Do this and I will do two things in turn for you."

"All I want is to stand in reach of Vess, with a dagger in hand
and the will to strike," Brit Arren said. "But no Sea-Raider ever
turned down coin."

Bendesevorian shook his head. "No coin. A better thing.

First, this." He held out a cloth bag. Brit Arren took it warily. "Carry it with you, when you enter her chambers, when you bring her down the passageway. Vess will not then sense your presence in that room, or your part in her escape."

Brit Arren laughed, without humor. "He will read all of us, until he finds his villain and kills him. But he must touch me to kill me, and if I had a dagger—"

"No. A better plan," the Nasath said. "If I could rearrange the outer semblance of your thought once Ylia was safely in my hands, make it that you had not seen or touched the woman, that you had never plotted to free her or to harm Vess? That your intentions toward him were—if not those of a man sworn to him, at least those of a man who examines his options and finds only one sensible course left to him?" Brit Arren felt for the edge of the table, sat on it and stared. "If by that he might grow to trust you and treat you as an ally—and if not one worthy to command, one worthy of again holding blades and fighting for him? But under that, your thought would be your own, still."

"I—" He closed his mouth, swallowed, tried again. No sound came.

"Think upon it, if you wish, but take the bag."

"No. Wait." Brit Arren closed his eyes, let his head fall back, tried to think. Too many branching futures, gods, how to choose? And this—like something from a mother's tales, how dared a man believe in such a thing? But—if it worked! If he could bring himself to patience and to playing the part. *But I can, if I must, for I will not die without one chance to kill Vess, as he made me kill Jon.*

The strange man was watching him with compassion. For some reason, it did not bother him. Such a man would not live by normal rules. *Man?* "Are you a god?" he blurted. Bendesevorian smiled faintly, shook his head.

"I? No. Merely one of those the Ylsans call Guardians, and not the strongest or the wisest of those. I am what Ylia of Nedao has—what *you* have. If you help us, I will give you what I can in return. I cannot promise Vess will grow to trust you. Know that."

"Of course not. That is my business. And he will," Brit Arren promised flatly. "I will aid you. Stay here, while I go and scout the hallway."

"No. Wait." The guard clattered across the landing and down the stairs to be greeted noisily by those in the lower hall. Brit

Arren stirred, but Bendesevorian again shook his head. "Wait. A little."

"Why?" *Get this over and done with!*

"Because—Vess is with her."

The key turned in the lock, rousing her from a long, blank study of the Plain: Barefoot children were herding goats across the brow of the hill; someone with a round net was fishing the river. Something to look at; better than walls. She didn't bother to turn; it was Vess' step. She'd see him soon enough.

"You look tired, sweet cousin." He bent down to kiss her throat. "You should be resting."

"Why? Have you another night planned for me like the last?"

He laughed, let his fingers trail down her arm. It took all the determination she had left not to pull away from him. "Perhaps. Perhaps not. I prefer to keep such things a surprise. They are more effective." Silence. "I nearly had you, last night."

"No."

"No?"

"No. You will not succeed. Too much, too often and you'll only kill me."

Vess laughed low in his throat. "Ah. And you would prefer that? You think so, perhaps, but you are merely confused about your desires, like most women. Nothing more."

"No."

His fingers dug into her shoulder, hard. "Have you not yet learned that you must not say 'no' to me?"

Ylia turned into his grip and met his eyes. "No." There was a chill little moment of quiet. Then Vess smiled, but he didn't look as confident, and he seemed to hesitate over various things he might say.

"My father will deal with you."

"I am certain you cannot wait to tell him you have failed so miserably!" His fingers dug in harder and he brought his face close to hers.

"Do not think you know me because you once knew one side of me, cousin," he whispered finally. He walked over to the table and poured himself wine. "I see you drank none of this. Did you think I would poison it?"

"Perhaps," she replied, consciously mocking his earlier words. "Perhaps not. I wish no wine today; my head aches."

Vess laughed, finished his wine and poured more. "Well." He

set the cup aside. Ylia caught at the windowsill with one hand and gripped it hard as he stood. She could not escape him here; she had to battle herself not to attempt to elude him. "There are men I must speak with before the ships leave port. But they must match the low tide, and so I have—an hour to spend with you, sweet cousin."

So hard to keep disgust from her face as he took her arm to lead her across the room as though she were a woman eager for him. She gave in to the pressure on her elbow, let him press her down onto the bed. *The knife—show nothing; give away nothing.* Vess' face almost touched hers. "I cannot think why you give me so much trouble, cousin. I am not unskilled, not ugly, not fat or soft. Not old."

"No. You are none of those things, Vess," she said quietly. Her hand touched the pillow, pulled it under her head. She let the hand remain there.

Vess' hand touched her shoulder. "That is the first nice thing you have said to me. And we have had so few days together. Perhaps you have had time to think, is that it? Do think, Ylia." His whisper tickled her ear. "Consider. Already sense convinces you not to fight me, and that has brought you fresh air, good food, clean clothing. I will obtain pretty gowns made just for you. Jewels, sapphires, to match your eyes. And for what? A little pleasure for both of us, once you accept what I give." He pulled back so he could meet her eyes. "Can you not simply enjoy what I give you, this once? There *is* no other choice for you. You know it. Why not make things pleasant?" Ylia gave no answer. *She is not stupid, only stubborn. Is it possible she has finally come to her senses?* Stubborn women so often capitulated suddenly and unexpectedly: He didn't dare believe his fortune, but when he clasped her hand, her fingers curled around his. He closed his eyes and kissed it and still she did not pull it away.

Move, she ordered herself. *Do it!* This would be the hardest part—not to convince him, who was more than prepared to be convinced, but to pretend compliance. She shifted slightly so her body pressed against his; tentatively at first. Vess made a happy little wordless sound, buried his face against the low throat of her gown.

She had the dagger now; inched it free and brought her arm down to rest it, even more tentatively, against his back.

Vess kissed the pulse in her throat. She was nervous as a maiden untried, by all the gods at once, her arm trembled as though she were afraid to touch him! Who would have thought the brave warrior so frightened in the face of pleasure? "Beloved," he murmured against her hair.

She tightened her grip, brought the blade through with all the strength in her. What warned him, she was never certain: the tightening of her muscles, some inner sense he'd set to protect himself—Power flared; there was a sudden aura around him, blood-red. She screamed in frustration as the blade bounced off something as ungiving as stone and slid along his back. She raised it for another try but Vess had already rolled away from her. His cry echoed through the room and through her head: The hilts went briefly red-hot, burning her palm. He slapped the knife away.

"Bastard!" she screamed. "Did you really think I would come to *you* willingly?"

Vess stumbled to his feet, ran a trembling hand across his back. It came away red. "You bitch! You cut me!"

"Come here and I'll *kill* you!" She scrambled across the bed after the dagger. Vess caught her arm, dragged her to her feet. She went for his eyes; he caught one hand, missed the other, yanked her off balance as she tried to blind him again. "You thought I'd want to sleep with you? You're not even good at what you pride yourself on!"

With a wordless howl, Vess slapped her, backhand and hard. The blow wrenched her from his grip and her head struck the bedpost with a loud crack.

He ignored her; *she* couldn't be any trouble for the moment. But where had that blade come from? He was dizzy from deflecting it, ill from the feel of his own blood running down his back. *I could kill her for that!* He glanced in her direction as his fingers closed on the hilts. Perhaps he had; she wasn't moving. There was blood on her mouth, a dark red thread of it running from her nose.

The blade was hers. But he had taken all her weapons: This dagger with its unusual hilts, her boot knife, even the nail knife that had a tinder-stone for its haft. How had this dagger come back to her? "Who touched it?" he whispered. He was deadly tired and the Power a mere flicker, but he *must* know.

He needed wine, needed it badly. It left a metallic taste in his mouth, but it steadied his nerves, and the cut was coagulating, finally. Fortunately it wasn't very deep, because he could not heal. *Don't think on it.* He couldn't; his skin sliced by this razor-sharp blade, *his* blood—

Ylia still had not moved. He sat, dagger hilts between his hands, and closed his eyes. When he opened them, there was an unpleasant little smile on his lips. "Jers. My good friend Jers."

He leaned into the hall and shouted for guard. The man who came running was dispatched for Jers and for more wine. Vess made it back to the chair and collapsed. *Hells! What good was Power when saving his life and testing the dagger drained him so?* And how was he to read Jers?

Of course, there were other ways of testing a man for truth, ways he had used before Power showed him an easier way. *You depend upon it too much, Vess. That is dangerous.* His thought was interrupted by a considerable amount of noise out in the hall. Jers was being brought, and by the sound of things, he was protesting wildly.

The door slammed against the wall and the guard came in with Jers in his fist, dangling by his grubby collar. The guard dropped him and stepped back.

"What do you know of this?" Vess demanded. The dagger dangled from his fingers. Jers watched it in wide-eyed fascination. "You gave it to her so she could kill me!" Vess advanced and Jers huddled into himself, flinching away from the expected blow. With a wordless snarl of disgust, Vess threw the dagger from him. "Why? Why would you do such a thing?"

Some of that got through: Jers drew himself upright, terror forgotten. Fury darkened his face. "You swore I should have the Nedaoan House! And you lied!"

"When Nedao is mine—!" Vess began.

"When? When you conquer it? Or when this witch *gives* it to you? She has blinded you to all but lust with her spells, she has—"

"Be silent!"

"I shall not be silent!" Jers roared. Vess, startled, fell back a step, and Jers came after him. "Did I not teach you the true way when you were a boy? Did you learn nothing? A man slays witches! He does not lay with them! She has ensorceled you! And you have succumbed willingly, my once pupil! Men call you lecher openly! They laugh at you, because you cannot control your lust for the Nedaoan witch!"

"I will kill you!" Vess snatched up the dagger and brought it high over his head. Jers shrieked and scrambled away from him.

The guard came forward but Jers dove under his arm and fled.

"Get him!" Vess shouted. The guard was already out the door. A shrill cry followed. Vess dropped Ylia's blooded dagger with a grimace of distaste, kicked it aside, drew his own as he stepped into the hall.

A glance toward the corner windows revealed a most curious situation. Vess fell back against the wall, laughing and shaking his head as Jers came toward him, dangling from Mal Brit Arren's oversized hands. Jers was shrieking nonsense, then simply wailing in terror. His nose ran, there was froth on his lips. He went suddenly, unnervingly still as Brit Arren came to a halt before the open door. "Is this your bit of mad priest? I found it down there; it seemed most anxious to get away from something."

"Its death," Vess replied grimly, but the laugh broke through again. He clapped a hand over it; it sounded too much like Jers' laugh.

But Brit Arren—! The laughter died out of him. *Why is he aiding me?* Why would he, of all men? Brit Arren's face gave him no clue, beyond the sardonic smile. "Why?" Vess demanded bluntly.

Brit Arren shrugged. "Why not? You wanted him, didn't you?" Blue eyes met his levelly.

"Why should I trust you? *She* just tried to buy my trust, only so she could knife me."

"Anything I say or do could have another motive, we both know it," Brit Arren countered flatly. "Trust or not, as you choose; I scarcely brought him to you to change how you think of me." Jers hung between them, nearly forgotten, whimpering and mumbling to himself. "I might be a fool, not as much of one as that. Is that your blood?" Vess nodded. "What did you expect? Sense? Thought? She's female. Women never understand kindness in men, they think it weakness, and take advantage of it." He hesitated, as though he had just realized to whom he spoke. "Well. So I have always seen." Another pause. Then, deliberately: "Lord Vess."

"I am learning," Vess replied sourly. He stared at Brit Arren for several long, silent moments. Brit Arren stared back. His face gave away nothing, his thought less. Jers—well, there was nothing to read in Jers. Dig through the man's mind however much he wished, once he had the strength, he'd find nothing but madness. It didn't matter. Jers had given her the knife, for whatever purpose of his own. She had used it the way a man might have expected. Jers would make no more such gifts, and Ylia would not have another chance; there would be no second dagger.

Dagger. He was still holding his own fine-bladed stiletto. He laughed and tossed it high. Brit Arren caught it. "If you truly would do me a service, rid me of this refuse."

Brit Arren tossed the dagger back. "Never dirty a good blade on refuse, Lord Vess." He dragged Jers to the open corner window and threw him out. There was no cry. Vess came up in time to hear him hit.

He stared down over the thick sill. Men were running, one of the kitchen women screamed and ran back inside. Brit Arren lounged against the wall, waiting. Vess smiled faintly. "I appreciate that. And I award what I appreciate."

Brit Arren shrugged. "It was nothing I would not have done for myself. You know that. Sir." Still that pause. Not quite the implied insult to it there once had been. But—

"Perhaps. But when he was under my protection, you let him be."

The two studied each other in silence. "That still was no true test—Lord Vess."

"No." Another, longer silence, broken only by the pandemonium in the courtyard. "I think you are a sensible man after all. A practical man."

Brit Arren smiled lazily. "Perhaps—a man who is becoming that, under provocation. Having found myself alive, I find I like being alive." He inclined his head slightly, and with only the least hint of mockery. "My Lord."

Vess watched him go. *It is all so simple, as though someone planned moves on a board! Life does not fall so neatly, I dare not trust him! And yet—if I have somehow tamed that man, of all men! Where could I not go, what could I not do, with the Sea-Raiders at my back and Mal Brit Arren my willing ally!*

He walked slowly into Ylia's chamber. She had not moved, but as he came in, she moaned. Her hand felt its way up the pillar, fell back again. "It's gone dark," she whispered, so low he could scarcely hear her. She brought up a trembling hand, held it close to her face, let it fall to her lap. It moved again, explored the floor around her feet, caught at the bed hangings. Clung there. "Oh, Mothers. I cannot see."

She moved her head cautiously; her eyes were wide, but gave no sign when they moved past him. The side of her face was purpled and swollen; the hair behind her ear was stiff and dark with dried blood. Her eyes closed and she slumped against the bedpost once again.

Vess turned and left the room, leaving her where she lay and the door wide open. Why bother to close it? She would never know. He was laughing as he stepped into the hall, still laughing as he reached the apartments that had been Brandt's and were now his.

He leaned against the door, found that he barely had strength to push it closed. *Reaction.* Somehow he managed the three steps that took him across to the bed, fell onto it. He winced, rolled cautiously onto his stomach; his back throbbed. He needed wine, needed someone to clean the cut. But—not just yet. Not—just —yet. He fell asleep between one breath and the next.

Brit Arren waited an additional count of a hundred after he saw Vess leave. He'd never be able to explain if the creature found him in *her* chambers. Likely Vess was already asleep; he'd been weaving like a drunk with the shock of his wound—that Vess was one of those odd men who went green and queasy at sight of his own blood! That was a thing worth knowing. A thing to remember. If he remembered things, once this Guardian with the unpronounceable name worked sorcery on his thought.

He hesitated. *Go. Get her out of here, the woman and her outland sorcerer both, so I can concentrate on the one task left to me before I die.*

He'd left his boots in the library—Jers' room no longer—and he ran silently down the deserted hallway to stop in surprise before the open door. *He can't have moved her, I was watching!* But she was there, a still, tiny form slumped against the bedframe. She stirred as he knelt beside her. "Who's there?" Her eyes looked right through him. "Who is it? I—please, whoever you are, help me, I cannot see."

"I will. It is I, Brit Arren." He took her hand; she clung to his with a tenacious grip. "We'll get you out of here, there's a friend, waiting."

"Friend?" She laughed breathily. "Friend?" That triggered something in her memory as he lifted her. "Dagger. There's a dagger somewhere, Vess took it. And—the sheath, it's in the bedding, under the pillows—"

"Woman, we haven't time for foolishness."

"Please! Pillow—red thread on white silk—please!" She

wouldn't be quiet. He cursed under his breath, set her on the bed, wrapped her hands around the post so she would not topple over, found it and pushed it into her hands. She felt it. "The dagger. It's—copper hilts, a ship on it."

"There isn't time for this—!"

"Please! It's—it was a—a last gift, from a man—a friend."

"He'll forgive you, come on!"

"He's dead. Lyiadd killed him."

"Ah, *gods*!" But he *had* to get it for her now. It was under the table, in plain sight. He shoved it into the sheath. "Hide it in your sleeve. If there is anyone in the hall, I can explain my presence and yours, but not that blade in your hands." When she made no move to indicate she'd understood, he yanked it impatiently out of her hands and shoved it up between the outer sleeve and the snug shift sleeve. She managed a faint nod, pushed it above her elbow and crooked her arm to hold it in place. He picked her up, careful that the bruised temple did not touch his arms or his shoulder.

It was silent in the hall, though he could still hear hysteria outside. Jers dead was causing more excitement here than Jers living ever had.

Brit Arren reached the little library, pressed the panel open with his shoulder and slammed it with his foot.

Ylia stirred. "What was that?"

"The panel in the library. I closed it. We're in a passageway, leading down and out." She settled against his arm with a little sigh. Brit Arren scowled down at her and took the stairs as rapidly as he dared.

It was dark in the main passageway. Bendesevorian moved out of thicker shadow, made a light that left the walls glowing faintly. Brit Arren could see no source for it and decided he did not want to know what it might be. He wordlessly held out his bundle and Bendesevorian took her. Ylia's hand touched his face; he kissed her brow. "Shhhh. You are safe, Ylia, I have you. And I will take you home. But can you stand so I may do a promised favor for this man who brought you here?" She tried to nod, grimaced as pain knifed through her head, pressed against his chest with her hands for answer. Bendesevorian set her hands on an outcropping in the wall, held her until she found her balance. "Time presses, Brit Arren. My friend, if I may call you that."

Brit Arren shrugged. "If it pleases you. You know why I did it. Not for her."

"Only the result matters in the end."

"Truly. Vess' death. Do what you must." He wiped suddenly damp hands down his breeches, let Bendesevorian cup his temples. A strange vibration ran through him.

"There. Your purpose is yours, and known now only to you and to me. It is locked behind a wall that Vess cannot tear down or sense. Nor can Lyiadd." Brit Arren merely nodded. "We must go. Five paces that way, there is an opening and within it is bricked, top to bottom. Kneel in front of that brick wall, find the lowest brick on the right side and count across four, up three, press hard. You will find yourself behind the great tapestry in one of the empty chambers near the kitchens."

"Thank you." The words didn't come easily, but he owed them.

"Wait." Ylia caught at his sleeve. She licked dry lips, swallowed. "You mean to kill Vess?"

"If you tell me you do not wish him dead," Brit Arren said stiffly. Fingers dug into his arm with surprising strength and there was suddenly color in her face, fury in those eyes, though they weren't aimed quite at his.

"If you kill him, if you *dare* to kill him, I will come for you, some day, and I will cut your throat!" she hissed. "He's mine! What does he owe you? A life, two lives? A son? He owed me that and more before I was brought here. Vess is *mine*." He glared down at her in a mixture of anger and astonishment.

"Then kill him before I can. And do not dally." He looked up at Bendesevorian. "There is no time for this, take her and go." He walked away. The passage was as simple to find and work as the Nasath had said; there was no one in the chamber. He hurried through it, bare feet silent on the polished wood floor. Down the hall, he heard men coming from outside, but he made the small library and collected his boots before anyone saw him.

When he came down the main stair moments later, he found himself the surprised object of celebration: That hall guard had already spread the tale of Jers' death and suddenly, their fallen Lord Captain was again a hero. Threw that slimy religious right out the window, and if it had been at Lord Vess' command, well, what of that? The thing had Brit Arren's old flair to it, and they'd sorely missed Mal's ways.

When he broke free an hour later, he had a full skin of wine in him, and a genuine, if drunken, smile plastered on his face. It took three false tries before he found the proper chamber, found his own blankets and fell across them. *A little sleep*, he thought blurrily, *aye, the old man has that coming*.

In a spacious chamber almost directly above him, Vess sprawled face down across his fur coverlet and slept like the dead.

It is no effort at all for an AEldra to read the thoughts of others and then to block them. Those are the first skills any of us learn. Perhaps fear buried long-trained ability, but that night, even I—with the strongest block among us— could not keep out the welter of emotions that were Ylia's: fear, guilt, pain, misery and anger. Even Bendesevorian could not.

22

It had been a long day; Ysian finally made herself quit counting moments after the Nasath left, and went to visit Grewl. The elderly Chosen Father was glad to see her, and after his first concerned inquiry, he led the conversation to innocent topics.

But though she found it temporarily pleasant to discuss simple matters, it was impossible to ignore realities. Ylia was gone; she must return to Galdan and wait. And she was aware of the bustle and excitement out in the hall, while she and Grewl drank tea and talked of the schools and of herbs and weaving. The Chosen Council would be meeting long hours this night to deal with the latest messages from Nar: threats from the Heirocracy and from Tevvro. And the messages from Osnera's Prince that had come in matched copies to Nedao's rulers and the Chosen Household, messages from Nalda on the same subject: Osnera had broken trade relations with Nar and refused Narran requests for Osneran warships to help defend against Lyiadd. Ysian privately doubted the Chosen could persuade either the Heirocrat or the Osneran Prince to countermand that ruling, but Grewl and his advisors would be awake làte trying to find a way to negotiate an easing of terms.

The sun was westering, nearly down when Ysian left. Nisana awaited her beyond the gate that separated Chosen land from Nedao, for Ysian seldom rode from the Tower to Grewl's halls. Like Ylia, she was scrupulous about utilizing the Power on Chosen grounds, and unless specifically invited by Grewl to visit the grain barns for mice, Nisana never went on Chosen land. Ysian pulled the cloak close as Nisana leaped to her shoulder: It was still day and summer, but the afternoon wind went right through her. Thinner air, higher mountains; she wondered if she'd ever adjust to it.

A sudden sense of presence brought her around sharply, and the cat nearly fell. "Ah, gods, what's that?"

'Don't fear, Ysian!' Nisana's thought overrode hers, and the cat leaped back to the ground. 'It is one of the Folk. Friend, what chances?' she added to their sudden companion—or what could be seen of it.

'Ye are needed.'

'Ylia?' But the cat already *knew*.

'She is safe. They wait for you, in the meadow you have trod before. Tell *no one*! Come soon.' It was gone. Ysian cried out faintly, and Nisana nudged her leg.

'You cannot go out into the woods like that. It will be dark soon and you would freeze. You need a shirt and breeches, a furred cloak. And quickly!' Ysian bridged back to her chamber, had her summer cloak thrown aside and low shoes kicked off almost before the Power faded. Nisana jumped up onto the narrow bed, watched as Ysian dragged her breeches from the chest at its foot and changed rapidly. She picked up her bow, set it down, tentatively picked it up again. "Ah, damn!" She pulled the arrow case from its shelf, strung the bow and hung it across her shoulder. Her warmest cloak went over all. She dragged her hair back and knotted it with a leather cord, wrapped the loose stuff around her hand and bundled it into her hood. "Ready?" Nisana touched her hand with a small paw for answer. Ysian glanced out into the half-lit hallway. "Galdan—we must tell him, poor man. Ylia—"

'No,' Nisana said shortly. 'Why would that Dreyz say to tell no one?' Ysian paled. Nisana butted her arm with a hard head. 'Go, now! Do not think, do it!'

Ysian started as Nisana's mind-speech reverberated through her, closed her eyes. 'You bridge. I do not know the way.' She dared not think what might await them.

Galdan sat up and yawned. He rubbed his eyes. He hadn't been sleeping this past hour, just trying to. Since Ysian was no longer drugging his food and water, it was all he could manage. But he feared to be in a drugged sleep when Ylia came back to him.

When.

He let a tendril of mind-touch loose as he ran a damp cloth over the back of his neck. Nisana and Ysian were back from visiting the Chosen. Perhaps he should go find the cat and try to persuade her to search with him. Waiting was killing him by slow inches.

But Bendesevorian had been gone less than a full day. It didn't seem possible. He wiped his face on his sleeve, realized the water jug was now empty. The wash water was slimy with soap, his mouth dry. *So get some, lazy beast! Who got water for ye when ye sold pelts for your salt and flour?*

He stepped into the hall and turned toward the stairs, but a flare of Power brought him back around. Nisana bridging— away. Nisana and Ysian. He frowned. It was nearly dinner hour, where were they going, and where in such a hurry? For there was urgency in the air, down in Ysian's room. Urgency/fear—secrecy...

He walked up the hall and stood irresolute outside Ysian's door, jug forgotten in his hand. Bits of conversation, half-heard, half-sensed while he was waking and washing, filtered back to him, and for once he was grateful it was harder for him to shield against AEldra mind-speech than it was for an AEldra.

The jug slipped from his fingers; he caught it just before it hit the floor. Bendesevorian had found her, a Dreyz had come for Nisana and Ysian—and no one wanted him to know. Fear rooted his feet to the tiles for what seemed forever.

Ysian's door was ajar. He moved to her bed, testing the air with his nose, letting his inner sense loose. His fingers prickled with the backwash from Nisana's bridging. They were gone— somewhere. He could have wept, could have slammed his fist through the door, or cried out until the stones of the outer wall cracked.

He stood still, letting his emotion wash through him, letting it go. Rage could not help Ylia, and it blocked thought. Inner silence replaced anger, grief and fear. And the thought he needed came. There was another way. Bridging left something behind: something as ethereal as smoke or a thin strand of breath and time, woven together. Something no AEldra even sensed, but a thing he might be able to follow.

He had to; it was all he had. "Mothers, aid me," he whispered, and closed his eyes.

•　•　•

Nisana insisted upon four small bridgings. 'Bendesevorian needs us, Ysian. We may not have time once there to wait to regain strength after bridging.' Unpalatable advice. Ysian was trembling with her desire to *be* there. She said nothing, let Nisana retain control and fed her energy.

There was no wind in the meadow and the moon was not yet up. A faint light illuminated the grass and the Folk who stood in hushed groups.

Bendesevorian sat in the very midst of the close-cropped clearing. Ylia lay beside him, hand in his, a mound of soft grass pillowing her head, his cloak wrapped around her. He looked up, alerted by the bridging, but Ylia was not aware of them until he leaned down to speak against her ear. He squeezed her hand reassuringly, got to his feet and came across the grass. Nisana passed him at a bound; all she saw was Ylia. Ysian would have followed, but Bendesevorian held out a hand to bar her. "I am glad they found you."

Ysian nodded but her attention was on the dark bundle on the grass: Nisana was lost in folds of cloak, Ylia's arms around her. "How bad is it?"

"Not as bad as it might be. Not—good." And he told her.

"I see why you did not want Galdan here," she said.

"No. That was her decision. She did not want him to see her so, and the other thing—"

Ysian gazed at her niece. "Vess. That's not good. If she thinks Galdan cannot accept—" She shook her head. "She is not thinking. But she cannot hide *that* from Galdan."

"No. She hurts. No one thinks well in such pain."

"Then—that is for me to repair." Ysian walked across the grass, but her pace was slow. *Coward, Ysian!* she thought furiously. She *was* afraid, though. Terribly afraid.

Nisana slowed as her feet touched the Nasath's cloak. 'Ylia?' No response. She put both front paws on Ylia's arm; Ylia cried out and her whole body jerked convulsively; Nisana scrambled for balance. 'Ylia?'

"Nisana? Where are you?"

'Here.' Nisana stepped back onto Ylia's forearm again, stepped onto her stomach and dropped down on her chest to bury her face against Ylia's throat. 'Ylia?' Her mind-speech was nearly a shout, but there was no response; Ylia could not sense her and Nisana fought panic. *Do not. Fear is no help at all. She spoke with me first, when she was a babe. My words were the first she heard, after Scythia's.*

"I can't hear you, cat. I can't!" She caught her breath in a sob, wrapped arms and cloak both around the cat. "But I thought you were dead! Oh, gods, Nisana!" Ylia's arms tightened, forcing a squeak out of the cat, and she was laughing and crying both, her tears wetting dark fur. For once Nisana made no objection, merely caught fully extended claws in cloak and loosened hair, and pushed her small round head hard under Ylia's chin.

Ysian gazed down at them. Ylia's face was swollen, black and angry red; dried blood covered her cheekbone, her chin, the left side of her throat. Her eyes were blank and she had no inner sense to warn her of Ysian's presence. *Temporary*, Bendesevorian had said. A Thullen bracelet and such close contact with Lyiadd's Power, for so long, had buried her own Power deep. Pain and Vess' drug had driven it even deeper.

The injuries themselves would heal; Ysian was certain Ylia's sight would return. But the rest—*Vess called it seduction, no doubt.* How Ylia ever hoped to keep Galdan unaware of *that!* Once she had a chance to think, and half a mind to think with, she'd surely see reason. And Ysian could understand Ylia's need. If it had been her, if Golsat were to see her in such a state: no. Let Galdan learn later what he must, at least he would not see; he would never have *this* to remember.

A wave of non-AEldra Power struck her and for half a shaken indrawn breath, she nearly panicked, thinking Lyiadd had found them. Realization that the Power was not *theirs* smote her almost at once, and she scrambled to her feet. Galdan. *Gods, gods, gods.* He'd found them.

Galdan stood at the edge of the clearing, half in shadow, clinging to a young maple as though he would strangle it. He was not aware of Ysian, the Nasath, the Dreyz—anything but Ylia. Terror for her faded; she lived. An unholy rage replaced it, and he would have fallen but for his grip on the sapling.

Ysian took his arm; he threw her hand off savagely. She tried to catch hold of him again but he struck her arm aside and turned on her. She winced as he grabbed her shoulder. "You left without telling me! You had no right!"

"I had no choice, it was what she wanted! And keep your voice low," Ysian hissed. "Or better yet, use mind-speech. She cannot hear *that*."

"She cannot—ah, gods!" He let go of her and buried his face in his hands.

'I am sorry.' Ysian's mind-speech was so soft even Nisana could barely have sensed it, had she been paying heed. 'It was Ylia's choice. She did not want *you* to hurt as you are hurting right now, seeing her and knowing.'

'No. *No*. How could she—how could she hope to hide all that from me?'

'You are thinking no more clearly than she is, Galdan. She is in pain, she cannot see, and the Power in her is dead, for the moment. Look at her. She does not sense you at all. Do what she wants, Galdan. Please. Return to the Tower.' Galdan shook his head, hard. 'Then listen to me. Listen! You are a man, and how-ever much you understand each other, you will not feel this the way she does. Do not let her feel your anger or your grief, she will think it is because of the thing Vess has done. Even *knowing* you would not blame her for that, she would feel blame gut-deep. She has enough to contend with, without that.' Silence, save for Galdan's harsh breathing. 'She wants to spare you. Do you un-derstand?'

Galdan drew a deep breath, let it out slowly and took another. His gaze was more rational, his thought less chaotic. 'No. You are right, I cannot understand. Perhaps one day, she can explain it so that I will. She is not thinking, but you are not thinking, either. She needs me. I cannot leave her.' He stepped past Ysian, walked into the meadow and knelt to gather Ylia into his arms.

"Galdan?" she whispered. "Galdan, no!" She momentarily fought him, then went limp against his chest, weeping. Over their bent heads, Ysian looked at Bendesevorian and Nisana and shrugged. "You weren't supposed—supposed to see—damn you, Galdan! I didn't want you to see me like this!"

"Shhh, beloved. They tried, I just came. I found a way, I had to. I couldn't not come. You need me."

"I—but you weren't—black hells, Galdan, I didn't want you to—didn't want—" She pressed her forehead against his shoulder and wrapped her hands in his shirt. He stroked her hair, and murmured against her ear. Slowly, so slowly, her grip re-laxed.

Galdan looked up finally. "Is there any reason to remain here? Since I have seen her after all? We can heal her as easily in our rooms."

Ysian shook her head. "No. It would be best, don't you think, that no one know anything? Except that they took Ylia and that Bendesevorian rescued her."

"Please," Ylia whispered. "I don't want people—staring at me. Thinking—thinking things. What they'll think, if I'm—if I go back like this, if they know Vess had me and I come back to the valley like this—" And as Galdan stirred, she added: "You don't understand! Everyone knows—Vess. I'll have to look at people, know they're thinking that. I—I can't."

"Shhh." Ysian laid a hand on her lips and spoke briskly. The air was charged with emotion; someone needed to bring things back to a sensible and swift path and get them home. "Let me mend your hurts. We won't take you home like this, then, you don't need anyone's pity, do you? No one will see you until you're clean and healed and in your clothes again. No one will think Vess raped you," she added flatly, voicing the word Ylia had been unable to speak. She and Galdan both shuddered. "Another woman, but never you, Ylia. We're wasting time here; it's chill and you worry the Dreyz. Give me your hands, niece."

As she had hoped, that simplified matters. Ylia held out her hands and let Ysian and Galdan help her sit, Galdan for support behind her and Nisana in her lap. Ylia flinched away as she sensed Ysian's fingers near her throbbing temple but forced herself to hold still. She could not sense the healing, only the lack of pain Bendesevorian had not been able to entirely block. Ysian's fingers were cool against her face and eyelids.

Ylia sagged into Galdan as Ysian finished, gripped his arms as he wrapped them around her. He leaned forward to kiss her hair. "Can you hear me?" he whispered, adding in mind-speech: 'Ylia? Can you?' She shook her head. Ysian's thought was faint, Nisana's stronger but still hard to understand. Bendesevorian—she could follow his thought only if he touched her. But Galdan—with his arms around her she could sense his love, his fear and the murderous fury he tried to hide from her. No words.

Ysian stood. "Never mind. The Power is there, undamaged. It will return. Niece, I daresay you would like your own bed now." Ylia nodded. She opened her eyes, cautiously. They were there, all of them—so blurred, it made her dizzy. But there. She let her eyes close again. *Dizzy. That's the need for sleep after a healing.*

But she opened her eyes once more as Eya's fingers touched her face. The Dreyz stood by her side, others behind her. "We will speak, soon. Things have begun, war is moving against us all, and we must bind our kinds together before many more days pass. Sleep, rest. Gather the strength that is in you."

"I will," Ylia whispered. She laid her hand over Eya's. "Bendesevorian said you aided him. Thank you."

"We did the duty of an ally," Eya said. "But we are friends, you and I." There was no answer Ylia could find to that, but the dryad's touch warmed her.

"Friends," she whispered. The faintest awareness told her the Folk were gone, the inner sense was not completely dead after all. Galdan wrapped her in Bendesevorian's cloak and picked her up.

"Forgive me?" he whispered against her ear.

"Never," she replied. "But I'm—glad you're here."

"That's a terrible answer, it makes no sense at all. Is that the best you can do?" She managed a faint smile; he was trying so hard for both of them. If she weren't so tired—she tightened her grip on his neck as they bridged.

He had her so few days—no time at all. So
little time to do such damage. She was afraid,
who had never let fear direct her before. Guilt
colored all her waking thought: That she had not
avoided Vess' trap, that she had not somehow
kept him from touching her. That her physical
strength had not sufficed against Vess'. Foolish?
Of course. And she knew it to be foolish, and
that made no difference.

She told no one, but her Swordmaster knew;
I saw that. And Marhan saw beyond the simple
explanation of rape and assault that other men
would have accepted. It still surprised me, that
he had such sensitivity, though no one ever saw
it but Ylia, and she rarely. But he had once been
powerless in the face of Lyiadd's greater
strength; I knew he would help her as no one
else could.

23

At dawn, Galdan called up a joint meeting of the Main and
War councils for second hour. By sunrise, word was already getting out that Ylia was home, safe and safely asleep in her own
bed. No one knew yet where she had been. There was an uncomfortable silence around the crowded table as Galdan told them
what more he dared. More than he wanted to tell.

"Vess holds Koderra." He had to wait a long time for the
outraged cries to die down. "He has his own army of Sea-
Raiders, mercenaries and Lyiadd's men. The Tehlatt have moved
back up-river, leaving the south to Vess. Bendesevorian went
there and saw that; he also has other news which he will tell you
shortly. Little of it is good, not surprisingly.

"But my news is largely good." He forced himself to continue
without hesitation, though he would have given anything to stop
with that. "Ylia is home again. She sleeps now, but she is un-

harmed and will be awake by evening. Vess took her prisoner and
held her in Koderra, in hopes he could use her against us. As part
of his plan, he gave her Ragnolan herb. We could do nothing
about the residue of that drug, unfortunately. It may impede her
vision or her thought, off and on. It was a strong dose and wears
off slowly."

He wondered as he looked from face to face, seeing only
concern and relief, fearing the thought that might hide behind the
faces. *Is it because she said folk would wonder and pity, knowing
Vess had kept her?* Pity. Was it for himself he feared, that men
would pity *him* for what Ylia had been unable to prevent?

He suddenly began to understand her fears, and it made him
intensely uncomfortable. *Gods, beloved.*

"So. Vess has Koderra." Marhan slapped the table with both
hands. "Could not wait, could he? Well! What do we do about
it?"

"Koderra?" Erken asked. "Vess? Should we do anything? Or
could we?" Marhan shrugged. "You said Vess could not wait; I
think that is all this means. He cannot readily attack us from
Koderra, as he perhaps might if he had taken Teshmor. No, he
has always wanted Brandt's City and now he has it."

"I wonder Lyiadd did not keep him in Yslar," Corlin said.
"For he *was* there—"

"He was." Galdan settled back into his chair. "But Yls is
taken; Vess may not be needed there. Perhaps Lyiadd did not
want the burden of Vess' armed upon the City, in addition to his
own armed. Perhaps the Three wield well together but do not
share close quarters willingly."

"He and Marrita loathe each other," Bendesevorian said.
"That was strong in his thought. But Vess will not attack this
place from Koderra, for that is not in Lyiadd's plan, and Vess is
loyal to his father. That is the rest of my news.

"I had to work my way slowly from the peak above the old
road to the walls, and from there to the ravine where the main
escape passage ends. There were many ships at anchor, and I
gathered from the thoughts and speech of those on the docks that
this was not normal, so many ships. There were fifteen of the
black-hulled hunter ships, and two enormous open ones, brightly
painted. There were faces on the hulls of these last, three banks
of oars per ship. I have not seen their like before."

"What color were the sails?" Corlin asked. Bendesevorian
closed his eyes briefly.

"Green and yellow, a pattern with no form to it."

Corlin nodded. "Those are Holthan warships, not their Emperor's ships. I remember those colors, they belong to—" He shrugged. "The name is unimportant. The man has money, power and many ships. I do not like Vess having Holthan warships, especially if he has an alliance with that particular noble."

"Vess was on the docks, arguing with men there, giving orders," Bendesevorian went on. "I could not sort the important from self-importance on his part, but it comes to this: The ships are no longer at Koderra's docks. Last night they were anchored near the mouth of the Torth, waiting for the tide and for other ships. They sailed this morning for Yslar. In a five-day, they will move north."

"Nar," Levren said. Bendesevorian nodded.

The Narran Ambassador struggled to his feet. "I must—send messages—" Galdan caught his arm and kept him from falling.

"Wait. We have paper here—Father, in the chest behind you on the black table." Erken brought the small box of paper, ink and pens. "Thank you, Father. My Lord Ambassador, write your messages. Bendesevorian will bridge to Nalda with them this evening." Ber'Sordes felt his way back into his chair, blindly pulled things from the box and blinked as Corlin lit candles for him. He shook himself, unstoppered the ink and began to write.

"Tell the Lord Mayor we will come to Nar's aid," Galdan said. Ber'Sordes nodded without looking up. "We would anyway. But with Osnera's new ultimatum they will need us more than ever—particularly since Prince Carthagus claims Nedao is the cause of the embargo."

"Carthagus is a fool," Ber'Sordes remarked flatly. He was still writing furiously. "He lets the Heirocrat dictate policy and thinks the sea full protection."

"The Heirocracy and the sea," Corlin said. "But the Chosen only control those who share their beliefs and fear their wrath, and Osnera's navy is no more match for Lyiadd's Power than Nedao's herders and villagers were for the Tehlatt." He turned to the Nasath. "I am curious about a thing. Did Vess go with his fleet?"

"No. He was going to remain with his prisoner, then bridge to Yslar as his ships arrived. He intended to break her with Power and with Ragnolan drugs; then, once Nedao was his, and Galdan and the child dead, he would wed Ylia. She *and* Nedao would both be his." Silence. "It does not matter now; he failed. And he will have no second chance. But Ylia knew, for he told her."

"Gods," Levren whispered. "You need never have told us that," he said aloud. "Ylia would not like it, knowing we knew."

"No." Galdan managed that much.

"D'ye think we would tell her?" Marhan demanded indignantly. Levren shook his head.

"Those of us who know her well—of course not." One of Brandt's old councilors stirred in his seat, subsided as Marhan glared at him. "No one in this room will indicate such knowledge, by word or look," Levren said flatly. He looked at each of those around the table. "I *trust* no one will."

"That is settled," Erken said. "The defense of Nar, however, we have little time to decide what to do, and who must go. We cannot leave the valley unprotected." Galdan waved him quiet.

"We will not. I think perhaps half our best fighters should go. That leaves behind many who can fight Mathkkra at need. We will be able to bridge armed near to Nalda. Remember Yslar, though. I doubt AEldra Power will work once Lyiadd's fleet arrives, even if he is not personally there. Even if none of them are, there will be men with Thullen brooches. Perhaps my own Power will be useless against those, perhaps not. We will no doubt learn."

"The brooches will not affect Nedaoans," Erken reminded him.

"No. Nor does bridging, not for many of our folk—not after this past year. Those are advantages. Against us, Lyiadd may remain in Yslar, and control his men and creatures with a focus. He will be able to remove tired men, send fresh ones to fight."

"An advantage to him," Corlin said. "But unless he is stronger than the tales say of the Night-Serpent, he cannot control ships by Power; a ship is too large to move about in such a way. Many ships must hold to a strategy of some kind, and that is perhaps an advantage to us."

"Since we have you, it is," Galdan said. "You've fought both Holthans and Sea-Raiders before. The Narrans know warfare on the seas even if they have not practiced it in long years."

"Another advantage to us, however small," Corlin said. "And another thing. However much he has changed this past while, Vess still sounds very familiar to me, and I doubt his personality is much different. We know Vess."

"Vess intends to lead Lyiadd's fleet against Nalda," Bendesevorian said. "What Lyiadd plans, I do not know. But if he does not choose to leave Yslar, he may well send Vess in his place."

"I know Lyiadd. As well as you know Vess." Ysian stood and everyone looked up at her—save Ber'Sordes, who was still writing at high speed. "Lyiadd will never go to Nalda until it is defeated. That would be to chance himself, and Lyiadd would never chance himself."

"He did once," Marhan growled.

"When Ylia fought him?" Ysian nodded. "His pride was always great; it must have been strong enough to overcome caution. I wager he does not let that happen again. Also, even though Yls is conquered, I doubt he believes her completely cowed. He may fear revolt, and what better time for a revolt than in his absence? Besides, why should he leave Yslar, when he can use a focus stone and control the battle through Vess?" She resumed her seat; Galdan stood.

"The War Council can spend more time tonight dealing with this matter; Ylia will be awake and able to contribute any knowledge she has. Those of you on the War Council, keep certain things in mind today as you think about our needs. Lyiadd may have more to send against us in Nalda—remember the creature that slew Ifney! I do not think he will simply rely on armsmen and ships, and he knows his Thullen brooches will only affect the AEldra among us—who are few indeed.

"Obviously, we cannot plan for all chances, and the Narrans will figure deeply in any plans we do make. But we should do what we are able, tonight, at once, to name difficulties and dispose of all such problems as we can."

Corlin pushed back his chair. "One thing. If Vess controls the enemy fleet at Nalda, he will be a weak link in Lyiadd's chain. Granted Vess has been with Lyiadd for some time now; granted he has skill as a swordsman, that he is brave. But he has no practical grasp of tactics."

"You cannot be certain of that," Erken began, but Corlin shook his head, silencing him.

"Consider: Nedao fought no wars when the Plain was still ours; you and I, Erken, we made an effort now and again to hold maneuvers so lads like your son would know how to plan a battle. Vess took no part in those. He took no part in that last battle against the Tehlatt—though there was little or no strategy involved in *that* fight. Since then, we have worked with our armed, we have planned and fought pitched battles against Mathkkra."

"But Vess—"

"Hear me out, my friend. We know certain things about Vess, even though he is no longer among us. He spent months asea and in Osnera, seeking aid from the Chosen. Once back in the Peopled Lands, he went to the Isles, and we believe he spent his time on the Isles. No man ever saw him on a Sea-Raider ship. He was part of the Three-fold attack on Yslar, but Lyiadd merely overwhelmed the AEldra with magic; there was no strategy involved in that." There was a silence. Corlin smiled grimly. "Erken, do you remember the first time you commanded fighting men in a battle?"

Erken grimaced. "Mothers, entirely too well. If Lyiadd entrusts Vess with Nalda, there is another advantage to us. Vess, for all his new Power and his pride, will find himself overwhelmed with detail before battle is ever joined. No matter if Lyiadd has planned Nalda's capture himself, to the placing of the least bowman; his plans still turn on the Narrans and on us. It will take a man of experience to control Lyiadd's plans, our movements, the constant shift and change of the fighting."

"But Lyiadd—" one of the Main Council men protested weakly. Erken shook his head.

"Lyiadd has little or no true battle experience, either. Mind, I do not think this will change the odds between us, not by itself! But it is, again, a small thing in our favor. We can do with such things. It cannot hurt us to remember that we know Vess. Yes, he now has Power, but fundamentally I daresay he has not changed much from Nala's bastard."

Less than you'd think, Father, Galdan thought savagely. He forced his hand to unclench. *I'd kill him, I will kill him, given the chance. For what he did to my Ylia, for the pain in her thought last night!* Something the Nasath had said came back to him, a saying among his own kind: Let three wish a man dead, and he is—though he still walks and breathes. He, Ylia—and Mal Brit Arren had condemned Vess. *Inniva's warp*, he thought, *to have been there, to see her stand down Mal Brit Arren himself, to have seen the look on his face!*

He was barely aware of men leaving; he somehow managed to respond politely when Lossana stopped to talk to him, though later he could not recall what either of them had said. There was a chatter of voices, bodies brushing by him. Then only he, Bendesevorian, his father and Ber'Sordes—the latter still writing, two folded papers at his elbow—were left in the council-room.

Erken called in the door-warder and sent him for wine, brushing aside Galdan's objection.

"Yes, it is early. You need it. Lady?" This as Ysian came back into the room.

"She still sleeps. I just—wanted to see." Erken nodded, shoved a cup into his son's hands and filled it. He turned to the Narran Ambassador then.

"My Lord Ber'Sordes, I think you need this also."

"I—yes. Thank you." Ber'Sordes drained the cup without tasting its contents, sealed the last of his letters and gathered them up in hands that wanted to tremble. Bendesevorian took the slender sheath of paper from him.

"Your Lord Mayor will have these before morning," he assured the Narran. "Sooner than a boat could reach the sea." Ber'Sordes seemed satisfied with that, but he was still anxious and pale when he left moments later. "I will deliver these messages and your own," Bendesevorian said to Galdan. "And then I will return here. But I am concerned about those in Yslar, and young Alxy is fretting himself ill."

"If you think it safe to go to Yslar," Galdan began. He shook his head as Bendesevorian would have responded. "Never mind. I know you have ways I do not; my mind is ready to worry any least thing, even the safest." He brooded on that, shook himself and pushed aside a second cup of wine Erken was urging on him. "Alxy should not worry so; even I was reassured by Geit's message."

He was also amazed by the tortuous route it had taken, from Geit in Yslar to Alxy: It had arrived late the previous afternoon. Four separate children—young and insignificant enough to be ignored by Lyiadd and his armsmen—had made the relay from the southern coastal city, passing the memorized oral message, until the last of them reached the unguarded northern village and the shepherd who could bridge. That man brought Geit's message to another, a herdsman summering his flocks in the mountains not far from the Ylsan border. He could not bridge, but his grandson could. The lad had appeared and spoke the message to Alxy as it had come down the chain from Geit: "Lyiadd's men still patrol the streets regularly. But they seldom take anyone away to the Sirdar's palace, and there are fewer of them. Those who patrol do not seem as worried for their hides as they once did. He is relaxing his guard, he is overconfident."

"Geit himself might be overconfident. But he should know

what chances; Lyiadd will only announce his war against Nar after Nar is his. I will warn them to caution, and to await further word. If they can aid us, they should have the right to do so."

Erken nodded. "One thinks of them as children; they are young but they have the right to fight for their own folk and their land. We can send that child messageless back to his village, if he is still intent upon return. Another thing, however, before Ylia wakens. We must agree, now, that she will *not* go to Nalda. What you told us is dreadful; she must have time to recover from that ordeal. And the House must not all be put in danger."

Galdan shrugged. "I agree with you, Father, you know that. But Ylia will never agree. *You* argue with her, I do not think I can, and I do not think you will win any more than I would."

"You will not win," Bendesevorian said. "Because she must go."

"She can't!" Erken protested.

"She *must*. Even if she were injured and unhealed, it would be necessary. Because she is Ylia of Nedao, because she carries that sword—Shelagn's weaponry—because she is Catalyst. I cannot say what will happen at Nalda if she is there. But if she is not— that would be truly disastrous."

"But she—" Erken's voice trailed away as Bendesevorian shook his head.

"Catalyst. As Shelagn was. And Shelagn was the cause of the Lammior's defeat and death, you know that. Because Ylia is who and what she is, Nedao is allied with the Dreyz, and with—well, at least two Nasath."

Erken shook his head. "Dreyz? What are Dreyz?"

"You call them naiads and dryads." Erken felt for a chair and sat, rather abruptly, and the Nasath smiled. "I am here because of her. Not much, I know. But any weapon is more than no weapon."

"You *found* her," Erken said somberly. "If you had not—" He shuddered, took the wine Ysian poured him and drank it.

"Do not think on it. I did, nothing else matters." He shook his head, looked at the packet of messages hanging forgotten in his hand. "I had better go find sleep, if I can. I will attend your War Council tonight and bridge to Nalda immediately after."

Ysian went with Erken but she left him in the main hall. Lisabetha was keeping watch over Ylia and she wanted fresh air.

And perhaps an hour or so with Golsat before she came back to sit with Nedao's sleeping Queen.

The Nasath stepped through the open door. Lisabetha sat in a thickly cushioned chair at the head of the bed, where she would hear if Ylia woke; her eyes were half-closed but she looked up at Bendesevorian's light step. Ylia lay on her back, one hand curled under her head, Nisana a small dark spot on her stomach. Bendesevorian smiled faintly as Selverra sat up, slid off the bed and tiptoed to the door. She contemplated him gravely as he knelt. "My mommy is home. Like you said."

"Yes. She's very tired."

"I know. Aunt 'Betha let me come into bed with her. I called to her with my thought, but she didn't hear me but Nisana did. *She* said to go to sleep." Silence. Bendesevorian, sensing what she wanted to ask, what she could not find words for in her child's vocabulary, patted her shoulder. He had never known a human child, and so had no basis for comparison, but he liked this one: Selverra was already a strong-willed individual, Ylia's and Galdan's but also her own person even at such a young age. The blend of Power she inherited from both parents would make an interesting mixture when she began to wield it.

"Your mother is all right, Selverra. Not hurt. Just very, very tired."

Selverra yawned. "I am, too. Chedra has baby Bren and she said I could hold him later, but they went to sleep again after Aunt 'Betha left. And I wanted to be sure my mommy was all right. So I better stay, in case she wakes up."

"Perhaps you had better," the Nasath replied gravely. He smiled as she hurried back across the room, planted a swift kiss on Lisabetha's cheek and pulled herself up onto the bed. Lisabetha covered them both; Selverra burrowed under the covers, little hands locked hard around her mother's arm.

He walked on up the hall. One of Ylia's women would be better than he to waken the child's nurse and let her know where Selverra was. It certainly wouldn't do to let the woman simply find her gone.

That accomplished, he turned into his own chamber, closed the door and felt his way to the bed. No point in lighting lights: He did not intend to be awake long enough for them to matter.

• • •

Over the next days, Bendesevorian went back and forth between Nedao and Nalda, serving as liaison between the two countries in their preparations for battle. He also made what search he dared of Yls and Yslar, and brought that news to the councils of both countries.

Counting Vess' ships, Yslar Harbor held a fleet of a hundred and fifty—as many from Holth and South Osnera as from the Isles—but only fifty sailed for Nar. Vess had taken the Sea-Raider vessel *Fury* for his own and it rode at the head of the fleet. Many hundreds of Lyiadd's armsmen gathered in the grounds of the Sirdar's palace, and strange lights and unpleasant odors emanated from the high towers there.

Nedao sent four companies of mounted armed down the Aresada—Corlin's and Erken's mostly, among them a scattering of Marckl's young men and women. Levren took a large company of bow in two Narran flat-boats. Brelian and Golsat would bridge to Nalda with the Elite Guard the day before Vess and his fleet reached the bay.

Marckl was named to lead the valley guard in Erken's absence and many of the strongest sword and bow were left with him. Lennet was one of those; Galdan had expected vehement objection from her but since Ylia's return she had been subdued. Perhaps it was as he and Levren both thought: The girl loved swords and fencing but she could not accept killing, however necessary it might be. It was just as well: Alxy could not be permitted to fight and he would hate it if Lennet went without him.

Ysian and Nisana were to remain in Nedao also: With their AEldra Power, they would be of little use in Nalda. Galdan planned to use them to bridge fighting companies back and forth to let them rest, if the battle went on for very long.

Ylia was pale and quiet during the War council, to no one's surprise. There was a faint mark on her right temple, barely visible against her hair. She looked tired and drawn but she told them what she knew readily enough and made her usual contributions to the discussions.

The meeting was a short one. Galdan left immediately with Corlin and Erken. Brelian was gone moments later and Levren had left early. Ylia found herself alone at the table. She got to her feet wearily, and stopped as she turned toward the door. Marhan stood there, waiting. "I'm going with ye, lass."

"With—" She dropped back into her seat. Marhan came over

to sit on the edge of the table and scowled down at her. "To Nar? Marhan, you don't have to," she protested faintly.

"Haven't slept enough yet, have ye?" he snapped. "Not thinking. I'll ignore the insult you just gave me, boy. Think I want to?" She shook her head. He wasn't making any sense, he was confusing her. But there was something wrong, something he was attempting to cover with his customary ill humor. "Don't want to. Don't ride comfortably, these days. Don't like your filthy bridging, makes me dizzy." He turned to spit, remembered where he was and refrained. "Have to."

"Why?" She reached for his hand. Marhan took it gently between his own.

"Thought I'd lost ye, lass. Know that?" She nodded. "You scared the old man. Don't do that again."

"I—won't."

"I know, lass. Not your fault, don't think it was." She looked up at him in surprise. "*Not* your fault," he repeated firmly. "That's how you think. Don't fuss at it. This other, though. I don't understand why. I have to go." He shifted uneasily on the hard table. "Never—never said anything about this before. No need. But—what he did for me. That man of yours."

"I remember what he did, Marhan," she said. Her voice sounded strangled.

"He said I wouldn't remember," Marhan whispered. "Lied." He tried to grin, but it wasn't much success. His eyes were too dark with remembered death.

"Oh, *Marhan.*" Her fingers tightened on his; he squeezed them, freed his hand and tried to glare, with even less success.

"Don't feel sorry for *me*, boy! Don't need it. Never did."

"I won't, old man."

"Well, then." He was silent again for some moments. "Because of that. Perhaps ye understand it better than I do. I *have* to go." His eyes glazed; he was staring beyond her shoulder— beyond in distance, leagues, time—she couldn't tell. "Not for Nalda. For what follows." He shook himself. "Nice thing, isn't it?"

"No." It wasn't; he'd hate it. "How long have you—? I mean—?"

"How long have I been sure that I was dead?" the old man demanded bluntly. "Since I was. He said I'd never remember, but I did. This other? Knowing? Since then. Sometimes I know things for no reason. I—Brandt spoke with me, once. I'm not mad," he added sharply.

"No. You're not." She gripped his arm hard, forced up a watery smile. "You're too foul-tempered and plain mean to go mad, Swordmaster." He stared at her, then began to chuckle. She grinned back; she simply couldn't help it. He did that for her, always. "I'd have asked you to come, Marhan, but I thought you'd be too frightened—"

That brought a towering snort. "Frightened! Huh! The old man doesn't fear anything, boy. Not for himself." He stood, helped her up. But just short of the door, he stopped again and she turned back toward him. "I'd kill him for ye, if I could, lass. For what he did to ye. Know that. If there were a way, I'd do that."

"Did to me. Did—?" She could feel the color draining from her face. Marhan caught hold of her arms as her knees gave way.

"Shhh. I know. No one said, no one thinks it. Don't fear that. I know ye do, but ye need not. *I* know. Because I know ye so well, and because there's a look to ye; the same one on our Lisabetha's face at the Caves, when Vess saw her. Think I don't notice such things?" He pulled her close and wrapped his arms around her. It was hard to breathe, his grip was so hard. "Does the boy know?"

"Galdan?" Her voice was muffled against his shirt.

"Aye. Does he?" She nodded. "We love ye, lass. Don't let it matter to ye, like 'Betha let it matter, it'll chew ye to rags." She pushed away, met his eyes and nodded. "I'm here, remember that."

"You always were," she whispered. He let go of her, opened the door.

"All right?"

"All right, Marhan." He walked away from her, moving across the polished tile of the hallway like a man with a purpose and no hellish secrets of hers and his own. Ylia leaned against the wall to watch him go. *Has to go. Gods. Poor old man. What new and dreadful thing is this?*

One of the first things they decided—or rather, one of the last that night—was that I should remain behind. In truth, I was content to do so, not the least because a cat in joined battle is a danger underfoot and even an AEldra cat of little use. Particularly here, where my AEldraness was not likely to be of use at all.

Beyond that: It was necessary that someone of Power remain in the valley—Ysian, I and Alxy could bridge armed to and from the battle, at need.

And there was Selverra, who was suddenly very worried indeed about her mother—who could blame the child?—and who needed company and comfort.

24

Three Narran boats came up the Aresada the next afternoon and left with a full load each—armsmen who would fight under Marhan, more of Levren's bow. The Lord Mayor had sent word for Ber'Sordes to remain where he was, and other messages for the War Council that he and his councilors would receive them gladly, whenever they came. The Narrans were hastily reinforcing three of their warships, fixing more catapults to the decks and adding iron rams below the waterline. It was all they had time to accomplish, for Lyiadd's fleet had passed the half-way point, and would reach Nalda by mid-morning, day after next.

The first of the Nedaoan army arrived at Nalda a full day beforehand, and Ylia, Galdan and their personal guard bridged to the south shore of the Bay of Nessea, across the water from Nalda's tall island, late that same afternoon.

Ylia hunched down in thick, soft sand, Galdan at her side, Eveya and the guard behind them. Eveya was already moving out, studying this new and unfamiliar terrain; Ylia was trying to shelter from the constant, chill wind. She gazed across the nar-

row arm of grey, choppy water. Nalda occupied the entire east
face of the island, its cottages, inns and shops hugging the shore
while prosperous houses and villas climbed the precipitous
wooded cliffs. Wharves and moles, docks and drydocks edged
the high tide mark. Shipwrights and drydocks occupied the only
other island, a much smaller and flatter one near the mouth of the
Aresada.

The little island was the site of furious activity: the *Shark*, the
Barracuda and the *Merman*—its original name had been *Gar*—
were pulled onto shore. A constant echoing clangor filled the
bay: the rams were not yet completed. They would be—had to
be—by nightfall. A faint reek of pitch and sulphur reached shore
whenever the west wind died down.

The beach was a long strip that ran from the point all the way
around to the Aresada and beyond it again to the north where it
merged into heavy marsh. Where she stood—half-way between
the point and the Aresada—it was broad, twenty lengths from
low tide mark to crumbly sandstone ridges topped with thick
forest. In some places it might be impassable at high tide. The
main island was almost sheer on its west face, forest on that side
a veritable thicket of trees, brush, undergrowth, brambles.
Lyiadd might send men against the west side of the island, but
they'd have to fire it first to get through.

Galdan squatted next to her, cloak snug around his shoulders.
"There'll be fighting here, I don't doubt, all the way down the
beach to the river. But Lyiadd's main target will be Nalda itself
and that won't be a landsman's fight. He'll be depending on his
fleet." He stood. "Brrr. The wind's terrible, goes right through
ye. Forgot how bad it was. Let's go find the Lord Mayor, get out
of this." They gathered their small guard together and bridged.

The Lord Mayor's Council wore an air of calm that threatened
to shatter on the moment, and the Lord Mayor himself—not long
from his sick bed—was no better. But there was an underlying
strength to men who fought the sea all their lives. And they had
once been Osneran, part of Osnera's armed fleet. There had been
other battles, a hundred and more years before, and some of
those had been fought in bays and inlets. A hastily assembled
War Council was working up strategies based on old tactics.

It was a simple plan, but it had often been effective for that
very reason; changes could be made at need and swiftly.

"The ships must come into harbor, either north or south of the island, so." The Lord Mayor rather self-consciously indicted open water on the enormous map spread across the table. "Both ways are narrow, but the north is near impassable at best, and we've had lads over there since your man brought us word. They're felling trees and snags, dragging them across the north inlet. They can't close it off entirely, not in such short time. So ships might pass through, but only one or two at a time.

"That would take a day or more; no one would attempt to win a battle in such a manner. In order to bring their fleet against us in less than a full day, they'll come through the south entry. They may send a ship or two north, to pincer us. We'll have lads ashore there, with catapults to make certain none reach us." He stirred uncomfortably, mopped his forehead and drank watery wine.

"You have no block for the south entry," Corlin said. "We have enough men to help you with that."

"No. We do not want to block the south entry; we want them to come through there. They must come here, between these two points. Kre'Darst's *Blue Conch* is waiting in a cove, here," he pointed, "and will warn us when they near. They will see him, of course, and know for certain we are aware of them."

"Lyiadd must know that anyway," Ylia said. The Lord Mayor looked at her unhappily.

"Aye. Even so. But not all of those aboard the ships have this man's Powers, have they? No," he answered his own question. "They are Sea-Raiders, Holthans, foemen we know. Seeing one fleeing ship, they may come at full speed, to take advantage of any surprise still left. Several of our ships will engage them just within the inlet, but in the face of their superior strength, our ships will back water as fast as the rowers can take them. An ordinary foe would see a frightened adversary that is beaten before it fights, and attack at speed.

"Once they are within the straits, our three warships will come out of hiding and ram whatever enemy they can. It will be difficult indeed to maneuver out of an attack formation, particularly in an enclosed place."

Erken shifted uncomfortably. This plan with its ifs and perhapses and goodly chances was not at all to his liking—even though his own plans had little more solid knowledge for a base. Then, too, he was no seaman, that was Corlin's territory. He cast a sidelong glance at his friend; Corlin looked interested in what he saw on the tabletop, but not overly concerned. Perhaps it could work, after all.

"None of this is graven upon stone, of course," the Lord Mayor said. "We all know how easily things go against plan, but we have allowed as much for that fleet's movements as we can. The bay and the inlet do limit their choices, a little." He emptied his cup, and Ang'Har, who hovered anxiously at his shoulder, refilled it. "If you have anything to add to this, please do. Our fathers' fathers once defeated a fleet four times their size with such a strategy, and it is the best we have."

Ylia leaned over the table to study the map. "This is more Lord Corlin's field. He would be more able to help you." she glanced at Galdan. "We would be better used on the docks, the beaches on the south shore, to see where to put our defenses. Lyiadd is certain to bridge armsmen here and we must plan to counter him."

"Good. Take any of the men here you need." He sighed wearily and let Ang'Har help him to his feet. "I fear I must rest again."

"I will come with you, if you'll permit," Ylia said. "Perhaps I can help." *Perhaps indeed!* she thought unhappily. The Power was still capricious, though it had returned to her. But the journey to Nalda had been all Galdan's work. She had reached for her own bridging and not found it; an hour later, on the south shore, it was there as if it had never gone. Even mind-speech came and went. *Time,* they assured her. Such close contact with Lyiadd's Power combined with Ragnolan herb had wreaked havoc with the innermost core of her Power. *Time! I haven't time!*

Hours later—cold and damp from walking Nar's beaches, bleary-eyed with the exhaustion of wielding the healing and arguing strategy and men with Galdan and his father—she had gratefully taken a cup of mulled wine and even more gratefully accepted the soft bed the Lord Mayor offered, with its heated stone for her feet and goose-down comforters.

It was still dark when Galdan woke her. She shivered out from under the warm bedding, dressed rapidly, dampened the sides of her hair and rubbed the loose ends off her face.

The Lord Mayor had hot tea, hot porridge, fresh bread and cold meat waiting for them. "Your War Council will be here momentarily. The boats came in late, the horsemen will arrive by dawn. By the way, the captain of the lead boat presents his compliments to your Lord Erken and says he hopes never again to navigate the lower Aresada by moon and torchlight!"

Ylia managed a smile; it was near impossible for her to be even civil at such an hour. But the Lord Mayor was nervous, showing it in a surfeit of speech. "We provided them what bedding and shelter we could; food for this morning, of course. Fortunate there were not more men." He *did* look nervous now; counting men on both sides must have done that for him.

"There will be more armsmen, fresh ones, if we need them," Galdan said. He never had Ylia's problem with early hours, and his smile seemed to go a long way toward reassuring the frightened Narran. "With your plan, we may do quite well as we are."

"We'll hope so." The Lord Mayor was busy then, offering tea and food to the four Nedaoans who came in. Erken was wet to the knees, and he and Corlin both looked thoroughly chilled. Levren showed little discomfort, though he left his cloak on until his second cup of Marran tea was gone. Marhan was grey with lack of sleep. Ylia opened her mouth, closed it again before she could say anything. Marhan had come with her, fighting his horror of magic and bridging. He'd take ill indeed any suggestion that he needed rest, and he'd never forgive her any outward show of concern before others. Lev—somehow, he managed to let the other men talk for him, managed to keep his eyes directed to his food or his cup, or otherwise off the Narrans. He was clammy-handed with it, she knew, but none of it showed. *Poor Lev. He's done so well, this past year or so, one forgets.* Marhan didn't forget though; he was running careful interference for his friend, as well as Golsat ever had.

"The weather," Erken broke a long silence. "How does it look?"

The Lord Mayor shrugged gloomily. "Who knows? It's been warm enough, days. Weather to shed cloaks but not heavy sleeves. Wind makes it cooler, of course. May be fog at sunrise —if there is sunrise. It's cloudy most mornings, this time of year."

"Could work to our advantage, on the water anyway," Corlin said. He downed a third cup of tea, set the cup aside and stood. "My thanks, that was needed. Erken, you had better dry your boots and breeches, you'll freeze out there otherwise." He held out a hand, gripped Galdan's, then Ylia's, then the Lord Mayor's. "I'll be on the *Shark*, I spoke with her captain, and it's all set." Corlin clapped Marhan's shoulder as he passed him, exchanged a "luck" with Levren and went out, taking the still cold-looking Erken with him. Galdan shook his head.

"What was he doing? Falling in?"

"You get wet, out there," the Lord Mayor answered simply. "Occupational hazard. Made worse by that wind. Right off the water. Winters—well, you can see why we put our houses on the lee side of the island."

There was dawn but no sun. A low fog blanketed the sand, the wharves and docks, the water itself, and a thick cloud cover obscured the sky. Ylia and Galdan huddled together at the base of the low cliff, well back from the point, a company of Erken's armed and their own guard around them. A short distance away were some of Levren's bow and beyond them another large company of armed. The rest of the Nedaoan armsmen and women were scattered around the bay, on the main island, but mostly along this southern beach. Bendesevorian moved tirelessly from one group to another, from the north point to the west face of the island, to the south point. He carried news; The welter of downed trees, snags, nets and lines across most of the north inlet had held through the night's high tide; the Narran warships were in place, ready to launch across the bay—and the enemy fleet would reach the Bay of Nessea within the hour. Far vision showed him another thing: companies of men waiting in the courtyards below the Sirdar's palace, clad for battle and armed. Lights had burned there the entire night.

Galdan caught Ylia's free hand in both of his as the Nasath went to alert Erken and the other commanders. "All right?" She nodded. "Ready?" She nodded again. He squeezed her fingers, let her have them back to wrap the cloak around her more snugly. Ylia shivered. Lossana's felt inner lining was an excellent idea, but it still wasn't enough against wind coming steadily off the sea. *Have to tell her that—if I get the chance.*

They walked up and down the sand. There was a hint of change to the air, finally; the least bit of warmth whenever the wind died down. Galdan caught Ylia's arm and pointed out to sea, and Eveya called out a warning. Kre'Darst's ship, running with all its sails, came hurtling across the bay. Ylia could see the strain on the near tillerman's face as he braced himself to bring the ship around and head for port. It cut directly across the path of twelve outbound Narran ships.

They were a brave sight, a pathetic sight: Twelve tubby little merchant ships, against an armada of hunters. But when the bow of the *Shark* rode above the waves, she saw the least gleam of metal casing. The ram itself was not visible, for it was well below the waterline and they had covered it with pitch.

A forest of black sails beyond the inlet caught her eye. As she watched, the neat formation turned, regrouped and came at the strait. Twenty ships made a tight line from point to point: all Sea-Raiders save the two deep-drafted Holthan ships in the middle. The remainder of the fleet came behind in three close lines.

It was a display of strength and navigational ability, intended to daunt. The Narran ships hesitated, came on more slowly, then men hauled down sails and lowered masts to the decks while other men shouted wildly and ran for the oars. The Narran line began to retreat, raggedly, and the enemy, with a whoop that must have been audible as far as the north inlet, came after them.

Another outcry, this one of rage, as one of the Holthan ships stopped abruptly in mid-strait. It had hung up on a submerged sandbar. The second Holthan reversed direction barely in time to avoid grounding. It fell in by itself behind the lighter Sea-Raider ships. The front line, still eighteen strong, closed formation. The Narran ships were pulling hard, but the Sea-Raiders were using full sail and were gaining on them by the moment.

Ylia could see Corlin aboard the *Shark*, high on the tillers' deck, vigorously waving a red flag on a long pole. The Narran warships suddenly came about and surged toward the enemy line.

"M'Lord Vess—look!" Gyseran, one of Vess' lieutenants— an older man who had been with Lyiadd all the years of his exile—pointed across the narrowing strip of water that separated their ships from the Narran cogs. Vess, his hands full of focus stone and his mind still ringing with Lyiadd's final orders, turned on him in irritation. "M'Lord, the Narrans are attacking!"

"So? Deal with it!" How, Vess wasn't going to try and tell him; ships were something Gyseran knew and so did these Sea-Raiders. Vess had enough to manage, between the focus, the land fighters and the *Fury*.

He glanced down at the main deck. Brit Arren was there, among his crew—in command under Gyseran and Vess. The man's gratitude was pathetic to see, though; he practically ate out of Vess' hand. Lyiadd had been furious, brushing aside Vess' assurances and certainties; it was more to placate his father than because of his own worry that he kept two Ylsan guard on Brit

Arren, kept him unarmed and forbade him access to the command deck.

Vess gazed along the shoreline, or what he could see of it from *Fury*'s place in mid-line. There were armed out there; he could see a few, sense others. That would be his most important task, bridging Lyiadd's armed to secure the land and deal with the Nedaoan army. Vess would have Lyiadd's aid via the focus stone, but only he was there to put men where they were needed most. His certainty he could manage that task had faded noticeably during the cold hours of early morning, and even more when they sailed into the bay.

Not for lack of skill or ability, no. But he had not expected so many distractions; even Gyseran bothered him with niggling details! The focus disturbed his thought by its mere presence, and Lyiadd had insisted upon constant contact. Of course, without such contact, he could not control the battle. Even Vess was willing to leave the overall control to his father. But he wished he had somehow not been given responsibility for the stone, and that it were not so awkward to hold. But Lyiadd said anything used to attach it to a cloak or arm interfered with the Power that flowed through it.

He looked up as men started shouting and the *Fury* jolted sideways as one of her fellow ships slammed into her. Gyseran was screaming furiously in one direction, Brit Arren in the other. "Separate, damn thee all for fools, separate! Give us room to maneuver!"

The Narran ships were moving faster than their bulk had indicated they could, faster than their earlier, sloppy motion had indicated. *Warships*. The Sea-Raiders recognized *Shark* as it swung out of line, then turned sharply to come straight at the south end of the line. As Gyseran paused for breath, Vess clearly heard the sound of splintering wood. *Shark* had rammed *Venom*, full amidships.

The second Narran was already coming in at an angle as *Shark* pulled back and *Venom* floundered to a halt. The rending, crackling sound of wood torn asunder reached them from the north end of the line. Men were shouting, screaming, cursing and the *Manta* listed badly. The ship that had rammed her was smoking but before Vess could open his mouth to point out that the cursed Narran was afire, he realized what the smoke was: The Narrans had a catapult, and were firing sulphur and pitch balls.

And suddenly the nine Narran ships were not retreating at all;

the smell of sulphur was overwhelming. The ship next to *Manta* was reversing when her sails went up in flames.

"*Do* something!" Vess screamed. Gyseran was half-way down the decks, bellowing orders above the outcry that was racing from ship to ship, trying to get the ships nearest him to haul sail and reverse. One of his subordinates was at the back railing, on the roof of what had been Mal Brit Arren's cabin, frantically signaling the ships behind to break formation and pull back, so the front line could break free of the Narran trap.

Smoke was so thick, it was nearly impossible for the second and third lines to see what the signals were—or that there was a signal at all, though most of them saw *Venom* listing heavily, trying to make shore. *Manta* had already heeled over and sunk. But retreat was impossible at the moment, though Vess could not see what they could: more Narran ships, hidden until now by the turn in the island and the bulk of the land itself, with skilled bowmen lining the rails. Men on board the northernmost of the ships in the second line died as a rain of arrows fell among them; sails smoldered and burst into flame as other bowmen shot arrows whose tips had been dipped in the sulphur and pitch mixture.

"Do something!" Vess screamed again. Gyseran, once again at his side, eyed him tiredly.

"M'Lord, the suggestion is yours. What would you like me to do?" Vess opened his mouth to speak; his hands twitched, and his father's lieutenant would likely have been dead the next moment, but the focus in his left hand grew uncomfortably warm and claimed all his attention. Gyseran had not been the only one who had heard Vess' cry.

Ylia's attention was drawn from the smoking, screaming maelstrom out on the bay by a sudden, fiercely intense burst of Power. Galdan dragged her around and shouted a warning to their following. "'Ware! Enemy foot!" Men stood between them and Erken's next company; more men behind them, and more further inland still. Up and down the shore, the cry was taken up, and Nedaoan armed moved to confront Lyiadd's armies.

With the shield that was her inner strength pierced as it had been and her Power so erratic, the child should have remained dangerously vulnerable for a long time. How could I have known how very little she needed to restore her sense of self?

25

It was a mixture of men who faced them: A melting pot of those Lyiadd had gathered to him—predominantly Holthan and Ragnolan, brown-faced men who wore short tunics and heavily padded, quilted cloth armor. Some were clean-shaven under bronze or copper round helmets, but most hid mouths and chins under red scarves. Many carried swords; more had lances and spears. As the aura of Lyiadd's Power faded, a few with throwing javelins ran forward.

"Nedao, 'ware!" Galdan bellowed. "Archers, now!" Swordsmen stepped aside to reveal half a dozen kneeling archers, arrows at the ready, another half dozen behind them. Spears and arrows passed each other; but most of the thrown weapons went into the sand; one struck a young swordsman, but fell aside, foiled by Nedaoan mail. Four enemy spearmen lay dead and the second rank of Nedaoan archers was in place. More javelin throwers came at the run. When another eight fell, the rest retreated.

Ylia waited impatiently in the midst of her guard, Galdan at her side. She didn't like hiding behind her guard. Three years of leading Nedao's armed had not lessened that sense, even though she knew it was necessary for her to oversee the fighting. But she couldn't even see what chanced beyond the double circle of sword until she found a windfallen tree trunk to climb.

Bendesevorian had insisted she be here; she would have insisted if he had not. But the rest was all riddles, as much to him as to her. *Catalyst. How am I to know when my time comes, and what to do about it?*

Out in the bay there was another loud, agonized, splintering crash: *Shark* had sliced through the next ship in the front lines. Or so she thought: The smoke was getting thicker by the moment,

238

making it hard to tell. Men were screaming and cursing out there, in Narran, Raider, Ylsan—and now and again she could make out the blaze of shot raining down on Lyiadd's fleet.

She couldn't *see*. *My fool Power, again? Or Lyiadd's toys?* There were no brooches among the enemy near her; she would know that. She ducked as a stone whizzed over her head; there were slingers at the rear of their lines. Their bowmen were bad shots, but the slingers had better aim and there were more of them.

Galdan dragged her down from her perch. "No sense making a target of yourself. Let me!" He clambered up where she had been, shouted, "Cover me!" The guard in front of him intensified its vigil, tightened rank. What a place to need total concentration! But his own answer to Baelfyr couldn't come otherwise. He stared intently at his fingertips, fought to keep balance on the teetering log. A tiny, wavering flame flickered at the tip of his thumb, spread across his fingers, and, as he summoned will and strength, grew. He swore as shot hurtled past his ear and he nearly fell. *Now.* Now or never, he couldn't bring it higher. He folded his fingers in to careful fists, held them together, concentrated. There was warmth there, becoming uncomfortable heat. He pulled his hands sharply apart, jerked his head back before the resulting fireball could take his beard with it. He cried out and flung it away from him with a snap: The fireball catapulted away from him. Fifty or sixty red-scarved men froze in terror for half a breath too long: The thing fell into their midst.

Nedaoan archers pulled back, arms flung protectively over their faces. Galdan fell backward off the log and Ylia took his place. "Sword!" she shouted. "Go!" Bowmen staggered wide and half the Nedaoan sword charged across the sand. There were few enemy left standing. But they would not surrender; the Nedaoans killed them to the last man.

"Gods and Mothers!" Ylia demanded as Galdan clambered back to his feet. "What was *that*?"

"Idea of—Bendesevorian's." He grinned and wiped his brow. "Effective as Baelfyr, don't you think?"

"Gods," she repeated fervently. "Look—there." She pivoted, pointed behind them. A company of at least a hundred—Ylsan and mercenary—badly outnumbered the Nedaoan. "There, next!"

"Half turn, west!" Galdan bellowed for reply. Their company

came back together and moved down the beach as quickly as they
could for the drag of dry sand.

There was no vantage point for her at first. The Osneran mercenaries and Ylsans were skilled and determined fighters. Many
of the Ylsans were using Power, instead of sword.

But they had no bow, and that told against them, finally: Nedaoan arrows cut them down from both sides, drove them back
into the cliffs. Ylia turned the Ylsan Power against them, Galdan
led the inner guard in a tight charge against the Osnerans. The
Osnerans fought back fiercely, then suddenly collapsed. Many
tried to scramble up the sandstone cliffs and most fell to Nedaoan
bow. Most of the Ylsans bridged; those who did not, died.

Ylia found a stump to climb and gazed across the bay. The
Holthan was still caught on the sandbar, and she could see men in
the water trying to work it free. There were only five enemy ships
in the front line now. *Shark* still threatened their southernmost,
but *Barracuda* was haring straight across the bay behind the Narran line, going to *Merman*'s aid. Ships in the rear enemy line
were spreading out, seeing the havoc ahead of them, and three
had turned for the docks. She thought she sensed Bendesevorian
there, but the Power was playing her false again, fading when she
needed it. *You still have eyes, fool; use them!* she admonished
herself tartly.

Power flared close to hand, bringing her around and Galdan
back to her side: Ylsan and Ragnolan swordsmen were racing for
them. Ylia leaped from her stump. For several long moments,
she could see nothing, could only hear shouting and swords, the
cries of the injured and dying. Galdan caught up a bow and
mounted her stump; he lit arrows with Wildfire as he launched
them.

The enemy broke, suddenly, a third as strong as they had
been, and the Ylsans bridged out, leaving their allies behind. The
Ragnolan mercenaries cried out in terror at finding themselves
suddenly deserted. As one man, they threw their swords aside
and fell to the ground.

Galdan swore. "Black hells! What do we do with prisoners?
We can't kill *that*!"

"Get them over to Nalda, bar them in one of the warehouses!"
Ylia shouted. It was hard to hear over the noise all around them
and out in the bay. "Let the Narrans watch them."

"Good idea." Galdan scowled at the huddle of red-scarved
mercenaries; they watched him nervously—those who were not

staring in alarm at his female companion. Forty pairs of black eyes—all that could be seen above the scarves—darted from one to another of their enemy, widening in fear and amazement as a swordsman turned out to be another woman. Grim-faced women, carrying bloody swords, seemed to send their morale even lower than Galdan's Wildfire had.

But Galdan took no chances, and when Bendesevorian bridged them across to the Narran docks, he also took ten sword and four bow with him.

"That's done, now where?" Galdan demanded. Ylia pointed.

"There, I think. Lev could use help. Wait." She pivoted, scanning the sand. She stopped abruptly. "What's he—black hells, what's he doing out there?" Galdan looked across the bay, but at first could not figure out what she was watching.

The rising wind was blowing the scattered rear line into the second line, creating even more havoc. Men hung from the lines, shouting at each other across the narrowing gap. Others fought to strap in the sails and lower the masts. The stranded Holthan ship was sideways to the incoming tide, and more men were in the frigid water, trying to pull her free. The mid-line of ships had its sails down and masts stowed, but their rowers could only hold where they were; there was no place to go until the third line retreated.

Debris from rammed ships littered the bay and washed ashore. Bodies and swimming men were everywhere. *Shark* was moving, taking the sharp veer to starboard that would put her ram through the bows of the next Sea-Raider ship in line. That ship worked its way forward, around the wreck of its southern neighbor. It turned, and *Shark* began to back away. Corlin was shouting up his archers; he was apparently running low on shot.

Fury had just pulled back and was partially protected by the second line, but the gap it left had not yet closed. Galdan saw what Ylia was gazing at, then: Vess. His inevitable black and silver were clearly visible; with the far vision, Galdan could make out more of him than he wanted to see. But Vess' habitual smirk was gone; grim purpose had replaced it and he held something in his hands that glittered red as a watery sun broke through thinning cloud cover. He was facing *Shark*, hands outstretched before him.

A high, painful scree knifed at Galdan's ears, an influx of Power left them ringing. A blood-red waterspout reared up where *Shark* had been only a moment before; the black-hulled ship that had been in pursuit of it was floundering as its rowers brought her about in desperate evasive maneuver. The waterspout was growing by the moment and the Sea-Raider vessel was directly between it and its prey. *Shark* swerved, and men ran to unlash the sails. The Narran line was edging back swiftly. With a blaze of light, the waterspout cut across the bows of the Sea-Raider vessel; the front two lengths of the ship simply vanished, and water spilled into the open end. Oarsmen threw themselves overboard. The tall swirl of blood-red water dwindled, was gone.

Vess stared open-mouthed at the broken and sinking *Dismay*. The Sea-Raiders aboard *Fury* were cursing and bellowing, and Gyseran could not silence them; his Ragnolans mumbled and rubbed their shoulder-stones in superstitious terror. 'Vess! What chanced, you have covered the stone again, I cannot *see*!' His father's thought reverberated through him.

'It took the wrong ship, Father! I *told* you, the Narrans are maneuvering too quickly! *Shark* is a warship, and Corlin of Teshmor commands it!'

'There are others ways,' Lyiadd replied grimly. And men cried out all along the shore, as a phalanx of Thullen came into being above them.

There, on the shore: Vess sensed Power there. Ylia's Power. His hands bunched into fists around the focus stone. How had she escaped Koderra? Galdan? Unlikely. It wasn't important. *Once this stone can reach him, he'll die*. As for her—he'd kill her himself. *Soon*. He smiled. He could feel her gaze, feel the hatred in her eyes. *All that for me, sweet cousin. Hate while you still can!* He laughed a little, and blew her a kiss.

"What's he doing?" Ylia whispered again.

"What? Don't worry him, come on!" Galdan gripped her arm; she turned as fingers bit into muscle.

"Ouch, don't! Look! That's *Fury*, isn't it?"

"I *see* Vess. He's too well protected to go against, don't even think it!"

"Not Vess," she said impatiently, and pointed. "Below him, on the bulwarks. See?" A red-haired man was edging his way around the outside of the ship, pulling himself along the network of ropes and grips, hand over hand. "It's Brit Arren. What is he doing?"

"I don't know. It isn't important—" But Galdan watched until Brit Arren swung himself around the stern, out of sight. He took

Ylia's arm again. "Don't worry about *him*, we've got—black hells, what's that?" But his sword was already at guard as multi-fold horror launched itself from the cliffs. Ylia tightened her grip on her sword; four Thullen broke away from the main body and dove at her and Galdan.

"Shelagn!" Her cry echoed across the water, bounced off the cliffs and came back again; silver fire seemed to tear itself free from her innermost being, to flare out through her arm and into the sword, leaving her momentarily drained and half-blind. Three of the four vanished, half a dozen arrows had the other. Three more came at them; the sword took one, Wildfire the others. Ylia shook her head, blinked dazzled tears out of her eyes and sheathed the blade. The rest of the pack had split, half going after Levren's archers, the rest soaring low toward the Aresada. Galdan flexed his fingers and laughed grimly.

"Next time warn a man to look aside, I could scarcely see to hit those I did!"

"Sorry!" Ylia had already turned back to the bay.

"Ylia, come *on*, now! Forget Vess!"

"Gods, Corlin! Galdan, they'll be killed!" *Shark* had moved through the Narran line and into the front line of the enemy ships to fill the hole *Fury* left, and was vigorously attacking Vess' command ship. Narran merchanters behind *Shark* kept their cata-pults working, making burning rubble of the ships on either side of *Shark*, keeping boarders few.

The Sea-Raiders were fighting hard, but only one of Vess' Ragnolan guard remained standing. Another knelt to tend a fallen companion, the rest were dead. Vess was turning back and forth frantically, focus stone gripped between his hands, and so he did not sense the silent figure on the rails behind him until Brit Arren closed the distance between them with a single leap and twisted the garrot around Vess' throat. The focus dropped and rolled across the deck.

"No!" Galdan stumbled backward, tripped over rubble and fell as Ylia's scream echoed across the bay. Power turned the air around her golden. "Damn you forever, Brit Arren, he's *mine*!" And she was gone. Galdan swore. Her cry echoed in his ears. He scrambled to his feet, stared out across the bay.

"Gods, no," he whispered as she appeared on the *Fury*'s deck. He would have bridged after her, but a hand restrained him. Ben-desevorian stood at his side. Sweat dotted his brow, cool as it was, and there were faint lines running from his nose to the corners of his mouth that had not been there earlier. "No. Wait. We can bring her back from here. Wait." Galdan shook his head unhappily, but subsided against the Nasath's grasp.

The focus stone fell from Vess' fingers as the rope looped down past his startled eyes and wrapped around his throat. He tried to get a hand under it, but Brit Arren had it too tight already. The one remaining guard shrieked in terror and fled. *Hit him—Power—* His vision was going, fast; consciousness would be next, he couldn't think! He lashed out with his feet, his elbows, fighting wildly, but the Sea-Raider laughed, dodged with ease and pulled the rope a little tighter.

He staggered then and nearly fell, as the guard who had been kneeling, forgotten by his wounded companion, launched himself sideways and caught Brit Arren's legs. Brit Arren cursed, kneed the Ragnolan in the chin, but the damage was already done. Vess forced his fingers under the garrot, half-twisted away from his would-be assassin and out from under the rope. A dagger was in his hand, pressing the Sea-Raider's throat.

"I was right not to fully trust you, wasn't I? I see you managed without access to the stairway and without blades, I commend you—dead man!" The point broke skin. Brit Arren looked at him coldly. His eyes widened as movement directly behind Vess caught his eye. Vess, sensing Power, tensed and began to pivot. He screamed as Ylia's dagger sliced across his back. He would have fallen into Brit Arren, but Ylia snatched hold of his shoulder and whirled him around.

"Greetings, *sweet cousin!*" she whispered. "By all the gods there are, but it pains me to kill you quick!" Vess screamed again, this time in rage; he brought up his dagger to block her, to hurt her if he could. But he was half-choked, bleeding profusely, and the Power wouldn't answer him.

Ylia slashed two-handed across his throat, scrambled back as blood shot across the upper deck, and Vess sprawled across the deck, dead before he ever touched it. Brit Arren stared at her blankly across the body; she, badly blooded, gasping for air, stared back. She was the first to recover; shouts on the lower deck and pounding feet warned her. "Here!" She caught up Vess' dagger and held it out; he ripped it from her fingers as he sped past. Ylia cast Vess one final look and glanced at the fallen Ragnolans. Neither seemed disposed to fight her.

Shark's bowmen were still shooting across the *Fury*'s decks;

Sea-Raiders crouched in the bows, waiting a chance to board her. But down on the main deck, twenty Ylsan swordsmen pelted toward the raised afterdeck. 'Galdan!' she sent urgently. Thullen stones, Lyiadd's focus or her own capricious Power, the bridging was gone again.

And an urgency beyond oncoming armsmen was pressing her. She shoved hair off her forehead, wiped her eyes clear. Brit Arren was standing near the bulwark, staring blankly across the deck of the *Fury*, and she realized in sudden horror that the focus stone was in his hands. "Mal Brit Arren, drop that thing!" He half-turned. The stone was beginning to change; he was also. She launched herself across the deck, threw herself on him and toppled them both over the side. The stone flew from his hand and went over with them.

It was a long way to the water, and she was somehow underneath when they hit. The air she'd taken in was driven from her, and they went below the surface, below the *Fury*'s mainbeam, down into blacker water. She saw the focus stone drift by on its way to the bottom. A strong hand caught at her cloak and dragged her upward. Her head broke the surface, she rubbed hair and water out of her eyes, choked as a wave broke over them.

"Watch the waves!" Brit Arren shouted against her ear. She nodded, but as she fought for air, the bridging caught them and hauled them ashore.

"You had no right!" Brit Arren made no attempt to stand, seemed to take no note of the sudden change of surroundings, the armed Nedaoans surrounding him—of anything but Ylia, who was still coughing up water. But at that, she sat upright and glared back at him.

"I *warned* you, Brit Arren! He was mine, I told you that! You tried, you failed. Should I have let him kill you first?"

"You interfered, I could have taken him!" he bellowed. Was this the same woman? The nervous, tentative air was gone as if it had never been. He barely noticed; his own formidable temper, buried for so long under grief and hopelessness, ignited. "I had it all worked out—!"

"He was mine, *you* had no right!" Ylia leaped to her feet, quarrel forgotten as Galdan shouted a warning. Where the focus had fallen, the water was boiling furiously; Power roared skyward. *Fury*'s men ran for the oars, risking Narran arrows in their haste to pull the ship away from this new terror. And the sky, which had been clearing rapidly with approaching mid-day, went dark: Lightning burst over the ships and wind howled through the bay, drowning even the thunder. As suddenly as the storm began, it was gone. The sea steamed where the focus stone had gone to the bottom.

Mal Brit Arren got slowly to his feet. He eyed the company around them warily. Galdan watched him impassively. There was no outward indication on his clothing, any more than there was on Ylia's, but Brit Arren had no doubt he stood before Nedao's King. His enemy.

"You are Mal Brit Arren, captain of the *Fury*?" Galdan asked.

"I'm Brit Arren."

"Then you are my prisoner," Galdan said.

"Prisoner," Ylia spat. She sheathed the dagger she'd held even when she hit the water. "He'll think prisoner!"

"He did nothing except help you," Galdan said mildly. Ylia glared at him. "Think on it when your brains overcome your rage, will you?"

Brit Arren had turned back to watch the ships. A sudden prickling ran over his skin. It had nothing to do with soaked clothes, salt water running down his neck from dripping hair, soggy boots or his present company. A pure fierce joy filled him and he turned to Galdan on impulse. "Do you want *Fury*? The other ships? Let me back out there."

"Let you out there. Why? Give me a good reason, I'll listen," Galdan said. Ylia stared at him in astonishment.

"Look." Brit Arren pointed. *Shark* had pulled back but there was still heavy fighting aboard *Fury*. *My* men. He ached with pride. "Look at them. They're killing Lyiadd's armed and throwing them into the bay. Let me out there. You can sink us all, but it will cost you. And there is no need. I owe no loyalty to Lyiadd. He will kill us because of Vess, or merely because we have failed him. Or you will kill us. We have nothing to lose." Galdan met his eyes, searchingly. "Let me out there. I can clear those filthy Ylsan sorcerers from our decks. My men can. But they need a leader."

"Go." Galdan held out a hand. Brit Arren gripped it. He hesitated, then faced Ylia. She gazed back at him with dark, hard eyes. But she met his hand half-way, then stood aside without comment as Galdan bridged him out to the *Fury*. A wild cheer rang across the water.

*So many deeds had been done for ven-
geance: For Brendan's death; for Lyiadd's near-
death. For Brandt's death, and Scythia's, against
the Tehlatt. Ylia's revenge against Vess and
against Lyiadd with Vess' death—and that
began the cycle once again.*

*For Ylia had in turn cost Lyiadd his only son:
Weak, vain, ruled by his loins instead of his
brains. Lyiadd never let himself see those flaws
—how often do human fathers see such flaws in
only sons, or sons of their age?*

26

Deathly silence held the topmost chamber of the Sirdar's palace: Lyiadd, his face ashen, stared into the oil basin. The focus
stone was on its way to the bottom of the bay, the oil a blank
sheet, but what was left of Vess still filled his vision. *My son! She
has dared!* "NO!" His outraged cry shook the stone walls of the
chamber. Tears spilled down his face, and he didn't even know
he wept. *Focus, find it, kill them—kill them all!* Power lashed
out: The stone was too far down in water for him to retrieve it,
but it reacted to his fury: Power set the mud around it to boiling;
Power erupted skyward, flame from the sea meeting the fullness
of his wrath: Lightning, thunder, a howl of wind.

He couldn't sustain it; couldn't, in his blind rage, control it. It
faded, was abruptly gone. Lyiadd fell back against the wall, covered his face with his hands and whirled away to lean against the
rough stones.

His two generals stood nearby, shifting nervously; they'd seen
little. It had been more than enough. "Barbarian," Delall whispered; Ylia's attack on Vess had shaken him badly. Ayater nodded faintly.

Marrita came alive at the single word, laid a tentative hand on
Lyiadd's arm; he shook it off. She set her jaw, touched him
again. "Beloved, do not."

"I will *kill* her, I will kill them all," he whispered, so softly even she barely caught the words. The generals, who could only see his profile, huddled together and away from him.

"Lyiadd—" He turned as she touched him again. This time he did not shake her off. "I am sorry, beloved."

"No." He shook his head, stopping her intended reply. "No. For me, perhaps, yes. Not because of Vess. *You* never liked him."

"No." No point to deny it. "That does not make it I wished him dead."

"Because of me only," he whispered. She shrugged.

"Is that not reason enough?" Her fingers tightened on his arm. slid down to his wrist. "Where is the focus? Can we retrieve it?" *We*, she said; *you*, she meant. She could only do certain things through a focus at such a distance. She could not control the jewel itself, not after a morning such as this. They had bridged men, whole companies of them; had bridged them up and down the beach. She had backed Lyiadd, helped him sustain Vess' Power when confusion and overwork caused it to go sporadic on him. It had been her Power, alone, that had brought together so many Thullen in full daylight and bridged them to the battle.

There was still strength in her. But for the first time in more than three years, she knew it wasn't bottomless.

Lyiadd was sweating; his shirt stuck to his breastbone; hair clung to his brow and tears still ran down his face. She could not sorrow for Vess' death, not even for the manner of it. But she'd wish Vess alive for Lyiadd's sake. If she could.

Lyiadd was concentrating, eyes closed. He opened them again, leaned back against the wall. "We cannot retrieve the stone. It lies nearly seven fathoms down, under a silt of mud. The water protects it from my efforts—but also from hers, if she was fool enough to take *that* one. Later, perhaps, we can use it again. Not—just now."

Marrita let go of his hand, walked over to the bowl and sank down on her knees beside it, wrapping her arms around it as far as they would reach. "I can activate this—for a few moments at a time." *Not for long.* She did not add that; they both knew it. She knew, Lyiadd was rapidly learning, that distance made even his Power awkward to wield. All the same, considering the total mess the Narrans had made of their fleet, she was glad Vess had taken the *Fury*, that she and Lyiadd had remained safe in Yslar. The bowl cleared and showed her an astonishing sight.

"Lyiadd. Come, quickly, look at this! It is not Ylia, *or* her man with his mountain Powers, who is thwarting us out there. Not only they, there is another Power, look!"

"Where?" With a curt gesture, Lyiadd motioned his generals to observe and knelt beside her.

"See." Silence. The bowl cleared a little more, showing fighting everywhere, and something else: a man—the shape and sense of him was blurred. "Can you not feel him? It is the Nasath, Bendesevorian. It must be. He has returned to aid them." Silence again. "And he has revealed himself to us, deliberately. Because otherwise, we could not see him at all."

Lyiadd shook his head impatiently. "One Nasath, what is that? Let me see the bay!" Marrita closed her eyes and tightened her grip on the rim of the bowl.

There was fighting aboard the *Fury*; the ships that had flanked it were both on fire. All along the south shore, Thullen harried Nedaoans and their enemies both, without regard to kind; near the mouth of the Aresada, some of the Holthan mercenaries had made truce with those they fought, and bowmen of both sides were shooting at the flying horrors.

"Pull the men back," Ayater said. His voice was high and thin in the silent chamber. Lyiadd glowered at him, and his man hesitated, but only briefly; Ayater had been with Lyiadd for long, had never feared to give his opinion. Nor would he now. "Do it, Lord! They are not without number; you will need them for the next fight!"

"Next?" Lyiadd's voice was ominously controlled.

"Lord, matters have gone beyond our plans and this battle is beyond repair; bring back your armsmen, your creatures, what of the mercenaries you can salvage. The fleet is half-destroyed, and as for the other half, it will not be long behind."

"No."

"The Nedaoans are not affected by the brooches, save one, and she does not only fight with Power." He could have bit his tongue, but the words were beyond recall. Lyiadd made no sign he had heard them. "Lord, pull back now, salvage all you can, and choose another site for battle. One you will win." Silence. They looked at each other, at Lyiadd, across his head to Marrita.

"No." Lyiadd's jaw was set, his eyes grim as he bent them to the bowl. "Not yet. One last thing. And then, if there is another battle, they will come to it fewer, and weakened—and afraid indeed!" His right hand dropped down to grip Marrita's. "Go!"

She bit back a sigh, cast Lyiadd's generals a resigned look over his head and complied.

The oil darkened, fogged, swirled and suddenly cleared, showing them the Bay of Nessea, and the battle that still raged there.

There had been a brief lull in the fighting after Lyiadd's fury broke over the fleet; Thullèn were everywhere, though by now many of them were down; Ylia, Galdan and their guard had moved down the beach, fighting mercenaries, pushing through those to deal with the Ylsans behind them. But the Ylsans once again bridged away.

There had been fighting on the docks, but Bendesevorian bridged over to find Kre'Darst and his men rounding up the Holthan crew. *Merman* had sheared its starboard oars and blocked its escape from one side while the *Blue Conch* came up from the other.

The Nasath rested before bridging back. He was beginning to worry: After that brief, furious outburst of murderous rage, Lyiadd had made no overt move against them. It had been too long; Lyiadd and Marrita must be planning, setting that plan into motion. He could not guard against all chance, and he was very worn.

He still grieved for Ylia, but it had been her presence in Koderra, and that only, that had brought about so much of what had happened: Vess' death, Brit Arren's switch of allegiance and with him, most of the Sea-Raiders. Things touched against each other in strange ways when a Catalyst joined them.

He gazed across the bay: Mal Brit Arren had secured *Fury*. Ylsans lay dead on her deck, a last Ragnolan flailed wildly as someone threw him overboard. The other ships across the middle line had been retaken and Brit Arren balanced precariously on the narrow railing above the afterdeck, clinging to the lines, bellowing orders to the rear line. The seaman at his side was echoing his words with signal flags. Three of the four ships left seemed disinclined to meet his demands, but neither did they seem willing to engage him; as one, they backed water, moved apart and turned. They went no further than the stranded Holthan, then turned back to wait.

Brit Arren had a wary eye for the sea and he could not be certain how much the ships had drifted since he'd boarded *Fury*.

Gods of the black depths, but that is no way to board a ship! he thought fervently. How far *had* she drifted? He had no intention of allowing his ships to stay anywhere near that drowned stone; whatever hellish magic was in it—whatever had burned the clouds, a ship would be no proof against *that*. Another signaler came hurtling across the deck at his command, flags in hand, and they warned the vessels to either side. With the rear line out of the way and the first line reduced to debris and two half-burned shells, it would be simple to peel off and separate.

And so it proved, even with the stiffening breeze that increased the chop, with the tide coming in, and with smoke thick from the two burning ships on the front line. Fortunately the wind blew most of the smoke eastward, but when that died, it fell back thick around all of them.

The northernmost ship of the third line came up into place and turned to port on signal; on the south arm, *Deadly* turned toward the beach. Another beat, and two more ships peeled away, pivoting and following the lead of the outer ship. Beat: *Fury* swung south as men strained at the oars; *Threat* went north.

If Nedao's King didn't warn those Narran ramships, Fury may well join that stone on the bottom! Brit Arren thought worriedly. But it was impossible to see where *Shark* was. They found her as they circled the burning ships and turned back into a line. *Shark* was there, on the south arm of the Narran line, *Barracuda* on the northern end.

Brit Arren leaped down from the afterdeck, ran forward to clamber the short front mast and clung there, staring across floating debris. A Nedaoan on *Shark*'s main deck gazed back at him. He held up a hand, palm out, as the ships passed each other. Brit Arren sagged for the space of one deep breath; pulled himself together again. Word had gone over. But that was Teshmor's Lord Corlin!

Brit Arren turned back to his crew and gave them the order to sit at the oars and wait. He could have laughed at it all, suddenly: Lord Corry himself! And it seemed that Lord Captain Mal Brit Arren was going to live to tell the tale.

Galdan spoke against Ylia's ear: "Pull back! Count of three!" Fighting had been heavy here, and they'd both been in the thick of it for a long time. She let him guide her back by her left shoulder, twisted aside as one of Erken's lads slid forward to take her place. "All right?" he shouted.

"All right!" she shouted back. He eyed her critically. He hadn't realized how unlike herself she had still been until they bridged her back from the *Fury*. Until she had killed Vess.

Fortunately the day had gone warmer and the sun was out: She was still soaked from her unexpected dunking in the bay.

Those they were fighting broke suddenly; the Nedaoan armed sprinted after them, bringing Ylia and Galdan in their midst. Someone in the fore shouted warning, and Nedaoan and Narran armed further down the beach turned to catch the enemy in a neat pincer. Ylsans bridged hastily away; several Ragnolans broke and ran for the water. None of them made it; the remainder—seven men in all—fell to their knees and waited for death.

"There can't be many more of these," Galdan said as he gazed down at them. "I wish *someone* spoke their language, though." He sighed. "Someone besides Corlin, before anyone says it again."

Ylia shook her head. "The Narrans must be running out of room. Has anyone kept count?" Shrugs. "Doesn't matter. We—" Galdan waved her silent, tipped his head back, shielding his eyes with his sword.

"Thullen," he announced tersely.

"Bow, at the ready!" Levren was nearby; she could not see him, but his voice was as unmistakable as the red-fletched, red-shafted arrow that killed the first of them. Ylia fell back a pace, sword ready, but there was no need: One spiraled into the bay, sending a geyser of water two lengths into the air; the other two went down moments later.

"They're a bother," Galdan said. Someone laughed. "However he intended them, they're a bother. Man can't see them, the way they pop in and out."

"Well, I can't see them any better," Ylia said dryly, "and I doubt Eveya or Sartha, or any of the other *women* can, either." Galdan laughed. Bendesevorian bridged into their midst moments later; one of the Ragnolans screamed and the rest fell flat. The Nasath paid them no heed: He was listening, testing the air. "What?"

"There's—something," Bendesevorian whispered. "They're about to try something, can you feel it?" Ylia shook her head.

A swimmer out in the bay shrieked in terror, a towering cry cut off abruptly as the waves above the focus stone erupted once again. Water began to spin, and the sky above the growing whirlpool darkened. Men, debris, bodies—the burning wreck of the *Venom*—all were dragged down. The greedy suck of the water rose above all other sounds. "Ah, gods and Mothers," Ylia whispered. "No!" The Ragnolan prisoners flung themselves frantically toward the cliff base, huddled together in a terrified clutch, not daring to look as the sky went from pale washed blue to deep purple. Shadow spread across the water, touching now on ships that were hauling wildly away from this new danger.

There were no broken ships left out there now; nothing but a vast whirlpool that dragged at everything near it. And far over-head, in the very midst of the darkness, *something* was forming. "No," Ylia whispered again. "It's—that *thing*! He's—made an-other. But the size of it! It will have us all!" She stumbled in the thick sand and would have fallen but for Galdan.

All fighting stopped; enemies turned from each other to gaze in fear at the bay. The whirlpool lapped greedily after the *Fury*; the shape overhead writhed against some unseen bond. Dull red light ran in a thin line from the vortex to the darkness, feeding it.

A deep growl came from the sky, growing by the moment. Then Bendesevorian's joyous shout suddenly topped it, momen-tarily drowning even the suck of water out in the bay. He ran past the Nedaoan armed and into the open to cry out in his own lan-guage. Ylia pushed through the Inner Guard, Galdan at her back, in time to see him surrounded by Nasath. He spoke quickly, words she could not understand, but the urgency needed no translation. Twenty heads lifted to where Bendesevorian pointed. The thing there was growing by the moment: It stared back at them out of blood-red eyes, and *something* came free.

Twenty-one Nasath simply vanished. Someone behind her wailed in despair as their last and only defense disappeared. "Wait!" Galdan bellowed; his own hand stabbed toward the sky. Flickering, golden light surrounded the darkness, pressing it in-ward. The whirlpool faltered; there was half a length more dis-tance between it and *Fury*'s retreating prow. "See!"

"Look to your backs!" Marhan roared, overtopping him easily. "Mathkkra!" Galdan thrust Ylia behind him and worked his way to the Swordmaster's side. It was visibly too light for the crea-tures' liking, but dark enough under that cloud that Lyiadd had loosed. Mathkkra poured down the sandstone in a wave, and flung themselves against the hated Nedaoans. On the ledge above them stood three red-clad shamans, acolytes crouched at their feet.

Ylia was still vibrating from Bendesevorian's outcry. Galdan shoved her into the very midst of the guard and took up his bow once again. She saw him teetering on a pile of rock so he could fire over the heads of the guard, saw the guard around both of them, fighting for all their lives. Two of her women fell and she thought she heard Eveya cry out—*Eveya fallen, ah, Mothers, no!* But the gap was sealed before she could be certain. Something ran light-foot across her inner being; she spun about, eyes on the sky.

The Nasath were fighting their own battle up there: The thing began to shrink, ever so little. Mathkkra squealed and gibbered as the light increased. But then certain of the faint points of light that opposed it would be scattered, or pressed back, and the thing swelled again. The whirlpool spread and shrank with it but the connecting thread of light never wavered. *The focus stone was exposed. If they could destroy it*—! But she could not and the Nasath had not attempted it. She groped under her cloak to touch the horn. No. It was not yet time for that.

Someone caught hold of her arm and was pulling her along, keeping her in the relative safety of the guard's protection. She stumbled, nearly fell as her heel caught on a small, fallen body; the hand hauled her upright by main strength. "Thank you!" she shouted.

"Lady!" someone shouted back.

"Look!" someone else cried. Eyes were dazzled as a blaze of light burst into the sky directly above them.

Eya. "They are ours!" Ylia cried out. Bars of red and blue and golden light, points and luminous bands of silver swirled, broke, formed and broke again overhead. The Folk rose in a single glorious pillar, arced over high above and plunged into the very heart of the vortex.

Water shot high; myriad lights gave it an iridescence as it cascaded back to the bay. The Folk, an intertwining ribbon of sound, color and motion, rose above it. In their midst, borne upon a pillow of water, was Lyiadd's focus stone. Almost before Ylia could realize what it was, it vanished in a whirl of fast-moving light. The thread of Power that connected it to the sky-born monstrosity shrank, thinned, faded. Was gone. For one brief, uncertain moment, she thought she saw the stone—a dull grey lump of beach pebble—waver mid-air. Light enclosed it again, hid it, and it vanished.

The far-spread ring of pinpoint golden lights closed in, driving darkness before it. Until it was gone, and there was only pale blue sky, and high overhead, the sun.

Mathkkra screamed in sudden terror. A wave of Lyiadd's Power swept over them, taking Mathkkra, what remained of the Thullen, Ylsans and southern mercenaries with it. Far out in the bay, near the mouth of the southern inlet, a deserted Holthan ship rocked as the incoming tide washed it to and fro.

But near the mouth of the Aresada, an army—Lyiadd's reserve Ylsans, fresh Holthan and Ragnolan and Osneran mercenaries—waited. The battle was not yet over.

"Lyiadd?" Marrita somehow gained her feet, staggered around the seeing bowl. Lyiadd had not moved since *they* unmade the stone; it had been her Power that bridged what was left of their armies and sent reinforcements to the river's end. Movement beyond Lyiadd caught her eye; his generals hovered there uncertainly. "Not your fault, we'll talk later. Go!" They went, hurriedly, before she could change her mind or Lyiadd could rescind the order. She braced herself, touched his shoulder. "Lyiadd?"

"I am all right," he whispered. "What was that, what did she do?" That sound had torn through him, left him huddling on the floor, hands vainly clapped to his ears. He'd felt everything disintegrating out there and had not been able to fight it. Ayater had been right, they should have pulled back, saved their strength for another day. It *would* be another day, now; they would both need rest before they dared try again.

Not that it made any difference to the end result. No. It merely extended the time that was theirs, not the outcome.

"Could you not tell?" Marrita had sensed them—had even *seen* them, for one brief moment. But then, they were no longer trying to hide. "The Guardians came to Nedao's aid." She fell silent as Lyiadd brought his head up; he stared at her incredulously, then began to laugh. "And the Folk," Marrita overrode him loudly. The laughter ceased as abruptly as it had begun.

"Catalyst," Lyiadd whispered. Somber eyes met Marrita's. "It cannot matter, not in the end." But for the first time, he sounded uncertain. A little. And it chilled her.

"No, it cannot." She could have believed it herself, hearing her own calmly assured voice. "Next time—next time, we will not try to control the battle from such a distance."

"No." *Vess. My son.* He had nothing of him, not even his body; that had gone overboard when Mal Brit Arren took back the *Fury*. The whirlpool had it, moments later. "No matter," he whispered, unaware that he spoke aloud. "There will be another son."

Marrita's free hand clutched at her skirts; the chill deepened and nearly stopped her heart. *A son—but not mine, who cannot bear sons*. She stared after him as he stood, walked unseeing from the chamber. *He cannot mean that. Another son*. But she could be certain of nothing. Nothing save the death that was regrouping on the south shores of that bay, the death that waited for her—and for him.

She would not tell him; he would never believe it. It would not matter to him; he would do no single thing different, knowing it. If he believed. *My knowledge, my burden*. She steadied herself against the wall, followed him out. In all the years since she had left this palace to follow him for the first time, she had never felt so alone.

She had brought together Folk and Nasath, Narrans, Sea-Raiders and Nedaoans, who could have foreseen such a thing? More than we could have foreseen that Nesrevera's arguments would bear fruit at that very hour, and that twenty of their kind had defied their Elders' decree to step across that threshold separating their world from the Peopled Lands. Or that once again it would be Ylia's blade and not her Power that so harmed the Power ranged against us?

27

Nalda was a hill ablaze with lights for most of the night, as deliriously happy folk celebrated. Even those Nedaoan sword who ranged the docks, keeping watch over the six black-hulled Sea-Raider vessels tied there, laughed and joked and traded wine-jugs and song with those aboard the ships.

Here and there, through the streets or above them, a few guards were posted, though Bendesevorian had assured them this was not necessary. He had not only *seen*, he and several of the others had gone to verify what he *saw*. Lyiadd and Marrita would not come against them this night. There was a strong allied force strung across the beach, north and south of Lyiadd's army. Three Sea-Raider ships and *Shark* blocked the mouth of the river, and Nasath watched there too.

The Lord Mayor's doors were open, and wine casks had been set by them so that anyone passing could have a cup, in celebration of the victory of the Battle of the Bay of Nessea. But inside there was a meeting somberly at odds with the celebration without. The Lord Mayor was there, surrounded by his own Council; Ylia and Galdan, with most of their own War Council; Bendesevorian, his cousin and the two older Nasath who had defied the Elders' thousand-year order; Eya and three of her Council, these last uncomfortable indeed at being inside a building. And, at

257

Ylia's left hand, at her own request, Lord Captain Mal Brit Arren, to represent their new ally.

The first flush of victory gone, the newly renamed Lord Captain was eyeing his so-called comrades uncertainly, hoping his face hid what he was thinking. None of *these* had any reason to love his kind. But at the moment, he was very aware of what he had deserted. Lyiadd was no one to cross, and in the heat of battle, heady with Vess' death and the scent of freedom, he had done precisely that. And Lyiadd lay squarely between Nalda and the Isles.

Ah well, he thought uncomfortably, it would have been an impossible situation, whatever he did; perhaps this way some of his men might survive this wizard's war. Whatever became of him. But he must have been mad to swear faith to Nar, and worse, to join hands and take oath with a woman!

These others at the table: Women, not only *her* but another, and she full Ylsan by the look of her. Nedao's King, but unlike any Nedaoan he had ever met, this one had Power. *Her* doing, perhaps, or that of one of the others, beyond him—it made his scalp crawl, even after all he'd seen of sorcery these past years, to look beyond Galdan at the creatures there: Guardians! Folk! Landlocked myth, all of it, but there they sat nonetheless, and he in their midst! Well, he wasn't the only one nervous about *them*. The old man at the Nedaoan King's elbow—Swordmaster, wasn't he?—looked like he'd be anywhere away from magic, looked unhappily aware that he was surrounded by it.

"We cannot let them recover." Lord Corlin spoke up from his place half-way down the table. "Nothing was destroyed but a stone—and Vess. Against what is left, that is not enough. There is a fresh army out there, and we know that is not all Lyiadd's armed."

"No," the Lord Mayor said uncertainly. He was out of his depth, but he had pledged Narrans to the fight to come, and felt obligated to say *something*. "Once that army is gone—do we take Yslar?" Erken shook his head.

"Not sense," Brit Arren found himself saying, though he'd intended to keep his mouth shut for present. "Beyond Lyiadd's Power, there are seventy more of *our* ships in Yslar Harbor. There are also Ylsan ships, those of the Osneran mercenaries. We haven't the strength of numbers to attack Yslar, and I cannot yet swear to the allegiance of half the men of *my* kind there."

"Not Yslar," Galdan said flatly. "As the Lord Captain says,

not sense." In spite of himself, Brit Arren smiled faintly. If this Nedaoan King had any grudge against Brit Arren and the ships and men under him, he gave no sign of it. He thought he could like the man, given half a chance. "Not yet. And if we destroy Lyiadd's army, we may never need go there."

"Perhaps," Corlin said dubiously. "He cannot leave us the advantage; we took that, here, no matter how strong his Power or his strength of armed in Yslar. And he lost allies." He glanced at Brit Arren. "But we cannot let him live!"

"There is a place—I will know it. We will destroy him there. Lyiadd." Ylia spoke for the first time in hours; she looked dazed. She shook herself. "Don't look at me like that, I'm neither mad nor possessed," she added flatly and much more like herself. "I will know. You of Nedao, at least, have trusted to my sword for a number of years now; trust to the Power that is mine also." *Can I blame them for such looks?* she wondered unhappily. Too many things were changing and she was so sensitive to so many kinds of Power. It frightened her, as the sword once had. *What will all this leave of me?* But what was left of her now? Friends dead, her son dead, her Power twisted and changed until she was no longer certain of all its form or its direction. Her body—

But *that* at least no longer mattered. Vess had done things, but he had paid for them all. It was past, gone. Another life. Other people, both of them, that Vess, that Ylia.

"Lass knows," Marhan growled. The dubious looks were transferred from her to him. The Swordmaster glared back at them. "She has Power, ye all know that. Hasn't played us false yet, has it?"

"We had best be ready to fight at first light," Galdan said before anyone could take up Marhan's argument. He, for one, was too tired to either listen to squabbling or to separate any who chose to fight tonight, and Erken looked tired enough to argue. "We have watch out; those of us in command will not watch tonight. I suggest those who have beds find them, and get what sleep we can."

"He's right," Erken said. "We had a certain advantage today; we cannot count on that tomorrow. Save that Vess is dead."

Bendesevorian leaned forward. "There are now more than twenty Nasath here, which will simplify certain matters for you. We can bridge full companies of Nedaoan armed back to the valley and bring fresh armed here. What we can do to help, we will. Also my sister is meeting with the Elders tonight, and while my cousin doubts she will succeed, there is that chance."

"We will count on what there is to count on," Galdan said. He smiled. "My friend, you and yours have already aided us greatly, and we are grateful. An exchange of armed will be most useful. Corlin, you should return to the valley to take charge there. Trade off as many companies as you can; remember Lyiadd's troop is fresh. Send Brel and Golsat back." Corlin nodded.

Brit Arren hesitated, then cleared his throat. "I do not have enough ships to harry Yslar, or even to be much use in a battle. But we can guard your backs." The wary looks he got were no more than he expected, and old Marhan looked just short of laughing aloud. His mouth twisted. "Even a lifelong enemy can have honor, according to his own lights. I have sworn to the Nedaoan Queen, and to King Galdan. Trust us or not, as you choose! But Lyiadd might think this good opportunity to burn Nalda to the ground. He is devious."

Like a cat, sneaking and sly, he would have added, but the four-footed creature down-table was watching him. Gods. Ylsan cat, AEldra and yet cat . . . and that full-blooded Ylsan noblewoman holding it. He pulled his gaze away from the cat's level, unblinking—he would almost have said measuring—gaze. The thing might be able to read his thought, and if it did not like what it saw—!

"We know he is devious," Corlin replied evenly. "Your plan is a good one; we accept your aid." *For now*, he implied. It hung in the air between them, but his eyes were not unfriendly. "We need a replacement for Eveya, Mothers rest the poor lass." There was a silence. Ylia toyed with her dagger moodily.

Galdan eyed her, the whole Council waited. Someone had to decide, though, if Ylia would not. "Lev, unless you have serious objection, or unless Ylia does, I'd like to put Lennet in her place. Temporarily at least." Levren considered this gravely.

"You want my opinion?" he said finally. "She's skilled with her blades and with a bow. On those counts, I would never worry for her. She is no tactician. But if she need only lead the Elite Guard, she can do that. I have no objection. Ylia?"

"Fine," she said faintly. Galdan shoved a winecup into her hand, watched as she drank. She opened her eyes, smiled in his direction, slumped back down in her chair. He couldn't quite make her out: She was tired, they all were. There was something else, though. Ylia was unaware of his concern, unaware of much at the moment unless someone held it immediately before her.

Lennet, Ylia thought tiredly. She'll do. She should have the chance to fight; it shames her being left behind. Poor Eveya.

She opened her eyes what seemed only a moment later to find the room nearly empty: Galdan was still there, but Marhan now sat where Brit Arren had and he had hold of her near hand. "Sleeping, boy? Supposed to do that on your watch, aren't ye?" She shook her head, brought up a smile.

"Not sleeping. Just—distracted."

"Hah." He pushed her cup toward her, raised his own in toast. "Nice bit of close fighting ye did today, or so I hear. Sorry I didn't see it." He'd been well down the beach, and *Shark's* bulk had been squarely in the way to boot. "Couldn't let someone else kill him, that it?"

Ylia drank. "He was mine, I told you that. I had to, Marhan. It was—messy." For one brief moment, it came back to her, real and messy indeed. A spasm crossed her face, was gone.

Marhan laughed grimly. "Not supposed to stand in front of a man when you cut his throat, didn't I teach ye that?"

"No. I'll remember for next time."

"Next time! Don't ye go making a habit of cutting men's throats, that's no sort of occupation for ye!" he snapped. He set aside his own cup, stood. "I'm off to find my bed; an old man needs his sleep." He turned a sharp glance Galdan's direction. "Don't think to send me back with Erken and Corlin, mind that!"

"I—" Galdan gazed at him, perplexed and a little irritated. There were currents here he couldn't fathom, odd things. Marhan of all men, insisting on bridging with them, insisting on remaining in the face of evils and more magic! "You go with us, Marhan."

"Good." His face was a study in conflicting wants as he left.

"Ylia?" She'd dozed off again; Galdan was shaking her shoulders. "You need real sleep, in a bed. Morning is not that far off, we need you awake and ready. Come." She shook her head. "Warm comforters?" he suggested. "Soft pillows?"

"Mmmm. It's not—I'm not really tired."

"Not much," he retorted. "Open your eyes and tell me that."

"Well," she let the word trail, leaned against him. "Well, I *am* tired, but that is—not all of it."

"I can see that straight on, even that red-haired pirate at your left elbow could see it. You've been strange for hours, what is it?"

"I don't know for certain." The words trailed off again. "Can you tell?"

"Only that something has half your attention, and exhaustion has the rest."

"This afternoon. The Folk. The Nasath. It's—still with me. But this other thing. I started to know then."

"Know what?" Galdan carried her from the council chamber.

"Lyiadd. There's a—a place. He'll come there."

"You told us that. You realized it then?"

"Began to," she said sleepily as he mounted the stairs leading to their small tower bedchamber. "The horn—" Her voice trailed away.

"What about the horn?" Galdan asked.

"Don't know yet. I thought it would call them—Nasath or Folk. Gods knew we needed them both. But—another thing." She sighed. "I'll know."

"Good," Galdan said as he dropped her on the bed. "No, don't try to help me, just lie back, let me get your boots. It caught you off guard, all this, and that on top of a long day. You sleep. Let it work itself off."

"Think so?" Her voice was muffled as he pulled the jerkin over her head. The shirt followed; he dug through her small pack to find the sleep shirt and helped her into it.

"Know so," he replied. "I've had experience with Power, too, remember?"

"Different," Ylia protested faintly as he bundled her under a mound of feather-filled comforters. She snuggled down and sighed happily.

"Not different," he retorted. "You'll see." But she didn't hear; she was already asleep. Galdan smoothed hair back from her brow—it was stiff with the salt she'd been too worn to wash out—kissed her lightly. He watched a moment, stood and went out. He needed to talk to Bendesevorian once more before he could rest.

Curious, after so long a time, dealing with Lyiadd's seemingly endless malice and Power, for us to realize that this was not so: Whatever else they might be, he and Marrita, there was yet some of both that had once been human and still was. Human emotion had ruled so many of their acts; and like other humans, they were mortal.

28

Battle was joined again not long after first light, when Lyiadd's strong Ylsan force attacked Erken's weakest position. The line crumbled briefly, allowing Lyiadd's men to regain a substantial length of beach. They lost what they had gained and more at sunrise as Bendesevorian and two of his fellows bridged Golsat, Brelian and a company of Nedaoan armed to the battle. These, though momentarily disoriented, were fresh, and the news Erken and Corlin had taken to the valley gave them heart. Erken's battleworn guard was bridged back to Nedao; the Nasath worked to shift armed thereafter, but it was mid-morning before the task was done.

There was no fog, no overcast this day; there were no Mathkkra—no Thullen once the sun rose, though in the pre-dawn hours one now and again swooped low to impartially terrorize the armed of either side.

But the battle itself, for most of the day, was largely a matter of sword and bow: Those siding with Nedao were withholding use of Power—AEldra, Nasath or Folkish—lest it be needed later in great strength. Among the Ylsans, now and again men bridged or made use of the Baelfyr, but less and less often as the day went on. Lyiadd and Marrita made no contribution to the fighting.

Lyiadd's force was larger, but the Nedaoan army was better trained and more unified. By mid-day, they had driven their enemy up the Aresada and into the cool, windy depths of the river canyon. Thullen harried them here, and Levren's bow were kept busy watching for them, shooting them down.

Ylia and Galdan remained near enough the front to direct the fighting, well enough back for protection, and for most of the day, Marhan stayed at her side. She didn't like it—magic and Marhan. And constant fighting could not be easy, at his age. But for all his near-fourscore years, he held his feet, led a charge or two and showed more stamina than some of the younger men who fought under him.

Things slowed during the early afternoon; the Ylsans and their Ragnolan allies had taken a position deep in rock from which it was difficult to dislodge them. Neither, however, could they push back down-river. Most of the armed on both sides managed time to eat and rest, and it was during Ylia's rest that Bendesevorian came to her.

"The valley has been beset by Mathkkra, a vast horde of them. But my sister is there, and she has reinforcements with her."

"How many?" Galdan swallowed bread hastily, washed it down with leather-flavored water from his bottle.

"Ten. All she could persuade." He shrugged, smiled faintly. "Enough. Your people are safe, for now."

"Ten." Ylia shook her head. "More exiles?" Bendesevorian shrugged again. "I—I'm sorry."

"We can talk of it later. But it does not matter, truly."

Lyiadd met Marrita's eyes across the oil-filled bowl. "Hold that vision for me. I need to speak with Nebyon—there." His voice echoed in the small chamber. Reflected in the oil, Marrita saw Lyiadd's captain start as his master's mind-speech touched him. "Continue to retreat slowly, as you have thus far: they must not suspect you are retreating deliberately. Lead them back, but slowly. Make no overt movement, except those needed to keep the Nedaoans fighting. You must not reach the proper place until second hour, tomorrow, I need that much time to prepare it. Do you *see* the place I have in mind? Do you understand what I ask of you?"

"My Lord, I do." The man looked harassed, but he was good; one of the best Lyiadd had left. Marrita sighed in tired relief as Lyiadd broke contact and she could let the bowl go dark. Lyiadd raised her to her feet. She brushed hair from her brow, leaned against him. One hand came around her shoulder automatically;

his attention was largely for the two men in the Tower with them.

"Stay here. Trade watch, monitor the fighting. If I am needed, send. Otherwise, the decisions are yours. There are many things I must do to prepare for events tomorrow. Do you understand me?" The men nodded. They carefully avoided looking at each other until after Lyiadd and Marrita were long gone.

The Ylsans and their allies retired behind a rock ledge that formed a natural keep wall at sunset; the Nedaoans pulled back a distance, made camp and set a heavy guard. Bendesevorian and several of his fellows went through the camp before evening-meal, sending the worn and the badly wounded to the valley, bringing others back. Ylia and Galdan healed the wounded who would stay—such as Golsat, who had taken a sword through his left hand but would not leave.

Ylia let Galdan walk through the forward ranks in her place and shared bread and a thick, hot soup with Golsat and Brelian.

"I don't like this place," Golsat said finally. Ylia shrugged, swallowed soup and tucked a bite of bread in her cheek.

"No. He can't send Mathkkra against our eastern flanks without sending them through his own men, though. They can't cross the Aresada, it's too high and fast, and we have heavy guard to the west and against the rock. Any problems among yours, any others we should send home?" Golsat shook his head. "Tomorrow—" She hesitated, shrugged as the two men looked at her inquiringly. "Tomorrow won't be good. Anyone who might break—send them back to protect the valley."

"One or two, then," Golsat said. He hesitated in turn. "Lennet—"

"She wouldn't thank you," Brelian said.

"No, perhaps not. She's not comfortable, trying to take Eveya's place."

"No one thinks she's trying to, do they?" Ylia drained her bowl, broke the last of her bread into bite-sized pieces.

"Doubt it. No."

Ylia sighed. "I know it's a problem. I need her, just now. I think she won't mind after this, though, if I take back the command. Eveya—poor Ev had what it takes to command guard; Len doesn't. She knows it now."

Brelian sopped up broth with his bread. "There isn't any shame in not wanting to kill. 'Betha should talk to her about that." He stood. "Going to walk through my company one more time, make certain everyone's set. Golsat?"

"Coming." He touched Ylia's knee. "Thank you."

"Thank—oh, your hand. Of course."

"Ysian would have been upset." He smiled. "Are you all right?" She nodded. "If you need me, send."

"I will." She watched him go.

Trap. She had sensed it all day; each length they drove Lyiadd's armsmen up-river brought it closer. They had no choice but to walk into it, though. His trap, her answer: They both lay in the same place—and that was not far away at all, now.

The battle was joined again as soon as it was light but the Nedaoan and Narran armed were not able to dislodge Lyiadd's men from their fastness until sunlight touched the upper ledges. Since then the enemy had been slowly giving ground, making an occasional feint but never bringing the fighting to a halt, never moving back down-stream.

Nearly a league up-river, they found the narrow entrance to a side ravine and dove through it. It took time, for the opening was no more than ten lengths across, and a deep tributary stream filled more than half of that. But even the Ylsans were in full flight by now. At Galdan's orders, two companies of Nedaoan sword led the pursuit, and the rest of the allied force came close behind.

The ravine was steep-sided, nearly treeless and shaded down near its river: Even though the sun was well above the horizon, it still only shone on the very tops of the rubble-strewn slopes. Footing was treacherous with fallen scree; boulders, branch and loose dirt from the ledges high above littered the ground.

A sudden, sharp turn and then another. The ravine widened abruptly, the stream meandered off eastward. There was a broad grassy meadow dotted with individual fir trees. It reminded Ylia of the ledge where they had first encountered Mathkkra, coming north from Koderra, and a chill touched her; it deepened as something else stirred deep down.

"Galdan." He couldn't hear her above the fighting. She caught at his sleeve, dragged him off balance and half around. "Galdan! It's—" She couldn't find the words, but Marhan was suddenly back at her side.

"This place reeks of trap!" he shouted. Golsat, who had just fallen back from the front lines, nodded.

"There is no way out up there, only the way we came! We dare not be cut off! Let me get a company of bow back there, in case!"

"Do it, find Lev," Galdan began; a blast of Power silenced him; someone from the rear cried out, "'Ware! Armsmen!" The cry came back from all sides.

Fighting suddenly ceased; the silence rang through them.

"Let me forward!" Ylia shouted, and the Elite Guard parted, came on behind her. The few armed between her and the short stretch of open ground hastily cleared a space. She gazed only briefly at the four new companies of armed facing them, spared no glance for those she knew to be on both sides of them, behind them. She lifted her eyes instead to the black pillars of stone rising above the valley floor. Lyiadd stood alone there. The Lammior's Sya'datha played around his head to form a thin haze of cloud between the sun and the ground.

"It was kind of you to come where I wanted you!" His voice echoed across the ravine. Someone back in the ranks drew his breath on a sob; there was no other sound. "You of Nedao! Give up the leaders of your armed to me, and I shall spare your lives!" Silence again.

"Did you think we would make it easy for you?" Ylia shouted back finally. "Or is it that you know you can take us in no other way?"

"I will hear no words from you, Ylia of Nedao. *Your* life is forfeit in any case, and as slowly as I can take it from you!"

She laughed wildly. "Come and try!" Galdan got one arm, Marhan the other, and they dragged her back. Lyiadd laughed; men cringed at the sound, and Lennet, who stood just behind Ylia, bit her hand to hold back tears.

Galdan left Ylia in Marhan's grip and stepped forward. "Lyiadd, we are not without allies." Bendesevorian moved to his side; four of his kin stood behind him.

Lyiadd glared down at them. "What—shall I simply place myself in the hands of these allies and give up all that is mine? Why should I?"

"Your thought is tainted, you are beyond reasoning. I grieve for you." Bendesevorian turned and walked away.

Lyiadd watched him go. "Grieve while you may," he jeered. "It will not be long."

"Your own life will be forfeit, if you continue in this fool's endeavor!" Galdan cried out. "You have lost, any man of sense can see that! Your ships are gone, your attempt to take Nalda a failure, your son is dead—"

"Do not speak to me of my son!" Lyiadd screamed; men cowered away from the sound of his voice. The rock at his feet turned blood-red and bubbled. "A man of sense, is it? But I am, perhaps, no longer simply a man. Ask your pet Nasath, there! Ask him of his kinsman who crossed the bridge they thought destroyed, *his* kinsman who became Lammior!

"Or judge for yourselves! Could a *man* do this?" He vanished; the armsmen fronting them vanished; the sky went black, and in the place of his companies of men stood a vast army of *seemings*. Hellish, dreadful *seemings* solidified, became real—and threw themselves into battle.

"Nedao!" Brelian's voice, from somewhere in the front lines. The archers under his command rallied. A volley of arrows flew, killing men where they struck men, but they passed through Lyiadd's *seemings* as though they were not there.

They were hard to see—a black fog surrounded them, and shapes changed frequently. But they could kill, as several stunned Nedaoans in the front lines discovered. "Back!" Galdan roared. "Fall back!" There was laughter all around them, echoing from the rocks, as they backed away, and the army of *seemings* came on. Black mist rose from the ground under the feet of Lyiadd's made creatures, surrounding them, dimming the sun.

Thunder rumbled. A Zahg hurtled down the western slope, but Nasath surrounded it, neutralized it. Another came close behind, and other Nasath moved against it. For a while, then, Lyiadd sent no more of those.

Lyiadd had bridged his human foreguard to block the ravine and all retreat to the rear. The Ylsans there were nervous, the mercenaries looked ready to bolt, even at a distance from the *seemings*. *Let them*, Lyiadd thought as he gathered a wisp of cloud, thickened it and sent it down the slope. *They do not matter.* They did not. His created army was pushing the Nedaoan and Narran force back, he had no doubt now of the outcome. The Nasath could contain whatever small things he sent out, but not his *seemings*, for they were all one spell. The Folk had made no attempt against it, and now he could not sense *them* at all.

"Galdan, brace me," Ylia shouted out. They were still retreating, the Nedaoans moving inward, slowly being pushed toward the river. Lyiadd's *seeming* army did not appear to be stopped by water, as many evil things were, but neither did it make any effort to block Nedao on that side. But it did not need to: Lyiadd's Ylsans waited at rest across the river several lengths back from it.

Ylia still had the sword in her right hand, though there was nothing it could touch, but as Galdan looked at her, she brought out the horn. He shook his head hopelessly. "What do you think to bring, the Elders themselves? Even the Nasath are helpless against *that*!" A wave of his sword indicated the horde advancing on them.

"I must," she replied grimly. "Lyiadd interrupted me, before I could tell you: I *know* this place." It took a moment for him to understand. Fear and hope balanced in him, then, and without a word, he set his shoulder against hers. She closed her eyes and raised the horn to her lips.

The cry rang out across the valley, shattering the darkness directly over her head so she stood in a pool of sunlight, the horn glittering in her fingers. The cry echoed, struck the cliffs and came back at her again, multi-fold, echoed—and *answered*. The air was alive with horncry, suddenly; Lyiadd's voice tried to rise above it but he was shouted down by horns. The Ylsan army on their left rose as one man and began edging away from the water.

For there was something there, suddenly; something wrapped in a cloud, or a fog of its own, something that moved and shifted like folk beyond a warped and smeared window. Ylia set the horn in Galdan's hands and walked steadily through her own armed. She stopped at the water's edge, river lapping gently at her feet. There were things—movement—folk there. Trying to get through, trying to reach her. She sensed them, sensed something familiar, but could do no more than that. She could not touch whatever was there.

Galdan came up behind her. He managed to go a little further, but only ankle-deep in the chill water. He reached cautiously. His hand stopped as though he'd hit glass.

"Someone," he whispered. "Someone help me." The world around them had stopped; Lyiadd was throwing coils of night at them, but they were moving too slowly, as though underwater, and the army of *seemings* was milling just in front of the Nedaoan line. Ylia's eyes were held to the shifting wall before her; her hands sought Galdan's. A faint surge of Power washed over them; Nisana came from nowhere to leap onto Ylia's shoulder. "Help me!" Galdan's vision was going black, no trick of

Lyiadd's, but the fierce drain on his Power; whatever was there was unable to get through, try though it might. And he could not reach it. His hands fell to his side, he tottered back a step into Bendesevorian.

"The horn." Ylia brought it up, but the Nasăth caught at her fingers and shook his head.

"No. Its purpose is done, it has called what aid it could, but its power is fading. If you cannot pull them through, then they cannot aid us." He turned in surprise as Marhan shouldered roughly past him. The old Swordmaster's eyes were black, his jaw set, and the hand that caught hold of Ylia's was damp. She opened her mouth, closed it as he glared at her.

"Don't say it! Think I want this? I *know* what's there, don't ye sense it? What good's that magic of yours, if ye cannot tell?" She shook her head dumbly. "My King," Marhan whispered. He was sweating freely, though the afternoon was cool. "Brandt is there. And others, those who never had—never got a good fight against that. Or the other one." He gave her one last black look. "All ye could ever have asked of me, boy, and it comes to this!" He spat. *"Magic!"* And before she could protest, he took two long strides forward, his fingers still twisted around hers, and he shoved his other hand through the wall.

It collapsed like shattered ice. Horns hurt her ears. "Marhan," she whispered in sudden agony, but he was nowhere in sight. And the Ylsans, if they were still there, were hidden from view by an army—white-clad, yellow-clad, so bright they burned the eye. Sun touched upon a hundred banners, and before all others were the Gyrfalcon of Brandt, and the Osprey and Ship of Shelagn.

Behind her, Nedaoans cried out in fear, and then in wonder as men or women once known to them passed through their line to attack Lyiadd's made armies. Men who had died on Koderra's walls, or who had ridden from her gates to die under Tehlatt axes, men from Teshmor and from Aresada. Tr'Harsen came there with his Narran ship-mates and the *Merman*'s banner. Beside him were young men of Nedaoan mien but ancient arms: Merreven, Kildres his brother and their following. Ifney there, sword-sworn at his heels, those lost at the Battle of the High Ridges and those dead at the hands of Mathkkra since following him. Nasath were there; and Folk; an Yderra.

Before all went Brandt, and at his side, the Power playing in rainbows about her shoulders, Scythia. Just behind them came a man scarcely of man's age, his reddish beard neatly trimmed on a face of unearthly beauty. Ylia cried out as Brendan passed, and he turned for the least of moments. The woman with him did also. Somehow, she could never say later which of them moved first, but they stood, she and Galdan, Brendan and Shelagn, and Brendan's fingers were momentarily warm in hers, hard on his friend's shoulder.

Shelagn smiled, brought up her sword in salute. In a daze, Ylia matched the gesture. The twin blades touched; the pool of daylight around them widened until it took in much of the Nedaoan army. And then they were gone, again taking their place behind Brandt, moving swiftly against Lyiadd's creations.

Ylia pushed her way through after the last of them, worked her way across the Nedaoan line and found a knoll from which to watch the fighting. Galdan came with her; the Elite Guard formed a barrier around them. But Lyiadd's human armsmen were frozen by his command or by fear of his *seemings*—or by fear of the dead.

There was little to see at first; fog and darkness held wherever the created beings were, and it was only as they were slain or unmade that the black fogs faded. The sun was again visible and starting down from mid-day when Brandt's army encircled the last of Lyiadd's *seemings* and began to move in on them.

"Ah, no," Marrita whispered. The oil clouded over, cleared briefly but went dark for good then. She pushed away from the bowl, stood. It took a great effort; suddenly, she was so very tired. *It's gone against us from the first time he opposed that child. Then she brought him a dagger, and now she brings him the very dead.* Her own mortality—until two nights ago, she had never thought about it. Now she saw little else, and she was so tired, it did not really matter. Lyiadd, though: *She* could not have him!

Lyiadd's generals were watching her from their corner. *Tell them?* No. She dared trust no one, just now; she sensed revolt in the City. These might not continue to serve, if they thought Lyiadd defeated.

"Wait," she ordered, and by some magic of its own, her voice sounded cool, unconcerned. They looked reassured, she thought. "I am going to Lyiadd's aid—to help him finish them."

"They are—?" Ayater began, hesitated. Perhaps not reassured after all.

"We will return shortly." She hesitated. "If somehow we do not, if chance turns things wrong, I give you one last order. Fire the palace. Destroy Yslar." They stared at her in silent fear. "Swear it!" she snapped. They knelt, bowed their heads in assent. Marrita caught up her cloak, threw it around her shoulders and vanished. Lyiadd's generals exchanged a wary look. *Wait*, it said.

"Look to the rear!" Levren's voice rose above the stunned whispers around her. "Archers, fall back, they're attacking!" The cry was taken up by a dozen other voices. Half the bow in the front lines turned and ran back through the huddled armed as, with a shout, the rearguard Ylsan army surged forward. They slowed as they found themselves facing a double line of Nedaoan bow, and their own line disintegrated when two-thirds of it fell dead. Others came across the river, filling in the gaps, pushing others forward ahead of them. A breath later, the Elite Guard came under attack from both sides.

But it was a last desperate attempt on Lyiadd's part. His mercenaries had either fled or fallen where they were when the wall that separated the dead from the living dissolved.

The *seeming* army was fading; Lyiadd flagging. A Zahg roared down the mountainside, wreathed in his black fogs, but Nasath surrounded it and easily unmade it.

The Elite Guard was hard beset for long moments: Ylia and Galdan fought shoulder to shoulder, Lennet braced with three of the guard against their backs. Shelagn's sword destroyed a Thullen and the three Ylsans controlling it. At that, the rest fled, and the guard quickly cut them down.

There were few of the dead left in the field; they were fading, vanishing as Lyiadd's armies dwindled, until only one small company remained below the crag where Lyiadd stood. Folk filled the air with a dazzle of light, unmaking the last of his fogs.

Fighting ceased. "Come down." Ylia stood at the head of the armies, Nedao's banners, Brandt's, Shelagn's behind her, Galdan at her side.

"No." Neither spoke above a whisper; in the sudden silence, it was all that was necessary. Lyiadd shimmered, but before he could bridge, Bendesevorian caught hold of his right arm, two others took his left. They brought him down to stand amid the banners. Lyiadd laughed grimly. "The next move is yours. What will it be? You dare not keep me alive, but you cannot kill me."

"We can kill you. Know that. We will, if we must." Bendesevorian spoke before Ylia or Galdan could. "But there is another way, for you and for her." Lyiadd heard him, but his eyes remained locked on Ylia's. "Let us rearrange your thought and your woman's. We could do that for you. You may not care for yourself, but she would not need to die." Whatever else he might have said went unsaid: Lyiadd's laughter drowned him.

"As though death mattered! Look at what stands with you, and tell me that death matters! But I will not go alone!" Sya'datha flared; the Nasath holding him cried out in pain and he leaped forward. Galdan brought his sword down but it slammed against Lyiadd's Power, dropping him to his hands and knees. His sword made two turns and quivered in the ground behind them; the blade was smoking. Lyiadd brushed past him, fingers raking Ylia's side where his blade had once cut. Sya'datha burned through her and she screamed in agony. Lyiadd laughed, lunged for her again.

A towering shriek ripped his concentration as something tangled in his feet and five needles drove into his knee; he stumbled, fought to right himself. Nisana scrambled out of the way as he fell.

Through a haze of burning agony, Ylia saw him go down. She staggered forward, brought the sword high over her head, two-handed. Galdan was back on his feet, hands gripping hers, his Power strengthening her arms and her will. She brought the blade down on the back of Lyiadd's unprotected neck with all two-fold strength in her.

The sword blazed, and those near her drew back in alarm as it slashed into the ground. Ylia started as something touched her foot, drew her breath in a faint scream as Lyiadd's head rolled past her toe and down the incline to stop at the water's edge. Blood soaked the grass. Her eyes closed, the sword dropped from nerveless fingers and she fell into Galdan's arms, but another scream echoed her cry, brought her eyes open, and she forced herself onto her feet again. Marrita. Marrita had come.

She dropped down to bury her face in Lyiadd's short red cloak. Ylia let Galdan take her weight. It hurt; everything hurt, and breathing was becoming difficult. Galdan's hands were warm, Nisana a warm pressure against her boot and then the cat's forefeet were hard on the muscle of her thigh as she sagged further and Galdan lowered her to the grass. The pain was spreading like fire, taking everything with it; she could not have remained

sitting without Galdan's support. Keeping her eyes open, focusing them on Marrita—she had to. But it took all the concentration left in her.

"You! All of you! It was your fault, all of it!" Marrita's voice
hurt her ears. "Laughing at him! You Nasath, withholding true
Power from him, until he must seek it himself! I—I could have
—could have—" She was weeping too hard to go on. She wiped
a hand across her eyes, careless of her appearance. One hand
gripped Lyiadd's unresponsive hand. "*You* did this to him! But he
killed you first with the Sya'datha, didn't he? You will not live
long enough to gloat." Ylia merely looked at her. She hurt too
much to argue; Marrita had never been worth that. Something,
though—she drew a breath, let the words out on it.

"For my son," she whispered. Marrita laughed hysterically.

"Son. Your son, his son. So stupid!" She brought dead fingers
to her lips, let them fall limply to her lap, let her head fall back.
A fireball of Baelfyr sent the onlookers in hasty retreat. Before
anyone could intervene, there were two bodies encircled in
flame. Galdan picked Ylia up and backed away with her.

If her life were a retelling of the old tales, as she so often thought it, she would have died. Much that happened to her had happened to Shelagn, certainly. But much is never all; and Shelagn had not had my like. Or, more importantly, such a one as Galdan.

29

She lay on her cloak and Galdan's, Lennet's pack and cloak under her head. Someone had rigged a shelter over her to keep the sun off. Galdan's fingers stayed tight around hers, and now and again she managed to smile at him, but she could see he was not reassured, even through the pain that was blurring everything. She could hear weeping out there, among her Nedaoans, and Galdan's eyes were red. *They think I am dying. Well—* She felt a pang of grief—for him and for them. Nothing for herself. There was only pain for her.

Someone knelt beside the little shelter and another hand took hers from Galdan's; small as hers, calloused. She opened her eyes to find dark blue ones staring into them. "Shelagn," she whispered. "It hurts. I—I'm dying of it, aren't I?"

Shelagn shook her head. "No. You will not die, heir of mine. Be well. Be content. And live for a fullness of years. Bear your Galdan a strong son."

"I—can't—"

"You will not die in this place. The Kabada will not deny you this one thing. You will not die of a child. A—" She smiled faintly. "A gift, Shelagn's gift. Think of it as that." She set Ylia's fingers back in Galdan's, laid her hands on his shoulders. "She will not die, because you are neither AEldra nor Nasath. Your Power is nearer the thing his was, because it came from the Foessa. You can heal her, so." Her eyes closed and her thought touched his. She stepped aside, and Ylia did not see her again. Brendan's hand touched her cheek. "Be well. Be content. And live for a fullness of years, first beloved," he whispered. And to Galdan, as they embraced, "Care for her, my good friend."

"Always," Galdan replied. His voice was rough, and he stared after them through blurring eyes.

I can heal her. He could. And did.

"Ah, gods, beloved." Ylia wiped tears from her face with a shaky hand and smiled up at him. "I thought I was dead." She hugged him hard.

"Ouch! My ribs, I think I've a cracked one," he protested, but his grip on her was at least as fierce. "Rest a while."

"No, help me up. I don't want anyone to think I *did* die."

"They don't—"

"Seeing is better than hearing," she insisted, and he finally laughed and dragged her out of the shelter and to her feet. At the sound of the heartfelt cheers that rang the valley, he smiled ruefully.

"So you were right again. Doesn't that bore you?"

"Nisana is the one always right, not me," she retorted. Galdan wrapped an arm around her shoulders while she put one around his waist, and they walked through the companies of Nedaoans and their allies.

There were dead, particularly where the army of *seemings* had been; there were many wounded. But of the captured Ylsans who could heal, most were willing to help any of the injured. Bendesevorian and his fellows bridged the Ylsan prisoners to Yslar, then, for Geit to hold awaiting the new Sirdar's justice. The Sirdar's palace was already in their hands; the generals had surrendered it once they realized Lyiadd was dead; across the City, men were fleeing if they could, surrendering if trapped. Only Lyiadd had kept them together and he was gone. The Sea-Raider ships in deep water were gone; the ships in harbor readied, only waiting for the tide to run with it.

Levren had been badly wounded. He had taken a sword through the arm, another low, and lost much blood before Lennet found him; Ylia sent them both back to the valley together, once the Bowmaster was healed and his frightened and weeping daughter calmed.

They found Marhan on the far side of the river, after the army of dead was gone. He lay on his side, on the grass, his eyes closed as though he slept, and there was no mark upon him. Galdan could have wept when they found him, remembering the Battle of the High Ridges, knowing this time there would be no return for the old Swordmaster. Ylia did weep for him, but she knew he would never thank her for that: He was with Brandt, now; magic no longer dogged his steps or warped his thought. But all Nedao would mourn him.

Nasath and Folk invaded the valley where Lyiadd had dwelt and the Lammior before him, to make certain before the end of that day that whatever Power had been left there could never again be used as Lyiadd had done. Bendesevorian went on to Nedao, to give folk there the news; others stayed behind to bridge the allied army back to the Bay of Nessea.

That night Narrans and Nedaoans alike danced through the hilly streets of Nalda, while the Folk played and danced among them.

Before they bridged home to Nedao the next morning, Ylia and Galdan went down to Nar's wharves. Most of the ships were already gone, but *Fury* lay against the docks, and Mal Brit Arren came down the plank to talk to them. "Give your Lord Corry a message for me. Tell him I am thinking on his notion, the idea he offered the night after the fight in the Bay, here. Tell him—perhaps, yes. Perhaps there will be trade for him and Nar, one day, silk and southern furs for other goods. Perhaps we will even occupy the City he offered us, and rebuild it in our own way."

"Riddles," Ylia said impatiently, but Brit Arren laughed.

"He will know! Tell him that whatever I decide, whatever my men decide, *his* ships are safe!"

"I will tell him that," Ylia replied. Brit Arren turned to Galdan then, held out a hand. Galdan clasped it.

"I'll give you something, if you like," Brit Arren said. "Found it off shore, waiting for good news. Doubt it got what it wanted." He whistled shrilly; two of his men came down the plank with a grey-clad third between them. Tevvro's eyes were furious, his mouth a thin, hard line. Ylia stepped in front of him. Pale eyes met hers, dropped away. Tevvro had lost badly enough that his confidence was shaken. For the moment.

"I have messages for you, and for your Heirocrat, from the Chosen House in Nedao," she said finally. "There will be no change in the House, Grewl will tolerate no fanatics. And a message from me, personally. I do not interfere with the Chosen, nor with any who follow that way, so long as they leave me alone. If your Heirocrat is intelligent, he will accept this; if your Prince is wise, he will reinstate trade with Nar before he loses all. There are other ports, other money as good as his." She gave him a shove. "Go." Tevvro, his shoulders sagging, turned. Brit Arren's men nodded him down the docks, where his ship waited.

She and Galdan stood, arm in arm, watching as *Fury* cleared the sandbar and the point to vanish out to sea. "Wonder what he meant," Galdan said finally.

"I don't know. What it sounded like, though—" She shook her head. "Flatly impossible. Not even Corlin could manage to turn a Sea-Raider from murder and plunder and make him into a trader!"

"Wager?" he demanded. But she merely laughed.

They bridged back to the Tower and into the midst of a joyous Fest: Most of Nedao was jammed into the City streets. At first, three minstrels and the royal musicians all held an awed, astonished silence as the Folk danced and piped and sang. But not for long: It was impossible to hold back from either the moment or the music. There was dancing in the square, dancing on the bridge and in the narrow lanes between cottages.

Somewhere in the midst of it all, Bendesevorian and his sister quietly disappeared; before middle night, there were no Nasath left in the City. Nisana, who was watching the festivities from the royal box, was not concerned by this. 'They will not return to their Elders. They will be about, in the mountains. We will see them often. And the Folk will come among us frequently now, for they no longer fear us.'

"Gone prescient in your old age, cat?" Ylia demanded aloud cheerfully. Lisabetha laughed and leaned back against Brelian; he brought her to her feet and took her out to dance. Lossana and Corlin followed moments later.

'Hah,' Nisana retorted. And when Ylia would have commented further, 'Shhh! They are singing the one about me again! The part where I felled Lyiadd!'

Ylia opened her mouth again, and Galdan laid a hand across it. "Well, didn't she?" And Ylia, who had managed to bury her last memory of that moment so deeply it could not hurt her to think of it, laughed. Nisana cast them both a very annoyed look, stretched and padded off after Ber'Sordes' minstrels.

Further down the street, near the barracks, Erken stared in mild astonishment at the merry little pipers with their bare, goat-like feet and hairy legs, the tiny horns on their heads. At those who accompanied him, spilling across the open grass in dance.

He knew they were at Nalda, but he hadn't seen them, had found it near impossible to believe. He wasn't certain he could now. Folk! But the music was touching something deep inside him. Not only him, for there was Marckl, capering like a lad with his lady. And there were Marckl's daughter and Ifney's Ivanha, clapping and cheering him on.

Nearby stood Lennet and Alxy, heads close together. Alxy, now Alxeidis XXIV, who had spoken only an hour before with the Nedaoan Main Council, to assure them of the honesty of his intentions, and to tell them that his own Council would be given to understand they could approve any bride for him—so long as that bride was Lennet, the Nedaoan Bowmaster's eldest daughter.

Erken blinked as a hand touched his: Ysian stood there smiling, her green gown caught up and knotted aside to keep it above her bare feet, her hair loose in a cascade of curls. Her eyes were alight, and she looked like a lass of twenty. "Here you are!"

"Well, yes," he replied doubtfully. Ysian laughed.

"Now, I have been reckoning it quite carefully, and as I see it, you are my sister's daughter's husband's father, and therefore kin to me. I insist that you take Father's betrothal dance with me!"

"Dance. Betrothal?" It took him a moment; he caught her by the waist, then, swung her around. "You and our Golsat? I would gladly dance with you for that." He took her hands; the music caught him up and warmed him as nothing in his life ever had.

The music faded with the stars, and folk moved from the streets to go home, to sleep. A few remained in the square, still dancing, or sitting and talking.

Ylia and Galdan stood on the southern balcony, watching the dawn spread across the line of eastern mountains, pale blue shading to peach-orange just above the deeper purple of peaks. Selverra slept in Ylia's arms, small fingers caught in her shirt; Ylia leaned back against Galdan so he could support them both.

"In another hour, the herds will be putting out to pasture. People will be harvesting the first grain next month. The apples after that. I think he'd hate that most of all, don't you?"

"Hate what most of all?" Galdan leaned forward to kiss Ylia's brow, Selverra's fingers.

"That—all he wanted to do, all the damage he did, he didn't really change anything." Her eyes went to the horizon; the gold was spreading, she could see well enough now to see the first early horseman riding out along Marckl's Road. "Not the things that really matter."

Not the things that really matter. Nedao—eight parts of her people dead, those that lived no longer Plainsfolk; Yls—her Sirdar a lad who had not thought to rule for another forty or fifty years, his grandsire's Council and half the First and Second Houses dead. *My son, dead. My Lady taken against her will.*

He gazed out over the valley. Selverra stirred against her mother's shoulder, subsided again. Just across the bridge, someone was awake, crossing his yard to milk a cow, his daughter to feed the geese. Not far away, two men pushed a small boat into the river and broke out nets as they slid under the bridge. And as the first rays of sun touched the trees on the high ridges behind them, the smallest bell in the Chosen's compound began its sweet tolling, to waken the household. He drew a deep breath, inhaled the heady fragrance of dust, cool river water and ripe peaches and apricots, all mixed.

Things that really count. Perhaps she was right.

And so my tale draws to an end, though for those of us who lived it, it was of course no end at all. Ordinary, everyday things prevailed, as they always do; though ordinary for Nedao now meant Bendesevorian and his kin, who dwelt in our mountains, and Folk who came to our Fests.

But as one who had lived through it all, I could not regret the commonplace, the routine of seasons and hours and days. We had fought for those things, after all.

Be well. Be content. And live for a fullness of years.